Garden of Beasts

Jeffery Deaver

GARDEN OF BEASTS

A NOVEL OF BERLIN 1936

Hodder & Stoughton

Copyright © 2004 by Jeffery Deaver

First published in the United States in 2004 by Simon & Schuster
First published in Great Britain in 2004 by Hodder and Stoughton
A division of Hodder Headline

The right of Jeffery Deaver to be identified as Author of the Work has been asserted by
him in accordance with the Copyright, Designs and Patents Act 1988

1 3 5 7 9 10 8 6 4 2

All characters in this publication are fictitious and any
resemblance to real persons, living or dead, is purely coincidental.

A CIP catalogue record for this title is available from the British Library

Trade Paperback ISBN 0 340 73454 X
Hardback ISBN 0 340 73453 1

Printed and bound by
Griffin Press

Hodder Headline's policy is to use papers that are natural, renewable and recyclable products
and made from wood grown in sustainable forests. The logging and manufacturing processes
are expected to conform to the environmental regulations of the country of origin.

Hodder and Stoughton Ltd
A division of Hodder Headline
338 Euston Road
London NW1 3BH

To the memories of Hans and Sophie Scholl, brother and sister, executed in 1943 for anti-Nazi protests; journalist Carl von Ossietzky, awarded the Nobel Peace Prize in 1935 while imprisoned in Oranienburg camp; and Wilhelm Kruzfeld, a Berlin police officer who refused to let a mob destroy a synagogue during the Nazi-sponsored anti-Jewish riots known as the Night of Broken Glass . . . four people who looked at evil and said, "No."

"[Berlin] was full of whispers. They told of illegal midnight arrests, of prisoners tortured in the S.A. barracks. . . . They were drowned by the loud angry voices of the Government, contradicting through its thousand mouths."

—Christopher Isherwood, *Berlin Stories*

I
THE BUTTON MAN

MONDAY, 13 JULY, 1936

Chapter One

As soon as he stepped into the dim apartment he knew he was dead.

He wiped sweat off his palm, looking around the place, which was quiet as a morgue, except for the faint sounds of Hell's Kitchen traffic late at night and the ripple of the greasy shade when the swiveling Monkey Ward fan turned its hot breath toward the window.

The whole scene was off.

Out of kilter . . .

Malone was supposed to be here, smoked on booze, sleeping off a binge. But he wasn't. No bottles of corn anywhere, not even the *smell* of bourbon, the punk's only drink. And it looked like he hadn't been around for a while. The New York *Sun* on the table was two days old. It sat next to a cold ashtray and a glass with a blue halo of dried milk halfway up the side.

He clicked the light on.

Well, there *was* a side door, like he'd noted yesterday from the hallway, looking over the place. But it was nailed shut. And the window that let onto the fire escape? Brother, sealed nice and tight with chicken wire he hadn't been able to see from the alley. The other window *was* open but was also forty feet above cobblestones.

No way out . . .

And where was Malone? Paul Schumann wondered.

Malone was on the lam, Malone was drinking beer in Jersey, Malone was a statue on a concrete base underneath a Red Hook pier.

Didn't matter.

Whatever'd happened to the boozehound, Paul realized, the punk had been nothing more than bait, and the wire that he'd be here tonight was pure bunk.

In the hallway outside, a scuffle of feet. A clink of metal.

Out of kilter . . .

Paul set his pistol on the room's one table, took out his handkerchief and mopped his face. The searing air from the deadly Midwest heat wave had made its way to New York. But a man can't walk around without a jacket when he's carrying a 1911 Colt .45 in his back waistband and so Paul was condemned to wear a suit. It was his single-button, single-breasted gray linen. The white-cotton, collar-attached shirt was drenched.

Another shuffle from outside in the hallway, where they'd be getting ready for him. A whisper, another clink.

Paul thought about looking out the window but was afraid he'd get shot in the face. He wanted an open casket at his wake and he didn't know any morticians good enough to fix bullet or bird-shot damage.

Who was gunning for him?

It wasn't Luciano, of course, the man who'd hired him to touch off Malone. It wasn't Meyer Lansky either. They were dangerous, yeah, but not snakes. Paul'd always done top-notch work for them, never leaving a bit of evidence that could link them to the touch-off. Besides, if either of them wanted Paul gone, they wouldn't need to set him up with a bum job. He'd simply be gone.

So who'd snagged him? If it was O'Banion or Rothstein from Williamsburg or Valenti from Bay Ridge, well, he'd be dead in a few minutes.

If it was dapper Tom Dewey, the death would take a bit longer—whatever time was involved to convict him and get him into the electric chair up in Sing-Sing.

More voices in the hall. More clicks, metal seating against metal.

But looking at it one way, he reflected wryly, everything was silk so far; he was still alive.

And thirsty as hell.

He walked to the Kelvinator and opened it. Three bottles of milk—two of them curdled—and a box of Kraft cheese and one of Sunsweet tenderized peaches. Several Royal Crown colas. He found an opener and removed the cap from a bottle of the soft drink.

From somewhere he heard a radio. It was playing "Stormy Weather."

Sitting down at the table again, he noticed himself in the dusty mirror on the wall above a chipped enamel washbasin. His pale blue eyes weren't as alarmed as they ought to be, he supposed. His face, though, was weary. He was a large man—over six feet and weighing more than two hundred pounds. His hair was from his mother's side, reddish brown; his fair complexion from his father's German ancestors. The skin was a bit marred—not from pox but from knuckles in his younger days and Everlast gloves more recently. Concrete and canvas too.

Sipping the soda pop. Spicier than Coca-Cola. He liked it.

Paul considered his situation. If it was O'Banion or Rothstein or Valenti, well, none of them gave a good goddamn about Malone, a crazy riveter from the shipyards turned punk mobster, who'd killed a beat cop's wife and done so in a pretty unpleasant way. He'd threatened more of the same to any law that gave him trouble. Every boss in the area, from the Bronx to Jersey, was shocked at what he'd done. So even if one of them wanted to touch off Paul, why not wait until *after* he'd knocked off Malone?

Which meant it was probably Dewey.

The idea of being stuck in the caboose till he was executed depressed him. Yet, truth be told, in his heart Paul wasn't too torn up about getting nabbed. Like when he was a kid and would jump impulsively into fights against two or three kids bigger than he was, sooner or later he'd eventually pick the wrong punks and end up with a broken bone. He'd known the same thing about his present career: that ultimately a Dewey or an O'Banion would bring him down.

Thinking of one of his father's favorite expressions: "On the best day, on the worst day, the sun finally sets." The round man would snap his colorful suspenders and add, "Cheer up. Tomorrow's a whole new horse race."

He jumped when the phone rang.

Paul looked at the black Bakelite for a long moment. On the seventh ring, or the eighth, he answered. "Yeah?"

"Paul," a crisp, young voice said. No neighborhood slur.

"You know who it is."

"I'm up the hall in another apartment. There're six of us here. Another half dozen on the street."

Twelve? Paul felt an odd calm. Nothing he could do about twelve. They'd get him one way or the other. He sipped more of the Royal Crown. He was so damn thirsty. The fan wasn't doing anything but moving the heat from one side of the room to the other. He asked, "You working for the boys from Brooklyn or the West Side? Just curious."

"Listen to me, Paul. Here's what you're going to do. You only have two guns on you, right? The Colt. And that little twenty-two. The others are back in your apartment?"

Paul laughed. "That's right."

"You're going to unload them and lock the slide of the Colt open. Then walk to the window that's not sealed and pitch them out. Then you're going to take your jacket off, drop it on the floor, open the door and stand in the middle of the room with your hands up in the air. Stretch 'em way up high."

"You'll shoot me," he said.

"You're living on borrowed time anyway, Paul. But if you do what I say you might stay alive a little longer."

The caller hung up.

He dropped the hand piece into the cradle. He sat motionless for a moment, recalling a very pleasant night a few weeks ago. Marion and he had gone to Coney Island for miniature golf and hot dogs and beer, to beat the heat. Laughing, she'd dragged him to a fortune teller at the amusement park. The fake gypsy had read his cards and told him a lot of things. The woman had missed this particular event, though, which you'd think should've showed up somewhere in the reading if she was worth her salt.

Marion . . . He'd never told her what he did for a living. Only that he owned a gym and he did business occasionally with some guys who had questionable pasts. But he'd never told her more. He realized suddenly that he'd been looking forward to some kind of future with her. She was a dime-a-dance girl at a club on the West Side, studying fashion design during the day. She'd be working now; she usually went till 1 or 2 A.M. How would she find out what happened to him?

If it was Dewey he'd probably be able to call her.

If it was the boys from Williamsburg, no call. Nothing.

The phone began ringing again.

Paul ignored it. He slipped the clip from his big gun and unchambered the round that was in the receiver, then he emptied the cartridges out of the revolver. He walked to the window and tossed the pistols out one at a time. He didn't hear them land.

Finishing the soda pop, he took his jacket off, dropped it on the floor. He started for the door but paused. He went back to the Kelvinator and got another Royal Crown. He drank it down. Then he wiped his face again, opened the front door, stepped back and lifted his arms.

The phone stopped ringing.

"This's called The Room," said the gray-haired man in a pressed white uniform, taking a seat on a small couch.

"You were never here," he added with a cheerful confidence that meant there was no debate. He added, "And you never heard about it."

It was 11 P.M. They'd brought Paul here directly from Malone's. It was a private town house on the Upper East Side, though most of the rooms on the ground floor contained desks and telephones and Teletype machines, like in an office. Only in the parlor were there divans and armchairs. On the walls here were pictures of new and old navy ships. A globe sat in the corner. FDR looked down at him from a spot above a marble mantel. The room was wonderfully cold. A private house that had air-conditioning. Imagine.

Still handcuffed, Paul had been deposited in a comfortable leather armchair. The two younger men who'd escorted him out of Malone's apartment, also in white uniforms, sat beside him and slightly behind. The one who'd spoken to him on the phone was named Andrew Avery, a man with rosy cheeks and deliberate, sharp eyes. Eyes of a boxer, though Paul knew he'd never been in a fistfight in his life. The other was Vincent Manielli, dark, with a voice that told Paul they'd probably grown up in the same section of Brooklyn. Manielli and Avery didn't look much older than the stickball kids in front of Paul's building, but they were, of all things, lieutenants in the navy. When Paul had been in France the lieutenants he'd served under had been grown men.

Their pistols were in holsters but the leather flaps were undone and they kept their hands near their weapons.

The older officer, sitting across from him on the couch, was pretty high up—a naval commander, if the gingerbread on his uniform was the same as it'd been twenty years ago.

The door opened and an attractive woman in a white navy uniform entered. The name on her blouse was Ruth Willets. She handed him a file. "Everything's in there."

"Thank you, Yeoman."

As she left, without glancing at Paul, the officer opened the file, extracted two pieces of thin paper, read them carefully. When he finished, he looked up. "I'm James Gordon. Office of Naval Intelligence. They call me Bull."

"This is your headquarters?" Paul asked. "'The Room'?"

The commander ignored him and glanced at the other two. "You introduced yourselves yet?"

"Yes, sir."

"There was no trouble?"

"None, sir." Avery was doing the talking.

"Take his cuffs off."

Avery did so while Manielli stood with his hand near his gun, edgily eyeing Paul's gnarled knuckles. Manielli had fighter's hands too. Avery's were pink as a dry-goods clerk's.

The door swung open again and another man walked inside. He was in his sixties but as lean and tall as that young actor Marion and Paul had seen in a couple of films, Jimmy Stewart. Paul frowned. He knew the face from articles in the *Times* and the *Herald Tribune*. "Senator?"

The man responded, but to Gordon: "You said he was smart. I didn't know he was well-informed." As if he wasn't happy about being recognized. The Senator looked Paul up and down, sat and lit a stubby cigar.

A moment later yet another man entered, about the same age as the Senator, wearing a white linen suit that was savagely wrinkled. The body it encased was large and soft. He carried a walking stick. He glanced once at Paul then, without a word to anyone, he retreated to the corner. He too looked familiar but Paul couldn't place him.

"Now," Gordon continued. "Here's the situation, Paul. We know you've worked for Luciano, we know you've worked for Lansky, a couple of the others. And we know what you do for them."

"Yeah, what's that?"

"You're a button man, Paul," Manielli said brightly, as if he'd been looking forward to saying it.

Gordon said, "Last March Jimmy Coughlin saw you . . ." He frowned. "What do you people say? You don't say 'kill.'"

Paul, thinking: Some of us people say "chill off." Paul himself used "touch off." It was the phrase that Sergeant Alvin York used to describe killing enemy soldiers during the War. It made Paul feel less like a punk to use the term that a war hero did. But, of course, Paul Schumann didn't share any of this at the moment.

Gordon continued. "Jimmy saw you kill Arch Dimici on March thirteenth in a warehouse on the Hudson."

Paul had staked out the place for four hours before Dimici showed up. He'd been positive the man was alone. Jimmy must've been sleeping one off behind some crates when Paul arrived.

"Now, from what they tell me, Jimmy isn't the most reliable witness. But we've got some hard evidence. A few revenue boys picked him up for selling hooch and he made a deal to rat on you. Seems he'd picked up a shell casing at the scene and was keeping it for insurance. No prints're on it—you're too smart for that. But Hoover's people ran a test on your Colt. The scratches from the extractor're the same."

Hoover? The FBI was involved? And they'd *already* tested the gun. He'd pitched it out of Malone's window less than an hour ago.

Paul rocked his upper and lower teeth against each other. He was furious with himself. He'd searched for a half hour to find that damn casing at the Dimici job and had finally concluded it'd fallen through the cracks in the floor into the Hudson.

"So we made inquiries and heard you were being paid five hundred dollars to . . ." Gordon hesitated.

Touch off.

" . . . eliminate Malone tonight."

"Like hell I was," Paul said, laughing. "You got yourself some bum wire. I just went to visit him. Where is he, by the way?"

Gordon paused. "Mr. Malone will no longer be a threat to the constabulary or the citizens of New York City."

"Sounds like somebody owes you five C-notes."

Bull Gordon didn't laugh. "You're in Dutch, Paul, and you can't beat the rap. So here's what we're offering. Like they say in those used-Studebaker ads: this's a one-time-only offer. Take it or leave it. We don't negotiate."

The Senator finally spoke. "Tom Dewey wants you as bad as he wants the rest of the scum on his list."

The special prosecutor was on a divine mission to clean up organized crime in New York. Crime boss Lucky Luciano, the Italian Five Families in the city and the Jewish syndicate of Meyer Lansky were his main targets. Dewey was dogged and smart and he was winning conviction after conviction.

"But he's agreed to give us first dibs on you."

"Forget it. I'm not a stool pigeon."

Gordon said, "We're not asking you to be one. That's not what this is about."

"Then what *do* you want me to do?"

A pause for a moment. The Senator nodded toward Gordon, who said, "You're a button man, Paul. What do you think? We want you to kill somebody."

Chapter Two

He held Gordon's eyes for a moment then he looked at the pictures of the ships on the wall. The Room . . . It had a military feel to it. Like an officers' club. Paul had liked his time in the army. He'd felt at home there, had friends, had a purpose. That was a good time for him, a simple time—before he came back home and life got complicated. When life gets complicated, bad things can happen.

"You're being square with me?"

"Oh, you bet."

With Manielli squinting out a warning to move slowly, Paul reached into his pocket and took out a pack of Chesterfields. He lit one. "Go on."

Gordon said, "You've got that gym over on Ninth Avenue. Not much of a place, is it?" He asked this of Avery.

"You been there?" Paul asked.

Avery said, "Not so swank."

Manielli laughed. "Real dive, I'd say."

The commander continued, "But you used to be a printer before you got into this line of work. You liked the printing business, Paul?"

Cautiously Paul said, "Yeah."

"Were you good at it?"

"Yeah, I was good. What's that got to do with the price of tea in China?"

"How'd you like to make your whole past go away. Start over. Be a printer again. We can fix it so nobody can prosecute you for anything you've done in the past."

"And," the Senator added, "we'll cough up some bucks too. Five thousand. You can get a new life."

Five *thousand?* Paul blinked. It took most joes two years to earn that kind of money. He asked, "How can you clean up my record?"

The Senator laughed. "You know that new game, Monopoly? You ever play it?"

"My nephews have it. I never played."

The Senator continued. "Sometimes when you roll the dice you end up in prison. But there's this card that says 'Get Out of Jail Free.' Well, we'll give you one for real. That's all you need to know."

"You want me to kill somebody? That's queer. Dewey'd never agree to it."

The Senator said, "The special prosecutor hasn't been informed about why we want you."

After a pause he asked, "Who? Siegel?" Of all the current mobsters Bugsy Siegel was the most dangerous. Psychotic, really. Paul had seen the bloody results of the man's brutality. His tantrums were legendary.

"Now, Paul," Gordon said, disdain on his face, "it'd be illegal for you to kill a U.S. citizen. We'd never ask you to do anything like that."

"Then I don't get the angle."

The Senator said, "This is more like a wartime situation. You were a soldier. . . ." A glance at Avery, who recited, "First Infantry Division, First American Army, AEF. St. Mihiel, Meuse-Argonne. You did some serious fighting. Got yourself some medals for marksmanship in the field. Did some hand-to-hand too, right?"

Paul shrugged. The fat man in the wrinkled white suit sat silently in his corner, hands clasped on the gold handle of his walking stick. Paul held his eye for a minute. Then turned back to the commander. "What're the odds I'll survive long enough to *use* my get-out-of-jail card?"

"Reasonable," the commander said. "Not great but reasonable."

Paul was a friend of the sports journalist and writer Damon Runyon. They'd drink together some in the dives near Broadway, go to fights and ball games. A couple of years ago Runyon had invited Paul to a party after the New York opening of his movie *Little Miss Marker,* which Paul thought was a pretty good flick. At the party afterward, where he got a kick out of meeting Shirley Temple, he'd asked Runyon to autograph a book. The writer had inscribed it, *To my pal, Paul—Remember, all of life is six to five against.*

Avery said, "How 'bout we just say your chances're a lot better than if you go to Sing-Sing."

After a moment Paul asked, "Why me? You've got dozens of button men in New York'd be willing to do it for that kind of scratch."

"Ah, but you're different, Paul. You're not a two-bit punk. You're good. Hoover and Dewey say you've killed seventeen men."

Paul scoffed. "Bum wire, I keep saying."

In fact, the number was thirteen.

"What we've heard about you is that you check everything two, three times before the job. You make sure your guns're in perfect shape, you read up about your victims, you look over their places ahead of time, you find their schedule and you make sure they stick to it, you know when they'll be alone, when they make phone calls, where they eat."

The Senator added, "And you're smart. Like I was saying. We need smart for this."

"Smart?"

Manielli said, "We been to your place, Paul. You got books. Damn, you got a lot of books. You're even in the Book of the Month Club."

"They're not smart books. Not all of 'em."

"But they *are* books," Avery pointed out. "And I'm betting a lot of people in your business don't read much."

"Or *can't* read," Manielli said and laughed at his own joke.

Paul looked over at the man in the wrinkled white suit. "Who're you?"

"You don't need to worry—" Gordon began.

"I'm asking him."

"Listen," the Senator grumbled, "we're calling the shots, my friend."

But the fat man waved his hand and then replied to Paul, "You know the comics? Little Orphan Annie, the girl without the pupils in her eyes?"

"Yeah, sure."

"Well, think of me as Daddy Warbucks."

"What's that mean?"

But he just laughed and turned to the Senator. "Keep pitching your case. I like him."

The rail-thin politician said to Paul, "Most important, you don't kill anybody innocent."

Gordon added, "Jimmy Coughlin told us you said one time that you only kill other killers. What'd you say? That you only 'correct God's mistakes'? That's what we need."

"God's mistakes," the Senator repeated, smiling in lip but not in spirit.

"Well, who is it?"

Gordon looked at the Senator, who deflected the question. "You have relatives in Germany still?"

"Nobody close. My family came over here a long time ago."

The Senator asked, "What do you know about the Nazis?"

"Adolf Hitler's running the country. Sounds like nobody's really crazy about it. There was this big rally against him at Madison Square Garden in March, two, three years ago. Traffic was a swell mess, I'll tell you. I missed the first three rounds of a fight up in the Bronx. Got under my skin. . . . That's about it."

"Did you know, Paul," the Senator said slowly, "that Hitler's planning another war?"

That brought him up short.

"Our sources've been giving us information from Germany since Hitler came to power in thirty-three. Last year, our man in Berlin got his hands on a draft of this letter. It was written by one of their senior men, General Beck."

The commander handed him a typed sheet. It was in German. Paul read it. The author of the letter called for a slow but steady rearmament of the German armed forces to protect and expand what Paul translated as "living area." The nation had to be ready for war in a few years.

Frowning, he put the sheet down. "And they're going ahead with this?"

"Last year," Gordon said, "Hitler started a draft and since then he's building up the troops to even higher levels than that letter recommends. Then four months ago German troops took over the Rhineland—the demil- itarized zone bordering France."

"I read about that."

"They're building submarines at Helgoland and're taking back control of the Wilhelm Canal to move warships from the North Sea to the Baltic. The man running the finances over there has a new title. He's head of the 'war economy.' And Spain, their civil war? Hitler's sending troops and equip- ment supposedly to help Franco. Actually he's using the war to train *his* sol- diers."

"You want me . . . you want a button man to kill Hitler?"

"Lord, no," the Senator said. "Hitler's just a crank. Funny in the head. He wants the country to rearm but he doesn't have a clue how to do it."

"And this man you're talking about does?"

"Oh, you bet he does," the Senator offered. "His name's Reinhard Ernst. He was a colonel during the War but he's civilian now. Title's a mouthful:

plenipotentiary for domestic stability. But that's hooey. He's the brains behind rearmament. He's got his finger in everything: financing with Schacht, army with Blomberg, navy with Raeder, air force with Göring, munitions with Krupp."

"What about the treaty? Versailles? They can't *have* an army, I thought."

"Not a big one. Same with the navy . . . and no air force at all," the Senator said. "But our man tells us that soldiers and sailors're popping up all over Germany like wine at Cana's wedding."

"So can't the Allies just stop them? I mean, *we* won the War."

"Nobody in Europe's doing a thing. The French could've stopped Hitler cold last March, at the Rhineland. But they didn't. The Brits? All they did was scold a dog that'd pissed on the carpet."

After a moment Paul asked, "And what've *we* done to stop them?"

Gordon's subtle glance was one of deference. The Senator shrugged. "In America all we want is peace. The isolationists're running the show. They don't want to be involved in European politics. Men want jobs, and mothers don't want to lose their sons in Flanders Fields again."

"And the president wants to get elected again this November," Paul said, feeling FDR's eyes peering down on him from above the ornate mantelpiece.

Awkward silence for a moment. Gordon laughed. The Senator did not.

Paul stubbed out his cigarette. "Okay. Sure. It's making sense now. If I get caught there's nothing to lead them back to you. Or to *him*." A nod toward Roosevelt's picture. "Hell, I'm just a crazy civilian, not a soldier like these kids here." A glance at the two junior officers. Avery smiled; Manielli did too but his was a very different smile.

The Senator said, "That's right, Paul. That's exactly right."

"And I speak German."

"We heard you're fluent."

Paul's grandfather was proud of his country of ancestry, as was Paul's father, who insisted the children study German and speak their native language in the house. He recalled absurd moments when his mother would shout in Gaelic and his father in German when they fought. Paul had also worked in his grandfather's plant, setting type and proofreading German-language printing jobs during the summers when he was in high school.

"How would it work? I'm not saying yes. I'm just curious. How would it work?"

"There's a ship taking the Olympic team, families and press over to Germany. It leaves day after tomorrow. You'd be on it."

"The Olympic team?"

"We've decided it's the best way. There'll be thousands of foreigners in town. Berlin'll be packed. Their army and police'll have their hands full."

Avery said, "You won't have anything to do with the Olympics officially—the games don't start till August first. The Olympic Committee only knows you're a writer."

"A sports journalist," Gordon added. "That's your cover. But basically you just play dumb and make yourself invisible. Go to the Olympic Village with everybody else and spend a day or two there then slip into the city. A hotel's no good; the Nazis monitor all the guests and record passports. Our man's getting a room in a private boardinghouse for you."

Like any craftsman, certain questions about the job slipped into his mind. "Would I use my name?"

"Yes, you'll be yourself. But we'll also get you an escape passport—with your picture but a different name. Issued by some other country."

The Senator said, "You look Russian. You're big and solid." He nodded. "Sure, you'll be the 'man from Russia.'"

"I don't speak Russian."

"Nobody there does either. Besides, you'll probably never need the passport. It's just to get you out of the country in an emergency."

"And," Paul added quickly, "to make sure nobody traces me to you if I *don't* make it out, right?"

The Senator's hesitation, followed by a glance at Gordon, said he was on the money.

Paul continued. "Who'm I supposed to be working for? All the papers'll have stringers there. They'd know I wasn't a reporter."

"We thought of that. You'll be writing freelance stories and trying to sell 'em to some of the sports rags when you get back."

Paul asked, "Who's your man over there?"

Gordon said, "No names just now."

"I don't need a name. Do you trust him? And why?"

The Senator said, "He's been living there for a couple of years and getting us quality information. He served under me in the War. I know him personally."

"What's his cover there?"

"Businessman, facilitator, that sort of thing. Works for himself."

Gordon continued. "He'll get you a weapon and whatever you need to know about your target."

"I don't have a real passport. In my name, I mean."

"We know, Paul. We'll get you one."

"Can I have my guns back?"

"No," Gordon said and that was the end of the matter. "So that's our general plan, my friend. And, I should tell you, if you're thinking of hopping a freight and laying low in some Hooverville out west? . . ."

Paul sure as hell had been. But he frowned and shook his head.

"Well, these fine young men'll be sticking to you like limpets until the ship docks in Hamburg. And if you should get the same hankering to slip out of Berlin, our contact's going to be keeping an eye on you. If you disappear, he calls us and we call the Nazis to tell them an escaped American killer's at large in Berlin. And we'll give them your name and picture." Gordon held his eye. "If you think *we* were good at tracking you down, Paul, you ain't seen nothing like the Nazis. And from what we hear they don't bother with trials and writs of execution. Now, we clear on that?"

"As a bell."

"Good." The commander glanced at Avery. "Now, tell him what happens after he finishes the job."

The lieutenant said, "We'll have a plane and a crew waiting in Holland. There's an old aerodrome outside of Berlin. After you've finished we'll fly you out from there."

"Fly me out?" Paul asked, intrigued. Flying fascinated him. When he was nine he broke his arm—the first of more times than he wanted to count—when he built a glider and launched himself off the roof of his father's printing plant, crash-landing on the filthy cobblestones two stories below.

"That's right, Paul," Gordon said.

Avery offered, "You like airplanes, don't you? You've got all those airplane magazines in your apartment. Books too. And pictures of planes. Some models too. You make those yourself?"

Paul felt embarrassed. It made him angry that they'd found his toys.

"You a pilot?" the Senator asked.

"Never even been in a plane before." Then he shook his head. "I don't know." This whole thing was absolutely nuts. Silence filled the room.

It was broken by the man in the wrinkled white suit. "I was a colonel in the War too. Just like Reinhard Ernst. And I was at Argonne Woods. Just like *you.*"

Paul nodded.

"You know the total?"

"Of what?"

"How many we lost?"

Paul remembered a sea of bodies, American, French and German. The wounded were in some ways more horrible. They cried and wailed and moaned and called for their mothers and fathers and you never forgot that sound. Ever.

The older man said in a reverent voice, "The AEF lost more than twenty-five thousand. Almost a hundred wounded. Half the boys under my command died. In a month we advanced seven miles against the enemy. Every day of my life I've thought about those numbers. Half my soldiers, seven miles. And Meuse-Argonne was our most spectacular *victory* in the War. . . . I do not want that to happen again."

Paul regarded him. "Who are you?" he asked again.

The Senator stirred and began to speak but the other man replied, "I'm Cyrus Clayborn."

Yeah, that was it. Brother . . . The old guy was the head of Continental Telephone and Telegraph—a real honest-to-God millionaire, even now, in the shadow of the Depression.

The man continued. "Daddy Warbucks, like I was saying. I'm the banker. For, let's say, *projects* like this it's usually better for the money not to come out of public troughs. I'm too old to fight for my country. But I do what I can. That satisfy your itch, boy?"

"Yeah, it does."

"Good." Clayborn looked him over. "Well, I've got one more thing to say. The money they mentioned before? The amount?"

Paul nodded.

"Double it."

Paul felt his skin crackle. *Ten* thousand dollars? He couldn't imagine it.

Gordon's head slowly turned toward the Senator. This, Paul understood, wasn't part of the script.

"Would you give me cash? Not a check."

For some reason the Senator and Clayborn laughed hard at this. "Whatever you want, sure," the industrialist said.

The Senator pulled a phone closer to him and tapped the hand piece. "So, what's it going to be, son? We get on the horn to Dewey, or not?"

The rasp of a match broke the silence as Gordon lit a cigarette. "Think about it, Paul. We're giving you the chance to erase the past. Start all over again. What kind of button man gets that kind of deal?"

II
THE CITY OF WHISPERS

FRIDAY, 24 JULY, 1936

Chapter Three

Finally, the man could do what he'd come here for.

It was six in the morning and the ship in whose pungent third-class corridor he now stood, the S.S. *Manhattan,* was nosing toward Hamburg harbor, ten days after leaving New York.

The vessel was, literally, the flagship of the United States Lines—the first in the company's fleet constructed exclusively for passengers. It was huge—over two football fields in length—but this voyage had been especially crowded. Typical transatlantic crossings found the ship carrying six hundred or so passengers and a crew of five hundred. On this trip, though, nearly four hundred Olympic athletes, managers and coaches and another 850 passengers, mostly family, friends, the press and members of the AOC, filled the three classes of accommodations.

The number of passengers and the unusual requirements of the athletes and reporters on board the *Manhattan* had made life hectic for the diligent, polite crew, but particularly so for this round, bald man, whose name was Albert Heinsler. Certainly his job as a porter meant long and strenuous hours. But the most arduous aspect of his day was due to his true role on board the ship, one that not a single soul here knew anything about. Heinsler called himself an A-man, which is how the Nazi intelligence service referred to their trusted operatives in Germany—their *Agenten.*

In fact, this reclusive thirty-four-year-old bachelor was merely a member of the German-American Bund, a group of ragtag, pro-Hitler Americans loosely allied with the Christian Front in their stand against Jews, Communists and Negroes. Heinsler didn't hate America but he could never forget the terrible days as a teenager when his family had been driven to poverty during the War because of anti-German prejudice; he himself had been relentlessly taunted—"Heinie, Heinie, Heinie the Hun"—and beaten up countless times in school yards and alleys.

No, he didn't hate his country. But he loved Nazi Germany with all his heart and was enraptured with the messiah Adolf Hitler. He'd make any sacrifice for the man—prison or even death if necessary.

Heinsler had hardly believed his good fortune when the commanding Stormtrooper at the New Jersey headquarters of the bund had noted the loyal comrade's past employment as a bookkeeper on board some passenger liners and had arranged to get him a job on the *Manhattan*. The brown-uniformed commandant had met him on the boardwalk at Atlantic City and explained that while the Nazis were magnanimously welcoming people from around the world they were worried about security breaches that the influx of athletes and visitors might allow. Heinsler's duty was to be the Nazis' clandestine representative on this ship. He wouldn't be doing his past job, though—keeping ledgers. It was important that he be free to roam the ship without suspicion; he'd be a porter.

Why, this was the thrill of his life! He immediately quit his job working in the back room of a certified public accountant on lower Broadway. He spent the next few days, until the ship sailed, being his typically obsessed self, preparing for his mission as he worked through the night to study diagrams of the ship, practice his role as a porter, brush up on his German and learn a variation of Morse code, called continental code, which was used when telegraphing messages to and within Europe.

Once the ship left port he kept to himself, observed and listened and was the perfect A-man. But when the *Manhattan* was at sea, he'd been unable to communicate with Germany; the signal of his portable wireless was too weak. The ship itself had a powerful radiogram system, of course, as well as short- and long-wave wireless, but he could hardly transmit his message those ways; a crew radio operator would be involved, and it was vital that nobody heard or saw what he had to say.

Heinsler now glanced out the porthole at the gray strip of Germany. Yes, he believed he was close enough to shore to transmit. He stepped into his minuscule cabin and retrieved the Allocchio Bacchini wireless-telegraph set from under his cot. Then he started toward the stairs that would take him to the highest deck, where he hoped the puny signal would make it to shore.

As he walked down the narrow corridor, he mentally reviewed his message once again. One thing he regretted was that, although he wanted to include his name and affiliation, he couldn't do so. Even though Hitler privately admired what the German-American Bund was doing, the group was so rabidly—and loudly—anti-Semitic that the Führer had been forced to publicly disavow it. Heinsler's words would be ignored if he included any reference to the American group.

And this particular message could most certainly not be ignored.

> *For the Obersturmführer-SS, Hamburg: I am a devoted National Socialist. Have overheard that a man with a Russian connection intends to cause some damage at high levels in Berlin in the next few days. Have not learned his identity yet but will continue to look into this matter and hope to send that information soon.*

He was alive when he sparred.

There was no feeling like this. Dancing in the snug leather shoes, muscles warm, skin both cool from sweat and hot from blood, the dynamo hum of your body in constant motion. The pain too. Paul Schumann believed you could learn a lot from pain. That really was the whole point of it, after all.

But mostly he liked sparring because, like boxing itself, success or failure rested solely on his own broad and slightly scarred shoulders and was due to his deft feet and powerful hands and his mind. In boxing, it's only you against the other guy, no teammates. If you get beat, it's because he's better than you. Plain and simple. And the credit's yours if you win—because you did the jump rope, you laid off the booze and cigarettes, you thought for hours and hours and hours about how to get under his guard, about what his weaknesses were. There's luck at Ebbets Field and Yankee Stadium. But there's no luck in the boxing ring.

He was now dancing over the ring that had been set up on the main deck of the *Manhattan;* the whole ship had been turned into a floating gymnasium for training. One of the Olympic boxers had seen him working out at the punching bag last night and asked if he wanted to do some sparring this morning before the ship docked. Paul had immediately agreed.

He now dodged a few left jabs and connected with his signature right, drawing a surprised blink from his opponent. Then Paul took a hard blow to the gut before getting his guard up again. He was a little stiff at first—he hadn't been in a ring for a while—but he'd had this smart, young sports doctor on board, a fellow named Joel Koslow, look him over and tell him he could go head-to-head with a boxer half his age. "I'd keep it to two or three rounds, though," the doc had added with a smile. "These youngsters're *strong*. They pack a wallop."

Which was sure true. But Paul didn't mind. The harder the workout the better, in fact, because—like the shadowboxing and jump rope he'd done every day on board—this session was helping him stay in shape for what lay ahead in Berlin.

Paul sparred two or three times a week. He was in some demand as a sparring partner even though he was forty-one, because he was a walking lesson book of boxing techniques. He'd spar anywhere, in Brooklyn gyms, in outdoor rings at Coney Island, even in serious venues. Damon Runyon was one of the founders of the Twentieth Century Sporting Club—along with the legendary promoter Mike Jacobs and a few other newspapermen—and he'd gotten Paul into New York's Hippodrome itself to work out. Once or twice he'd actually gone glove to glove with some of the greats. He'd spar at his own gym too, in the little building near the West Side docks. Yeah, Avery, it's not so swank, but the dingy, musty place was a sanctuary, as far as Paul was concerned, and Sorry Williams, who lived in the back room, always kept the place neat and had ice, towels and beer handy.

The kid now feinted but Paul knew immediately where the jab was coming from and blocked it then laid a solid blow on the chest. He missed the next block, though, and felt the leather take him solidly on the jaw. He danced out of the man's reach before the follow-through connected and they circled once more.

As they moved over the canvas Paul noted that the boy was strong and fast, but he couldn't detach himself from his opponent. He'd get overwhelmed with a lust to win. Well, you needed desire, of course, but more important was calmly observing how the other guy moved, looking for clues as to what he was going to do next. This detachment was absolutely vital in being a great boxer.

And it was vital for a button man too.

He called it touching the ice.

Several years ago, sitting in Hanrahan's gin mill on Forty-eighth Street, Paul was nursing a painful shiner, courtesy of Beavo Wayne, who couldn't hit a midsection to save his soul but, Lord above, could he open eyebrows. As Paul pressed a piece of cheap beefsteak to his face, a huge Negro pushed through the door, making the daily delivery of ice. Most icemen used tongs and carried the blocks on their back. But this guy carried it in his hands. No gloves even. Paul watched him walk behind the bar and set the block in the trough.

"Hey," Paul'd asked him. "You chip me off some of that?"

The man looked at the purple blotch around Paul's eye and laughed. He pulled an ice pick out of a holster and chipped off a piece, which Paul wrapped in a napkin and held to his face. He slid a dime to the deliveryman, who said, "Thanks fo' that."

"Let me ask," Paul said. "How come you can carry that ice? Doesn't it hurt?"

"Oh, look here." He held up his large hands. The palms were scar tissue, as smooth and pale as the parchment paper that Paul's father had used when printing fancy invitations.

The Negro explained, "Ice can burn you too, juss like fire. Like leavin' a scar. I been touchin' ice fo' so long I ain't got no feelin' left."

Touching the ice . . .

That phrase stuck with Paul. It was, he realized, exactly what happened when he was on a job. There's ice within all of us, he believed. We can choose to grip it or not.

Now, in this improbable gymnasium, thousands of miles from home, Paul felt some of this same numbness as he lost himself in the choreography of the sparring match. Leather met leather and leather met skin, and even in the cool air of dawn at sea these two men sweated hard as they circled, looking for weaknesses, sensing strengths. Sometimes connecting, sometimes not. But always vigilant.

There's no luck in the boxing ring. . . .

Albert Heinsler perched beside a smokestack on one of the high decks of the *Manhattan* and hooked the battery to the wireless set. He took out the tiny black-and-brown telegraph key and mounted it to the top of the unit.

He was slightly troubled to be using an Italian transmitter—he thought Mussolini treated the Führer with disrespect—but this was mere sentiment; he knew that the Allocchio Bacchini was one of the best portable transmitters in the world.

As the tubes warmed up he tried the key, *dot dash, dot dash.* His compulsive nature had driven him to practice for hours on end. He'd timed himself just before the ship sailed; he could send a message of this length in under two minutes.

Staring at the nearing shore, Heinsler inhaled deeply. It felt good to be up here, on the higher deck. While he hadn't been condemned to his cabin, retching and moaning like hundreds of the passengers and even some crew, he hated the claustrophobia of being below. His past career as shipboard bookkeeper had had more status than the job of porter and he'd had a larger cabin on a high deck. But no matter—the honor of helping his surrogate country outweighed any discomfort.

Finally a light glowed on the face plate of the radio unit. He bent forward, adjusted two of the dials and slipped his finger onto the tiny Bakelite key. He began transmitting the message, which he translated into German as he keyed.

Dot dot dash dot . . . dot dot dash . . . dot dash dot . . . dash dash dash . . . dash dot dot dot . . . dot . . . dot dash dot . . .

Für Ober—

He got no further than this.

Heinsler gasped as a hand grabbed his collar from behind and pulled him backward. Off balance, he cried out and fell to the smooth oak deck.

"No, no, don't hurt me!" He started to rise to his feet but the large, grim-faced man, wearing a boxing outfit, drew back a huge fist and shook his head.

"Don't move."

Heinsler sank back to the deck, shivering.

Heinie, Heinie, Heinie the Hun . . .

The boxer reached forward and ripped the battery wires off the unit. "Downstairs," he said, gathering up the transmitter. "Now." And he yanked the A-man to his feet.

"What're you up to?"

"Go to hell," the balding man said, though with a quavering voice that belied his words.

They were in Paul's cabin. The transmitter, battery and the contents of the man's pockets were strewn on the narrow cot. Paul repeated his question, adding an ominous growl this time. "Tell me—"

A pounding on the cabin door. Paul stepped forward, cocked his fist and opened the door. Vince Manielli pushed inside.

"I got your message. What the hell is—?" He fell silent, staring at their prisoner.

Paul handed him the wallet. "Albert Heinsler, German-American Bund."

"Oh, Christ . . . Not the bund."

"He had that." A nod at the wireless telegraph.

"He was spying on *us*?"

"I don't know. But he was just about to transmit something."

"How'd you tip to him?"

"Call it a hunch."

Paul didn't tell Manielli that, while he trusted Gordon and his boys up to a point, he didn't know how careless they might be at this sort of game; they could've been leaving behind a trail of clues a mile wide—notes about the ship, careless words about Malone or another touch-off, even references to Paul himself. He hadn't thought there was much of a risk from the Nazis; he was more concerned that word might get to some of his old enemies in Brooklyn or Jersey that he was on the ship, and he wanted to be prepared. So he'd dipped into his own pocket just after they'd left port and slipped a senior mate a C-note, asking him to find out about any crew members who were strangers to the regular crew, kept to themselves, were asking unusual questions. Any passengers too who seemed suspicious.

A hundred dollars buys a hell of a lot of detective work but throughout the voyage the mate had heard of nothing—until this morning, when he'd interrupted Paul's sparring match with the Olympian to tell him that some of the crew had been talking about this porter, Heinsler. He was always skulking around, never spent time with fellow crew members and—weirdest of all—would start spouting hooey about the Nazis and Hitler at the drop of a hat.

Alarmed, Paul tracked down Heinsler and found him on the top deck, hunched over his radio.

"Did he send anything?" Manielli now asked.

"Not this morning. I came up the stairs behind him and saw him setting the radio up. He didn't have time to send more than a few letters. But he might've been transmitting all week."

Manielli glanced down at the radio. "Probably not with that. The range is only a few miles. . . . What does he know?"

"Ask *him*," Paul said.

"So, fella, what's your game?"

The bald man remained silent.

Paul leaned forward. "Spill."

Heinsler gave an eerie smile. He turned to Manielli. "I heard you talking. I know what you're up to. But they'll stop you."

"Who put you up to this? The bund?"

Heinsler scoffed. "Nobody put me up to anything." He was no longer cringing. He said with breathless devotion, "I'm loyal to the New Germany. I love the Führer and I'd do anything for him and the Party. And people like you—"

"Oh, can it," Manielli muttered. "What do you mean, you heard us?"

Heinsler didn't answer. He smiled smugly and looked out the porthole.

Paul said, "He heard you and Avery? What were you saying?"

The lieutenant looked down at the floor. "I don't know. We went over the plan a couple of times. Just talking it through. I don't remember exactly."

"Brother, not in your cabin?" Paul snapped. "You should've been up on deck where you could see if anybody was around."

"I didn't think anybody'd be listening," the lieutenant said defensively.

A trail of clues a mile wide . . .

"What're you going to do with him?"

"I'll talk to Avery. There's a brig on board. I guess we'll stow him there until we figure something out."

"Could we get him to the consulate in Hamburg?"

"Maybe. I don't know. But . . ." He fell silent, frowning. "What's that smell?"

Paul too frowned. A sudden, bittersweet scent filled the cabin.

"No!"

Heinsler was falling back on the pillow, eyes rolling up in his sockets, bits of white foam filling the corner of his mouth. His body was convulsing horribly.

The scent was of almond.

"Cyanide," Manielli whispered. He ran to the porthole and opened it wide.

Paul took a pillowcase and carefully wiped the man's mouth, fished inside for the capsule. But he pulled out only a few shards of glass. It had shattered completely. He was dead by the time Paul turned back from the basin with a glass of water to wash the poison out of his mouth.

"He killed himself," Manielli whispered manically, staring with wide eyes. "Just . . . Right there. He killed himself."

Paul thought angrily: And there goes a chance to find out anything more.

The lieutenant stared at the body, shaken. "This's a jam all right. Oh, brother . . ."

"Go tell Avery."

But Manielli seemed paralyzed.

Paul took him firmly by the arm. "Vince . . . tell Avery. You listening to me?"

"What? . . . Oh, sure. Andy. I'll tell him. Yeah." The lieutenant stepped outside.

A few dumbbells from the gymnasium tied to the waist would be heavy enough to sink the body in the ocean but the porthole here was only eight inches across. And the *Manhattan*'s corridors were now filling with passengers getting ready to disembark; there was no way to get him out through the interior of the ship. They'd have to wait. Paul tucked the body under the blankets and turned its head aside, as if Heinsler were asleep, then washed his own hands carefully in the tiny basin to make sure all the traces of poison were off.

Ten minutes later there was a knock on the door and Paul let Manielli back inside.

"Andy's contacting Gordon. It's midnight in D.C. but he'll track him down." He couldn't stop staring at the body. Finally the lieutenant asked Paul, "You're packed? Ready to go?"

"Will be, after I change." He glanced down at his athletic shirt and shorts.

"Do that. Then go up top. Andy said we don't want things to look bum, you disappearing and this guy too, then his supervisor can't find him. We'll meet you on the port side, main deck, in a half hour."

With a last glance toward Heinsler's body, Paul picked up his suitcase and shaving kit and headed down to the shower room.

After washing and shaving he dressed in a white shirt and gray flannel slacks, forgoing his short-brimmed brown Stetson; three or four landlubbers had already lost their straw boaters or trilbies overboard. Ten minutes later he was strolling along the solid oak decks in the pale early morning light. Paul stopped, leaned on the rail and smoked a Chesterfield.

He thought about the man who'd just killed himself. He'd never understood that, suicide. The look in the man's eyes gave a clue, Paul supposed. That fanatic's shine. Heinsler reminded him of something he'd read recently, and after a moment he recalled: the people suckered in by the revivalist minister in *Elmer Gantry,* that popular Sinclair Lewis book.

I love the Führer and I'd do anything for him and the Party. . . .

Sure, it was nuts that a man would just take his own life like that. But what was more unsettling was what it told Paul about the gray strip of land he was now gazing at. How many people there had this same deadly passion? People like Dutch Schultz and Siegel were dangerous, but you could understand them. What this man had done, that look in his eyes, the breathless devotion . . . well, they were nuts, way out of kilter. Paul'd never been up against anyone like that.

His thoughts were interrupted as he looked to his side and noticed a well-built young Negro walking toward him. He wore a thin blue Olympic team jacket and shorts, revealing powerful legs.

They nodded greetings.

"Excuse me, sir," the man said softly. "How you doing there?"

"Fine," Paul answered. "Yourself?"

"Love the morning air. Lot cleaner than in Cleveland or New York." They looked over the water. "Saw you sparring earlier. You pro?"

"An old man like me? Just do it for the exercise."

"I'm Jesse."

"Oh, yes, sir, I know who *you* are," Paul said. "The Buckeye Bullet from Ohio State." They shook hands. Paul introduced himself. Despite the shock of what had happened in his cabin, he couldn't stop grinning. "I saw the newsreels of the Western Conference Meet last year. Ann Arbor. You beat three world records. And tied another one, right? Must've seen that film a dozen times. But I'll bet you're tired of hearing people tell you that."

"I don't mind it one bit, no, sir," Jesse Owens said. "Just, I'm always surprised people keep up so close with what I do. Just running and jumping. Haven't seen much of you on the trip, Paul."

"I've been around," Paul said evasively. He wondered if Owens knew something about what'd happened to Heinsler. Had he overheard them? Or seen Paul grab the man on the top deck by the smokestack? But he decided the athlete would've been more troubled if that had been the case. It seemed he had something else in mind. Paul nodded toward the deck behind them. "This is the biggest damn gym I've ever seen. You like it?"

"I'm glad for the chance to train but a track shouldn't move. And it definitely shouldn't rock up and down like we were doing a few days ago. Give me dirt or cinders any day."

Paul said, "So. That's our boxer I was up against."

"That's right. Nice fellow. I spoke to him some."

"He's good," Paul said without much enthusiasm.

"Seems to be," the runner said. It was clear he too knew boxing wasn't the strong suit of the American team but Owens wasn't inclined to criticize a fellow athlete. Paul had heard that the Negro was among the most genial of the Americans; he'd come in second in the most-popular-athlete-on-board contest last night, after Glenn Cunningham.

"I'd offer you a ciggie . . ."

Owens laughed. "Not for me."

"I've pretty much given up offering butts and hits from my flask. You folks're too damn healthy."

Another laugh. Then silence for a moment as the solid Negro looked out to sea. "Say, Paul. I got a question. You here officially?"

"Officially?"

"With the committee, I mean? Maybe like a guard?"

"Me? Why do you say that?"

"You sort of seemed like a, well, soldier or something. And then, the way you were fighting. You knew what you were doing."

"I was in the War. That's probably what you noticed."

"Maybe." Then Owens added, "Course that was twenty years ago. And those two fellows I've seen you talking with. They're navy. We heard 'em talking to one of the crew."

Brother, another trail of clues.

"Those two guys? Just bumped into 'em on board. I'm bumming a ride with you folks. . . . Doing some stories about sports, boxing in Berlin, the Games. I'm a writer."

"Oh, sure." Owens nodded slowly. He seemed to debate for a moment. "Well, if you're a reporter, you still might know something 'bout what I was going to ask you. Just wondering if you heard anything about those two fellows?" He nodded at some men on the deck nearby, running in tandem, passing the relay baton. They were lightning fast.

"Who're they?" Paul asked.

"Sam Stoller and Marty Glickman. They're good runners, some of the best we've got. But I heard a rumor they might not run. Wondered if you knew anything about that."

"Nope, nothing. You mean some qualification problem? Injury?"

"I mean because they're Jewish."

Paul shook his head. He recalled there was a controversy about Hitler not liking Jews. There was some protest and talk about moving the Olympics. Some people even wanted the U.S. team to boycott the Games. Damon Runyon had been all hot under the collar about the country even participating. But why would the *American* committee pull some athletes because they were Jewish? "That'd be a bum deal. Doesn't seem right by a long shot."

"No, sir. Anyway, I was just thinking maybe you'd heard something."

"Sorry, can't help you, friend," Paul said.

They were joined by another Negro. Ralph Metcalfe introduced himself. Paul knew about him too. He'd won medals in the Los Angeles Olympics in '32.

Owens noticed Vince Manielli looking down at them from an upper deck. The lieutenant nodded and started for the stairs.

"Here comes your buddy. That you *just* met on board." Owens had a sly grin on his face, not completely convinced that Paul'd been on the level. The Negro's eyes looked forward, at the growing strip of land. "Imagine that. We're almost in Germany. Never thought I'd be traveling like this. Life can be a pretty amazing thing, don't you think?"

"That it can," Paul agreed.

The runners said good-bye and jogged off.

"Was that Owens?" Manielli asked, walking up and leaning against the railing. He turned his back to the wind and rolled a cigarette.

"Yep." Paul pulled a Chesterfield out of a pack, lit it in cupped hands and offered the matches to the lieutenant. He too lit up. "Nice man."

Though a little too sharp, Paul thought.

"Damn, that man can run. What'd he say?"

"We were just shooting the breeze." In a whisper: "What's the situation with our friend down below?"

"Avery's handling it," Manielli said ambiguously. "He's in the radio room. Be here in a minute." A plane flew overhead, low. They watched it for several minutes in silence.

The kid still seemed shaken by the suicide. Not in the same way Paul was, though: because the death told him something troubling about the people he was going up against. No, the sailor was upset because he'd just seen death up close—and for the first time, it was pretty clear. Paul knew there were two kinds of punks. They both talked loud and they both blustered and they both had strong arms and big fists. But one kind would leap for the chance to give knuckle and take it—touching the ice—and the other wouldn't. It was the second category that Vince Manielli fell into. He was really just a good boy from the neighborhood. He liked to sling out words like "button man" and "knock off" to show he knew what they meant, but he was as far from Paul's world, though, as Marion was—Marion, the good girl who flirted with bad.

But, like the mob boss Lucky Luciano had once told him, "Flirting ain't fucking."

Manielli seemed to be waiting for Paul to comment on the dead sap, Heinsler. Something about the guy deserving to die. Or that he was nuts in the head. People always wanted to hear that about somebody who died. That it was their own fault or they deserved it or it was inevitable. But death is never symmetrical and tidy, and the button man had nothing to say. A thick silence filled the space between them and a moment later Andrew Avery joined them. He was carrying a folder of papers and an old battered leather briefcase. He looked around. There was no one within earshot. "Pull up a chair."

Paul found a heavy wooden white deck chair and carried it over to the sailors. He didn't need to carry it in one hand, would've been easier in two, but he liked seeing Manielli's blink when he hefted the furniture and swung it over without a grunt. Paul sat down.

"Here's the wire," the lieutenant whispered. "The commander's not so worried about this Heinsler guy. The Allocchio Bacchini's a small wireless; it's made for fieldwork and airplanes, short range. And even if he got a message off, Berlin probably wouldn't pay it much attention. The bund's an embarrassment to them. But Gordon said it's up to you. If you want out, that's okay."

"But no get-out-of-jail card," Paul said.

"No card," Avery said.

"This deal just keeps getting sweeter and sweeter." The button man gave a sour laugh.

"You're still in?"

"I'm in, yeah." A nod toward the deck below. "What'll happen to the body?"

"After everybody disembarks, some marines from the Hamburg consulate'll come on board and take care of it." Then Avery leaned forward and said in a low voice, "Okay, here's what's going to happen about your mission, Paul. After we dock, you get off and Vince and I'll take care of the situation with Heinsler. Then we're going on to Amsterdam. You stay with the team. There'll be a brief ceremony in Hamburg and then everybody takes the train to Berlin. The athletes'll have another ceremony tonight but you go straight to the Olympic Village and stay out of sight. Tomorrow morning take a bus to the Tiergarten—that's the Central Park of Berlin." He handed the briefcase to Paul. "Take this with you."

"What is it?"

"It's part of your cover. Press pass. Paper, pencils. A lot of background about the Games and the city. A guide to the Olympic Village. Articles, clippings, sports statistics. The sort of stuff a writer'd have. You don't need to look at it now."

But Paul opened the case and spent some minutes looking carefully, going through the contents. The pass, Avery assured him, was authentic and he could spot nothing suspicious about the other materials.

"You don't trust anybody, do you?" Manielli asked.

Thinking it'd be fun to sock the punk once, really hard, Paul clicked the briefcase closed and looked up. "What about my other passport, the Russian one?"

"Our man'll give that to you there. He's got a forger who's an expert with European documents. Now, tomorrow, make sure you have the satchel with you. It's how he'll recognize you." He unfurled a colorful map of Berlin and traced a route. "Get off here and go this way. Make your way to a café called the Bierhaus."

Avery looked at Paul, who was staring at the map. "You can take it with you. You don't have to memorize it."

But Paul shook his head. "Maps tell people where you've been or where you're going. And looking at one on the street draws everybody's attention to you. If you're lost, better just to ask directions. That way only one person knows you're a stranger, not a whole crowd."

Avery lifted an eyebrow, and even Manielli couldn't find anything to razz him about on this point.

"Near the café there's an alley. Dresden Alley."

"It'll have a name?"

"In Germany the alleys have names. Some of them do. It's a shortcut. Doesn't matter where to. At noon walk into it and stop, like you're lost. Our man'll come up to you. He's the guy the Senator was telling you about. Reginald Morgan. Reggie."

"Describe him."

"Short. Mustache. Darkish hair. He'll be speaking German. He'll strike up a conversation. At some point you ask, 'What's the best tram to take to get to Alexanderplatz?' And he'll say, 'The number one thirty-eight tram.' Then he'll pause and correct himself and say, 'No, the two fifty-four is better.' You'll know it's him because those aren't real tram numbers."

"You look like this's funny," Manielli added.

"It's right out of Dashiell Hammett. *The Continental Op*."

"This ain't a game."

No, it wasn't, and he didn't think the passwords were funny. But it *was* unsettling, all this intrigue stuff. And he knew why: because it meant he was relying on other people. Paul Schumann hated to do that.

"All right. Alexanderplatz. Trams one thirty-eight, two fifty-four. What if he flubs the tram story? It's not him?"

"I'm getting to that. If something seems fishy, what you do is you don't hit him, you don't make a scene. Just smile and walk away as casually as you can and go to this address."

Avery gave him a slip of paper with a street name and number on it. Paul memorized it and handed the paper back. The lieutenant gave him a key, which he pocketed. "There's an old palace just south of Brandenburg Gate. It was going to be the new U.S. embassy but there was a bad fire about five years ago and they're still repairing it; the diplomats haven't moved in. So the French, Germans and British don't bother to snoop around the place. But we've got a couple of rooms there we use from time to time. There's a wireless in the storeroom next to the kitchen. You can radio us in Amsterdam and we'll place a call to Commander Gordon. He and the Senator'll decide what to do next. But if everything's silk, Morgan'll take care of you. Get you into the boardinghouse, find you a weapon and get all the information you need on the . . . the man you're going to visit."

We people say touch-off . . .

"And remember," Manielli was pleased to announce, "you don't show up in Dresden Alley tomorrow or you give Morgan the slip later, he calls us and we make sure the police come down on you like a ton of bricks."

Paul said nothing and let the boy have his bluster. He could tell Manielli was embarrassed about his reaction to Heinsler's suicide and he needed to jerk some leash. But in fact there was no possibility that Paul was going to lam off. Bull Gordon was right; button men never got a second chance like he was being given—and a pile of dough that would let him make the most of it.

Then the men fell silent. There was nothing more to say. Sounds filled the damp, pungent air around them: the wind, the shusssh of the waves, the baritone grind of the *Manhattan*'s engines—a blend of tones that he found oddly comforting, despite Heinsler's suicide and the arduous mission that lay ahead. Finally the sailors went below.

Paul rose, lit another cigarette and leaned against the railing once more as the huge ship eased into the harbor in Hamburg, his thoughts wholly focused on Colonel Reinhard Ernst, a man whose ultimate importance, to Paul Schumann, had little to do with his potential threat to peace in Europe and to so many innocent lives but could be found in the fact that he was the last person that the button man would ever kill.

Several hours after the *Manhattan* docked and the athletes and their entourage had disembarked, a young crewman from the ship exited German passport control and began wandering through the streets of Hamburg.

He wouldn't have much time ashore—being so junior, he had a leave of only six hours—but he'd spent all his life on American soil and was bound and determined to enjoy his first visit to a foreign country.

The scrubbed, rosy-cheeked assistant kitchen mate supposed there were probably some swell museums in town. Maybe some all-right churches too. He had his Kodak with him and was planning to ask locals to take some snapshots of him in front of them for his ma and pa. (*"Bitte, das Foto?"* he'd been rehearsing.) Not to mention beer halls and taverns . . . and who knew what else he might find for diversion in an exotic port city?

But before he could sample some local culture he had an errand to complete. He'd been concerned that this chore would eat into his precious time ashore but as it turned out he was wrong. Only a few minutes after leaving the customs hall, he found exactly what he was looking for.

The mate walked up to a middle-aged man in a green uniform and a black-and-green hat. He tried out his German. *"Bitte . . ."*

"Ja, mein Herr?"

Squinting, the mate blundered on, *"Bitte, du bist ein Polizist,* uhm, or a *Soldat?"*

The officer smiled and said in English, "Yes, yes, I am a policeman. And I *was* a soldier. What can I help you for?"

Nodding down the street, the kitchen mate said, "I found this on the ground." He handed the man a white envelope. "Isn't that the word for 'important'?" He pointed to the letters on the front: *Bedeutend.* "I wanted to make sure it got turned in."

Staring at the front of the envelope, the policeman didn't respond for a moment. Then he said, "Yes, yes. 'Important.'" The other words written on the front were *Für Obersturmführer-SS, Hamburg.* The mate had no idea what this meant but it seemed to trouble the policeman.

"Where was this falling?" the policeman asked.

"It was on the sidewalk there."

"Good. You are thanked." The officer continued to look at the sealed envelope. He turned it over in his hand. "You were seeing perhaps who dropped it?"

"Nope. Just saw it there and thought I'd be a Good Samaritan."

"Ach, yes, Samaritan."

"Well, I better scram," the American said. "So long."

"Danke," the policeman said absently.

As he headed back toward one of the more intriguing tourist sites he'd passed, the young man was wondering what exactly the envelope contained. And why the man he'd met on the *Manhattan,* the porter Al Heinsler, had asked him last night to deliver it to a local policeman or soldier after the ship docked. The fellow was a little nuts, everybody agreed, the way everything in his cabin was perfectly ordered and clean, nothing out of line, his clothes pressed all the time. The way he kept to himself, the way he got all wet-eyed talking about Germany.

"Sure, what is it?" the mate had asked.

"There was a passenger on board who seemed a little fishy. I'm letting the Germans know about him. I'm going to try to send a wireless message but sometimes they don't go through. I want to make sure the authorities get it."

"Who's the passenger? Oh, hold up, I know—that fat guy in the check-ered suit, the one who passed out drunk at the captain's table."

"No, it was somebody else."

"Why not go to the sergeant-at-arms on board?"

"It's a German matter."

"Oh. And you can't deliver it?"

Heinsler had folded his pudgy hands together in a creepy way and shook his head. "I don't know how busy I'll be. I heard you had leave. It's real important the Germans get it."

"Well, I guess, sure."

Heinsler had added in a soft voice, "One other thing: It'd be better to say you found the letter. Otherwise they might take you into the station and question you. That could take hours. It could use up all your shore leave."

The young mate had felt a little uneasy at this intrigue.

Heinsler had picked up on that and added quickly, "Here's a twenty."

Jesus, Mary and Joseph, the man had thought, and told the porter, "You just bought yourself a special delivery."

Now, as he walked away from the policeman and headed back toward the waterfront, he wondered absently what had happened to Heinsler. The young man hadn't seen him since last night. But thoughts about the porter vanished quickly as the mate approached the venue he'd spotted, the one that seemed like a perfect choice for his first taste of German culture. He was, however, disappointed to find that Rosa's Hot Kitten Club—the enticing name conveniently spelled in English—was permanently closed, just like every other such attraction on the waterfront.

So, the mate thought with a sigh, looks like it'll be churches and museums after all.

Chapter Four

He awoke to the sound of a hazel grouse fluttering into the sky from the gooseberry bushes just outside the bedroom window of his home in suburban Charlottenburg. He awoke to the smell of magnolia.

He awoke to the touch of the infamous Berlin wind, which, according to young men and old housewives, was infused with an alkaline dust that aroused earthy desires.

Whether it was the magic air, or being a man of a certain age, Reinhard Ernst found himself picturing his attractive, brunette wife of twenty-eight years, Gertrud. He rolled over to face her. And he found himself looking at the empty indentation in their down bed. He could not help but smile. He was forever exhausted in the evenings, after working sixteen-hour days, and she always rose early because it was her nature. Lately they had rarely even shared so much as a word or two in bed.

He now heard, from downstairs, the clatter of activity in the kitchen. The time was 7 A.M. Ernst had had just over four hours of sleep.

Ernst stretched, lifting his damaged arm as far as he could, massaging it and feeling the triangular piece of metal lodged near the shoulder. There was a familiarity and, curiously, a comfort about the shrapnel. Ernst believed in embracing the past and he appreciated all the emblems of years gone by, even those that had nearly taken his limb and his life.

He climbed from the bed and pulled off his nightshirt. Since Frieda would be in the house by now Ernst tugged on beige jodhpurs and, forgoing a shirt, stepped into the study next to the bedroom. The fifty-six-year-old colonel had a round head, covered with cropped gray hair. Creases circled his mouth. His small nose was Roman and his eyes set close together, making him seem both predatory and savvy. These features had earned him the nickname "Caesar" from his men in the War.

During the summer he and his grandson Rudy would often exercise together in the morning, rolling the medicine ball and lifting Indian clubs, doing press-ups and running in place. On Wednesdays and Fridays, though, the boy had holiday-child-school, which began early, so Ernst was relegated to solo exercise, which was a disappointment to him.

He began his fifteen minutes of arm press-ups and knee bends. Halfway through, he heard: "Opa!"

Breathing hard, Ernst paused and looked into the hallway. "Good morning, Rudy."

"Look what I've drawn." The seven-year-old, dressed in his uniform, held up a picture. Ernst didn't have his glasses on and he couldn't make out the design clearly. But the boy said, "It's an eagle."

"Yes, of course it is. I can tell."

"And it's flying through a lightning storm."

"Quite a brave eagle you've drawn."

"Are you coming to breakfast?"

"Yes, tell your grandmother I'll be down in ten minutes. Did you eat an egg today?"

The boy said, "Yes, I did."

"Excellent. Eggs are good for you."

"Tomorrow I'll draw a hawk." The slight, blond boy turned and ran back down the stairs.

Ernst returned to his exercising, thinking about the dozens of matters that needed attending to today. He finished his regimen and bathed his body with cold water, wiping away both sweat and alkaline dust. As he was drying, the telephone buzzed. His hands paused. In these days no matter how high one was in the National Socialist government, a telephone call at an odd hour was a matter of concern.

"Reinie," Gertrud called. "Someone has telephoned for you."

He pulled on his shirt and, not bothering with stockings or shoes, walked down the stairs. He took the receiver from his wife.

"Yes? This is Ernst."

"Colonel."

He recognized the voice of one of Hitler's secretaries. "Miss Lauer. Good morning."

"And to you. I am asked to tell you that your presence is required by the

Leader at the chancellory immediately. If you have any other plans I'm asked to tell you to alter them."

"Please tell Chancellor Hitler that I will leave at once. In his office?"

"That is correct."

"Who else will be attending?"

There was a moment's hesitation then she said, "That's all the information I have, Colonel. Hail Hitler."

"Hail Hitler."

He hung up and stared at the phone, his hand on the receiver.

"Opa, you have no shoes on!" Rudy had come up beside Ernst, still clutching his drawing. He laughed, looking at his grandfather's bare feet.

"I know, Rudy. I must finish dressing." He looked for a long moment at the telephone.

"What is it, Opa? Something is wrong?"

"Nothing, Rudy."

"Mutti says your breakfast is getting cold."

"You ate *all* your egg, did you?"

"Yes, Opa."

"Good fellow. Tell your grandmother and your mutti that I'll be downstairs in a few moments. But tell them to begin their breakfast without me."

Ernst started up the stairs to shave, observing that his desire for his wife and his hunger for the breakfast awaiting him had both vanished completely.

Forty minutes later Reinhard Ernst was walking through the corridors of the State Chancellory building on Wilhelm Street at Voss Street in central Berlin, dodging construction workers. The building was old—parts of it dated to the eighteenth century—and had been the home of German leaders since Bismarck. Hitler would fly into tirades occasionally about the shabbiness of the structure and—since the new chancellory was not close to being finished—was constantly ordering renovations to the old one.

But construction and architecture were of no interest to Ernst at the moment. The one thought in his mind was this: What will the consequences of my mistake be? How bad was my miscalculation?

He lifted his arm and gave a perfunctory "Hail Hitler" to a guard, who had enthusiastically saluted the plenipotentiary for domestic stability, a title as heavy and embarrassing to wear as a wet, threadbare coat. Ernst continued down the corridor, his face emotionless, revealing nothing of the turbulent thoughts about the crime he had committed.

And what *was* that crime?

The infraction of not sharing all with the Leader.

This would be a minor matter in other countries, perhaps, but here it could be a capital offense. Yet sometimes you *couldn't* share all. If you *did* give Hitler all the details of an idea, his mind might snag on its most insignificant aspect and that would be the end of it, shot dead with one word. Never mind that you had no personal gain at stake and were thinking only of the good of the fatherland.

But if you didn't tell him . . . Ach, that could be far worse. In his paranoia he might decide that you were withholding information for a reason. And then the great piercing eye of the Party's security mechanism would turn toward you and your loved ones . . . sometimes with deadly consequences. As, Reinhard Ernst was convinced, had now occurred, given the mysterious and peremptory summons to an early, unscheduled meeting. The Third Empire was order and structure and regularity personified. Anything out of the ordinary was cause for alarm.

Ach, he should have told the man *something* about the Waltham Study when Ernst had first conceived it this past March. Yet the Leader, Defense Minister von Blomberg, and Ernst himself had been so occupied with retaking the Rhineland that the study had paled beside the monumental risk of reclaiming a portion of their country stolen away by the Allies at Versailles. And, truth be told, much of the study was based on academic work that Hitler would find suspect, if not inflammatory; Ernst simply hadn't *wanted* to bring the matter up.

And now he was going to pay for that oversight.

He announced himself to Hitler's secretary and was admitted.

Ernst walked inside the large ante-office and found himself standing before Adolf Hitler—leader, chancellor and president of the Third Empire and ultimate commander of the armed forces. Thinking as he often did: If charisma, energy and canniness are the prime ingredients of power, then here is the most powerful man in the world.

Wearing a brown uniform and glossy black knee boots, Hitler was bending over a desk, leafing through papers.

"My Leader," Ernst said, nodding respectfully and offering a gentle heel tap, a throwback to the days of the Second Empire, which had ended eighteen years before, with Germany's surrender and the flight of Kaiser Wilhelm to Holland. Though giving the Party salute with "Hail Hitler" or "Hail victory" was expected from citizens, the formality was rarely seen among the higher echelon of officials, except from the drippier sycophants.

"Colonel." Hitler glanced up at Ernst with his pale blue eyes beneath drooping lids—eyes that for some reason left the impression that the man was considering a dozen things at once. His mood was forever unreadable. Hitler found the document he sought and turned and walked into his large but modestly decorated office. "Please join us." Ernst followed. His still, soldier's face gave no reaction but his heart sank when he saw who else was present.

Sweating and massive, Hermann Göring lounged on a couch that creaked under his weight. Claiming he was always in pain, the round-faced man was continually adjusting himself in ways that made one want to cringe. His excessive cologne filled the room. The air minister nodded a greeting to Ernst, who reciprocated.

Another man sat in an ornate chair, sipping coffee, his legs crossed like a woman's: the clubfooted scarecrow Paul Joseph Goebbels, the state propaganda minister. Ernst didn't doubt his skill; he was largely responsible for the Party's early, vital foothold in Berlin and Prussia. Still, Ernst despised the man, who couldn't stop gazing at the Leader with adoring eyes and smugly dishing up damning gossip about prominent Jews and Socis one moment then dropping the names of famous German actors and actresses from UFA Studios the next. Ernst said good morning to him and then sat, recalling a recent joke that had made the rounds: Describe the ideal Aryan. Why, he's as blond as Hitler, as slim as Göring and as tall as Goebbels.

Hitler offered the document to puffy-eyed Göring, who read it, nodded and then put it into his sumptuous leather folder without comment. The Leader sat and poured himself chocolate. He lifted an eyebrow toward Goebbels, meaning he should continue with whatever he had been discussing, and Ernst realized his fate regarding the Waltham Study would have to remain in limbo for sometime longer.

"As I was saying, my Leader, many of the visitors to the Olympics will be interested in entertainment."

"We have cafés and theater. We have museums, parks, movie theaters. They can see our Babelsberg films, they can see Greta Garbo and Jean Harlow. And Charles Laughton and Mickey Mouse." The impatient tone in Hitler's voice told Ernst he knew exactly what kind of entertainment Goebbels had meant. There followed an excruciatingly long and edgy debate about letting legal prostitutes—licensed "control girls"—out on the streets again. Hitler was against this idea at first but Goebbels had thought through the matter and argued persuasively; the Leader relented eventually, on the condition that there be no more than seven thousand women throughout the metropolitan area. Similarly, the penal code provision banning homosexuality, Article 175, would be relaxed temporarily. Rumors abounded about Hitler's own preferences—from incest to boys to animals to human waste. Ernst had come to believe, though, that the man simply had no interest in sex; the only lover he desired was the nation of Germany.

"Finally," Goebbels continued suavely, "there is the matter of public display. I am thinking that perhaps we might permit women's skirts to be shortened somewhat."

As the head of Germany's Third Empire and his adjutant debated, in centimeters, the degree to which Berlin women might be allowed to conform to world fashion, the worm of ill ease continued to eat away at Ernst's heart. Why hadn't he at least mentioned the *name* of the Waltham Study some months ago? He could have sent a letter to the Leader, with a glancing reference to it. One *had* to be savvy about such things nowadays.

The debate continued. Then the Leader said firmly, "Skirts may be raised five centimeters. That settles it. But we will not approve makeup."

"Yes, my Leader."

A moment of silence as Hitler's eyes settled in the corner of the room, as they often did. He then glanced sharply at Ernst. "Colonel."

"Yes, sir?"

Hitler rose and walked to his desk. He lifted a piece of paper and walked slowly back to the others. Göring and Goebbels kept their eyes on Ernst. Though each believed he had the special ear of the Leader, deep within him was the fear that the grace was temporary or, more frightening, illusory and at any moment he would be sitting here, like Ernst, a tethered badger, though probably without the quiet aplomb of the colonel.

The Leader wiped his mustache. "An important matter."

"Of course, my Leader. However I may help." Ernst held the man's eyes and answered in a steady voice.

"It involves our air force."

Ernst glanced at Göring, ruddy cheeks framing a faux smile. A daring ace in the War (though dismissed by Baron von Richthofen himself for repeatedly attacking civilians), he was presently both air minister and commander in chief of the German air force—the latter currently being his favorite among the dozen titles he held. It was on the subject of the German air force that Göring and Ernst met most frequently and clashed the most passionately.

Hitler handed the document to Ernst. "You read English?"

"Some."

"This is a letter from Mr. Charles Lindbergh himself," Hitler said proudly. "He will be attending the Olympics as our special guest."

Really? This was exciting information. Both smiling, Göring and Goebbels leaned forward and rapped on the table in front of them, signifying approval of this news. Ernst took the letter in his right hand, the back of which, like his shoulder, was shrapnel scarred.

Lindbergh . . . Ernst had avidly followed the story of the man's transatlantic flight, but he'd been far more moved by the terrible account of the death of the aviator's son. Ernst knew the horror of losing a child. The accidental explosion on a ship's magazine that had taken Mark was tragic, wrenching, yes; but at least Ernst's son had been at the helm of a combat ship and had lived to see his own boy, Rudy, born. To lose an *infant* to the hands of a criminal—that was appalling.

Ernst scanned the document and was able to make out the cordial words, which expressed an interest in seeing Germany's recent developments in aviation.

The Leader continued. "This is why I have asked for you, Colonel. Some people think that it would be of strategic value to show the world our increasing strength in the air. I am inclined to feel this way myself. What do you think about a small air show in honor of Mr. Lindbergh, in which we demonstrate our new monoplane?"

Ernst was greatly relieved that the summons had not been about the Waltham Study. But the relief lasted only a moment. His concerns rose once again as he considered what he was being asked . . . and the answer he had to give. The "some people" Hitler was referring to was, of course, Hermann Göring.

"The monoplane, sir, ah . . ." The Me 109 by Messerschmitt was a superb killing machine, a fighter with a speed of three hundred miles per hour. There were other monowing fighters in the world but this was the fastest. More important, though, the Me 109 was of all-metal construction, which Ernst had long advocated because it allowed easy mass production and field repair and maintenance. Large numbers of the planes were necessary to support the devastating bombing missions that Ernst planned as precursors for any land invasion by the Third Empire's army.

He cocked his head, as if considering the question, though he'd made his decision the instant he'd heard it. "I would be against that idea, my Leader."

"Why?" Hitler's eyes flared, a sign that a tantrum might follow, possibly accompanied by what was nearly as bad: an endless, ranting monologue about military history or politics. "Are we not allowed to protect ourselves? Are we ashamed to let the world know that we reject the third-class role the Allies keep trying to push us into?"

Careful, now, Ernst thought. Careful as a surgeon removing a tumor. "I'm not thinking of the backstabbers' treaty of 1918," Ernst answered, filling his voice with contempt for the Versailles accord. "I am thinking of how wise it might be to let others know about this aircraft. It's constructed in a way that those familiar with aviation would spot as unique. They could deduce that it is being mass produced. Lindbergh could easily recognize this. He himself designed his *Spirit of St. Louis,* I believe."

Avoiding eye contact with Ernst, Göring predictably said, "We must begin to let our enemies know our strength."

"Perhaps," Ernst said slowly, "a possibility would be to display one of the *prototypes* of the one-oh-nine at the Olympics. They were constructed more by hand than our production models and have no armament mounted. And they're equipped with British Rolls-Royce engines. The world could then see our technological achievement yet be disarmed by the fact that we are using our former enemy's motors. Which would suggest that any offensive use is far from our thoughts."

Hitler said, "There is something to your point, Reinhard. . . . Yes, we will not put on an air show. And we will display the prototype. Good. That is decided. Thank you for coming, Colonel."

"My Leader." Bathed in relief, Ernst rose.

He was nearly to the door when Göring said casually, "Oh, Reinhard, a matter occurs to me. I believe a file of yours was misdirected to my office."

Ernst turned back to examine the smiling, moonish face. The eyes, however, seethed from Ernst's victory in the fighter debate. He wanted revenge. Göring squinted. "I believe it had to do with . . . what was it? The Waltham Study. Yes."

God in heaven . . .

Hitler was paying no attention. He unfurled an architectural drawing and studied it closely.

"Misdirected?" Ernst asked. Filched by one of Göring's spies was the true meaning of this word. "Thank you, Mr. Minister," he said lightly. "I'll have someone pick it up immediately. Good day to—"

But the deflection, of course, was ineffectual. Göring continued. "You were fortunate that the file was delivered to me. Imagine what some people might've thought to see Jew writing with your name on it."

Hitler looked up. "What is this?"

Sweating prodigiously, as always, Göring wiped his face and replied, "The Waltham Study that Colonel Ernst has commissioned." Hitler shook his head and the minister persisted. "Oh, I assumed our Leader knew about it."

"Tell me," Hitler demanded.

Göring said, "I know nothing about it. I only received—mistakenly, as I say—several reports written by those Jew mind doctors. One by that Austrian, Freud. Someone named Weiss. Others I can't recall." He added with a twist of his lips, "Those psychologists."

In the hierarchy of Hitler's hatred, Jews came first, Communists second and intellectuals third. Psychologists were particularly disparaged since they rejected racial science—the belief that race determined behavior, a cornerstone of National Socialist thought.

"Is this true, Reinhard?"

Ernst said casually, "As part of my job I read many documents on aggression and conflict. That's what these writings deal with."

"You've never mentioned this to me." And with his characteristic instinct for sniffing out the merest hint of conspiracy Hitler asked quickly, "Defense Minister von Blomberg? Is he familiar with this study of yours?"

"No. There's nothing to report at this time. As the name suggests it's merely a study being conducted through Waltham Military College. To gather information. That's all. Nothing may come of it." Ashamed to be playing this game, he added, putting some of Goebbels's sycophantic shine in his eyes, "But it is possible that the results will show us ways in which to create a much stronger, more efficient army to achieve the glorious goals you've established for our fatherland."

Ernst could not tell if this bootlicking had any effect. Hitler rose and paced. He walked to an elaborate model of the Olympic stadium grounds and stared at it for a long moment. Ernst could feel his heartbeat thudding all the way to his teeth.

The Leader turned and shouted, "I wish to see my architect. Immediately."

"Yes, sir," his aide said and hurried to the ante-office.

A moment later a man entered the room, though it was not Albert Speer, but black-uniformed Heinrich Himmler, whose weak chin, diminutive physique and round black-rimmed glasses nearly made you forget that he was the absolute ruler of the SS, Gestapo and every other police force in the country.

Himmler gave his typical stiff salute and turned his adoring, blue-gray eyes toward Hitler, who responded with his own standard greeting, a limp over-the-shoulder flap.

The SS leader glanced around the room and concluded that he could share with them whatever news had brought him here.

Hitler gestured absently toward the coffee and chocolate service. Himmler shook his head. Usually in utter control—aside from the fawning looks sent the Leader's way—the police chief today had an edginess about him, Ernst observed. "I have a security matter to report. An SS commander in Hamburg received a letter this morning, dated today. It was addressed to him by title, but not name. It claimed that some Russian was going to cause some 'damage' in Berlin in the next few days. At 'high levels,' it said."

"Written by whom?"

"He described himself as a loyal National Socialist. But gave no name. It was found in the street. We don't know any more about its origin." Revealing perfectly white, even teeth, the man gave a wince, like a child disappointing his parent. He removed his glasses, wiped the lenses and replaced them. "Whoever sent it said that he was continuing to investigate and would send the man's identity when he learned it. But we never heard anything further. Finding the note in the street suggests the sender was intercepted and perhaps killed. We might never learn more."

Hitler asked, "The language? German?"

"Yes, my Leader."

"'Damage.' What sort of damage?"

"We don't know."

"Ach, the Bolsheviks would love to disrupt our Games." Hitler's face was a mask of fury.

Göring asked, "You think it's legitimate?"

Himmler replied, "It may be nothing. But tens of thousands of foreigners are passing through Hamburg these days. It's possible someone learned of a plot and didn't want to get involved so he wrote an anonymous note. I would urge everyone here to exercise particular caution. I will contact military commanders too and the other ministers. I've told all our security forces to look into the matter."

His voice raw with anger, Hitler raged, "Do what you must! Everything! There will be no taint on our Games." And, unnervingly, a fraction of a second later, his voice was calm and his blue eyes bright. He leaned forward to refill his cup with chocolate and place two zwieback biscuits on the saucer. "Please, now, you may all leave. Thank you. I need to consider some building matters." He called to the aide in the doorway, "Where is Speer?"

"He will be here momentarily, my Leader."

The men walked to the door. Ernst's heart had resumed its normal, slow beat. What had just happened was typical of the way the inner circle of the National Socialist government worked. Intrigue, which could have disastrous results, simply vanished like crumbs swept over the door stoop. As for Göring's plotting, well, he—

"Colonel?" Hitler's voice called.

Ernst stopped immediately and looked back.

The Leader was staring at the mock-up of the stadium, examining the newly constructed train station. He said, "You will prepare a report on this Waltham Study of yours. In detail. I will receive it on Monday."

"Yes, of course, my Leader."

At the door Göring held his arm out, palm upward, letting Ernst exit first. "I will see that you receive those misdirected documents, Reinhard. And I do hope you and Gertrud will attend my Olympic party."

"Thank you, Mr. Minister. I will make a point of being there."

Friday evening, misty and warm, fragrant with the scent of cut grass, overturned earth and sweet, fresh paint.

Paul Schumann strolled by himself through the Olympic Village, a half hour west of Berlin.

He'd arrived not long before, after the complicated journey from Hamburg. It had been an exhausting day, yes. But invigorating too and he was stoked by the excitement of being in a foreign land—his ancestral home— and the anticipation of his mission. He had shown his press pass and been admitted to the American portion of the village—dozens of buildings housing fifty or sixty people each. He'd left his suitcase and satchel in one of the small guestrooms in the back, where he'd stay for a few nights, and was now walking through the spotless grounds. As he looked around the village he was amused. Paul Schumann was used to a lot rougher venues for sports—his own gym, for instance, which hadn't been painted in five years and smelled of sweat and rotten leather and beer, no matter how energetically Sorry Williams scrubbed and mopped. The village was, however, just what the name suggested: a quaint town all its own. Set in a birch forest, the place was beautifully laid out in sweeping arcs of low, immaculate buildings, with a lake and curved paths and trails for running and walking, training fields and even its own sports arena.

According to the guidebook Andrew Avery had included in his satchel, the village had a customs office, stores, pressroom, a post office and bank, gas station, sporting goods store, souvenir stands, food shops and travel office.

The athletes were presently at the welcoming ceremony, which he'd been urged to attend by Jesse Owens, Ralph Metcalfe and the young boxer he'd sparred with. But now that he was in the locale of the touch-off, he needed to lay low. He'd begged off, saying he had to get some work done for interviews the next morning. He'd eaten in the dining hall—had one of the best steaks of his life—and after a coffee and a Chesterfield was now finishing his walk through the village.

The only thing troubling to him, considering the reason he was in the country, was that each nation's dorm complex was assigned a German soldier, a "liaison officer." In the U.S. facility this was a stern, young, brown-haired man in a gray uniform that seemed unbearably uncomfortable in the heat. Paul stayed as clear of him as possible; the contact here, Reginald Morgan, had warned Avery that Paul should be wary of anyone in uniform. He used only the back door to his dorm and made sure the guard never got a close look at him.

As he strolled along the swept sidewalk he saw one of the American track athletes with a young woman and baby; several team members had brought wives and other relatives with them. This put Paul in mind of the conversation with his brother last week, just before the *Manhattan* had sailed.

Paul had distanced himself from his brother and sister and their families for the past decade; he didn't want to visit the violence and danger tainting his own life on theirs. His sister lived in Chicago and he got there rarely but he did see Hank sometimes. He lived on Long Island and ran the printing plant that was the descendant of their grandfather's. He was a solid husband and father, who didn't know for sure what his brother did for a living, except that he associated with tough guys and criminals.

Although Paul hadn't shared any personal information with Bull Gordon or the others in The Room, the main reason he'd decided to agree to come to Germany for this job was that wiping his record clean and getting all that scratch might let him reconnect with the family, which he'd dreamed about doing for years.

He'd had a shot of whisky, then another, and finally picked up the phone and called his brother at home. After ten minutes of nervous small talk about the heat wave and the Yankees and Hank's two boys, Paul had taken the plunge and asked if Hank might be interested in having a partner at Schumann Printing. He quickly reassured, "I'm not having anything to do with my old crowd anymore." Then he added that he could bring $10,000 into the business. "Legit dough. One hundred percent."

"Mother of pearl," Hank said. And they'd both laughed at the expression, a favorite of their father's.

"There's one problem," Hank added gravely.

Paul understood that the man was about to say no, thinking of his brother's shady career.

But the elder Schumann added, "We'll have to buy a new sign. There's not enough room for 'Schumann *Brothers* Printing' on the one I got."

The ice broken, they talked about the plan some more. Paul was surprised that Hank sounded almost tearfully touched at this overture. Family was key to Hank and he couldn't understand Paul's distance in the past ten years.

Tall, beautiful Marion, Paul had decided, would like that life too. Oh, she played at being bad, but it was an act, and Paul knew enough to give her only a small taste of the seamy life. He'd introduced her to Damon Runyon, served her beer in a bottle at the gym, taken her to the bar in Hell's Kitchen where Owney Madden used to charm ladies with his British accent and show off his pearl-handled pistols. But he knew that like a lot of renegade college girls, Marion would get tired of the tough life if she actually had to live it. Dime-dancing would wear thin as well, and she'd want something more stable. Being the wife of a well-off printer would be aces.

Hank had said he was going to talk to his lawyer and have a partnership agreement drawn up for Paul to sign as soon as he got back from his "business trip."

Now, returning to his room at the dorm, Paul noticed three boys in shorts, brown shirts and black ties, wearing brown, military-style hats. He'd seen dozens of such youngsters here, assisting the teams. The trio marched toward a tall pole, at the top of which flew the Nazi flag. Paul had seen the banner in newsreels and in the papers but the images had always been in black and white. Even now, at dusk, the flag's crimson was striking, brilliant as fresh blood.

One boy noticed him watching and asked in German, "You are an athlete, sir? Yet you're not at the ceremony we are hosting?"

Paul thought it better not to give away his linguistic skills, even to Boy Scouts, so he said in English, "Sorry, I don't speak German so well."

The boy switched to Paul's language. "You are an athlete?"

"No, I'm a journalist."

"You are English or American?"

"American."

"Ach," the cheerful youngster said in a thick accent, "welcome to Berlin, *mein Herr.*"

"Thank you."

The second boy noted Paul's gaze and said, "You are liking our Party's flag? It is, would you say, impressing, yes?"

"Yeah, it is." The Stars and Stripes was somehow softer. This flag sort of punched you.

The first boy said, "Please, each parts is having a meaning, an important meaning. Do you know what are those?"

"No. Tell me." Paul looked up at the banner.

Happy to explain, he said enthusiastically, "Red, that is socialism. The white is, no doubt, for nationalism. And the black . . . the hooked cross. You would say swastika. . . ." He looked at Paul with a raised eyebrow and said nothing more.

"Yes," Paul said. "Go on. What does that mean?"

The boy glanced at his companions then back to Paul with a curious smile. He said, "Ach, surely you know."

To his friends he said in German, "I will lower the flag now." Smiling, he repeated to Paul, "Surely you know." And frowning in concentration, he brought the flag down as the other two extended their hands in one of those stiff-armed salutes you saw everywhere.

As Paul walked toward the dorm, the boys broke into a song, which they sang with uneven, energetic voices. He heard snatches of it rising and falling on the hot air as he strolled away: *"Hold high the banner, close the ranks. The SA marches on with firm steps. . . . Give way, give way to the brown battalions, as the Stormtroopers clear the land. . . . The trumpet calls its final blast. For battle we stand ready. Soon all streets will see Hitler's flag and our slavery will be over. . . ."*

Paul looked back to see them fold the flag reverently and march off with it. He slipped through the back entrance of his dorm and returned to his room, where he washed, cleaned his teeth then stripped and dropped onto his bed. He stared at the ceiling for a long time, waiting for sleep as he thought about Heinsler—the man who'd killed himself that morning on the ship, making such a passionate, foolish sacrifice.

Thinking too of Reinhard Ernst.

And finally, as he began to doze, thinking of the boy in the brown uniform. Seeing his mysterious smile. Hearing his voice over and over: *Surely you know . . . surely you know. . . .*

III
GÖRING'S HAT

SATURDAY, 25 JULY, 1936

Chapter Five

The streets of Berlin were immaculate and the people pleasant, many nodding as he walked past. Carting the beat-up old briefcase, Paul Schumann was walking north through the Tiergarten. It was late morning on Saturday and he was on his way to meet Reggie Morgan.

The park was beautiful, filled with dense trees, walkways and lakes, gardens. In New York's Central Park, you were forever aware of the city around you; the skyscrapers were visible everywhere. But Berlin was a low city, very few tall buildings here, "cloud catchers," he overheard a woman say to a young child on the bus. On his walk through the park with its black trees and thick vegetation he lost any sense that he was in the city at all. It reminded Paul of the dense woods in upstate New York where his grandfather had taken him hunting every summer until the old man's failing health had prevented them from making the trips.

An uneasiness crept over him. This was a familiar feeling: the heightened senses at the beginning of a job, when he was looking over the touchoff's office or apartment, following him, learning what he could about the man. Instinctively he paused from time to time and would glance casually behind him, as if orienting himself. No one seemed to be following. But he couldn't tell for sure. The forest was very dim in places and someone might easily have been eyeing him. Several scruffy men looked his way suspiciously and then slipped into the trees or bushes. Probably hoboes or bums but he took no chances and changed direction a number of times to throw off anyone who might be tailing him.

He crossed the murky Spree River and found Spener Street then continued north, away from the park, noting that, curiously, the homes were in vastly different states of repair. Some were grand while right next door might be others that were abandoned and derelict. He passed one in which brown weeds filled the front yard. At one point the house had clearly been very luxurious. Now, most of the windows were broken and someone, young punks, he assumed, had splashed yellow paint on it. A sign announced that a sale of the contents would be taking place on Saturday. Tax problems, maybe, Paul thought. What had happened to the family? Where had they gone? Hard times, he sensed. Changed circumstances.

The sun finally sets . . .

He found the restaurant easily. He saw the sign but didn't even notice the word "Bierhaus." To him it was "Beer House." He was already thinking in German. His upbringing and the hours of typesetting at his grandfather's plant made the translations automatic. He looked over the place. A half dozen lunchers sat on the patio, men and women, solitary for the most part, lost in their food or newspapers. Nothing out of kilter that he could see.

Paul crossed the street to the passageway Avery had told him about, Dresden Alley. He walked into the dark, cool canyon. The time was a few minutes before noon.

A moment later he heard footsteps. Then a heavyset man in a brown suit and waistcoat strode up behind him, working a toothpick in his teeth.

"Good day," the man said cheerfully in German. He glanced at the brown leather briefcase.

Paul nodded. He was the way Avery'd described Morgan, though he was heavier than Paul had expected.

"This is a good shortcut, don't you think? I use it often."

"It certainly is." Paul glanced at him. "Maybe you can help me. What's the best tram to take to get to Alexander Plaza?"

But the man frowned. "The tram? Do you mean from here?"

Paul grew more alert. "Yes. To Alexander Plaza."

"Why would you take the tram? The underground is much faster."

Okay, Paul thought; he's the wrong one. Get away. Now. Just walk slowly. "Thank you. That's most helpful. Good day to you."

But Paul's eyes must have revealed something. The man's hand strayed to his side, a gesture Paul knew well, and he thought: pistol!

Goddamn them for sending him out here without his Colt.

Paul's fists clenched and he started forward but, for a fat man, his adversary was surprisingly quick and leapt back, out of Paul's reach, deftly pulling a black pistol from his belt. Paul could only turn and flee. He sprinted around a corner into a short offshoot of the alley.

He stopped fast. It was a dead end.

A scrape of shoe behind him and he felt the man's weapon against his back, level with his heart. . . .

"Don't move," the man announced in guttural German. "Drop the bag."

He dropped the briefcase on the cobblestones, feeling the gun leave his back and touch his head, just below the sweatband of his hat.

Father, he thought—not to the deity but to his own parent, gone from this earth twelve years.

He closed his eyes.

The sun finally sets . . .

The shot was abrupt. It echoed briefly off the walls of the alley and then was smothered by the brick.

Cringing, Paul felt the muzzle of the gun press harder into his skull and then the weapon fell away; he heard it clatter on the cobblestones. He stepped away fast, crouching, and turned to see the man who'd been about to kill him crumpling to the ground. His eyes were open but glazed. A bullet had struck him in the side of the head. Blood spattered the ground and brick wall.

He looked up and saw another man, in a charcoal-gray flannel suit, approaching him. Instinct took over and Paul swept up the dead man's pistol. It was an automatic of some sort with a toggle on the top, a Luger, he believed. Aiming at the man's chest, Paul squinted. He recognized the fellow from the Beer House. He'd been sitting on the patio, lost in his newspaper—Paul had assumed. He held a pistol, a large automatic of some kind, but it wasn't pointed at Paul; he was still aiming at the man on the ground.

"Don't move," Paul said in German. "Drop the gun."

The man didn't drop it but, convinced the man he'd shot wasn't a threat, slipped his own weapon into his pocket. He looked up and down Dresden Alley. "Shhhh," he whispered then cocked his head to listen. He slowly approached. "Schumann?" he asked.

Paul said nothing. He kept the Luger aimed at the stranger, who crouched in front of the shot man. "My watch." The words were in German, a faint accent.

"What?"

"My watch. That's all I'm reaching for." He pulled out his pocket watch, opened it and held the crystal in front of the man's nose and mouth. There was no condensation of breath. He put the timepiece away.

"You're Schumann?" the man repeated, nodding at the briefcase on the ground. "I'm Reggie Morgan." He too fit the description Avery had given him: dark hair and mustache, though he was much thinner than the dead man.

Paul looked up and down the alley. No one.

The exchange would seem absurd, with a dead body in front of them, but Paul asked, "What's the best tram to take to get to Alexander Plaza?"

Morgan replied quickly, "The number one thirty-eight tram . . . No, actually, the two fifty-four is better."

Paul glanced at the body. "So then who's *he?*"

"Let's find out." He bent over the corpse and began to rifle through the dead man's pockets.

"I'll keep watch," Paul said.

"Good."

Paul stepped away. Then he turned back and touched the Luger to the back of Morgan's head.

"Don't move."

The man froze. "What's this?"

In English Paul said, "Give me your passport."

Paul took the booklet, which confirmed that he was Reginald Morgan. Still, as he handed it back, he kept the pistol where it was. "Describe the Senator to me. In English."

"Just easy on the trigger, you don't mind," the man said in a voice that placed his roots somewhere in New England. "Okay, the Senator? He's sixty-two years old, got white hair, a nose with more veins than he ought to have, thanks to the scotch. And he's thin as a rail even though he eats a whole T-bone at Delmonico's when he's in New York and at Ernie's in Detroit."

"What's he smoke?"

"Nothing the last time I saw him, last year. Because of the wife. But he told me he was going to start again. And what he *used* to smoke were Dominican cigars that smelled like burning Firestones. Give me a break, pal. I don't want to die 'cause some old man took up a bad habit again."

Paul put the gun away. "Sorry."

Morgan resumed his examination of the corpse, unfazed by Paul's test. "I'd rather work with a cautious man who insults me than a careless one who doesn't. We'll both live longer." He dug through the pockets of the dead man. "Any visitors yet?"

Paul glanced up and down Dresden Alley. "Nothing."

He was aware that Morgan was staring in chagrin at something he'd found in the dead man's pockets. He sighed. "Okay. Brother, here's a problem."

"What?"

The man held up an official-looking card. On the top was a stamp of an eagle and below it, in a circle, a swastika. The letters "SA" appeared on the top.

"What does that mean?"

"It means, my friend, that you've been in town for less than a day and already we've managed to kill a Stormtrooper."

Chapter Six

"A what?" Paul Schumann asked.

Morgan sighed. "*Sturmabteilung.* Stormtrooper. Or Brownshirt. Sort of the Party's own army. Think of them as Hitler's thugs." He shook his head. "And it's worse for us. He's not in uniform. That means he's a Brown Elite. One of their senior people."

"How did he find out about me?"

"I'm not sure he did, not you specifically. He was in a phone booth, checking up on everybody on the street."

"I didn't see him," Paul said, angry with himself for missing the surveillance. Everything was too damn out of kilter here; he didn't know what to look for and what to ignore.

Morgan continued. "As soon as you started into the alley, he came after you. I'd say he just took it on himself to see what you were up to—a stranger in the neighborhood. The Brownshirts have their fiefdoms. This must've been his." Morgan frowned. "But still, it's unusual for them to be so vigilant. The question is why is a senior SA man looking into ordinary citizens? They leave that to their underlings. Maybe some alert has gone out." He gazed at the corpse. "In any event, this is a problem. If the Brownshirts find out one of their own has been killed they won't stop searching until they find the murderer. Oh, and they *will* search. There are tens of thousands of them in the city. Like roaches."

The initial shock of the shooting had worn off. Paul's instincts were returning. He walked from the cul-de-sac to the main portion of Dresden Alley. It was still empty. The windows were dark. No doors were open. He held up a finger to Morgan and returned to the mouth of the alley, then looked around the corner, toward the Beer House. None of the few people on the street seemed to have heard the shot.

He returned and told Morgan that everything seemed clear. Then he said, "The casing."

"The what?"

"The shell casing. From your pistol." They looked over the ground and Paul spotted the small yellow tube. He picked it up with his handkerchief, rubbed it clean, just in case Morgan's prints were on it, and dropped it down a drainpipe. He heard it rattle for a moment until there was a splash.

Morgan nodded. "They said you were good."

Not good enough to keep from getting nabbed back in the United States, thanks to a little bit of brass just like that one.

Morgan opened a well-worn pocketknife. "We'll cut the labels out of his clothes. Take all his effects. Then get away from here as fast as possible. Before they find him."

"And who is 'they'?" Paul asked.

A hollow laugh from Morgan's lips. "In Germany now, 'they' is everybody."

"Would a Stormtrooper wear a tattoo? Maybe of that swastika? Or the letters 'SA'?"

"Yes, it's possible."

"Look for any. On his arms and chest."

"And if I find one?" Morgan asked, frowning. "What can we do about it?"

Paul nodded at the knife.

"You're joking."

But Paul's face revealed that, no, he wasn't.

"I can't do that," Morgan whispered.

"I will then. If it's important he's not identified, we have to." Paul knelt on the cobblestones and opened the man's jacket and shirt. He could understand Morgan's queasiness but being a button man was a job like any other. You gave it one hundred percent or you found a new line of work. And a single, small tattoo could mean the difference between living and dying.

But no flaying was required, as it turned out. The man's body was free of markings.

A sudden shout.

Both men froze. Morgan looked up the alley. His hand went to his pistol again. Paul too gripped the weapon he'd taken from the Stormtrooper.

The voice called again. Then silence, except for the traffic. A moment later, though, Paul could detect an eerie siren, rising and falling, growing closer.

"You should leave," Morgan said urgently. "I'll finish with him." He thought for a moment. "Meet me in forty-five minutes. There's a restaurant called the Summer Garden on Rosenthaler Street, northwest of Alexander Plaza. I have a contact who's got information about Ernst. I'll have him meet us there. Go back to the street in front of the beer hall. You should be able to get a taxi there. Trams and buses often have police on them. Stick to taxis, or walk, when you can. Look straight ahead and don't make eye contact with anyone."

"The Summer Garden," Paul repeated, picking up the briefcase and brushing dust and grime off the leather. He dropped the Stormtrooper's pistol inside. "From now on, let's stick to German. Less suspicious."

"Good idea," Morgan said in the local tongue. "You speak well. Better than I expected. But soften your *G*'s. It will make you sound more like a Berliner."

Another shout. The siren grew closer. "Oh, Schumann—if I'm not there in an hour? The radio that Bull Gordon told you about, in the embassy building they're working on?"

Paul nodded.

"Call in and tell them that you need new instructions." A grim laugh. "And you may as well give them the news that I'm dead. Now, get out of here. Keep your eyes forward, look casual. And whatever happens, don't run."

"Don't run? Why?"

"Because there are far too many people in this country who will chase you simply because you are running. Now hurry!" Morgan turned back to his task with the quick precision of a tailor.

The dusty, pitted black car pulled onto the sidewalk near the alleyway, where three Schupo officers stood, wearing spotless green uniforms with bright orange collar tabs and tall green-and-black shako hats.

A middle-aged mustachioed man in a three-piece, off-white linen suit climbed out of the passenger side of the vehicle, which rose several inches, relieved of his considerable weight. He placed his Panama hat on his thinning salt-and-pepper hair, which was swept back, and tapped the smoldering tobacco from his meerschaum pipe.

The engine stuttered, coughed and finally went silent. Pocketing the yellowing pipe, Inspector Willi Kohl glanced at their vehicle with some exasperation. The top SS and Gestapo investigators had Mercedes and BMWs. But Kripo inspectors, even senior ones like Kohl, were relegated to Auto Union cars. And, of the four interlocking rings representing the combined companies—Audi, Horch, Wanderer and DKW—it was, naturally, a two-year-old model of the most modest of those lines that had been made available to Kohl (while his car ran, to be generous, on petrol, it was telling that the initials "DKW" stood for the words "steam-powered vehicle").

Konrad Janssen, smooth-shaven and hatless like so many of today's young inspector candidates, emerged from the driver's seat and buttoned his double-breasted, green silk suit jacket. He took a briefcase and the Leica case from the trunk.

Patting his pocket to make sure he had his notebook and evidence envelopes, Kohl wandered toward the Schupos.

"Hail Hitler, Inspector," the older of the trio said, a familiarity in his voice. Kohl didn't recognize him and wondered if they'd met before this. The Schupo—city patrolmen—might assist inspectors occasionally but they were not technically under the command of the Kripo. Kohl had little regular contact with any of them.

Kohl lifted his arm in a semblance of a Party salute. "Where's the body?"

"Through there, sir," the man said. "Dresden Alley." The other officers stood at half attention. They were cautious. Schupo officers were very talented at traffic offenses and catching pickpockets and holding back crowds when Hitler rode down the broad avenue of Under the Lindens, but murder today called for discernment on their part. A killing by a robber would require them to protect the scene carefully; a murder by the Stormtroopers or the SS meant they should disappear as quickly as they could and forget what they'd seen.

Kohl said to the older Schupo, "Tell me what you know."

"Yes, sir. That's not much, I'm afraid. A call came into the Tiergarten precinct and I came immediately here. I was the first to arrive."

"Who called?" Kohl walked into the alley then looked back at the other officers and impatiently gestured for them to follow.

"She gave no name. A woman. She heard a shot from around here."

"The time she called?"

"Around noon, sir."

"You arrived when?"

"I left as soon as my commander alerted me."

"And you arrived when?" Kohl repeated.

"Perhaps twenty minutes past noon. Perhaps thirty." He gestured down a narrow offshoot that ended in a cul-de-sac.

Lying on his back on the cobblestones was a man in his forties, overweight. The wound in the side of his head was clearly the cause of death and he'd bled profusely. His clothes were disheveled and his pockets turned out. There was no doubt he'd been killed here; the blood pattern made this conclusion obvious.

The inspector said to the two younger Schupos, "Please, see if you can find witnesses, particularly anyone at the mouths of this alley. And in these buildings here." He nodded to the two surrounding brick structures—noting, though, that they were windowless. "And that café we passed. The Beer House, it was called."

"Yes, sir." The men walked off sharply.

"Did you search him?"

"No," the senior Schupo said then added, "Only to verify that he was not Jewish, of course."

"Then you *did* search him."

"I simply opened his trousers. Which I refastened. As you can see."

Kohl wondered whether whoever had decided that the deaths of circumcised men were to be given low priority had considered that sometimes the procedure was performed for medical reasons, even presumably on the most Aryan of babies.

Kohl searched the pockets and found no identification. Nothing at all, in fact. Curious.

"You took nothing from him? There were no documents? No personal effects?"

"No, sir."

Breathing heavily as he knelt, the inspector examined the body carefully and found the man's hands to be soft, free of calluses. He spoke, half to himself, half to Konrad Janssen. "With these hands, trimmed nails and hair and residue of talcum on his skin, he doesn't work labor. I see ink on his fingers but not much, which suggests he's not in the printing trade. Besides, the patterns suggest the ink comes from handwriting, probably ledgers and correspondence. He's not a journalist, for he would have traces of pencil lead on his hands and I can see none." Kohl knew this because he'd investigated the deaths of a dozen reporters just after the National Socialists came to power. Not one of the cases had been closed; not one was being actively investigated. "Businessman, professional, civil servant, government . . ."

"Nothing *under* his nails either, sir."

Kohl nodded then probed the man's legs. "An intellectual man most likely, as I said. But his legs are very muscular. And look at those excessively worn shoes. Ach, they make my own feet burn just to glance at them. My guess is that he is a walker and a hiker." The inspector grunted as he rose with some effort.

"Out for a stroll after an early lunch."

"Yes, very likely. There is a toothpick, which might be his." Kohl retrieved and smelled it. Garlic. He bent down and smelled the same scent near the victim's mouth too. "Yes, I believe so." He dropped the toothpick into one of his small brown paper envelopes and sealed it.

The young officer continued. "So, a robbery victim."

"Certainly a possibility," Kohl said slowly. "But I think not. A robber taking *everything* that the man had on him? And there aren't any gunpowder burn patterns on the neck or ear. That means the bullet was fired from some distance. A robber would have been closer and confronted him face-to-face. This man was shot from behind and the side." A lick of the stubby pencil tip, and Kohl recorded these observations in his crinkled notebook. "Yes, yes, I'm sure there are robbers who would lie in wait and shoot a victim then rob him. But that doesn't fit what we know about most thieves, does it?"

The wound also suggested that the killer had not been the Gestapo, SS or Stormtroopers. The bullet in such cases usually was fired from point-blank range into the front of the brain or the back.

"What was he doing in the alley?" the inspector candidate mused, looking around as if the answer were lying on the ground.

"That question doesn't interest us yet, Janssen. This is a popular shortcut between Spener Street and Calvin Street. His purpose may have been illicit but we'll have to learn that from evidence other than his route." Kohl examined the head wound again then walked to the wall of the alley, on which a considerable amount of blood was spattered.

"Ah." The inspector was delighted to find the bullet, sitting where the cobblestones met the brick wall. He picked it up carefully with a tissue. It was only slightly dented. He recognized immediately that it was a 9mm slug. This meant it most likely came from an automatic pistol, which would have ejected the spent brass cartridge.

He said to the third Schupo, "Please, Officer, look over the ground there, every centimeter. Look for a brass shell casing."

"Yes, sir."

Pulling his magnifying monocle from his waistcoat pocket and squinting through it, Kohl examined the projectile. "The bullet is in very good shape. That's encouraging. We'll see what the lands and grooves tell us back at the Alex. They're quite sharp."

"So the killer has a new gun," Janssen offered, then qualified his comment. "Or an old gun that has rarely been fired."

"Very good, Janssen. Those were to be my very next words." Kohl put the slug in another brown envelope and sealed this one too. Writing more notes.

Janssen again looked over the corpse. "If he wasn't robbed, sir, then why are they turned out?" he asked. "His pockets, I am referring to."

"Oh, I didn't mean he wasn't robbed. I simply am not sure that robbery was the primary motive. . . . Ah, there. Open the jacket again."

Janssen pulled open the garment.

"See, the threads?"

"Where?"

"Right here!" Kohl pointed.

"Yes, sir."

"The label has been cut out. Is that true of all his garments?"

"Identification," the young man said, nodding, as he looked at the trousers and shirt. "The killer doesn't want us to know whom he has killed."

"Markings in the shoes?"

Janssen took them off and examined them. "None, sir."

Kohl glanced at them and then felt the deceased's jacket. "The suit is made of . . . ersatz fabric." The inspector had nearly made the mistake of using the phrase "Hitler fabric," a reference to fake cloth made of fibers from trees. (A popular joke: If you have a tear in your suit, water and expose it to sunlight; the cloth will grow back.) The Leader had announced plans to make the country independent of foreign imports. Elastic, margarine, gasoline, motor oil, rubber, cloth—all were being made from alternative materials found in Germany. The problem, of course, was the same with substitutes everywhere—they simply weren't very good, and people some-times referred to them disparagingly as "Hitler" goods. But it was never wise to use the term in public; one could be reported for uttering it.

The import of the discovery was that the man was probably German. Most foreigners in the country nowadays had their own currency to convert, which meant their buying power was quite strong, and none would willingly purchase cheap clothing like this.

But why would the killer wish to keep his victim's identity secret? The ersatz clothing suggested there was nothing particularly important about him. But then, Kohl reflected, many senior people in the National Socialist Party were poorly paid, and even those who had decent salaries often wore substitute clothing out of loyalty to the Leader: Could the victim's job within the Party or the government have been the motive for his death?

"Interesting," Kohl said, rising stiffly. "The killer shoots a man in a crowded part of the city. He knows someone might hear the report of the gun and yet he risks detection to slice the labels out of his clothing. This makes me all the more intrigued to learn who this unfortunate gentleman is. Take his fingerprints, Janssen. It will be forever if we wait for the coroner to do so."

"Yes, sir." The young officer opened his briefcase and removed the equipment. He started to work.

Kohl gazed at the cobblestones. "I have been saying 'killer,' singular, Janssen, but of course there could have been a dozen. But I can see noth-ing of the choreography of this event on the ground." In more open crime scenes the infamously gritty Berlin wind conveniently spread telltale dust on the ground. But not in this sheltered alley.

"Sir . . . Inspector," the Schupo officer called. "I can find no casings here. I have scoured the entire area."

This fact troubled Kohl, and Janssen caught his boss's expression.

"Because," the inspector explained, "he not only cut the labels from his victim, he took the time to find the shell casing."

"So. He is a professional."

"As I say, Janssen, when making deductions, never state your conclu-sions as if they are certainties. When you do that, your mind instinctively closes out other possibilities. Say, rather, that our suspect *may* have a high degree of diligence and attention to detail. Perhaps a professional criminal, perhaps not. It could also be that a rat or bird made off with the shiny object, or a schoolboy picked it up and fled at the terrifying sight of a dead man. Or even that the killer is a poor man who wishes to reuse the brass."

"Of course, Inspector," Janssen said, nodding as if memorizing Kohl's words.

In the short time they'd worked together, the inspector had learned two things about Janssen: that the young man was incapable of irony and that he was a remarkably fast learner. The latter quality was a godsend to the impatient inspector. Regarding the former, though, he wished the boy joked more frequently; policing is a profession badly in need of humor.

Janssen finished taking the fingerprints, which he'd done expertly.

"Now dust the cobblestones around him and take photographs of any prints you find. The killer might've been clever enough to take the labels but not so smart to avoid touching the ground when he did so."

After five minutes of spreading the fine powder around the body, Janssen said, "I believe there are some here, sir. Look."

"Yes. They're good. Record them."

After he photographed the prints the young man stood back and took additional pictures of the corpse and the scene. The inspector walked slowly around the body. He pulled his magnifying monocle from his vest's watch pocket again and placed around his neck its green cord, braided for him as a Christmas present by young Hanna. He examined a spot on the cobblestones near the body. "Flakes of leather, it seems." He looked at them carefully. "Old and dry. Brown. Too stiff to be from gloves. Maybe shoes or a belt or old satchel or suitcase that either the killer or victim was carrying."

He scooped these flakes up and placed them in another brown envelope then moistened the gum and sealed it.

"We have a witness, sir," one of the younger Schupo officers called. "Though he's not very cooperative."

Witness. Excellent! Kohl followed the man back toward the mouth of the alley. There, another Schupo officer was prodding forward a man in his forties, Kohl estimated. He was dressed in worker's clothes. His left eye was glass and his right arm dangled uselessly at his side. One of the four million who survived the War but were left with bodies forever changed by the unfathomable experience.

The Schupo officer pushed him toward Kohl.

"That will do, Officer," the inspector said sternly. "Thank you." Turning to the witness, he asked, "Now, your card."

The man handed over his ID. Kohl glanced at it. He forgot everything on the document the instant he returned it, but even a cursory examination of papers by a police officer made witnesses extremely cooperative.

Though not in all cases.

"I wish to be helpful. But as I told the officer, sir, I didn't actually see much of anything." He fell silent.

"Yes, yes, tell me what you actually *did* see." An impatient gesture from Kohl's thick hand.

"Yes, Inspector. I was scrubbing the basement stairs at Number forty-eight. There." He pointed out of the alley to a town house. "As you can see. I was below the level of the sidewalk. I heard what I took to be a backfire."

Kohl grunted. Since '33 no one but an idiot assumed backfires; they assumed bullets.

"I thought nothing of it and continued scrubbing." He proved this by pointing to his damp shirt and trousers. "Then ten minutes later I heard a whistle."

"Whistle? A police whistle?"

"No, sir, I mean, as someone would make through his teeth. It was quite loud. I glanced up and saw a man walk out of the alley. The whistle was to hail a taxi. It stopped in front of my building and I heard the man ask the driver to take him to the Summer Garden restaurant."

Whistling? Kohl reflected. This was unusual. One whistled for dogs and horses. But to summon a taxi this way would demean the driver. In Germany all professions and trades were worthy of equal respect. Did this suggest that the suspect was a foreigner? Or merely rude? He jotted the observation into his notebook.

"The number of the taxi?" Kohl had to ask, of course, but received the expected response.

"Oh, I have no idea, sir."

"Summer Garden." This was a common name. "Which one?"

"I believe I heard 'Rosenthaler Street.'"

Kohl nodded, excited to find such a good lead this early in an investigation. "Quickly—what did the man look like?"

"I was below the stairs, sir, as I said. I saw only his back as he hailed the car. He was a large man, more than two meters tall. Broad but not fat. He had an accent, though."

"What kind? From a different region of Germany? Or a different country?"

"Similar to someone from the south, if anything. But I have a brother near Munich and it sounded different still."

"Outside the country, perhaps? Many foreigners here now, with the Olympics."

"I don't know, sir. I've spent all my life in Berlin. And I've only been out of the fatherland once." He nodded toward his useless arm.

"Did he have a leather satchel?"

"Yes, I believe so."

To Janssen, Kohl said, "The likely source of the leather flakes." He turned back. "And you didn't see his face?"

"No, sir. As I say."

Kohl's voice lowered. "If I were to tell you that I won't take your name, so you would not be further involved, could you perhaps remember better what he looked like?"

"Honestly, sir, I did not see his face."

"Age?"

The man shook his head. "All I know is that he was a big man and was wearing a light suit. . . . I can't say the color, I'm afraid. Oh, and on his head was a hat like Air Minister Göring wears."

"What kind is that?" Kohl asked.

"With a narrow brim. Brown."

"Ah, something helpful." Kohl looked the janitor up and down. "Very well, you may go now."

"Hail Hitler," the man said with pathetic enthusiasm and offered a powerful salute, perhaps in compensation for the fact he needed to use his left arm for the gesture.

The inspector offered a distracted "Hail" and returned to the body. They quickly collected their equipment. "Let's hurry. To the Summer Garden."

They started back to the car. Willi Kohl winced, glancing down at his feet. Even wearing overpriced leather shoes stuffed with the softest of lamb's wool did little to help his distraught toes and arches. Cobblestones were particularly brutal.

He was suddenly aware of Janssen, at his side, slowing. "Gestapo," the young man whispered.

Dismayed, Kohl looked up and saw Peter Krauss, in a shabby brown suit and matching felt trilby hat, approach. Two of his assistants, younger men, about Janssen's age, held back.

Oh, not now! The suspect might be at the restaurant this very moment, not suspecting that he'd been detected.

Krauss walked toward the two Kripo inspectors leisurely. Propaganda Minister Goebbels was always sending out Party photographers to stage pictures of model Aryans and their families to use in his publications. Peter

Krauss could easily have been a subject for a hundred such pictures: He was a tall, slim, blond man. A former colleague of Kohl's, Krauss had been invited to join the Gestapo because of his experience in the old Department 1A of the Kripo, which investigated political crimes. Just after the National Socialists came to power the department was spun off and became the Gestapo. Krauss was like many Prussian Germans: Nordic with some Slav blood in his veins but office gossip had it that he'd been invited to leave the Kripo for the job on Prince Albrecht Street only after changing his first name from Pietr, which sniffed of the Slavic.

Kohl had heard Krauss was a methodical investigator though they had never worked together; Kohl had always refused to handle political crimes, and now the Kripo was forbidden to.

Krauss said, "Willi, good afternoon."

"Hail. What brings you here, Peter?"

Janssen nodded and the Gestapo investigator did the same. He said to Kohl, "I received a phone call from our boss."

Did he mean Heinrich Himmler himself? Kohl wondered. It was possible. One month ago, the SS leader had consolidated every police force in Germany under his own control and had created the Sipo, the plain-clothed division, which included the Gestapo, the Kripo, and the notorious SD, which was the SS's intelligence division. Himmler had just been named state chief of police, a rather modest description, Kohl had thought at the time of the announcement, for the most powerful law enforcer on earth.

Krauss continued. "He's been instructed by the Leader to keep our city blemish-free during the Olympics. We're to look into all serious crimes near the stadium, Olympic Village and city center and make sure the perpetrators are swiftly caught. And here, a murder within shouting distance of the Tiergarten." Krauss clicked his tongue in dismay.

Kohl glanced obviously at his watch, desperate to get to the Summer Garden. "I'm afraid I have to leave, Peter."

Examining the body closely, crouching down, the Gestapo man said, "Unfortunately with all the foreign reporters in town . . . So difficult to control them, to monitor them."

"Yes, yes, but—"

"We need to make sure this is solved before they learn of the death." Krauss rose and walked in a slow circle around the dead man. "Who is he, do we know?"

"Not yet. His ID is missing. Tell me, Peter, this wouldn't have anything to do with an SS or SA matter, would it?"

"Not that I know of," Krauss replied, frowning. "Why?"

"On the way here, Janssen and I noticed many more patrols. Random stops to check papers. Yet we've heard no word about an operation."

"Ach, that's nothing," the Gestapo inspector said, waving his hand dismissively. "A minor security matter. Nothing the Kripo need worry about."

Kohl looked again at his pocket watch. "Well, I really must go, Peter."

The Gestapo officer rose to his feet. "Was he robbed?"

"Everything's missing from his pockets," Kohl said impatiently.

Krauss stared at the body for a long moment and all Kohl could think of was the suspect sitting at the Summer Garden, halfway through a meal of schnitzel or wurst. "I must be getting back," Kohl said.

"One moment." Krauss continued to study the body. Finally, without looking up, he said, "It would make sense if the killer was a foreigner."

"A foreigner? Well—" Janssen spoke quickly, eyebrows rising in his youthful face. But Kohl shot him a sharp look and he fell silent.

"What's that?" Krauss asked him.

The inspector candidate made a fast recovery. "I'm curious why you think it would make sense."

"The deserted alley, missing identification, a cold-blooded shooting . . . When you've been in this business for a time, you get a feel for the perpetrators in murders such as this, Inspector Candidate."

"A murder such as what?" Kohl could not resist asking. A man shot to death in a Berlin alley was hardly sui generis these days.

But Krauss didn't respond. "A Roma or Pole very likely. Violent people, to be sure. And with motives galore to murder innocent Germans. Or the killer might be Czech, from the east, of course, not the Sudetenland. They're known for shooting people from behind."

Kohl nearly added: as are the Stormtroopers. But he merely said, "Then we can hope that the perpetrator turns out to be a Slav."

Krauss gave no reaction to the reference to his own ethnic origins. Another look at the corpse. "I will make inquiries about this, Willi. I will have my people make contact with the A-men in the area."

Kohl said, "I am encouraged by the thought of using National Socialist informants. They're very good at it. And there are so many of them."

"Indeed."

Bless him, Janssen too looked impatiently at his watch, grimaced and said, "We're very late for that meeting, sir."

"Yes, yes, we are." Kohl started back up the alley. But he paused and called to Krauss, "One question?"

"Yes, Willi?"

"What kind of hat does Air Minister Göring wear?"

"You are asking . . . ?" Krauss frowned.

"Göring. What kind of hat?"

"Oh, I have no idea," he replied, looking momentarily stricken, as if this were knowledge that every good Gestapo officer should be versed in. "Why?"

"No matter."

"Hail Hitler."

"Hail."

As they hurried back to the DKW, Kohl said breathlessly, "Give the film to one of the Schupo officers and have him rush it to headquarters. I want the pictures immediately."

"Yes, sir." The young man diverted his course and handed the film to an officer, gave him the instructions, then caught up with Kohl, who called to a Schupo, "When the coroner's men get here, tell them that I want the autopsy report as soon as possible. I want to know about diseases our friend here might have had. The clap and consumption in particular. And how advanced. And the contents of his stomach. Tattoos, broken bones, surgical scars, as well."

"Yes, sir."

"Remember to tell them it's urgent."

So busy was the coroner these days that it might take eight or ten hours for the body even to be picked up; the autopsy could take several days.

Kohl winced in pain as he hurried to the DKW; the lamb's wool in his shoes had shifted. "What's the fastest route to the Summer Garden? Never mind, we'll figure it out." He looked around. "There!" he shouted, pointing to a newsstand. "Go buy every newspaper they have."

"Yes, sir, but why?"

Willi Kohl dropped into the driver's seat and pushed the ignition button. His voice was breathless but still managed to convey his impatience. "Because we need a picture of Göring in a hat. Why else?"

Chapter Seven

Standing on the street corner, holding a limp *Berlin Journal*, Paul studied the Summer Garden café: women who drank their coffees with gloved hands, men who would down their beers in large gulps and tap their mustaches with pressed linen napkins to lift away the foam. People enjoying the afternoon sun, smoking.

Paul Schumann remained perfectly still, looking, looking, looking.

Out of kilter . . .

Just like setting type, plucking the metal letters from a California job case and assembling words and sentences. "Mind your *p*'s and *q*'s," his father would call constantly—those particular letters easy to confuse because the piece of type was the exact reverse of the printed letter.

He was now looking over the Summer Garden just as carefully. He'd missed the Stormtrooper watching him from the phone booth outside Dresden Alley—an inexcusable mistake for a button man. He wasn't going to let that happen again.

After a few minutes, he sensed no immediate danger but, he reflected, how could he tell? Maybe the people he was watching were nothing more than they seemed: normal joes eating meals and going about their errands on a hot, lazy Saturday afternoon, with no interest in anyone else on the street.

But maybe they were as suspicious and murderously loyal to the Nazis as the man on the *Manhattan,* Heinsler.

I love the Führer . . .

He tossed the paper into a bin then crossed the street and entered the restaurant.

"Please," he said to the captain, "a table for three."

"Anywhere, anywhere," the harried man said.

Paul took a table inside. A casual glance around him. No one paid any attention to him.

Or appeared to.

A waiter sailed past. "You wish to order?"

"A beer for now."

"Which beer?" He started to name brands Paul had never heard of.

He said, "The first. A large."

The waiter walked toward the bar and returned a moment later with a tall pilsner glass. Paul drank thirstily but found he disliked the taste. It was almost sweet, fruity. He pushed it aside and lit a cigarette, having shaken the Chesterfield out of the pack below the tabletop so no one could see the American label. He glanced up to see Reginald Morgan strolling casually into the restaurant. Looking around, he noticed Paul and walked up to him, saying in German, "My friend, so good to see you again."

They shook hands and he sat down across the table.

Morgan's face was damp and he wiped it with his handkerchief. His eyes were troubled. "It was close. The Schupo pulled up just as I got away."

"Anyone see you?"

"I don't think so. I left by the far end of the alley."

"Is it safe to stay here?" Paul asked, looking around. "Should we leave?"

"No. It would be more suspicious at this time of day to arrive at a restaurant then leave quickly without eating. Not like New York. Berliners won't be rushed when it comes to meals. Offices close down for two hours so people can have a proper lunch. Of course, they also eat two breakfasts." He patted his stomach. "Now you can see why I was happy to be posted here." Looking around casually, Morgan said, "Here." He pushed a thick book toward Paul. "See, I remembered to return it." The German words on the cover were *Mein Kampf*, which Paul translated as "My Struggle." Hitler's name was on it. He'd written a book? Paul wondered.

"Thank you. But there was no hurry."

Paul stubbed out the cigarette in the ashtray but, when it was cool, slipped it into his pocket, ever careful not to leave traces that might place him somewhere.

Morgan leaned forward, smiling as if whispering a bawdy joke. "Inside the book's a hundred marks. And the address of the place you'll be staying, a boardinghouse. It's near Lützow Plaza, south of the Tiergarten. I wrote down directions too."

"Is it on the ground floor?"

"The apartment? I don't know. I didn't ask. You're thinking of escape routes?"

Specifically he was thinking of Malone's binge-nest with its sealed doors and windows and a welcoming party of armed sailors. "That's right."

"Well, have a look at it. Maybe you can swap if there's a problem. The landlady seems agreeable. Her name is Käthe Richter."

"Is she a Nazi?"

Morgan said softly, "Don't use that word here. It will give you away. 'Nazi' is Bavarian slang for 'simpleton.' The proper abbreviation is 'Nazo,' but you don't hear that much either. Say 'National Socialist.' Some people use the initials, NSDAP. Or you can refer to the 'Party.' And say it reverently. . . . Regarding Miss Richter, she doesn't seem to have any sympathies one way or the other." Nodding at the beer, Morgan asked, "You don't care for that?"

"Piss water."

Morgan laughed. "It's wheat beer. Children drink it. Why did you order it?"

"There were a thousand kinds. I'd never heard of any of them."

"I'll order for us."

When the waiter arrived he said, "Please, bring us two Pschorr ales. And sausage and bread. With cabbage and pickled cucumbers. Butter if you have any today."

"Yes, sir." He took away Paul's glass.

Morgan continued. "In the book there's also a Russian passport with your picture in it and some rubles, about a hundred dollars' worth. In an emergency make your way to the Swiss border. The Germans'll be happy to get another Russian out of their country and they'll let you pass. They won't take the rubles because they won't be allowed to spend them. The Swiss won't care that you're a Bolshevik and will be delighted to let you in to spend the money. Go to Zurich and get a message to the U.S. embassy. Gordon will get you out. Now, after Dresden Alley we must be extremely careful. Like I said, something is clearly going on in town. There are far more patrols on the street than usual: Stormtroopers, which is not particularly odd—they have nothing to do with their time but march and patrol—but SS and Gestapo too."

"They are . . . ?"

"SS . . . Did you see the two out on the patio? In the black uniforms?"

"Yes."

"They were originally Hitler's guard detail. Now they're another private army. Mostly they wear black but some of the uniforms are gray. The Gestapo is the secret police force, plainclothes. They're small in number but very dangerous. Their jurisdiction is political crimes mostly. But in Germany now anything can be a political crime. You spit on the sidewalk, it's an offense to the honor of the Leader so off you go to Moabit Prison or a concentration camp."

The Pschorr beers and food arrived and Paul drank down half of the brew at once. It was earthy and rich. "Now, that's good."

"You like it? After I got here I realized I could never drink American beer again. To be able to brew beer, it takes years of learning. It's as respected as a university degree. Berlin is the brewing capital of Europe but they make the best in Munich, down in Bavaria."

Paul ate hungrily. But beer and food were not the first things on his mind. "We have to move fast," he whispered. In his profession every hour you were near the site of the touch-off increased the risk of getting caught. "I need information and I need a weapon."

Morgan nodded. "My contact should be here any minute. He has details about . . . the man you're here to visit. Then this afternoon we'll go to a pawnshop. The owner has a good rifle for you."

"Rifle?" Paul frowned.

Morgan was troubled. "You can't shoot a rifle?"

"Yes, I can shoot one. I was infantry. But I always work up close."

"Close? That's easier for you?"

"It's not a question of easy. It's more efficient."

"Well, believe me, Paul, it may be possible, though very difficult, to get close enough to your target to kill him with a pistol. But there are so many Brownshirts and SS and Gestapo hovering about that you'd without doubt be caught. And I guarantee that your death would be lengthy and unpleasant. But there's another reason to use a rifle—he has to be killed in public."

"Why?" Paul asked.

"The Senator said that everybody in the German government and the Party knows how crucial Ernst is to rearming. It's important to make certain that whoever replaces him knows they'll be in danger too if they take up where he left off. If Ernst dies in private, Hitler would cover it up, claim he'd been killed in an accident or died of some illness."

"Then I'll do it in public," Paul said. "With a rifle. But I'll need to sight-in the gun, get a feel for it, find a good killing field, examine it ahead of time, see what the breezes are like, the light, the routes to and from the place."

"Of course. You're the expert. Whatever you want."

Paul finished his meal. "After what happened in the alley, I need to go to ground. I want to get my things from the Olympic Village and move to the boardinghouse as soon as possible. Is the room ready now?"

Morgan told him that it was.

Paul sipped more beer then pulled Hitler's book toward him, rested it in his lap, flipped through it, found the passport, money and address. He took out the slip of paper on which was jotted the information on the boarding-house. Dropping the book in his briefcase, he memorized the address and directions, casually wiped the note in beer spilled on the table and kneaded it in his strong hands until it was a wad of pulp. He slipped this into his pocket with the cigarette butts for later disposal.

Morgan lifted an eyebrow.

They told me you were good.

Paul nodded toward his satchel, whispering, "*My Struggle.* Hitler's book. What exactly is it?"

"Somebody called it a collection of 160,000 grammatical errors. It's sup-posedly Hitler's philosophy but basically it's impenetrable nonsense. But you might want to keep it." Morgan smiled. "Berlin is a city of shortages and at the moment toilet tissue is hard to find."

A brief laugh. Then Paul asked, "This man we're about to meet . . . why can we trust him?"

"In Germany now trust is a curious thing. The risk is so grave and so prevalent that it's not enough to trust someone just because they believe in your cause. In my contact's case, his brother was a union organizer mur-dered by Stormtroopers, so he sympathizes with us. But I am not willing to risk my life on that alone. So I have paid him a great deal of money. There is an expression here: 'Whose bread I eat is whose song I sing.' Well, Max eats a great deal of my bread. And he's in the precarious position of having already sold me some very helpful and, for him, compromising material. This is a perfect example of how trust works here: You must either bribe someone or threaten him, and I prefer to do both simultaneously."

The door opened and Morgan squinted in recognition. "Ah, that's he," he whispered. A thin man in worker's coveralls entered the restaurant, a small rucksack slung over his shoulder. He looked around, blinking to acclimate his vision to the dimness. Morgan waved his hand and the man joined them. He was clearly nervous, eyes darting from Paul to the other patrons to the waiters to the shadows in the corridors that led to the lavatory and the kitchen, then back to Paul.

"They" is everybody in Germany now. . . .

He sat at the table, first with his back to the door, then switched seats so that he could see the rest of the restaurant.

"Good afternoon," Morgan said.

"Hail Hitler."

"Hail," Paul replied.

"My friend here has asked that he be called Max. He has done work for the man you've come to see. Around his house. He delivers goods there and knows the housekeeper and gardener. He lives in the same town, Charlottenburg, west of here."

Max declined food or beer and had only coffee, into which he poured sugar that left a dusty scum on the surface. He stirred vigorously.

"I need to know everything you can tell me about him," Paul whispered.

"Yes, yes, I will." But he fell silent and looked around again. He wore his suspicion like the lotion that plastered down his thinning hair. Paul found the uneasiness irritating, not to mention dangerous. Max opened the rucksack and offered a dark green folder to Paul. Sitting back so no one could see the contents, he opened it and found himself looking at a half dozen wrinkled photographs. They depicted a man in a business suit, which was tailored, the clothing of a meticulous, conscientious man. He was in his fifties and had a round head and short gray or white hair. He wore wire-rimmed glasses.

Paul asked, "These are definitely of him? What about doubles?"

"He doesn't use doubles." The man took a sip of coffee with shaking hands and looked around the restaurant again.

Paul finished studying them. He was going to tell Max to keep the photos and destroy them when he got home but the man seemed too nervous and the American imagined him panicking and leaving them on the tram or subway. He slipped the folder into his satchel, next to Hitler's book; he'd dispose of them later.

"Now," Paul said, leaning forward, "tell me about him. Everything you know."

Max relayed what he knew about Reinhard Ernst: The colonel retained the discipline and air of a military man though he'd been out of the service for some years. He would rise early and work long, long hours, six or seven days a week. He exercised regularly and was an expert shot. He often carried a small automatic pistol. His office was on Wilhelm Street, in the Chancellory building, and he drove himself to and from the office, rarely accompanied by a guard. His car was an open-air Mercedes.

Paul was considering what the man had said. "This Chancellory? He's there every day?"

"Usually, yes. Though sometimes he travels to shipyards or, recently, to Krupp's works."

"Who's Krupp?"

"His companies make munitions and armor."

"At the Chancellory, where would he park?"

"I don't know, sir. I've never been there."

"Can you find out where he'll be in the next few days? When he might go to the office?"

"Yes, I'll try." A pause. "I don't know if . . ." Max's voice faded.

"What?" Paul asked.

"I know some things about his personal life too. About his wife, daughter-in-law, his grandson. Do you want to know that side of his life? Or would you rather not?"

Touching the ice . . .

"No," Paul said in a whisper. "Tell me everything."

They drove down Rosenthaler Street, as quickly as the tiny engine could carry them, toward the Summer Garden restaurant.

Konrad Janssen asked his boss, "Sir, a question?"

"Yes?"

"Inspector Krauss was hoping to find that a foreigner was the killer and we have evidence that the suspect is one. Why didn't you tell him that?"

"Evidence that *suggests* that he *might be* one. And not very strongly. Merely that he might have had an accent and that he whistled for a taxi."

"Yes, sir. But shouldn't we have mentioned it? We could use the Gestapo's resources."

Heavyset Kohl was breathing hard and sweating furiously in the heat. He liked the summer because the family could enjoy the Tiergarten and Luna Park or drive to Wannsee or the Havel River for picnics. But for climate he was an autumn person at heart. He wiped his forehead and replied,

"No, Janssen, we should *not* have mentioned it nor should we have sought the Gestapo's help. And this is why: First, since the consolidation last month, the Gestapo and SS are doing whatever they can to strip the Kripo of its independence. We must retain as much as we can and that means we need to do our job alone. And second, and much, much more important: The Gestapo's 'resources' are often simply arresting anyone who seems in the least guilty—of anything. And sometimes arresting those who are clearly innocent but whose arrests might be *convenient*."

Kripo headquarters contained six hundred holding cells, whose purpose had once been like those in police stations everywhere: to detain criminal arrestees until they were released or tried. Presently these cells—filled to overflowing—held those accused of vague political crimes and were overseen by Stormtroopers, brutal young men in brown uniforms and white armbands. The cells were merely temporary stops on the way to a concentration camp or Gestapo headquarters on Prince Albrecht Street. Sometimes to the cemetery.

Kohl continued. "No, Janssen, we're craftsmen practicing the refined art of police work, not Saxon farmers armed with sickles to mow down dozens of citizens in the pursuit of a single guilty man."

"Yes, sir."

"Never forget that." He shook his head. "Ach, how much harder it is to do our job in this moral quicksand around us." As he pulled the car to the curb he glanced at his assistant. "Janssen, you could have me arrested, you know, and sent to Oranienburg for a year for saying what I just did."

"I wouldn't say anything, sir."

Kohl killed the ignition. They climbed out, then trotted quickly up the broad sidewalk toward the Summer Garden. As they got closer Willi Kohl detected the scent of well-marinated sauerbraten, for which this place was known. His stomach growled.

Janssen was carrying a copy of the National Socialist newspaper, *The People's Observer,* which featured Göring prominently on the front page, wearing a jaunty hat of a cut that wasn't common in Berlin. Thinking of these particular accessories, Kohl glanced at his assistant; the inspector candidate's fair face was growing red from the July sun. Did today's young people not realize that hats had been created for a purpose?

As they approached the restaurant Kohl motioned Janssen to slow. They paused beside a lamppost and studied the Summer Garden. There were not many diners remaining at this hour. Two SS officers were paying and leaving, which was just as well, since, for the reasons he'd just explained to Janssen, he preferred to say nothing about the case. The only men remaining were a middle-aged fellow in lederhosen and a pensioner.

Kohl noted the thick curtains, protecting them from surveillance from inside. He nodded to Janssen and they stepped onto the deck, the inspector asking each diner if he'd seen a large man in a brown hat enter the restaurant.

The pensioner nodded. "A big man? Indeed, Detective. I didn't look clearly but I believe he walked inside about twenty minutes ago."

"He's still there?"

"He hasn't come out, not that I saw."

Janssen stiffened like a beagle on a scent. "Sir, shall we call the Orpo?"

These were the uniformed Order Police, housed in barracks, ready, as the name suggested, to keep order by use of rifles, machine pistols and truncheons. But Kohl thought again of the mayhem that could erupt if they were summoned, especially against an armed suspect in a restaurant filled with patrons. "No, I think we won't, Janssen. We'll be more subtle. You go around the back of the restaurant and wait at the door. If anyone comes out, whether in a hat or not, detain him. Remember—our suspect is armed. Now move surreptitiously."

"Yes, sir."

The young man stopped at the alley and, with an extremely unsurreptitious wave, turned the corner and vanished.

Kohl casually started forward and paused, as if perusing the posted menu. Then he moved closer, feeling uneasiness, feeling too the weight of his revolver in his pocket. Until the National Socialists came to power few Kripo detectives carried weapons. But several years ago, when then Interior Minister Göring had expanded the many police forces in the country, he'd ordered every policeman to carry a weapon and, to the shock of Kohl and his colleagues in the Kripo, to use them liberally. He'd actually issued an edict saying that a policeman would be reprimanded for failing to shoot a suspect, but not for shooting someone who turned out to be innocent.

Willi Kohl hadn't fired a weapon since 1918.

Yet, picturing the shattered skull of the victim in Dresden Alley, he now was pleased that he had the gun with him. Kohl adjusted his jacket, made sure he could grab the gun quickly if he needed to and took a deep breath. He pushed through the doorway.

And froze like a statue, panicked. The interior of the Summer Garden was quite dark and his eyes were used to the brilliant sunlight outside; he was momentarily blinded. Foolish, he thought angrily to himself. He should have considered this. Here he stood with "Kripo" written all over him, a clear target for an armed suspect.

He stepped further inside and closed the door behind him. In his cottony vision, people moved throughout the restaurant. Some men, he believed, were standing. Someone was moving toward him.

Kohl stepped back, alarmed. His hand went toward the pocket containing his revolver.

"Sir, a table? Sit where you like."

He squinted and slowly his vision began returning.

"Sir?" the waiter repeated.

"No," he said. "I'm looking for someone."

Finally the inspector was able to see normally again.

The restaurant contained only a dozen patrons. None was a large man with a brown hat and light suit. He started into the kitchen.

"Sir, you can't—"

Kohl displayed his identification card to the waiter.

"Yes, sir," the man said timidly.

Kohl walked through the stupefyingly hot kitchen and to the back door. He opened it. "Janssen?"

"No one came through the door, sir."

The inspector candidate joined his boss and they returned to the dining room.

Kohl motioned the waiter over to them.

"Sir, what is your name?"

"Johann."

"Well, Johann, have you seen a man in here, within the past twenty minutes, wearing a hat like this?" Kohl nodded at Janssen, who displayed the picture of Göring.

"Why, yes, I have. He and his companions just left moments ago. It seemed rather suspicious. They left by the side door."

He pointed to the empty table. Kohl sighed with disgust. It was one of the two tables next to the windows. Yes, the curtain was thick but he noted a tiny gap at the side; their suspect had undoubtedly seen them canvassing the patrons on the patio.

"Come, Janssen!" Kohl and the inspector candidate rushed out the side door and through an anemic garden typical of the tens of thousands throughout the city; Berliners loved growing flowers and plants but land was at such a premium that they were forced to use any scraps of dirt they could find for their gardens. There was only one route out of the patch; it led to Rosenthaler Street. They trotted to it and looked up and down the congested street. No sign of their suspect.

Kohl was furious. Had he not been distracted by Krauss they would likely have had more of a chance to intercept the large man in the hat. But mostly he was angry with himself for his carelessness on the patio a moment earlier.

"In our haste," he muttered to Janssen, "we've burnt the crust, but perhaps we can salvage some of the remaining loaf." He turned and stalked back toward the front door of the Summer Garden.

Paul, Morgan and the skinny, nervous man known as Max stood fifty feet up Rosenthaler Street in a small cluster of linden trees.

They were watching the man in the white suit and his younger associate in the garden, beside the restaurant, looking up and down the street, then they returned to the front door.

"They couldn't be after us," Morgan said. "Impossible."

"They were looking for *someone*," Paul said. "They came out the side door a minute after we did. That's not a coincidence."

In a shaky voice, Max asked, "You think they were Gestapo? Or Kripo?"

"What's Kripo?" Paul asked.

"Criminal police. Plainclothes detectives."

"They were *some* sort of police," Paul announced. There was no doubt. He'd suspected it from the moment he'd seen the two men approach the Summer Garden. He'd taken the window table specifically to keep an eye on the street and, sure enough, he'd noticed the men—a heavyset one in a Panama hat and a slimmer, younger one in a green suit—asking diners on the patio questions. Then the younger one had stepped away—probably to cover the back door—and the white-suited cop had walked to the posted menu, examining it for far longer than one normally would.

Paul had stood suddenly, tossed down money—paper bills only, on which fingerprints would be nearly impossible to find—and snapped, "Leave now." With Morgan and a panicked Max behind him, he'd pushed through the side door and waited at the front of a small garden until the cop had gone inside the restaurant, then walked fast down Rosenthaler Street.

"Police," Max now muttered, sounding near tears. "No . . . no . . ."

Too many people to chase you here . . . and too many people to follow you, too many people to rat on you.

I'd do anything for him and the Party. . . .

Paul looked again down the street, back toward the Summer Garden. No one was in pursuit. Still, he felt an electric current of urgency to learn information of Ernst's whereabouts from Max and get on with the touch-off. He turned, saying, "I need to know . . ." His voice faded.

Max was gone.

"Where is he?"

Morgan too turned. "Goddamn," he muttered in English.

"Did he betray us?"

"I can't believe that he would—it would mean his arrest too. But . . ." Morgan's voice faded as he looked past Paul. "No!"

Spinning around, Paul saw Max about two blocks away. He was among several people stopped by two men in black uniforms, whom he apparently hadn't seen. "An SS security stop."

Max looked around nervously, waiting his turn to be questioned by the SS troopers. He wiped his face, looking guilty as a teenager.

Paul whispered, "There's nothing for him to worry about. His papers are fine. He gave us Ernst's photos. As long as he doesn't panic he'll be all right."

Calm down, Paul told the man silently. Don't look around. . . .

Then Max smiled and stepped closer to the SS.

"He's going to be fine," Morgan said.

No, he's not, Paul thought. He's going to shank it.

And just at that moment the man turned and fled.

The SS troops pushed aside a couple they'd been speaking with and began running after him. "Stop, you will stop!"

"No!" Morgan whispered. "Why did he do that? Why?"

Because he was scared witless, Paul thought.

Max was slimmer than the SS guards, who were in bulky uniforms, and was beginning to pull away from them.

Maybe he can make it. Maybe—

A shot echoed and Max tumbled to the concrete, blood blossoming on his back. Paul looked behind him. A third SS officer across the street had drawn his pistol and fired. Max started to crawl toward the curb when the first two guards caught up to him, gasping for breath. One drew his pistol, fired a shot into the poor man's head and leaned against a lamppost to catch his breath.

"Let's go," Paul whispered. "Now!"

They turned back onto Rosenthaler Street and walked north, along with the other pedestrians moving steadily away from the site of the shooting.

"God in heaven," Morgan muttered. "I've spent a month cultivating him and holding his hand while he got details on Ernst. Now what do we do?"

"Whatever we decide, it's got to be fast; somebody might make the connection between him"—a glance back at the body in the street—"and Ernst."

Morgan sighed and thought for a moment. "I don't know anyone else close to Ernst. . . . But I do have a man in the information ministry."

"You have somebody inside *there?*"

"The National Socialists are paranoid but they have one flaw that offsets that: their ego. They have so many agents in place that it never occurs to them that somebody might infiltrate *them.* He's just a clerk but he may be able to find out something."

They paused on a busy corner. Paul said, "I'm going to get my things at the Olympic Village and move to the boardinghouse."

"The pawnshop where we're getting the rifle is near Oranienburger Station. I'll meet you in November 1923 Square, under the big statue of Hitler. Say, four-thirty. Do you have a map?"

"I'll find it."

The men shook hands and, with a glance back at the crowd standing around the body of the unfortunate man, they started their separate ways as another siren filled the streets of a city that was clean and orderly and filled with polite, smiling people—and that had been the site of two killings in as many hours.

No, Paul reflected, the unfortunate Max hadn't betrayed him. But he realized that there was another implication that was far more troubling: These two cops or Gestapo agents had tracked Morgan or Paul or both of them from Dresden Alley to the Summer Garden on their own and come within minutes of capturing them. This was police work far better than any he'd seen in New York. Who the hell are they? he wondered.

"Johann," Willi Kohl asked the waiter, "what exactly was this man with the brown hat wearing?"

"A light gray suit, a white shirt and a green tie, which I found rather garish."

"And he was large?"

"Very large, sir. But not fat. He was a bodybuilder perhaps."

"Any other characteristics?"

"Not that I noticed."

"Was he foreign?"

"I don't know. But he spoke German flawlessly. Perhaps a faint accent."

"His hair color?"

"I couldn't say. Darker rather than lighter."

"Age?"

"Not young, not old."

Kohl sighed. "And you said 'companions'?"

"Yes, sir. He arrived first. Then he was joined by another man. Considerably smaller. Wearing a black or dark gray suit. I don't recall his tie. And then yet another, a man in brown overalls, in his thirties. A worker, it seemed. He joined them later."

"Did the big man have a leather suitcase or satchel?"

"Yes. It was brown."

"His companions spoke German too?"

"Yes."

"Did you overhear their conversation?"

"No, Inspector."

"And the man's face? The man in the hat?" Janssen asked.

A hesitation. "I didn't see the face. Or his companions'."

"You waited on them but you did not see their faces?" Kohl asked.

"I didn't pay any attention. It's dark in here, as you can see. And in this business . . . so many people. You look but you rarely see, if you understand."

That was true, Kohl supposed. But he also knew that since Hitler had come to power three years ago, blindness had become the national malady. People either denounced fellow citizens for "crimes" they hadn't witnessed, or else were unable to recall the details of offenses they actually had seen. Knowing too much might mean a trip to the Alex—the Kripo headquarters—or the Gestapo's on Prince Albrecht Street—to examine endless pictures of known felons. No one would willingly go to either of those places; today's witness could be tomorrow's detainee.

The waiter's eyes swept the floor, troubled. Sweat broke out on his forehead. Kohl pitied him. "Perhaps in lieu of a description of his face, you could give us some other observations and we could dispense with a visit to police headquarters. If you happen to think of something helpful."

The man looked up, relieved.

"I'll try to assist you," the inspector said. "Let's start with some specifics. What did he eat and drink?"

"Ah, that's something. He at first ordered a wheat beer. He must not have ever drunk it before. He only sipped it and pushed it aside. But he drank all of the Pschorr ale that his companion ordered for him."

"Good." Kohl never knew at first what these details about a suspect might ultimately reveal. Perhaps the man's state or country of origin, perhaps something more specific. But it was worth noting, which Willi Kohl now did in his well-thumbed notebook, after a lick of the pencil tip. "And his food?"

"Our sausage and cabbage plate. With much bread and margarine. They had the same. The big man ate everything. He seemed ravenous. His companion ate half."

"And the third man?"

"Coffee only."

"How did the big man—as we'll call him—how did he hold his fork?"

"His fork?"

"After he cut a piece of sausage, did he change his fork from one hand to another and then eat the bite? Or did he lift the food to his mouth without changing hands?"

"I . . . I don't know, sir. I would think possibly he *did* change hands. I say that because it seemed he was always placing his fork down to drink the beer."

"Good, Johann."

"I am happy to aid my Leader in any way I can."

"Yes, yes," Kohl said wearily.

Switching forks. Common in other countries, less so in Germany, like whistling for taxis. So the accent may have indeed been foreign.

"Did he smoke?"

"I believe so, sir."

"Pipe, cigar, cigarette?"

"Cigarette, I believe. But I—"

"Didn't see the brand of the manufacturer."

"No, sir. I didn't."

Kohl walked across the room and examined the suspect's table and the chairs around it. Nothing helpful. He frowned to see that the ashtray contained ash but no cigarette stubs.

More evidence of their man's cleverness?

Kohl then crouched and struck a match over the floor beneath the table.

"Ah, yes, look, Janssen! Some flakes of the same brown leather we found earlier. Indeed it is our man. And there are marks in the dust here that suggest he set a satchel down."

"I wonder what it contains," Janssen said.

"That does not interest us," Kohl said, scooping up these flakes and depositing them in an envelope. "Not at this point. The importance is the bag itself, the connection it establishes between this man and Dresden Alley."

Kohl thanked the waiter and, with a longing glance at a plate of wiener schnitzel, he walked outside, Janssen behind him.

"Let's inquire around the neighborhood to see if anyone saw our gentlemen. You take the far side of the street, Janssen. I'll take the flower vendors." Kohl laughed grimly. Berlin flower sellers were notoriously rude.

Janssen removed his handkerchief and wiped his brow. He seemed to give a faint sigh.

"Are you tired, Janssen?"

"No, sir. Not at all." The young man hesitated then added, "It's just that it seems our work sometimes is hopeless. All this effort for a fat dead man."

Kohl dug his yellow pipe out of his pocket, frowning to see that he'd put his pistol into the same pocket and had nicked the bowl. He filled it with tobacco. He said, "Yes, Janssen, you're right. The victim *was* a fat middle-aged man. But we're clever detectives, aren't we? We know something else about him, as well."

"What's that, sir?"

"That he was somebody's son."

"Well . . . of course he was."

"And perhaps he was somebody's brother. And maybe somebody's husband or lover. And, if he was lucky, he was a father of sons and daughters. I would hope too that there are past lovers who think of him occasionally. And in his future other lovers might have awaited. And three or four more children he could have brought into the world." He rasped a match on the side of the box and got a smolder going in the meerschaum. "So, Janssen, when you look at the incident in this way we don't have merely a curious mystery about a stocky dead man. We have a tragedy like a spiderweb reaching many different lives and many different places, extending for years and years. How sad that is. . . . Do you see why our job is so important?"

"Yes, sir."

And Kohl believed that the young man did indeed understand.

"Janssen, you must get a hat. But for now, I've changed my mind. You take the shady side of the street. It will mean, of course, that *you* must interview the flower vendors. They'll treat you to some words you won't hear outside of a Stormtrooper barracks but at least you won't return to your wife tonight with skin the shade of fresh beetroot."

Chapter Eight

Walking toward the busy square to find a taxi, Paul glanced behind him from time to time. Smoking his Chesterfield, looking at the sights, stores, passersby, once again searching for anything out of kilter.

He slipped into a public rest room, which was immaculate, and stepped into a stall. He stubbed out his cigarette and dropped it, along with the cigarette butts and wad of pulp that had held the address of Käthe Richter's boardinghouse, into the toilet. Then he tore the pictures of Ernst up into dozens of tiny pieces and flushed everything away.

Outside on the street again, he put aside the difficult images of Max's sad and unnecessary death and concentrated on the job ahead of him. It had been years since he'd killed anyone with a rifle. He was a good shot with a long weapon. People call guns "equalizers." But that's not completely true. A pistol weighs perhaps three pounds, a rifle twelve or more. To hold a weapon absolutely still requires strength, and Paul's solid arms had helped make him the best shot in his squadron.

Yet now, as he'd explained to Morgan, when he had to touch off someone, he preferred to do it with a pistol.

And he always came in close, close as breath.

He never said a word to his victim, never confronted him, never even let him know what was about to happen. He would appear, as silently as a big man could, behind the victim, if possible, and fire the shot into his head, killing him instantly. He would never think of behaving like the sadistic Bugsy Siegel or the recently departed Dutch Schultz; they'd slowly beat people to death, torment them, taunt them. What Paul did as a button man had nothing to do with anger or pleasure or the gritty satisfaction of revenge; it was simply about committing an evil act to eliminate a greater evil.

And Paul Schumann insisted on paying the price for this hypocrisy. He suffered from the proximity of killing. The deaths sickened him, sent him into a tunnel of sorrow and guilt. Every time he killed, another part of him died too. Once, drunk in a shabby West Side Irish bar, he concluded that he was the opposite of Christ; he died so that others might die too. He wished he'd been too smoked on hooch to remember that thought. But it'd stuck with him.

Still, he supposed Morgan was right about using the rifle. His buddy Damon Runyon had once said that a man could be a winner only if he was willing to step over the edge. Paul sure did that often enough, but he also knew when to stop walking. He'd never been suicidal. On a number of occasions he'd postponed the touch-off when he sensed the odds were bad. Maybe six to five against was acceptable. But worse than that? He didn't—

A loud crash startled him. Something flew through a bookstore window onto the sidewalk a few yards away. A bookcase. Some books followed. He glanced inside the shop and saw a middle-aged man holding his bloody face. He appeared to have been struck on the cheek. A woman, crying, gripped his arm. They were both terrified. Four large men in light brown uniforms stood around them. Paul supposed they were Stormtroopers, Brownshirts. One of them was holding a book and shouting at the man. "You are not allowed to sell this shit! They're illegal. They're a ticket to Oranienburg."

"It's Thomas Mann," the man protested. "It means nothing against the Leader or our Party. I—"

The Brownshirt slapped the bookseller in his face with the open book. He spoke in a mocking voice. "It's . . ." Another furious slap. "Thomas . . ." Another, and the spine of the book broke. "Mann. . . ."

The bullying angered Paul but it wasn't his problem. He could hardly afford to draw attention to himself here. He started on. But suddenly one of the Brownshirts grabbed the woman by the arm and pushed her out the door. She fell hard into Paul and dropped to the sidewalk. She was so terrified she didn't even seem to notice him. Blood ran from her knees and palms where the window glass had cut her skin.

The apparent leader of the Stormtroopers dragged the man outside. "Destroy the place," he called to his friends, who began to push over the counters and shelves, rip the pictures from the walls, slam the sturdy chairs onto the floor, trying to break them. The leader glanced at Paul then delivered a powerful blow to the midsection of the bookseller, who gave a grunt, rolled over on his stomach and vomited. The Brownshirt stepped toward the woman. He grabbed her by the hair and was about to strike her in the face when Paul, out of instinct, grabbed his arm.

The man spun around, spittle flying from his mouth, set in a large, square face. He stared into Paul's blue eyes. "Who are you? Do you know who I am? Hugo Felstedt of the Berlin Castle Stormtrooper Brigade. Alexander! Stefan!"

Paul eased the woman aside. She bent and helped up the other bookseller, who was wiping his mouth, tears falling from the pain, the humiliation.

Two Stormtroopers emerged from the store. "Who is this?" one asked.

"Your card! Now!" Felstedt cried.

Although he'd boxed all his life, Paul avoided street brawls. His father used to sternly lecture the boy that he should never compete in any event where no one oversaw the rules. He was forbidden to fight in school yards and alleyways. "You listening to me, son?" Paul had dutifully replied, "Sure, Pa, you bet." But sometimes there was nothing to do but meet Jake McGuire or Little Bill Carter and take and give some knuckle. He wasn't sure what made those times different. But somehow you knew without a doubt that you couldn't walk away.

And sometimes—maybe a lot of times—you *could*, but you just plain didn't want to.

He sized up the man; he was like the kid lieutenant, Vincent Manielli, Paul decided. Young and muscled, but mostly talk. The American eased his weight to his toes, balanced himself and struck Felstedt's midsection with a nearly invisible straight right.

The man's jaw dropped and he backed up, struggling for breath, tapping his chest as if searching for his heart.

"You swine," one of the others cried in a high voice, shocked, reaching for his pistol. Paul danced forward, grabbed the man's right hand, pulled it from the holster cover, and popped a left hook into his face. In boxing there is no pain worse than a solid blow to the nose and, as the cartilage snapped and the blood flowed onto his camel-brown uniform, the man gave a keening howl and staggered back against the wall, tears pouring from his eyes.

Hugo Felstedt had by now dropped to his knees and was no longer interested in his heart; he was gripping his belly as *he* retched pathetically.

The third trooper went for his gun.

Paul stepped forward fast, fists closed. "Don't," he warned calmly. The

Brownshirt suddenly bolted up the street, crying, "I'll get some help. . . . I'll get some help. . . ."

The fourth Stormtrooper stepped outside. Paul moved toward him and he cried, "Please, don't hurt me!"

Eyes fixed on the Brownshirt, Paul knelt, opened the satchel and began rummaging through the papers inside to find the pistol.

His eyes dipped for a moment and the Stormtrooper bent suddenly, grabbed some shards of window glass and flung them toward Paul. He ducked but the man launched himself into the American and caught him on the cheek with his brass-knuckled fist. It was a glancing blow but Paul was stunned and fell backward over his briefcase into a small weedy garden next to the store. The Brownshirt leapt after him. They grappled. The man was not particularly strong nor was he a trained fighter but, still, it took Paul a moment to struggle to his feet. Angry that he'd been caught off guard, he grabbed the man's wrist, twisted sharply and heard a snap.

"Oh," the man whispered. He sagged to the ground and passed out.

Felstedt was rolling into a sitting position, wiping vomit from his face.

Paul pulled the man's pistol from his belt and flung it onto the roof of a low building nearby. He turned to the bookseller and the woman. "Leave now. Go."

Speechless, they stared at him.

"Now!" he muttered sharply.

A whistle sounded up the street. Some shouts.

Paul said, "Run!"

The bookseller wiped his mouth again and glanced at the remains of their shop one last time. The woman put her arm around his shoulders and they hurried away.

Looking in the opposite direction down Rosenthaler Street, Paul noted a half dozen Brownshirts running in his direction.

"You Jew swine," the man with the broken nose muttered. "Oh, you're done for now."

Paul grabbed the satchel, scooped the scattered contents back inside and began running toward a nearby alley. A glance behind. The clutch of large men was in pursuit. Where the hell had they all come from? Breaking from the alley, he found himself on a street of residential buildings, pushcarts, decrepit restaurants and tawdry shops. He paused, looking around the crowded street.

He stepped past a vendor selling secondhand clothing and, when the man was looking away, slipped a dark green jacket off a rack of men's garments. He rolled it up and started into another alley to put it on. But he heard shouts from nearby. "There! Is that him? . . . You! Stop!"

To his left he saw three more Stormtroopers pointing his way. Word had spread of the incident. He hurried into the alley, longer and darker than the first. More shouts behind him. Then a gunshot. He heard a sharp snap as the bullet hit brick near his head. He glanced back. Another three or four uniformed men had joined his pursuers.

There are far too many people in this country who will chase you simply because you are running. . . .

Paul spit hard against the wall and struggled to suck air into his lungs. A moment later he burst out of the alley into another street, more crowded than the first. He inhaled deeply and lost himself in the crowds of Saturday shoppers. Looking up and down the avenue, he saw three or four alleys branching off.

Which one?

Shouts behind him as the Stormtroopers poured into the street. No time to wait. He picked the nearest alleyway.

Wrong choice. The only exits from it were five or six doors. They were all locked.

He started to run back out of the cul-de-sac but stopped. There were now a dozen Brownshirts prowling through the crowds, moving steadily toward this alley. Most of them held pistols. Boys accompanied them, dressed like the flag-lowering youngsters he'd met yesterday at the Olympic Village.

Steadying his breathing, he pressed flat against the brick.

A swell mess this is, he thought angrily.

He stuffed his hat, tie and suit jacket into the satchel, then pulled on the green jacket.

Paul set the bag at his feet and took out the pistol. He checked to make certain the gun was loaded and a round chambered. Bracing his arm against the wall, he rested the weapon on his forearm and leaned out slowly, aiming at the man who was in the lead—Felstedt.

It would be difficult for them to figure out where the shot had come from and Paul hoped they'd scatter for cover, giving him the chance to lam through the rows of nearby pushcarts. Risky . . . but they'd be at this alley in a few minutes; what other choices did he have?

Closer, closer . . .

Touching the ice . . .

Pressure slowly increasing on the trigger as he aimed at the center of the man's chest, the sights floating on the spot where the diagonal leather strap from belt to shoulder covered his heart.

"No," the voice whispered urgently in his ear.

Paul spun around, leveling the pistol at the man who'd come up silently behind him. He was in his forties, dressed in a well-worn suit. His thick hair was swept back with oil and he had a bushy mustache. He was some inches shorter than Paul, his belly protruding over his belt. In his hands was a large cardboard carton.

"You may point that elsewhere," he said calmly, nodding down at the pistol.

The American didn't move the gun. "Who are you?"

"Perhaps we may converse later. We have more urgent matters now." He stepped past Paul and looked around the corner. "A dozen of them. You must have done something quite irksome."

"I beat up three of them."

The German lifted a surprised eyebrow. "Ach, well, I assure you, sir, if you kill one or two, there will be hundreds more here within minutes. They'll hunt you down and they may kill a dozen innocent people in the process. I can help you escape."

Paul hesitated.

"If you don't do as I say they *will* kill you. Murder and marching are the only things they do well."

"Put the box down." The man did and Paul lifted his jacket, looked at the waistband then gestured for him to turn in a circle.

"I have no gun."

The same gesture, impatient.

The German turned. Paul patted his pockets and ankles. He was unarmed.

The man said, "I was watching you. You removed your jacket and hat— that's good. And you stood out like a virgin on Nollendorf Plaza in that gauche tie. But it is likely you'll be searched. You must discard the clothes." A nod toward the satchel.

Running footsteps sounded nearby. Paul stepped back, considering the words. The advice made sense. He dug the items out of the satchel and stepped to a trash bin.

"No," the man said. "Not there. If you wish to dispose of something in Berlin don't throw it into food bins because people foraging for scraps will find it. And don't throw it into the waste containers or the Gestapo or the V-men or A-men from the SD will find it; they regularly go through garbage. The only safe place is the sewer. No one goes through the sewers. Not yet, in any case."

Paul glanced down at a nearby grating and reluctantly shoved in the items.

His luck-of-the-Irish tie . . .

"Now I'll add something to your role as an escaper-from-dung-shirts." He reached into his jacket pocket and extracted several hats. He selected a light-colored canvas crush hat. He unfurled and handed it to Paul then replaced the others. "Put it on." The American did so. "Now, the pistol too. You must get rid of it. I know you are hesitant, but in truth it will do you little good. No gun carries enough bullets to stop all the Stormtroopers in the city, let alone a puny Luger."

Yes or no?

Instinct again told him the man was right. He crouched down and tossed the gun down the grating as well. He heard a splash far below street level.

"Now, follow me." The man picked up the carton. When Paul hesitated he whispered, "Ach, you're thinking, how can you possibly trust me? You don't know me at all. But, sir, I would say that under the circumstances the real question is, how can you *not* trust me? Still, it's your choice. You have about ten seconds to decide." He laughed. "Doesn't that always seem to be the way? The more important the decision, the less the time to make it." He walked to a door, fiddled with a key and unlocked it. He glanced back. Paul followed. They stepped into a storeroom and the German swung the door shut and locked it. Watching through the greasy window, Paul saw the band of Stormtroopers step into the alley, look around, then continue on.

The room was densely packed with boxes and crates, dusty bottles of wine. The man paused, nodding to a carton. "Take that. It will be a prop for our storytelling. And perhaps a profitable one too."

Paul looked at the man angrily. "I could have left my clothes and the gun in your warehouse here. I didn't have to throw them out."

The man jutted out his lower lip. "Ach, yes, except that this isn't exactly *my* warehouse. Now, that carton. Please, sir, we must hurry." Paul set the satchel on top, hefted the box and followed. They emerged into a dusty front room. The man glanced out the filthy window. He began to open the door.

"Wait," Paul said. He touched his cheek; the cut from the brass knuckles was bleeding slightly. He ran his hands over some dirty shelves and patted his face, covering the wound, and his jacket and slacks. The smudges would draw less attention than the blood.

"Good," the German said and pushed the door wide. "You are now a sweaty laborer. And I will be your boss. This way." He turned directly toward a cluster of three or four Stormtroopers, speaking to a woman who lounged against a street lamp, holding a tiny poodle on a red leash.

Paul hesitated.

"Come on. Don't slow up."

They were almost past the Brownshirts when one of them called to the two men, "You there, stop. We will see your papers." One of his friends joined him and they stepped in front of Paul and the German. Seething that he'd given up his gun, Paul glanced to his side. The man from the alley frowned. "Ach, our cards, yes, yes. I am very sorry, gentlemen. You must understand we're forced to work today, as you can see." A nod toward the cartons. "It was unplanned. An urgent delivery."

"You must carry your card with you at all times."

Paul said, "We are only going a short way."

"We are looking for a large man in a gray suit and brown hat. He is armed. Have you seen anyone like that?"

A consulting glance. "No," Paul said.

The second Brownshirt patted both the German and Paul for weapons then grabbed the satchel and opened it, glanced inside. He lifted out the copy of *Mein Kampf*. Paul could see the bulge where the Russian passport and rubles were hidden.

The German from the alley said quickly, "Nothing of interest in there. But now I recall that we *do* have our identification. Look in my man's carton."

The Brownshirts glanced at each other. The one holding Hitler's book tossed it back inside, set the satchel down and ripped open the top of the carton that Paul held.

"As you can see, we are the Bordeaux Brothers."

A Brownshirt laughed, and the German continued. "But you can never be too sure. Perhaps you should take two of those with you for verification."

Several bottles of red wine were lifted out. The Stormtroopers waved the men on. Paul picked up the satchel and they continued up the street.

Two blocks farther on, the German nodded across the street. "In there." The place he indicated appeared to be a nightclub decorated with Nazi flags. A wooden sign read: *The Aryan Café*.

"Are you mad?" Paul asked.

"Have I been right so far, my friend? Please, inside. It's the safest place to be. Dung-shirts aren't welcome here, nor can they afford it. As long as you haven't beaten any SS officers or senior Party officials, you'll be safe. . . . You haven't, have you?"

Paul shook his head. He reluctantly followed the man inside. He saw immediately what the man meant about the price of admission. A sign said: *$20 U.S./40 DM.* Jesus, he thought. The ritziest place he went to in New York, the Debonair Club, had a five-buck cover.

How much dough did he have on him? That was nearly half the money Morgan had given him. But the doorman looked up and recognized the mustachioed German. He nodded the men inside without charging them.

They pushed through a curtain into a small dark bar, cluttered with antiques and artifacts, movie posters, dusty bottles. "Otto!" the bartender called, shaking the man's hand.

Otto set his carton on the bar and gestured for Paul to do the same with his.

"I thought you were delivering one case only."

"My comrade here helped me carry a second one, ten bottles only in his. So that makes the total seventy marks now, does it not?"

"I asked for one case. I need only one case. I will pay for only one case."

As the men dickered, Paul focused on the loud words coming from a large radio behind the bar. "*. . . modern science has found myriad ways to protect the body from disease and yet if you don't apply those simple rules of hygiene, you can fall greatly ill. With our foreign visitors in town, it is likely that there may be new strains of infection, so it is vital to keep in mind rules of sanitation.*"

Otto finished the negotiation, apparently to his satisfaction, and glanced out the window. "They're still there, prowling. Let us have a beer. I will let you buy me one." He noticed Paul looking at the radio, which no one in the bar seemed to be paying attention to, despite the high volume. "Ach, you like the deep voice of our propaganda minister? It's dramatic, yes? But to see him, he's a runt. I have contacts all over Wilhelm Street, all the government buildings. They call him 'Mickey Mouse' behind his back. Let us go in the back. I can't stand the droning. Every establishment must have a radio to broadcast the Party leaders' speeches and must turn the sound up when they are transmitting. It's illegal not to. Here they keep the radio up front to satisfy the rules. The real club is in the back rooms. Now, do you like men or women?"

"What?"

"Men or women? Which do you prefer?"

"I'm not interested in—"

"I understand, but since we must wait for the Brownshirts to grow tired of their pursuit, please tell me: Which would you rather look at while we have the beer you've so generously agreed to buy me? Men dancing as men, men dancing as women or women dancing as themselves?"

"Women."

"Ach, me too. It's illegal to be a homosexual in Germany now. But you would be surprised how many National Socialists seem to enjoy one another's company for reasons other than discussing rightist politics. This way." He pushed through a blue velvet curtain.

The second room was for men who enjoyed women, it seemed. They sat down at a rickety wicker table in the black-painted room, decorated with Chinese lanterns, paper streamers and animal trophies, as dusty as the Nazi flags hanging from the ceiling.

Paul handed back the canvas cap; it disappeared into the man's pocket with the others. "Thanks."

Otto nodded. "Ach, what are friends for?" He looked for a waiter or waitress.

"I'll be back in a moment." Paul rose and went to the lavatory. He washed the smudges and blood off his face and combed his hair back with lotion, which shortened and darkened it, making him appear somewhat different from the man the Brownshirts were seeking. His cheek was not badly cut but a bruise had formed around it. He stepped out of the washroom and slipped backstage. He found the dressing room for performers. A man sat at the far end, smoking a cigar and reading a newspaper. He didn't pay any attention as Paul dipped his finger into a pot of makeup. Returning to the lavatory he smoothed the cosmetic over the bruise. He had some experience with makeup; all good boxers knew the importance of concealing injuries from their opponents.

He returned to the table, where he found Otto gesturing toward the waitress, a pretty, dark-haired young woman. But she was busy and the man sighed in irritation. He turned back, regarding Paul closely. "Now, you are obviously not from here because you know nothing of our 'culture.' I'm speaking of the radio. And of the dung-shirts, whom you would not have antagonized by fighting had you been a German. But your language is perfect. The faintest of accents. And not French or Slav or Spanish. What breed of dog are you?"

"I appreciate the help, Otto. But some matters I'll keep to myself."

"No matter. I've decided you're American or English. Probably American. I know from your movies—the way you make your sentences . . . Yes, you are American. Who else would have a troop of dung-shirts after him but a brash American with big balls? You are from the land of heroic cowboys, who take on a tribe of Indians alone. Where *is* that waitress?" He looked about, smoothing his mustache. "Now, introductions. I am presenting myself to you. Otto Wilhelm Friedrich Georg Webber. And you? . . . But perhaps you wish to keep your name to yourself."

"I think that's wiser."

Webber chuckled. "So you beat up three of them and earned the endless affection of the Brownshirts and the bitch brood?"

"The what?"

"Hitler Youth. The boys scurrying among the legs of the Stormtroopers." Webber eyed Paul's red knuckles. "You perhaps enjoy the boxing matches, Mr. Nameless? You look like an athlete. I can get you Olympic tickets. There are none left, as you know. But I can get them. Day seats, good ones."

"No thanks."

"Or I can get you into one of the Olympic parties. Max Schmeling will be at some."

"Schmeling?" Paul raised an eyebrow. He admired Germany's most successful heavyweight champ and had been in the bleachers at Yankee Stadium just last month to see the bout between Schmeling and Joe Louis. Shocking everyone, Schmeling knocked out the Brown Bomber in the twelfth round. The evening had cost Paul $608, eight for the ticket and the six C-notes for the bum bet.

Webber continued. "He will be there with his wife. She is so beautiful. Anny Ondra. An actress, you know. You will have a truly memorable evening. It would be quite expensive but I can arrange it. You need a dinner jacket, of course. I can provide that too. For a small fee."

"I'll pass."

"Ach," Webber muttered, as if Paul had made the mistake of his life.

The waitress stopped at their table and she stood close to Paul, smiling down at him. "I am Liesl. Your name is?"

"Hermann," Paul said.

"You would like what?"

"Beers for us both. A Pschorr for me."

"Ach," Webber said, sneering at the choice. "Berlin lager for me. Bottom-fermented. A large." When she glanced at him her look was cool, as if he'd recently stiffed her on a check.

Liesl gazed into Paul's eyes a moment longer then offered a flirtatious smile and walked to another table.

"You have an admirer, Mr. Not-Hermann. Pretty, yes?"

"Very."

Webber winked. "If you like, I can—"

"No," Paul said firmly.

Webber raised an eyebrow and turned his attention to the stage, where a topless woman gyrated. She had loose disks of breasts and flabby arms, and even from a distance Paul could see creases around her mouth, which kept up a fierce smile as she moved to the scratchy sound of a gramophone.

"There is no live music here now, in the afternoon," Webber explained. "But at night they have good bands. Brass . . . I love brass. I have a gramophone disk I play often. The great British bandleader, John Philip Sousa."

"Sorry to tell you: He's American."

"No!"

"It's true."

"What a country that must be, America. They have such wonderful cinema and millions of motorcars, I hear. And now I learn they have John Philip Sousa too."

Paul watched the waitress approach, slim hips rocking back and forth. Liesl set the beers down. She'd put on fresh perfume, it seemed, in the three or four minutes she'd been away. She smiled at Paul and he grinned back then glanced at the check. Not familiar with German currency and not wishing to draw attention to himself fumbling with coins, Paul gave her a five-mark note, which was about two bucks, four bits, he guessed.

Liesl took the difference to be a tip and thanked him heartily, gripping his hand in both of hers. He was afraid she'd kiss him. He didn't know how to ask for the rest of the money back and decided to put the loss down to a lesson about German customs. With another adoring glance, Liesl left the table then instantly grew sullen at the prospect of waiting on other tables. Webber clinked his stein against Paul's and both men drank deeply.

Webber eyed Paul closely and said, "So. What kind of cons do you run?"

"Cons?"

"When I first saw you in the alley, with that gun, I thought: Ach, he's no Soci or Kosi—"

"What?"

"Soci—a Social Democrat. It used to be a big political party until it was outlawed. Kosis are the Communists. They're not only outlawed; they're dead. No, I knew you were not an agitator. You were one of us, a con runner, an artist-of-dark-dealings." He glanced around the room. "Don't worry. As long as we're quiet it's safe to talk. No microphones here. No Party loyalty either, not inside these walls. After all, a man's dick is always more reliable than his conscience and National Socialists have no consciences to start with." Webber persisted: "So what kind of cons?"

"I don't do cons. I came over for the Olympics."

"You did?" He winked. "There must be a new event this year that I've not heard of."

"I'm a sportswriter."

"Ach, a writer . . . yet one who fights Brownshirts, keeps his name to himself, walks around with a peashooter of a Luger, changes clothes to avoid pursuers. And then slicks back his hair and puts on pancake." Webber tapped his own cheek and smiled knowingly.

"I happened to run into some Stormtroopers attacking this couple. I stopped them. As for the Luger, it was one of theirs. I stole it."

"Yes, yes, so you say. . . . Do you know Al Capone?"

"Of course not," Paul said, exasperated.

Webber sighed loudly, genuinely disappointed. "I follow American crime. Many of us do, here in Germany. We are always reading crime shockers—novels, you understand? Many are set in America. I followed with great interest the fate of John Dillinger. He was betrayed by a woman in a red dress and shot down in an alley after they'd been to the cinema. I think it was good he saw the film *before* they killed him. He died with that small pleasure within him. Though it would have been better yet had he seen the film, gotten drunk, bedded the woman and *then* been shot. That would have been a perfect death. Yes, I think that, despite what you say, you are a real mobster, Mr. John Dillinger. Liesl! Beautiful Liesl! More beer here! My friend is buying two more."

Webber's stein was empty; Paul's was three-quarters full. He called to Liesl, "No, not for me. For him only."

As she disappeared toward the bar she tossed Paul another adoring look, the brightness in her eyes, the slim figure reminding him of Marion. He wondered how she was, what she was doing at the moment, which would be six or seven hours earlier in America. Call me, she'd said in their last conversation, thinking he was bound for Detroit on business. Paul had learned you could actually place a telephone call across the Atlantic Ocean but it cost almost $50 a minute. Besides, no competent button man would think of leaving such evidence of his whereabouts.

He looked over the Nazis in the audience: some SS or soldiers in their immaculate black or gray uniforms, some businessmen. Most were tipsy, some were well into their afternoon drunks. All smiled gamely but seemed bored as they watched a very unsexy sex show.

When the waitress arrived she did indeed have two beers. She set one in front of Webber, whom she otherwise ignored, and said to Paul, "You may pay for your friend's but yours is a present from me." She took his hand and placed it around the handle of the stein. "Twenty-five pfennigs."

"Thank you," he said, reflecting that the extra marks from the fiver would probably have bought him a keg. He gave her a mark this time.

She shivered with pleasure, as if he'd slipped her a diamond ring. Liesl kissed his forehead. "Please enjoy." And headed off again.

"Ach, you got the familiar discount. Me, I have to pay fifty. Of course, most foreigners pay a mark seventy-five."

Webber drained a third of the stein. He wiped the residue from his mustache with the back of his arm and pulled out a pack of cigars. "These are vile but I rather like them." He offered the pack to Paul, who shook his head. "They are cabbage leaves soaked in tobacco water and nicotine. It's hard now to find real cigars."

"What line are you in?" Paul asked. "Aside from being a wine importer."

Webber laughed and squinted a coy gaze at Paul. He worked to inhale the acrid smoke and then said thoughtfully, "Many different things. Much of what I do is to acquire and sell hard-to-find items. Military goods are in demand lately. Not weapons, of course. But insignias, canteens, belts, boots, uniforms. Everyone here loves uniforms. When husbands are at work, their women go out and buy them uniforms, even if they have no rank or any affiliation. Children wear them. Infants! Medals, bars, ribbons, epaulets, collar tabs. And I sell them to the government for our real soldiers too. We have conscription again. Our army is swelling. They need uniforms, and cloth is hard to come by. I have people from whom I acquire uniforms and then I alter them somewhat and sell them to the army."

"You steal them from one government source and sell them back to another."

"Ach, Mr. John Dillinger, you are very funny." He looked across the room. "One moment . . . Hans, come here. Hans!"

A man dressed in a tuxedo appeared. He looked suspiciously at Paul but Webber assured him that they were friends and then said, "I have come into possession of some butter. Would you like it?"

"How much?"

"How much butter or how much the price?"

"Both, naturally."

"Ten kilos. Seventy-five marks."

"If it's like last time, you mean you have *six* kilos of butter mixed with four kilos of coal oil, lard, water and yellow dye. That is too much to pay for six kilos of butter."

"Then trade me two cases of French champagne."

"One case."

"Ten kilos for one case?" Webber looked indignant.

"Six kilos, as I explained."

"Eighteen bottles."

With a dismissing shrug the maître d' said, "Add more dye and I'll agree. A dozen patrons refused to eat your white butter last month. And who could blame them?"

After he had left, Paul finished his beer and shook a Chesterfield out of the pack, once again keeping it below the level of the table so that no one could see the American brand. It took him four tries to light the cigarette; the cheap matches the club provided kept breaking.

Webber nodded at them. "I didn't supply those, my friend. Don't blame me."

Paul inhaled long on the Chesterfield and then asked, "Why did you help me, Otto?"

"Because, of course, you were in need."

"You do good deeds, do you?" Paul raised an eyebrow.

Webber stroked his mustache. "All right, let us be honest: In these days one must look much harder for opportunities than in the past."

"And I'm an opportunity."

"Who can say, Mr. John Dillinger? Perhaps no, perhaps yes. If no, then I've wasted nothing but an hour drinking beer with a new friend and that is no waste at all. If yes, then perhaps we can both profit." He rose, walked to the window and looked out past a thick curtain. "I think it is safe for you to leave. . . . Whatever you are doing in our vibrant city, I may be just the man for you. I know many people here, people in important places—no, not the men at the top. I mean the people it is best to know for those in our line of work."

"What people?"

"The *little* people, well placed. Did you hear the joke about the town in Bavaria that replaced its weathervane with a civil servant? Why? Because civil servants know better than anyone which way the wind is blowing. Ha!" He laughed hard. Then his face grew solemn again and he finished the stein of beer. "In truth, I'm dying here. Dying of boredom. I miss the old days. So, leave a message or come see me. I'm usually here. In this room or at the bar." He wrote the address down on a napkin and pushed it forward.

Glancing at the square of paper, Paul memorized the address and pushed the paper back.

Webber watched him. "Ah, you're quite the savvy sportswriter, aren't you?"

They walked to the door. Paul shook his hand. "Thank you, Otto."

Outside, Webber said, "Now, my friend, farewell. I hope to see you again." Then he scowled. "And for me? A quest for yellow dye. Ach, this is what my life has become. Lard and yellow dye."

Chapter Nine

Reinhard Ernst, sitting in his spacious office in the Chancellory, looked over the carelessly formed characters in the note once again.

> Col. Ernst:
>
> I await the report you have agreed to prepare on your Waltham Study. I have devoted some time to review it on Monday.
>
> Adolf Hitler

He cleaned his wire-rimmed glasses, replaced them. He wondered what the careless lettering revealed of the writer. The signature was particularly distinctive. The "Adolf" was a compressed lightning bolt; "Hitler" was somewhat more legible but it sloped curiously, and severely, downward to the right.

Ernst spun around in his chair and stared out the window. He felt just like an army commander who knew that the enemy was approaching, about to attack, but not knowing when he would strike, what his tactics would be, how strong was his force, where he would establish the lines of assault, where the flanking maneuver would come.

Aware too that the battle would be decisive and the fate of his army—indeed, of the whole nation—was at stake.

He wasn't exaggerating the gravity of his dilemma. Because Ernst knew something about Germany that few others sensed or would admit out loud: that Hitler would not be in power long.

The Leader's enemies, both within the country and without, were too many. He was Caesar, he was Macbeth, he was Richard. As his madness played itself out he would be ousted, murdered, or even die by his own hand (so astonishingly manic were his rages), and others would step into the immense vacuum after his demise. And not Göring either; greed of soul and greed of body were in a footrace to bring him down. Ernst's own feeling was that, with the two leaders gone (and Goebbels pining away for his lost love, Hitler), the National Socialists would wither, and a centrist Prussian states-man would emerge—another Bismarck, imperial perhaps but reasonable and a brilliant statesman.

And Ernst might even have a hand in that transformation. For, short of a bullet or bomb, the only sure threat to Adolf Hitler and the Party was the German army.

In June of '34, Hitler and Göring murdered or arrested much of the Stormtrooper leadership during the so-called Night of the Long Knives. The purge was felt necessary largely to appease the regular army, which had become jealous of the huge Brownshirt militia. Hitler had regarded the horde of thugs on one side and the German military—the direct heirs of the nineteenth century's Hohenzollern battalions—on the other, and without a moment's hesitation chose the latter. Two months later, upon President Hindenburg's death, Hitler took two steps to solidify his position. First, he declared himself the unrestricted leader of the nation. Second—and far more important—he required the German armed forces to pledge a per-sonal oath of loyalty to him.

De Tocqueville had said that there would never be a revolution in Ger-many for the police would not allow it. No, Hitler wasn't concerned about a popular uprising; his only fear was the army.

And it was a new, enlightened military that Ernst had devoted his life to since the end of the War. An army that would protect Germany and its citi-zens from all threats, perhaps ultimately even from Hitler himself.

Yet, he reflected, Hitler was not gone yet, and Ernst couldn't afford to ignore the author of this note, which was as troubling to him as the distant rumble of armor approaching through the night.

Col. Ernst: I await the report. . . .

He had hoped that the intrigue Göring set in motion would fade away, but this piece of onionskin paper meant that it would not. He understood that he had to act quickly to prepare for and repel the attack.

After a difficult debate, the colonel came to a decision. He pocketed the letter, rose from his desk and left his office, telling his secretary that he would return within a half hour.

Down one hall, down another, past the ubiquitous construction work in the old, dusty building. Workers, busy even on the weekend, were everywhere. Building was *the* metaphor for the new Germany—a nation rising from the ashes of Versailles, being reconstructed according to Hitler's often-quoted philosophy of "bringing-into-line" with National Socialism every citizen and institution in the country.

Down another hallway, under a stern portrait of the Leader in three-quarter view, looking slightly upward, as if at his vision for the nation.

Ernst stepped outside into the gritty wind, hot from the broiling afternoon sun.

"Hail, Colonel."

Ernst nodded to the two guards, armed with bayonet-mounted Mausers. He was amused at their greeting. It was customary for anyone near cabinet rank to be addressed by his full title. But "Mr. Plenipotentiary" was laughably cumbersome.

Down Wilhelm Street, past Voss Street then Prince Albrecht Street, with a glance to his right at No. 8—Gestapo headquarters in the old hotel and arts-and-crafts school. Continuing south to his favorite café, he ordered a coffee. He sat for only a moment and then walked to the phone kiosk. He called a number, dropped some pfennigs into the slot and was connected.

A woman's voice answered. "Good day."

"Please, Dame Keitel?"

"No, sir. I am the housekeeper."

"Is Doctor-professor Keitel available? This is Reinhard Ernst."

"One moment, please."

A moment later a man's soft voice came through the line. "Good day, Colonel. Though a hot one."

"Indeed, Ludwig. . . . We need to meet. Today. An urgent matter has come up about the study. You can make yourself available?"

"Urgent?"

"Extremely so. Can you come to my office? I'm awaiting word on some matters from England. So I must be at my desk. Four P.M. would be convenient?"

"Yes, of course."

They rang off and Ernst returned to his coffee.

What ridiculous measures he needed to resort to simply to find a phone not monitored by Göring's minions. I have seen war from the inside and from the out, he thought. The battlefield is horrible, yes, inconceivably horrible. But how much purer and cleaner, even angelic, is war, compared with a struggle where your enemies are beside, not facing, you.

On the fifteen-mile ride from downtown Berlin to the Olympic Village, along a wide, perfectly smooth highway, the taxi driver whistled happily and told Paul Schumann that he was anticipating many well-paying fares during the Olympics.

Suddenly the man grew silent as some ponderous classical music poured from a radio; the Opel was equipped with two, one to dispatch the driver and one for public transmissions. "Beethoven," the driver commented. "It precedes all official broadcasts. We will listen." A moment later the music faded and a raw, passionate voice began speaking.

"In the first place, it is not acceptable to treat this question of infection frivolously; it must be understood that good health would depend and does depend on finding ways to treat not only the symptoms of the disease, but the source of the illness, as well. Look at the tainted waters of a stagnant pond, a breeding ground for germs. But a fast-moving river does not offer the same climate for such danger. Our campaign will continue to locate and drain these stagnant pools, thereby offering germs and the mosquitoes and flies that carry them no place to multiply. Moreover—"

Paul listened for a moment longer but the repetitious rambling bored him. He tuned out the meaningless sound and looked at the sun-baked landscape, the houses, the inns, as the pretty suburbs west of the city gave way to more sparse areas. The driver turned off the Hamburg highway and pulled up in front of the Olympic Village's main entrance. Paul paid the man, who thanked him by lifting an eyebrow but said nothing, remaining fixed on the words streaming from the radio. He considered asking the driver to wait but decided it would be wiser to find someone else to take him back to town.

The village was hot in the afternoon sun. The wind smelled salty, like ocean air, but it was dry as alum and carried a fine grit. Paul displayed his pass and continued down the perfectly laid sidewalk, past rows of narrow trees perfectly spaced, rising straight from round disks of mulch in the perfect, green grass. The German flag snapped smartly in the hot wind: red and white and black.

Ach, surely you know . . .

At the American dorms he bypassed the reception area, with its German soldier, and slipped into his room through the back door. He changed his outfit, burying the green jacket in a basket full of dirty laundry, there being no sewers handy, and putting on cream-colored flannels, a tennis shirt and a light cable-knit sweater. He brushed his hair differently—to the side. The makeup had worn off but there was nothing he could do about that now. As he stepped out the door with his suitcase and satchel a voice called, "Hey, Paul."

He glanced up to see Jesse Owens, dressed in gymnasium clothes, returning to the dorm. Owens asked, "What're you doing?"

"Heading into town. Get some work done."

"Naw, Paul. We were hoping you'd stay around. You missed an all-right ceremony last night. You've gotta see the food they got here. It's swell."

"I know it's grand, but I gotta skip. I'm doing some interviews in town."

Owens stepped closer then nodded at the cut and bruise on Paul's face. Then the runner's sharp eyes dropped down to the man's knuckles, which were raw and red from the fight.

"Hope the rest of your interviews go better than the one this morning. Dangerous to be a sportswriter in Berlin, looks like."

"I took a spill. Nothing serious."

"Not for *you* maybe," Owens said, amused. "But what about the fellow you landed on?"

Paul couldn't help but smile. The runner was just a kid. But there was something worldly about him. Maybe growing up a Negro in the South and Midwest made you mature faster. Same with putting yourself through school on the heels of the Depression.

Like stumbling into his own line of work had changed Paul. Changed him real fast.

"What exactly *are* you doin' here, Paul?" the runner whispered.

"Just my job," he answered slowly. "Just doing my job. Say, what's the wire on Stoller and Glickman? Hope they haven't been sidelined."

"Nope, they're still scheduled," Owens said, frowning, "but the rumors aren't sounding good."

"Good luck to them. And to you too, Jesse. Bring home some gold."

"We'll do our best. See you later?"

"Maybe."

Paul shook his hand and walked off toward the entrance to the village, where a line of taxis waited.

"Hey, Paul."

He turned to see the fastest man in the world saluting him, a grin on his face.

The poll of the vendors and bench-sitters along Rosenthaler Street had been futile (though Janssen confirmed that he'd learned some new curses when a flower seller found out he was troubling her only to ask questions, not to buy anything). There had been a shooting not far away, Kohl had learned, but that was an SS matter—perhaps about their jealously guarded "minor security matter"—and none of the elite guard would deign to speak to the Kripo about it.

Upon their return to headquarters, however, they found that a miracle had occurred. The photographs of the victim and of the fingerprints from Dresden Alley were on Willi Kohl's desk.

"Look at this, Janssen," Kohl said, gesturing at the glossy pictures, neatly assembled in a file.

He sat down at his battered desk in his office in the Alex, the Kripo's massive, ancient building, nicknamed for the bustling square and sur-rounding neighborhood where it was located: Alexander Plaza. All the state buildings were being renovated except theirs, it seemed. The criminal police were housed in the same grimy building they'd been in for years. Kohl did not mind this, however, since it was some distance from Wilhelm Street, which at least gave some practical autonomy to the police, even if none now existed administratively.

Kohl was also fortunate to have an office of his own, a room that mea-sured four meters by six and contained a desk, a table and three chairs. On the oak plain of the desk were a thousand pieces of paper, an ashtray, a pipe rack and a dozen framed photographs of his wife, children and parents.

He rocked forward in his creaking wooden chair and looked over the crime scene photographs and the ones of the fingerprints. "You're talented, Janssen. These are quite good."

"Thank you, sir." The young man was looking down at them, nodding.

Kohl regarded him closely. The inspector himself had taken a traditional route up through the police ranks. The son of a Prussian farmer, young Willi had become fascinated with both Berlin and police work from the story-books he'd read growing up. At eighteen he'd come to the city and gotten a job as a uniformed Schupo officer, went through the basic training at the famed Berlin Police Institute and worked his way up to corporal and sergeant, receiving a college degree along the way. Then, with a wife and two children, he'd gone on to the institute's Officers School and joined Kripo, rising over the years from detective-inspector assistant to senior detective-inspector.

His young protégé, on the other hand, had gone a different route, one that was far more common nowadays. Janssen had graduated from a good university several years ago, passed the qualifying exam in jurisprudence, then, after attending the police institute, he was accepted at this young age as a detective-inspector candidate, apprenticed to Kohl.

It was often hard to draw the inspector candidate out; Janssen was reserved. He was married to a solid, dark-haired woman who was now pregnant with their second child. The only time Janssen grew animated was when he talked about his family or about his passion for bicycling and hiking. Until all police were put on overtime because of the approaching Olympics, detectives worked only half days on Wednesday and Janssen would often change into his hiking shorts in a Kripo lavatory at noon and go off on a wander with his brother or his wife.

But whatever made him tick, the man was smart and ambitious and Kohl was very fortunate to have him. Over the past several years the Kripo had been hemorrhaging talented officers to the Gestapo, where the pay and opportunities were far better. When Hitler came to power the number of Kripo detectives around the country was twelve thousand. Now, it was down to eight thousand. And of those, many were former Gestapo investigators sent to the Kripo in exchange for the young officers who'd transferred out; in truth, they were largely drunks and incompetents.

The telephone buzzed and he picked it up. "This is Kohl."

"Inspector, it is Schreiber, the clerk you spoke to today. Hail Hitler."

"Yes, yes, hail." On the way back to the Alex from the Summer Garden, Kohl and Janssen had stopped at the haberdashery department at Tietz, the massive department store that dominated the north side of Alexander Plaza, near Kripo headquarters. Kohl had shown the clerk the picture of Göring's hat and asked what kind it was. The man didn't know but would look into the matter.

"Any luck?" Kohl asked him.

"Ach, yes, yes, I have found the answer. It's a Stetson. Made in the United States. As you know, Minister Göring shows the finest taste."

Kohl made no comment on that. "Are they common here?"

"No, sir. Quite rare. Expensive, as you can imagine."

"Where could I buy one in Berlin?"

"In truth, sir, I don't know. The minister, I'm told, special-orders them from London."

Kohl thanked him, hung up and told Janssen what he'd learned.

"So perhaps he's an American," Janssen said. "But perhaps not. Since Göring wears the same hat."

"A small piece of the puzzle, Janssen. But you will find that many small pieces often give a clearer picture of a crime than a single large piece." He took the brown evidence envelopes from his pocket and selected the one containing the bullet.

The Kripo had its own forensics laboratory, dating back to when the Prussian police force had been the nation's preeminent law enforcer (if not the world's; in the Weimar days, the Kripo closed 97 percent of the murder cases in Berlin). But the lab too had been raided by the Gestapo both for equipment and personnel, and the technical workers at headquarters were harried and far less competent than they had once been. Willi Kohl, therefore, had taken it upon himself to become an expert in certain areas of criminal science. Despite the absence of his personal interest in firearms, Kohl had made quite a study of ballistics, modeling his approach on the best firearms laboratory in the world—the one at J. Edgar Hoover's Federal Bureau of Investigation in Washington, D.C.

He shook the bullet out onto a clean piece of paper.

Placing the monocle in his eye he found a pair of tweezers and examined the slug carefully. "Your eyes are better," he said. "You look."

The inspector candidate carefully took the bullet and the monocle while Kohl pulled a binder from his shelf. It contained photographs and sketches of many types of bullets. The binder was large, several hundred pages, but the inspector had organized it by caliber and by number of grooves and lands—the stripes pressed into a lead slug by the rifling in the barrel—and whether they twisted to the left or the right. Only five minutes later Janssen found a match.

"Ach, this is good news," Kohl said.

"How so?"

"It is an unusual weapon our killer used. Look. It's a nine-millimeter Largo round. Most likely from the Spanish Star Modelo A. Good for us, it is rare. And as you pointed out, it is either a new weapon or one that has been fired little. Let us hope the former. Janssen, you have a way with words: Please send a telegram to all police precincts in the area. Have them query gun shops and see if any have sold a new or little-used Star Modelo A in the past several months, or ammunition for such a gun. No, make that the past year. I want names and addresses of all purchasers."

"Yes, sir."

The young inspector candidate took down the information and started for the Teletype room.

"Wait, add as a postscript to your message a description of our suspect. And that he is armed." The inspector gathered up the clearest photographs of the suspect's fingerprints and the inked card of the victim's. Sighing, he said, "And now I must try to be diplomatic. Ach, how I hate doing that."

Chapter Ten

"I am sorry, Inspector Kohl, the department is engaged."

"Entirely?"

"Yes, sir," said the prim bald man in a tight suit, buttoned high on his chest. "Several hours ago we were ordered to stop all other investigations and compile a list of everyone in the files with a Russian background or pronounced appearance."

They were in the ante-office of the Kripo's large identification division, where fingerprint analysis and anthropometry were performed.

"*Everyone* in Berlin?"

"Yes. There is some alert going on."

Ah, the security matter again, the one that Krauss had deemed too insignificant to mention to the Kripo.

"They're using *fingerprint* examiners to check personal files? And *our* fingerprint examiners, no less?"

"Drop everything," the buttoned-up little man replied. "Those were my orders. From Sipo headquarters."

Himmler again, Kohl thought. "Please, Gerhard, these are vital." He showed him the fingerprint card and the photos.

"They are good pictures." Gerhard examined them. "Very clear."

"Put three or four examiners on it, please. That's all I'm asking."

A pinched-face laugh crossed the administrator's face. "I cannot, Inspector. Three? Impossible."

Kohl felt the frustration. A student of foreign criminal science, he looked with envy at America and England, where forensic identification was now done almost exclusively by fingerprint analysis. Here, yes, fingerprints were used for identification but, unlike in the United States, the

Germans had no uniform system of analyzing prints; each area of the country was different. A policeman in Westphalia might analyze a print in one way; a Berlin Kripo officer would analyze it differently. By posting the samples back and forth it was possible to achieve an identification but the process could take weeks. Kohl had long advocated standardizing fingerprint analysis throughout the country but had met with considerable resistance and lethargy. He'd also urged his supervisor to buy some American wire-photo machines, remarkable devices that could transmit clear facsimile photographs and pictures, such as of fingerprints, over telephone lines in minutes. They were, however, quite expensive and his boss had turned down the request without even taking the matter up with the police president.

More troubling to Kohl, though, was that once the National Socialists came to power fingerprints took on less importance than the antiquated system of Bertillon anthropometry, in which measurements of the body, face and head were used to identify criminals. Kohl, like most modern detectives, rejected Bertillon analysis as unwieldy; yes, each person's body structure was largely different from another's, but dozens of precise measurements were needed to categorize someone. And, unlike fingerprints, criminals rarely left sufficient bodily impressions at the scene to link any individual to the site of the crime through Bertillon data.

But the National Socialists' interest in anthropometry went beyond merely identifying someone; it was the key to what they termed the "science" of criminobiology: categorizing people as criminal irrespective of their behavior, solely on their physical characteristics. Hundreds of Gestapo and SS labored full-time to correlate size of nose and shade of skin, for instance, to proclivity to commit a crime. Himmler's goal was not to bring criminals to justice but to eliminate crime *before* it occurred.

To Kohl this was as frightening as it was foolish.

Looking out over the huge room of long tables, filled with men and women hunched over documents, Kohl now decided that the diplomacy he'd summoned up on the way here would have no effect. A different tactic was required: deceit. "Very well. Tell me a date you can begin your analysis. I must tell Krauss *something*. He's been nagging me for hours."

A pause. "Our Pietr Krauss?"

"The *Gestapo's* Krauss, yes. I'll tell him . . . what shall I tell him, Gerhard? It will take you a week, ten days?"

"The Gestapo is involved?"

"Krauss and I investigated the crime scene together." At least this much was true. More or less.

"Perhaps this incident relates to the security situation," the man said, uneasy now.

"I'm sure it does," Kohl said. "Perhaps those very prints are from the Russian in question."

The man said nothing but looked over the pictures. He was so slim; why did he wear such a tight suit?

"I will submit the prints to an examiner. I will call you with any results."

"Whatever you can do will be appreciated," Kohl said, thinking: Ach, *one* examiner? Most likely useless, unless he happened to find a lucky match.

Kohl thanked the technician and walked back up the stairs to his floor. He entered the office of his superior, Friedrich Horcher, who was chief of inspectors for Berlin-Potsdam.

The lean, gray-haired man, with a throwback of a waxed mustache, had been a good investigator in his early days and had weathered the seas of recent German politics well. Horcher had been ambivalent about the Party; he'd been a secret member in the terrible days of the Inflation, then he quit because of Hitler's extreme views. Only recently had he joined again, reluctantly perhaps, drawn along inexorably by the course the nation was taking. Or perhaps he was a true convert. Kohl had no idea which was the case.

"How is this case coming, Willi? The Dresden Alley case?"

"Slowly, sir." He added grimly, "Resources are occupied, it seems. *Our* resources."

"Yes, something is going on. An alert of some sort."

"Indeed."

"Have you heard anything about it, I wonder?" Horcher asked.

"No, nothing."

"But still we are under such pressure. They think the world is watching and one dead man near the Tiergarten might ruin the image of our city forever." At Horcher's level, irony was a dangerous luxury and Kohl could detect none in the man's voice. "Any suspects?"

"Some aspects of his appearance, some small clues. That's all."

Horcher straightened the papers on his desk. "It would be helpful if the perpetrator was—"

"—a foreigner?" Kohl supplied.

"Exactly."

"We shall see. . . . I would like to do one thing, sir. The victim is as yet unidentified. This is a handicap. I would like to run a picture in *The People's Observer* and the *Journal* and see if anyone recognizes him."

Horcher laughed. "A picture of a dead body in the paper?"

"Without knowing the victim we are largely disadvantaged in the investigation."

"I will send the matter to the propaganda office and see what Minister Goebbels has to say. It would have to be cleared with him."

"Thank you, sir." Kohl turned to leave. Then he paused. "One other matter, Chief of Inspectors. I am still waiting for that report from Gatow. It's been a week. I was wondering if you perhaps had received it."

"What was in Gatow? Oh, that shooting?"

"Two," Kohl corrected. "Two shootings."

In the first, two families, picnicking by the Havel River, southwest of Berlin, had been shot to death: seven individuals, including three children. The next day there'd been a second slaughter: eight laborers, living in caravans between Gatow and Charlottenburg, the exclusive suburb west of Berlin.

The police commandant in Gatow had never handled such a case and had one of his gendarmes call the Kripo for help. Raul, an eager young officer, had spoken to Kohl, and had sent photos of the crime scene to the Alex. Willi Kohl, hardened to homicide investigations, had nonetheless been shocked at the sight of the mothers and children gunned down. The Kripo had jurisdiction over all nonpolitical crimes anywhere in Germany, and Kohl wished to make the murders a priority.

But legal jurisdiction and allocation of resources were two very different matters, particularly in these crimes, where the victims were, Raul informed him, Jews and Poles, respectively.

"We'll let the Gatow gendarmerie handle it," Horcher had told him last week.

"Homicides of this magnitude?" Kohl had asked, both troubled and skeptical. The suburban and rural gendarmes investigated automobile accidents and stolen cows. And the chief of the Gatow constabulary, Wilhelm Meyerhoff, was a dull, lazy civil servant who couldn't find his breakfast zwieback without help.

So Kohl had persisted with Horcher until he got permission to at least review the crime scene report. He'd called Raul and coached him in basic investigation techniques and had asked him to interview witnesses. The gendarme promised to send the report to Kohl as soon as his superior approved it. Kohl had received the photographs but no other materials.

Horcher now said, "I've heard nothing, Willi. But, please—Jews, Poles? We have other priorities."

Kohl said thoughtfully, "Of course, sir. I understand. I only care that the Kosis don't get away with anything."

"The Communists? What does this have to do with them?"

"I didn't form the idea until I saw the photographs. But I observed there was something organized about the killings—and there was no attempt to cover them up. The murders were too obvious to me. They seemed almost staged."

Horcher considered this. "You're thinking the Kosis wanted to make it appear that the SS or Gestapo were behind the killings? Yes, that's clever, Willi. The red bastards would certainly stoop to that."

Kohl added, "Especially with the Olympics, the foreign press in town. How the Kosis would love to mar our image in the eyes of the world."

"I will look into the report, Willi. I'll make some calls. A good thought on your part."

"Thank you, sir."

"Now, go clear the Dresden Alley case. If our chief of police wants a blemish-free city, he shall have one."

Kohl returned to his office and sat heavily in his chair, massaging his feet as he stared at the photographs of the two murdered families. It was nonsense what he had told Horcher. Whatever had happened in Gatow, it was not a Communist plot. But the National Socialists went for conspiracies like pigs for slop. These were games that had to be played. Ach, what an education he'd had since January of '33.

He put the pictures back into the file folder labeled *Gatow/Charlottenburg* and set it aside. He then placed the brown envelopes of the evidence he'd collected that afternoon into a box, on which he wrote *Dresden Alley Incident*. He added the extra photographs of the fingerprints, the crime scene and the victim. He placed the box prominently on his desk.

Ringing up the medical examiner, he learned the doctor was at coffee. The assistant told him that Unidentified Corpse A 25-7-36-Q had arrived from Dresden Alley but he had no idea when it would be examined. By that night possibly. Kohl scowled. He had hoped the autopsy was at least in progress, if not finished. He hung up.

Janssen returned. "The Teletypes went out to the precincts, sir. I told them urgent."

"Thank you."

His phone buzzed and he answered. It was Horcher again.

"Willi, Minister Goebbels has said that we cannot display the picture of the dead man in the newspaper. I tried to convince him. I was at my most persuasive, I can tell you. I thought I would prevail. But in the end, I was not successful."

"Well, Chief of Inspectors, thank you." He hung up, thinking cynically: most persuasive, indeed. He doubted the call had even been made.

Kohl told his inspector candidate what the man had said. "Ach, and it will be days or weeks before a fingerprint examiner can even narrow down the prints we found. Janssen, take that picture of the victim. . . . No, no, the other one—where he looks slightly *less* dead. Take it to our printing department. Have them print up five hundred etchings. Tell them we're in a great hurry. Say it's a joint Kripo/Gestapo matter. We can at least exploit Inspector Krauss since it was he who made us late for the Summer Garden. About which I am still perturbed, I must say."

"Yes, sir."

Just as Janssen returned, ten minutes later, the phone buzzed once more and Kohl lifted the handset. "Yes, Kohl here."

"It is Georg Jaeger. How are you?"

"Georg! I am fine. Working this Saturday, when I'd hoped for the Lustgarten with my family. But so it goes. And you?"

"Working too. Always work."

Jaeger had been a protégé of Kohl's some years before. He was a very talented detective and after the Party had come to power had been asked to join the Gestapo. He'd refused and his blunt rejection had apparently offended some officials. He found himself back at the uniformed Order Police—a step down for a Kripo detective. As it turned out, though, Jaeger excelled at his new job too and soon rose to be in charge of the Orpo precinct in north-central Berlin; ironically he seemed far happier in his banished territory than in the intrigue-mired Alex.

"I am calling with what I hope is some help, Professor."

Kohl laughed. He recalled that this was how Jaeger had referred to Kohl when they were working together. "What might that be?"

"We just received a telegram about a suspect in a case you are working on."

"Yes, yes, Georg. Have you found a gun shop that sold a Spanish Star Modelo A? Already?"

"No, but I heard of some SA complaining that a man attacked them at a bookshop on Rosenthaler Street not long ago. He fit the description in your message."

"Ach, Georg, this is most helpful. Can you have them meet me where the assault occurred?"

"They won't want to cooperate but I keep the fools in line if they're in my precinct. I'll make sure they're there. When?"

"Now. Immediately."

"Certainly, Professor." Jaeger gave the address on Rosenthaler Street. Then he asked, "And how is life back at the Alex?"

"Perhaps we'll save that conversation for another time, over schnapps and beer."

"Yes, of course," the Orpo commander said knowingly. The man would be thinking that Kohl was reluctant to discuss certain matters over a telephone line.

Which was certainly true. Kohl's motive for ending the call, though, had less to do with intrigue than with the pitched urgency he felt to find the man in Göring's hat.

"Ach," the Brownshirt muttered sarcastically, "a Kripo detective has come to help us? Look, comrades, here's an odd sight."

The man was over two meters tall and, like many Stormtroopers, quite solid: from day labor before he joined the SA and from the constant, mindless parading he would now do. He sat on the curb, his can-shaped, light brown hat dangling from his fingers.

Another Brownshirt, shorter but just as stocky, leaned against the storefront of a small grocery. The sign in the window said, *No butter, no beef today.* Next door was a bookshop whose window was shattered. Glass and torn-up books littered the sidewalk. This man winced as he held his bandaged wrist. A third sat sullenly by himself. Dried blood stained his shirtfront.

"What got you out of your office, Inspector?" the first Brownshirt continued. "Not us, surely. Communists could have shot us down like Horst Wessel and it wouldn't've pried you away from your cake and coffee at Alexander Plaza."

Janssen stiffened at their offensive words but Kohl's glance restrained him and the detective looked the men over sympathetically. A police or government official at Kohl's level could insult most low-level Stormtroopers to their faces with no consequences. But he now needed their cooperation. "Ah, my good gentlemen, there's no reason for words like that. The Kripo is as concerned about your well-being as everyone else's. Please tell me about the ambush."

"Ach, you're right, Inspector," the larger man said, nodding at Kohl's carefully chosen word. "It *was* an ambush. He came up from behind while we were enforcing the law against improper books."

"You are . . . ?"

"Hugo Felstedt. I command the barracks at Berlin Castle."

This was a deserted brewery warehouse, Kohl knew. Two dozen Stormtroopers had taken it over. "Castle" could be read "flophouse."

"Who were they?" Kohl asked, nodding at the bookstore.

"A couple. A husband and wife, it seemed."

Kohl struggled to maintain a look of concern. He looked around. "They escaped too?"

"That's right."

The third Stormtrooper finally spoke. Through missing teeth he said, "It was a plan, of course. The two distracted us and then the third came up behind. He laid into us with a truncheon."

"I see. And he wore a Stetson hat? Like Minister Göring wears? And a green tie?"

"That's right," the larger one agreed. "A loud, Jew tie."

"Did you see his face?"

"He had a huge nose and fleshy jowls."

"Bushy eyebrows. And bulbous lips."

"He was quite fat," Felstedt contributed. "Like on last week's *The Stormer*. Did you see that? He looked just like the man on the cover."

This was Julius Streicher's pornographic, anti-Semitic magazine that contained fabricated articles about crimes that Jews had committed and nonsense about their racial inferiority. The covers featured grotesque caricatures of Jews. Embarrassing even to most National Socialists, it was published only because Hitler enjoyed the tabloid.

"Sadly, I missed it," Kohl said dryly. "And he spoke German?"

"Yes."

"Did he have an accent?"

"A Jew accent."

"Yes, yes, but perhaps *another* accent. Bavarian? Westphalian? Saxon?"

"Maybe." A nod of the big man's head. "Yes, I think so. You know, he would not have hurt us if he'd come at us like a man. Not a cowardly—"

Kohl interrupted. "Might his accent have been from another country?"

The three regarded one another. "We wouldn't know, would we? We've never been out of Berlin."

"Maybe Palestine," one offered. "That could have been it."

"All right, so he attacked you from behind with his truncheon."

"And these too." The third held up a pair of brass knuckles.

"Are those his?"

"No, they're mine. He took his with him."

"Yes, yes. I see. He attacked you from behind. Yet it's your nose that has bled, I see."

"I fell forward after he struck me."

"And where was this attack exactly?"

"Over there." He pointed to a small garden jutting into the sidewalk. "One of our comrades went to summon aid. He returned and the Jew coward took off, fleeing like a rabbit."

"Which way?"

"There. Down several alleys to the east. I will show you."

"In a moment," Kohl said. "Did he carry a satchel?"

"Yes."

"And he took it with him?"

"That's right. It's where he had his truncheons hidden."

Kohl nodded to the garden. He and Janssen walked to it. "That was useless," his assistant whispered to Kohl. "Attacked by a huge Jew with brass knuckles and truncheons. And probably fifty of the Chosen People right behind him."

"I feel, Janssen, that the account of witnesses and suspects is like smoke. The words themselves are often meaningless but they might lead you to the fire."

They walked around the garden, looking down carefully.

"Here, sir," Janssen called excitedly. He'd found a small guidebook to the men's Olympic Village, written in English.

Kohl was encouraged. It would be odd for foreign tourists to be in this bland neighborhood and coincidentally lose the booklet in just the spot where the struggle had taken place. The pages were crisp and unstained, suggesting it had lain in the grass for only a short time. He lifted it with a handkerchief (sometimes one could find fingerprints on paper). Opening it carefully, he found no handwriting on the pages and no clue to the identity of the person who'd possessed it. He wrapped up the booklet and placed it in his pocket. He called to the Stormtroopers. "Come here, please."

The three men wandered to the garden.

"Stand there, in a row." The inspector pointed to a spot of bare earth.

They lined up precisely, as Stormtroopers were exceedingly talented at doing. Kohl examined their boots and compared the size and shape to the sole prints in the dirt. He saw that the assailant had larger feet than they and that his heels were well worn.

"Good." Then to Felstedt he said, "Show us where you pursued him. You others can leave now."

The man with the bloody face called, "When you find him, Inspector, you will call us. We have a cell at our barracks. We will deal with him there."

"Yes, yes, perhaps that can be arranged. And I will give you plenty of time so that you can have more than three men to handle him."

The Stormtrooper hesitated, wondering if he was being insulted. He examined his crimson-stained shirt. "Look at this. Ach, when we get him, we'll *drain* all the blood out of him. Let's go, comrade."

The two walked off down the sidewalk.

"This way. He ran this way." Felstedt led Kohl and Janssen down two alleys into crowded Gormann Street.

"We were sure he went down one of these other alleys. We had men covering the far ends of them all but he disappeared."

Kohl surveyed them: Several alleys branched off from the street, one a cul-de-sac, the others connecting to different streets. "All right, sir, we will take over from here."

With his comrades gone, Felstedt was more candid. In a low voice he said, "He *is* a dangerous man, Inspector."

"And you feel that your description is accurate?"

A hesitation. Then: "A Jew. Clearly he was a Jew, yes. Crinkly hair like an Ethiopian, a Jew nose, Jew eyes." The Stormtrooper brushed at the stain on his shirt and swaggered away.

"Cretin," Janssen muttered, glancing cautiously at Kohl, who said, "To be kind." The inspector was looking up and down the alleys, musing, "Despite his own strain of blindness, though, I believe what 'commandant' Felstedt told us. Our suspect *was* cornered but managed to escape—and from dozens of SA. We will look in the trash containers in the alleys, Janssen."

"Yes, sir. You think he discarded some clothing or the satchel to escape?"

"It is logical."

They inspected each of the alleys, looking into the trash bins: nothing but old cartons, papers, cans, bottles, rotting food.

Kohl stood for a moment with his hands on his hips, glancing around and then asked, "Who does your shirts, Janssen?"

"My shirts?"

"They are always impeccably washed and pressed."

"My wife, of course."

"Then my apologies to her for having to clean and mend the one you are presently wearing."

"Why should she need to clean and mend my shirt?"

"Because you are going to lie down on your belly and fish into that sewer grating."

"But—"

"Yes, yes, I know. But I've done so, many times. And with age, Janssen, comes some privilege. Now off with your jacket. It's lovely silk. No need to repair that as well."

The young man handed Kohl his dark green suit jacket. It was quite nice. Janssen's family was well off and he had some money independent of his monthly inspector candidate salary—which was fortunate, considering the paltry compensation Kripo detectives received. The young man knelt on the cobblestones and, supporting himself with one hand, reached into the dark opening.

As it turned out, though, the shirt was not badly soiled after all, for the young man called out only a moment later, "Something here, sir!" He stood up and displayed a crumpled brown object. Göring's hat. And a bonus: Inside it was the tie, indeed gaudy green.

Janssen explained that they'd been resting on a ledge only a half meter below the sewer opening. He searched once more but found nothing else.

"We have some answers, Janssen," Kohl said, examining the inside of the hat. The manufacturer's label read, *Stetson Mity-Lite*. Another had been stitched inside by the store. *Manny's Men's Wear, New York City*.

"More to add to our portrait of the suspect." Kohl took the monocle from his vest pocket, squinted it into his eye and examined some hairs caught in the sweatband. "He has medium-length dark brown hair with a bit of red in it. Not black or 'crinkly' at all. Straight. And there are no stains from cream or hair oil."

Kohl handed the hat and tie to Janssen, licked the tip of his pencil and jotted these latest observations into his notebook, which he then folded closed.

"Where to now, sir? Back to the Alex?"

"And what would we do there? Eat biscuits and sip coffee, as our Stormtrooper comrades think we do all day long? Or watch the Gestapo siphon off our resources as they round up every Russian in town? No, I think we'll go for a drive. I hope the DKW doesn't overheat again. The last time Heidi and I took the children to the country we sat outside Falkenhagen for two hours with nothing to do but watch the cows."

Chapter Eleven

The taxi he'd taken from the Olympic Village dropped him at Lützow Plaza, a busy square near a brown, stagnant canal south of the Tiergarten.

Paul stepped out, smelling fetid water, and stood for a moment, orienting himself as he looked about slowly. He saw no lingering eyes peering at him over newspapers, no furtive men in brown suits or uniforms. He began walking east. This was a quiet, residential neighborhood, with some lovely houses and some modest. Recalling perfectly Morgan's directions, he followed the canal for a time, crossed it and turned down Prince Heinrich Street. He soon came to a quiet road, Magdeburger Alley, lined with four- and five-story residential buildings, which reminded him of the quainter tenements on the West Side of Manhattan. Nearly all of the houses flew flags, most of them National Socialist red, white and black, and several with banners bearing the intertwined rings of the Olympics. The house he sought, No. 26, flew one of the latter. He pressed the doorbell. A moment later footsteps sounded. The curtain in a side window wafted as if in a sudden breeze. Then a pause. Metal snapped and the door opened.

Paul nodded at the woman, who looked out cautiously. "Good afternoon," he said in German.

"You are Paul Schumann?"

"That's right."

She was in her late thirties, early forties, he guessed. A slim figure in a flowery dress with a hemline well below the knees, which Marion would have labeled "pretty unstylish," a couple of years out of date. Her dark blonde hair was short and waved and, like most of the women he'd seen in Berlin, she wore no makeup. Her skin was dull and her brown eyes tired, but those were superficial qualities that a few square meals and a couple of nights' undisturbed sleep would take care of. And, curiously, because of these distractions it made the woman behind them appear all the more attractive to him. Not like Marion's friends—Marion herself too—who sometimes got so dolled up that you never knew what they really looked like.

"I am Käthe Richter. Welcome to Berlin." She thrust a red, bony hand forward and shook his firmly. "I didn't know when you'd be arriving. Mr. Morgan said sometime this weekend. In any case, your quarters are ready. Please, come in."

He stepped into the foyer, smelling naphtha from moth repellent and cinnamon and just a hint of lilac, perhaps her perfume. After she closed and locked the door she looked through the curtained side window once again and examined the street for a moment. Then she took the suitcase and the leather satchel from him.

"No, I—"

"I will carry them," she said briskly. "Come this way."

She led him to a door halfway down the dim corridor, which still had the original gas lamps installed next to the newer electric fixtures. A few faded oil paintings of pastoral scenes were on the walls. Käthe opened the door and motioned him inside. The apartment was large, clean and sparsely furnished. The front door opened onto the living room, a bedroom was in the back, to the left, and along the wall was a small kitchen, separated from the rest of the living area by a stained Japanese screen. Tables were covered with figurines of animals and dolls, chipped, lacquered boxes and cheap paper fans. There were two unsteady electric lamps. A gramophone was in the corner, next to a large console radio, which she walked to and turned on.

"The smoking room is in the front of the building. I am sure you are used to a men-only smoking room but here everyone may use it. I insist on that."

He wasn't used to smoking rooms at all. He nodded.

"Now, tell me if you like the rooms. I have others if you do not."

Glancing quickly at the place, he said, "It will suit me fine."

"You don't wish to see more? The closets, run the water, examine the view?"

Paul had noted that the place was on the ground floor, the windows were not barred and he could make a quick exit from the bedroom window, the living room window or the hallway door, which would lead to other apartments and other means of escape. He said to her, "Provided the water doesn't come out of that canal I passed, I'm sure it will be fine. As for the view I'll be working too hard to enjoy it."

The radio tubes warmed up and a man's voice filled the room. Brother! The health lecture was still going on, more talk of draining swamps and spraying to kill mosquitoes. At least FDR's fireside chats were short and sweet. He walked over to the set and turned the dial, looking for music. There was none. He shut it off.

"You don't mind, do you?"

"It's your room. Do as you wish." She glanced at the silent radio uncertainly then said, "Mr. Morgan said you're an American. But your German is very good."

"Thanks to my parents and grandparents." He took the suitcase from her, walked into the bedroom and set it on the bed. The bag sank deep into the mattress, and he wondered if it was filled with down. His grandmother had told him that she'd had a down bed in Nuremberg before they immigrated to New York, and as a boy Paul had been fascinated at the thought of sleeping on bird feathers.

When he returned to the living room Käthe said, "I serve a light breakfast, across the hall, from seven to eight A.M. Please let me know the night before when you'd like to be served. And there is coffee in the afternoon, of course. You'll find a basin in the bedroom. The bathroom is up the hall, to be shared, but for now you are our only guest. Closer to the Olympics it will be much more crowded. Today you are the king of number twenty-six Magdeburger Alley. The castle is yours." She walked to the door. "I will get afternoon coffee now."

"You don't have to. I actually—"

"Yes, yes, I will. It's part of the price."

When she stepped into the hall Paul went into the bedroom, where a dozen black beetles roamed the floor. He opened his briefcase and placed the copy of Hitler's *Mein Kampf*, containing the fake passport and rubles, on the bookcase. Removing his sweater, he rolled up the sleeves of his tennis shirt, washed his hands then dried them on a threadbare towel.

Käthe returned a moment later with a tray containing a dented silver coffeepot, a cup and a small plate covered with a lace doily. She set this on the table in front of a well-worn couch.

"Please, you will sit."

He did, rebuttoning his sleeves. He asked, "Do you know Reggie Morgan well?"

"No, he just answered an advertisement for the room and paid in advance."

This was the answer Paul had been hoping for. He was relieved to learn that *she* had not contacted Morgan, which would have made her suspect. From the corner of his eye he felt her glance at his cheek. "You are hurt?"

"I'm tall. I'm always banging my head." Paul touched his face lightly, as if he were hitting himself, to illustrate his words. The pantomime made him feel foolish and he lowered his hand.

She rose. "Please, wait." A few minutes later she'd returned with a sticking plaster, which she offered him.

"Thanks."

"I have no iodine, I'm afraid. I looked."

He went into the bedroom, where he stood in front of the mirror behind the washstand and pressed the plaster to his face.

She called, "We have no low ceilings here. You will be safe."

"Is this your building?" he asked, returning.

"No. It is owned by a man who is presently in Holland," Käthe replied. "I manage the house in exchange for room and board."

"Is he connected to the Olympics?"

"Olympics? No, why?"

"Most of the flags on the street are the Nazi—National Socialist, I mean. But you have an Olympic flag here."

"Yes, yes." She smiled. "We are in the spirit of the Games, aren't we?"

Her German grammar was flawless and she was articulate; she'd had a different, and much better, career in the past, he could tell, but the ragged hands and cracked nails and such tired, tired eyes told a story of recent difficulties. But he could also sense an energy within her, a determination to see life through to better times. This, he decided, was part of the attraction he felt.

She poured him coffee. "There is no sugar at the moment. The stores have run out."

"I don't take sugar."

"But I have strudel. I made it before the supplies ran short." She took the doily off the plate, on which sat four small pieces of pastry. "Do you know what strudel is?"

"My mother made it. Every Saturday. My brother and sister would help her. They'd pull the dough so thin that you could read through it."

"Yes, yes," she said enthusiastically, "that is how I make it too. You did not help them stretch the dough?"

"No, I never did. I'm not so talented in the kitchen." He took a bite and said, "But I *ate* plenty of it. . . . This is very good." He nodded toward the pot. "Would you like coffee? I'll pour you some."

"Me?" She blinked. "Oh, no."

He sipped the brew, which was weak. It had been made from used grounds.

"We will speak your language," Käthe announced. And launched into: "I have never been over to your country but I want very much to go."

He could detect only a slight *v*'ing of her *w*'s, which is the hardest English sound for Germans to form.

"Your English is good," Paul said.

"You mean 'well,'" she blurted, smiling to have caught him in a mistake.

Paul said, "No. Your English is *good*. You speak English *well*. 'Good' is an adjective. 'Well' is an adverb—most of the time."

She frowned. "Let me think. . . . Yes, yes, you are right. I am blushing now. Mr. Morgan said you are a writer. And you've been to university, of course."

Two years at a small college in Brooklyn before he dropped out to enlist and go fight in France. He'd never gotten around to finishing his studies. When he'd returned, that was when life got complicated, and college fell by the wayside. In fact, though, he'd learned more about words and books working for his grandfather and father in the printing plant than he figured he'd ever learn in college. But he told her none of this.

"I am a teacher. That is to say, I *was* a teacher. I taught literature to youngsters. As well as the difference between 'will' and 'shall' and 'may' and 'can.' Oh, and 'good' and 'well.' Which I am now embarrassed about."

"English literature?"

"No, German. Though I love many English books."

There was silence for a moment. Paul reached into his pocket, took out his passport, handed it to her.

She frowned, turning it over in his hand.

"I'm really who I say I am."

"I don't understand."

"The language . . . You asked me about speaking English to see if I'm really an American. Not a National Socialist informer. Am I right?"

"I . . ." Her brown eyes quickly examined the floor. She was embarrassed.

"It's all right." He nodded. "Look at it. The picture."

She started to return it. But then she paused, opened it up and compared the picture to his face. He took the booklet back.

"Yes, you are right. I hope you will forgive me, Mr. Schumann."

"Paul."

Then a smile. "You must be quite a successful journalist to be so . . . 'perceptive' is the word?"

"Yes, that's the word."

"The Party is not so diligent, nor so wealthy, as to hire Americans to spy on little people like me, I am thinking. So I can tell you that I am not in favor." A sigh. "It was my fault. I was not thinking. I was teaching Goethe, the poet, to my students and I mentioned simply that I respected his courage when he forbade his son to fight in the German war of independence. Pacifism is a crime in Germany now. I was fired for saying that, and all my books were confiscated." She tossed her hand. "Forgive me. I am complaining. Have you read him? Goethe?"

"I don't think so."

"You would like him. He is brilliant. He spins colors out of words. Of all the books taken from me, his are the ones I miss the most." Käthe glanced hungrily at the plate of strudel. She hadn't eaten any. Paul held the plate out to her. She said, "No, no, thank you."

"If you don't eat one, then I'll think that *you're* the National Socialist agent trying to poison me."

She eyed the pastry and took one. She ate it quickly. When Paul looked down to reach for his coffee cup he noted from the corner of his eye that she touched up pastry flakes from the tabletop on her fingertips and lifted them to her mouth, staring at him to make sure he wasn't looking.

When he turned back, she said, "Ah, but now, we have been careless, you and I, as often happens on first meetings. We must be more cautious. This reminds me." She pointed toward the telephone. "Always keep it unplugged. You must be aware of listening devices. And if you do make a call, assume that you are sharing your conversation with a National Socialist lackey. That is true especially for any long-distance calls you make from the post office, though phone kiosks on the street are, I'm told, relatively private."

"Thanks," Paul said. "But if anybody listened to my conversations all they'd hear is pretty boring talk: What's the population of Berlin, how many steaks will the athletes eat, how long did it take to build the stadium? Things like that."

"Ach," Käthe said softly, rising to leave, "what we have said this afternoon, you and I, would be considered boring by many but would easily merit a visit from the Gestapo. If not worse."

Chapter Twelve

Willi Kohl's battered Auto Union DKW managed the twenty kilometers to the Olympic Village west of the city without overheating, despite the relentless sunlight that forced both officers to shed their jackets—contrary both to their natures and to Kripo regulations.

The route had taken them through Charlottenburg and, had they continued southwest, would have led them toward Gatow, the two towns near which the Polish workers and the Jewish families had died. The terrible pictures of the murders continued to toss about in Kohl's memory like bad fish in his gut.

They arrived at the main entrance of the village, which was bustling. Private cars, taxis and buses were dropping off athletes and other personnel; trucks were delivering crates, luggage and equipment. Jacketed once more, they walked to the gate, showed their ID cards to the guards—who were regular army—and were let inside the spacious, trimmed grounds. Around them men carted suitcases and trunks along the wide sidewalks. Others, in shorts and sleeveless shirts, exercised or ran.

"Look," Janssen said enthusiastically, nodding toward a cluster of Japanese or Chinese men. Kohl was surprised to see them in white shirts and flannel trousers and not . . . well, he didn't know what. Loincloths, perhaps, or embroidered silk robes. Nearby several dark, Middle Eastern men walked together, two of them laughing at what the third had said. Willi Kohl stared like a schoolboy. He would certainly enjoy watching the Games themselves when they began next week but he was also looking forward to seeing people from nearly every country on earth, the only major nations not represented being Spain and Russia.

The policemen located the American dormitories. In the main building was a reception area. They approached the German army liaison officer.

"Lieutenant," Kohl said, noting the rank on the man's uniform. He stood immediately and then grew even more attentive when Kohl identified himself and his assistant. "Hail Hitler. You are here on business, sir?"

"That's right." He described the suspect and asked if the officer had seen such a man.

"No, sir, but there are many hundreds of people in the American dormitories alone. As you can see, the facility is quite large."

Kohl nodded. "I need to speak to someone who is with the American team. Some official."

"Yes, sir. I will arrange it."

Five minutes later he returned with a lanky man in his forties, who identified himself in English as one of the head coaches. He wore white slacks and, although the day was very hot, a white chain-knit sweater vest over his white shirt. Kohl realized that while the reception area had been nearly empty a short time before, now a dozen athletes and others had eased into the room, pretending to have some business there. As he remembered from the army, nothing spread faster than news among men housed together.

The German officer was willing to interpret but Kohl preferred to speak directly to those he was interviewing and said in halting English, "Sir, I am being a police inspector with the German criminal police." He displayed his ID.

"Is there some problem?"

"We are not certain yet. But, uhm, we try to find a man we would like to speak to. Perhaps you are knowing him."

"It's quite a serious matter," Janssen offered with perfect English pronunciation. Kohl had not known he spoke the language so well.

"Yes, yes," the inspector continued. "He had seemingly this book he lost." He held up the guidebook, unfurled the handkerchief around it. "It is given to persons with the Olympic Games, is it?"

"That's right. Not just athletes, though, everybody. We've given out maybe a thousand or so. And a lot of the other countries give out the English version too, you know."

"Yes, but we have located too his hat and it was purchased in New York, New York. So, mostly likely, he is Americaner."

"Really?" the coach asked cautiously. "His hat?"

Kohl continued. "He is being a large man, we are believing, with red, black brown hair."

"Black brown?"

Frustrated at his own lack of foreign vocabulary, Kohl glanced at Janssen, who said, "His hair is dark brown, straight. A reddish tint."

"He wears a light gray suit and this hat and tie." Kohl nodded toward Janssen, who produced the evidence from his case.

The coach looked at them noncommittally and shrugged. "Maybe it would help if you told us what this was about."

Kohl thought again how different life was in America. No German would dare ask *why* a policeman wished to know something.

"It is a matter of state security."

"State security. Uh-huh. Well, I'd like to help. I sure would. But unless you've got something more specific . . ."

Kohl looked around. "Perhaps some person here might be knowing this man."

The coach called, "Any of you boys know who these belong to?"

They shook their heads or muttered "No" or "Nope."

"Perhaps then I am in hopes you are having a . . . yes, yes, a *list* of peoples who came with you here. And addresses. To see who would be living in New York."

"We do but only the members of the team and the coaches. And you're not suggesting—"

"No, no." Kohl believed that the killer was not on the team. The athletes were in the spotlight; it would be unlikely for one of them to slip away from the village unseen on his first full day in Berlin, murder a man, visit several different places in the city on a mission of some sort, then return without arousing suspicion. "I am doubting this man is an athlete."

"So. I can't be much help, I'm afraid." The coach crossed his arms. "You know, Officer, I'll bet your immigration department has information on visitors' addresses. They keep track of everybody entering and leaving the country, don't they? I heard you fellows in Germany are real good at that."

"Yes, yes, I was considered that. But, unfortunate, the information does not present a person's address in his home. Only his nationality."

"Oh, tough break."

Kohl persisted. "What I am also been hoping: perhaps a manifest of the ship, the *Manhattan* passenger list? Often it is giving addresses."

"Ah, yeah. That I'll bet we do have. Although you realize there were close to a thousand people on board."

"Please, I am understanding. But still I would most hopefully like to see it."

"You bet. Only . . . I sure hate to be difficult, Officer, but I think this dorm . . . you know, I think we might have diplomatic status. Sovereign territory. So, I think you'd need a search warrant."

Kohl remembered when a judge needed to approve the search of a suspect's house or the demand to turn over evidence. The Weimar Constitution, creating the Republic of Germany after the War, had many such protections, most borrowed from the American. (It contained a single, rather significant flaw, though, one that Hitler seized upon immediately: the right of the president to indefinitely suspend all civil rights.)

"Oh, I'm merely looking at a few matters here. I am having no warrant."

"I'd really feel better if you got one."

"This is a matter of certain urgency."

"I'm sure it is. But, hey, it might be better for you too. We sure don't want to ruffle any feathers. Diplomatically. 'Ruffle feathers,' you know what I mean?"

"I am understanding the words."

"So how 'bout if your boss called the embassy or the Olympic Committee. They give me the okay, then whatever you want, I'll hand it to you on a silver platter."

"The okay. Yes, yes." The U.S. embassy probably would agree, Kohl reflected, if he handled the request properly. The Americans would not want the story to circulate that a killer had gotten into Germany with their Olympic team.

"Very good, sir," Kohl said politely. "I am be contacting the embassy and the committee as you suggest."

"Good. You take care now. Hey, and good luck at the Games. Your boys're going to give us a run for our money."

"I will be in attendance," Kohl said. "I am having my tickets for more than a whole year."

They said good-bye and Kohl and the inspector candidate stepped outside. "We will call Horcher from the radio in the car, Janssen. He can contact the American embassy, I am sure. This could be—" Kohl stopped speaking. He'd detected a pungent smell. Something familiar, yet out of place. "Something's wrong."

"What do—?"

"This way. Quickly!" Kohl began walking fast, around the back of the main American building. The smell was of smoke, not cooking smoke, which one detected often in the summer from grilling braziers, but wood smoke from a stove, rare in July.

"What is that word, Janssen? On the sign? I cannot make out the English."

"It says *Showers/steam room.*"

"No!"

"What's the matter, sir?"

Kohl ran through the door into a large tiled area. The lavatory was to the left, showers to the right, and a separate door led to the steam room. It was this door that Kohl ran to. He flung it open. Inside was a stove on top of which was a large tray filled with rocks. Nearby were buckets of water, which could be ladled onto the hot rocks to produce steam. Two young Negroes in navy blue cotton exercising outfits stood at the stove, in which a fire was blazing. One, bending down to the door, had a round, handsome face with a high hairline, the other was leaner and had thicker hair that came down farther on his forehead. The round-faced one stood and closed the metal stove door. He turned around, cocking his eyebrow toward the inspector with a pleasant smile.

"Good afternoon, sirs," Kohl said, once again in dreaded English. "I am being—"

"We heard. How are you doing, Inspector? Grand place you fellows made for us here. The village, I mean."

"I smelled smoke and was grown concerned."

"Just getting the fire going."

"Nothing like steam for achin' muscles," added his friend.

Kohl stared through the glass door of the stove. The damper was wide open and the flames raged. He saw some sheets of white paper curling to ash inside.

"Sir," Janssen began sharply in German, "what are they—?" But Kohl cut him off with a shake of his head and glanced at the first man who'd spoken. "You are . . . ?" Kohl squinted and his eyes went wide. "Yes, yes, you are Jesse Owens, the great runner." In Kohl's German-accented English, the name came out "Yessa Ovens."

The surprised man extended his sweaty hand. Shaking the firm grip, Kohl glanced to the other Negro.

"Ralph Metcalfe," the athlete said, introducing himself. A second handshake.

"He's on the team too," Owens said.

"Yes, yes, I have heard of you, as well. You won in Los Angeles in the California state at the last Games. Welcome to you too." Kohl's eyes dipped to the fire. "You take the steam bath *before* you exercise?"

"Sometimes before, sometimes after," Owens said.

"You a steam man, Inspector?" Metcalfe asked.

"Yes, yes, from time to time. Mostly now I soak my feet."

"Sore feet," Owens said, wincing. "I know all about that. Say, why don't we get outa here, Inspector? It's a heck of a lot cooler outside."

He held the door open for Kohl and Janssen. The Kripo men hesitated then followed Metcalfe into the grassy area behind the dorm.

"You've got a beautiful country, Inspector," Metcalfe said.

"Yes, yes. That is true." Kohl watched the smoke rise from the metal duct above the steam room.

"Hope you have luck finding that fellow you're looking for," Owens said.

"Yes, yes. I am supposed it is not useful to ask if you know of anyone who weared a Stetson hat and a green tie. A man of large size?"

"Sorry, I don't know anyone like that." He glanced at Metcalfe, who shook his head.

Janssen asked, "Would you know *anyone* who came here with the team and perhaps left soon? Went on to Berlin or somewhere else?"

The men glanced at each other. "Nope, afraid not," Owens replied.

"I sure don't either," Metcalfe added.

"Ach, well, it is being an honor to meet you both."

"Thank you, sir."

"I was followed news of your races in, was it the Michigan state? Last year—the trials?"

"Ann Arbor. You heard about that?" Owens laughed, again surprised.

"Yes, yes. World records. Sadly, now we are not getting much news from America. Still, I look forward to the Games. But I am having four tickets and five children and my wife and future son-in-law. We will be present and attending in . . . shifts, you would say? The heat will not be bothering you?"

"I grew up running in the Midwest. Pretty much the same weather there."

With sudden seriousness Janssen said, "You know, there are a lot of people in Germany who hope you don't win."

Metcalfe frowned and said, "Because of that bull—what Hitler thinks about the coloreds?"

"No," the young assistant said. Then his face broke into a smile. "Because our bookmakers will be arrested if they accept bets on foreigners. We can only bet on German athletes."

Owens was amused. "So you're betting against us?"

"Oh, we would bet in *favor* of you," Kohl said. "But, alas, we can't."

"Because it's illegal?"

"No, because we are only poor policemen with no money. So run like the *Luft*, the wind, you Americans say, right? Run like the wind, Herr Owens and Herr Metcalfe. I will be in the stands. And cheering you on, though perhaps silently. . . . Come, Janssen." Kohl got several feet then stopped and turned back. "I must ask again: You are being certain no one has worn the brown Stetson hat? . . . No, no, of course not, or you would have told me. Good day."

They walked around to the front of the dormitory and then toward the exit to the village.

"Was that the ship's manifest with the name of our killer on it, sir? What the Negroes burned in the stove?"

"It is possible. But say 'suspect,' remember. Not 'killer.'"

The smell of the burning paper wafted through the hot air and stung Kohl's nose, taunting him and adding to the frustration.

"What can we do about it?"

"Nothing," Kohl said simply, sighing angrily. "We can do nothing. And it was my fault."

"Your fault, sir?"

"Ach, the subtleties of our job, Janssen . . . I wished to give nothing away about our purpose and so I said we wished to see this man about a matter of 'state security,' which we say far too readily nowadays. My words suggested that the crime wasn't the murder of an innocent victim but perhaps an offense against the government—which, of course, was at war with their country less than twenty years ago. Many of those athletes undoubtedly lost relatives, even fathers, to the Kaiser's army, and might feel a patriotic interest in protecting such a man. And now it is too late to retract what I so carelessly said."

When they reached the street in front of the village, Janssen turned toward where they had parked the DKW. But Kohl asked, "Where are you going?"

"Aren't we returning to Berlin?"

"Not yet. We've been denied our passenger manifest. But destruction of evidence implies a reason to destroy it, and that reason might logically be found near the point of its loss. So we'll make some inquiries. We must continue our trail the hard way, by using our poor feet. . . . Ach, that food smells good, doesn't it? They're cooking well for the athletes. I remember when I used to swim daily. Years ago. Why, then I could eat whatever I wanted and never gain a gram. Those days are long behind me, I'm afraid. To the right here, Janssen, to the right."

Reinhard Ernst dropped his phone into its cradle and closed his eyes. He leaned back in the heavy chair in his Chancellory office. For the first time in several days he felt content—no, he felt joyous. A sense of victory swept through him, as keen as when he and his sixty-seven surviving men successfully defended the northwestern redoubt against three hundred Allied troops near Verdun. That had earned him the Iron Cross, first-class—and an admiring look from Wilhelm II (only the Kaiser's withered arm had prevented him from pinning the decoration on Ernst's chest himself)—but this success today, which would be greeted with no public accolades, of course, was far sweeter.

One of the greatest problems he'd faced in rebuilding the German navy was the section in the Versailles treaty that forbade Germany to have submarines and limited the number of warships to six battleships, six light cruisers, twelve destroyers and twelve torpedo boats.

Absurd, of course, even for basic defense.

But last year Ernst had engineered a coup. He and brash Ambassador-at-Large Joachim von Ribbentrop had negotiated the Anglo-German Naval Treaty, which allowed submarine construction and lifted the limitation on Germany's surface navy to 35 percent of the size of England's. But the most important part of the pact had never been tested until now. It had been Ernst's brainstorm to have Ribbentrop negotiate the percentage not in terms of *number* of ships, as had been the measure at Versailles, but in *tonnage*.

Germany now had the legal right to build even *more* ships than Britain had, as long as the total tonnage never exceeded the magic 35 percent. Moreover, it had been the goal all along of Ernst and Erich Raeder, commander in chief of the navy, to create lighter, more mobile and deadlier fighting vessels, rather than behemoth battleships that made up the bulk of the British war fleet—ships that were vulnerable to attack by aircraft and submarines.

The only question had been: Would England claim a foul when they reviewed the shipyard construction reports and realized that the German navy would be far bigger than expected?

The caller on the other end of the line, though, a German diplomatic aide in London, had just reported that the British government had reviewed the figures and approved them without a second thought.

What a success this was!

He drafted a note to the Leader to give him the good news and had a runner deliver it in person.

Just as the clock on the wall was striking four, a bald, middle-aged man wearing a brown tweed jacket and ribbed slacks stepped into Ernst's office. "Colonel, I just—"

Ernst shook his head and touched his lips, silencing Doctor-professor Ludwig Keitel. The colonel spun around and glanced out the window. "What a delightful afternoon it is."

Keitel frowned; it was one of the hottest days of the year, close to thirty-four degrees, and the wind was filled with grit. But he remained silent, an eyebrow raised.

Ernst pointed toward the door. Keitel nodded and together they stepped into the hallway outside and then left the Chancellory. Turning north on Wilhelm Street they continued to Under the Lindens and turned west, chatting only of the weather, the Olympics, a new American movie that was supposed to open soon. Like the Leader, both men admired the American actress Greta Garbo. Her film *Anna Karenina* had just been approved for release in Germany, despite its Russian setting and questionable morality. Discussing her recent films, they entered the Tiergarten just past the Brandenburg Gate.

Finally, looking around for tails or surveillance, Keitel spoke. "What is this about, Reinhard?"

"There is madness among us, Doctor." Ernst sighed.

"No, are you making a joke?" asked the professor sardonically.

"Yesterday the Leader asked me for a report on the Waltham Study."

Keitel took a moment to digest this information. "The Leader? Himself?"

"I was hoping he would forget it. He has been wholly preoccupied with the Olympics. But apparently not." He showed Keitel Hitler's note and then related the story of how the Leader had learned of the study. "Thanks to the man of many titles and more kilos."

"Fat Hermann," Keitel said loudly, sighing angrily.

"Sssh," Ernst said. "Speak through flowers." A common expression nowadays, meaning: Say only good things when mentioning Party officials by name in public.

Keitel shrugged. In a softer voice he continued, "Why should he care about us?"

Ernst had neither the time nor the energy to discuss the machinations of the National Socialist government to a man whose life was essentially academic.

"Well, my friend," Keitel said, "what are we going to do?"

"I've decided that we go on the offensive. We hit back hard. We'll give him a report—by Monday. A detailed report."

"Two days?" Keitel scoffed. "We have only raw data and even that's very limited. Can't you tell him that in a few months we'll have better analysis? We could—"

"No, Doctor," Ernst said, laughing. If one could not speak through flowers, a whisper would do. "One does not tell the Leader to wait a few months. Or a few days or minutes. No, it's best for us to do this now. A lightning strike. That's what we must do. Göring will continue his intriguing and may meddle enough so that the Leader digs deeper, doesn't like what be sees and stops the study altogether. The file he stole was some of Freud's writings. That's what he mentioned in the meeting yesterday. I think the phrase was 'Jew mind-doctor.' You should have seen the Leader's face. I thought I was on my way to Oranienburg."

"Freud was brilliant," Keitel whispered. "The ideas are important."

"We can use his *ideas*. And those of the other psychologists. But—"

"Freud is a psycho*analyst*."

Ach, academics, Ernst thought. Worse than politicians. "But we won't attribute them in our study."

"That's intellectually dishonest," Keitel said sullenly. "Moral integrity is important."

"Under these circumstances, no, it's not" was Ernst's firm response. "We're not going to publish the work in some university journal. That's not what this is about."

"Fine, fine," Keitel said impatiently. "That still doesn't address my concern. Not enough data."

"I know. I've decided we must find more volunteers. A dozen. It will be the biggest group yet—to impress the Leader and make him ignore Göring."

The doctor-professor scoffed. "We won't have time. By Monday morning? No, no, we can't."

"Yes, we can. We have to. Our work is too important to lose in this skirmish. We'll have another session at the college tomorrow afternoon. I'll write up our magnificent vision of the new German army for the Leader. In my best diplomatic prose. I know the right turn of phrase." He looked around. Another whisper: "We'll cut the air minister's fat legs out from underneath him."

"I suppose we can try," Keitel said uncertainly.

"No, we *will* do it," Ernst said. "There is no such thing as 'trying.' Either one succeeds or one does not." He realized he was sounding like an officer lecturing a subordinate. He smiled wistfully and added, "I'm no happier about it than you, Ludwig. This weekend I had hoped to relax. Spend some time with my grandson. We were going to carve a boat together. But there'll be time for recreation later." The colonel added, "After we're dead."

Keitel said nothing but Ernst felt the doctor-professor's head turn uncertainly toward him.

"I am joking, my friend," the colonel said. "I am joking. Now, let me tell you some marvelous news about our new navy."

Chapter Thirteen

The greened bronze of Hitler, standing tall above fallen but noble troops, in November 1923 Square, was impressive but it was located in a neighborhood very different from the others Paul Schumann had seen in Berlin. Papers blew in the dusty wind and there was a sour smell of garbage in the air. Hawkers sold cheap merchandise and fruit, and an artist at a rickety cart would draw your portrait for a few pfennigs. Aging unlicensed prostitutes and young pimps lounged in doorways. Men missing limbs and rigged with bizarre leather and metal prosthetic braces limped or wheeled up and down the sidewalks, begging. One had a sign pinned to his chest: *I gave my legs for my country. What can you give me?*

It was as if he'd stepped through the curtain behind which Hitler had swept all the trash and undesirables of Berlin.

Paul walked through a rusty iron gate and sat facing the statue of Hitler on one of the benches, a half dozen of which were occupied.

He noticed a bronze plaque and read it, learning that the monument was dedicated to the Beer Hall Putsch, in the fall of 1923, when, according to the turgid prose set in metal, the noble visionaries of National Socialism heroically took on the corrupt Weimar state and tried to wrest the country out of the hands of the stabbers-in-the-back (the German language, Paul knew, was very keen on combining as many words as possible into one).

He soon grew bored with the lengthy, breathless accolades for Hitler and Göring and sat back, wiped his face. The sun was lowering but it was still bright and mercilessly hot. He'd been sitting for only a minute or two when Reggie Morgan crossed the street, stepped through the gate and joined Paul.

"You found the place all right, I see." Again speaking his flawless German. He laughed, nodding at the statue, and lowered his voice. "Glorious, hmm? The truth is a bunch of drunks tried to take over Munich and got swatted like flies. At the first gunshot Hitler dove to the ground and he only survived because he pulled a body of a 'comrade' on top of him." Then he looked Paul over. "You look different. Your hair. Clothes." Then he focused on the sticking plaster. "What happened to you?"

He explained about the fight with the Stormtroopers.

Morgan frowned. "Was it about Dresden Alley? Were they looking for you?"

"No. They were beating these people who ran a bookshop. I didn't want to get involved but I couldn't let them die. I've changed clothes. My hair too. But I'll need to steer clear of Brownshirts."

Morgan nodded. "I don't think there's a huge danger. They won't go to the SS or Gestapo about the matter—they prefer to mete out revenge by themselves. But the ones you tangled with will stay close to Rosenthaler Street. They never go far afield. You're not hurt otherwise? Your shooting hand is all right?"

"Yes, it's fine."

"Good. But be careful, Paul. They'd have shot you for that. No questions asked, no arrest. They'd have executed you on the spot."

Paul lowered his voice. "What did your contact at the information ministry find about Ernst?"

Morgan frowned. "Something odd is going on. He said there are hushed meetings all over Wilhelm Street. Usually it's half deserted on a Saturday but the SS and SD are everywhere. He's going to need more time. We're to call him in an hour or so." He looked at his watch. "But for now, our man with the rifle is up the street. He closed his shop today because we are coming in. But he lives nearby. He's waiting for us. I'll call him now." He rose and looked around. Of the divey bars and restaurants here, only one, the Edelweiss Café, advertised a public telephone.

"I'll be back in a moment."

As Morgan crossed the street, Paul's eyes followed him and he saw one of the disabled veterans ease close to the patio of the restaurant, begging for a handout. A burly waiter stepped to the railing and shooed him away.

A middle-aged man, who'd been sitting several benches away, rose and sat next to Paul. He offered a grimace, which revealed dusky teeth, and grumbled, "Did you see that? A crime how some people treat heroes."

"Yes, it is." What should he do? Paul wondered. It might be more suspicious to stand up and leave. He hoped the man would fall silent.

But the German eyed him closely and continued. "You're of an age. You fought."

This was not a question and Paul assumed it would have taken extraordinary circumstances for a German in his twenties to have avoided combat during the War.

"Yes, of course." His mind was racing.

"At which battle did you get that?" A nod toward the scar on Paul's chin.

That battle had involved no military action whatsoever; the enemy had been a sadistic button man named Morris Starble, who inflicted the scar with a knife in the Hell's Kitchen tavern behind which Starble died five minutes later.

The man looked at him expectantly. Paul had to say something so he mentioned a battle he was intimately familiar with: "St. Mihiel." For four days in September of 1918 Paul and his fellow soldiers in the First Infantry Division, IV Corps, slogged through driving rain and soupy mud to assault eight-foot-deep German trenches protected by wire obstacles and machine-gun nests.

"Yes, yes! I was there!" The beaming man shook Paul's hand warmly. "What a coincidence this is! My Comrade!"

Good choice, Paul thought bitterly. What were the odds that this would happen? But he tried to look pleasantly surprised at this happenstance. The German continued to his brother-in-arms: "So you were part of Detachment C! That rain! I have never seen so much rain before or since. Where were you?"

"At the west face of the salient."

"I faced the Second French Colonial Corps."

"We had the Americans against us," Paul said, searching fast through two-decade-old memories.

"Ah, Colonel George Patton! What a mad and brilliant man he was. He would send troops racing all over the battlefield. And his tanks! They would suddenly appear as if by magic. We never knew where he was going to strike next. No infantryman ever troubled me. But tanks . . ." He shook his head, grimacing.

"Yes, that was quite a battle."

"If that's your only wound you were lucky."

"God was looking out for me, that's true." Paul asked, "And you were wounded?"

"A bit of shrapnel in my calf. I carry it to this day. I show my nephew the wound. It is shaped like an hourglass. He touches the shiny scar and laughs with delight. Ah, what a time that was." He sipped from a flask. "Many people lost friends at St. Mihiel. I did not. Mine had all died before then." He fell silent and offered the flask to Paul, who shook his head.

Morgan stepped out of the café and gestured.

"I must go," Paul said to the man. "A pleasure meeting a fellow veteran and sharing these words."

"Yes."

"Good day, sir. Hail Hitler."

"Ach, yes. Hail Hitler."

Paul joined Morgan, who said, "He can meet us now."

"You didn't tell him anything about why I need the gun?"

"No, not the truth, at least. He thinks you're German and you want it to kill a crime boss in Frankfurt who cheated you."

The two men continued up the street for six or seven blocks, the neighborhood growing even shabbier, until they came to a pawnbroker's shop. Musical instruments, suitcases, razors, jewelry, dolls, hundreds of other items filled the grimy, iron-barred windows. A "Closed" sign was on the door. They waited only a few minutes in the vestibule before a short, balding man showed up. He nodded to Morgan, ignored Paul, looked around then let them inside. He glanced back, closed and locked the door, then pulled the shade.

They walked farther into the musty, dust-filled shop. "Come this way." The shopkeeper led them through two thick doors, which he closed and bolted, then down a long stairway into a damp basement, lit only by two small yellow bulbs. When his eyes grew accustomed to the dim light Paul noted that there were two dozen rifles in racks against the wall.

He handed Paul a rifle with a telescopic sight on it. "It's a Mauser Karabiner. A 7.92-millimeter. This one breaks down easily so you can carry it in a suitcase. Look at the scope. The best optics in the world."

The man clicked a switch and lights illuminated a tunnel, perhaps one hundred feet long, at the end of which were sandbags and, pinned to one, a paper target.

"This is completely soundproofed. It is a supply tunnel that was dug through the ground years ago."

Paul took the rifle in his hands. Felt the smooth wood of the sanded and varnished stock. Smelled the aroma of oil and creosote and the leather of the sling. He rarely used rifles in his job and the combination of sweet scents and solid wood and metal took him back in time. He could smell the mud of the trenches, the shit, kerosene fumes. And the stink of death, like wet, rotting cardboard.

"These are special bullets too, which are hollowed out at the tip, as you can see. They are more likely to cause death than standard cartridges."

Paul dry-fired the gun several times to get a feel for the trigger. He pressed bullets into the magazine then sat down at a bench, resting the rifle on a block of wood covered with cloth. He began to fire. The report was ear-splitting but he hardly noticed. Paul just stared through the scope, concentrating on the black dots of the target. He made a few adjustments to the scope and then slowly fired the remaining twenty rounds in the box of ammunition.

"Good," he said, shouting because his hearing was numb. "A good weapon." Nodding, he handed the rifle back to the pawnbroker, who took it apart, cleaned it and packed the gun and ammunition into a battered fiber-board suitcase.

Morgan took the case and handed an envelope to the shopkeeper, who shut the lights out in the range and led them upstairs. A look out the door, a nod that all was clear and soon they were outside again, strolling down the street. Paul heard a metallic voice filling the street. He laughed. "You can't escape it." Across the street, at a tram stop, was a speaker, from which a man's voice droned on and on—yet more information about public health. "Don't they ever stop?"

"No, they don't," Morgan said. "When we look back, that will be the National Socialist contribution to culture: ugly buildings, bad bronze sculpture and endless speeches. . . ." He nodded at the suitcase holding the Mauser. "Now let's go back to the square and call my contact. See if he's found enough information to let you put this fine piece of German machinery to use."

The dusty DKW turned onto November 1923 Square and, unable to find a place to park on the hectic street, narrowly avoided a vendor selling questionable fruit as it drove halfway over the curb.

"Ach, here we are, Janssen," Willi Kohl said, wiping his face. "Your pistol is convenient."

"Yes, sir."

"Then let's go hunting."

They climbed out.

The purpose of the inspector's diversion after they left the U.S. dormitory was to interview the taxi drivers stationed outside the Olympic Village. With typical National Socialist foresight, only cabdrivers who were multilingual were allowed to serve the village, which meant both that there was a limited number of them and that they would return to the village after dropping off fares. This, in turn, Kohl reasoned, meant that one of them might have driven their suspect somewhere.

After dividing the taxis up between them, and speaking to two dozen drivers, Janssen found one who'd had a story that did indeed interest Kohl. The fare had left the Olympics not long before with a suitcase and an old brown satchel. He was a burly man with a faint accent. His hair did not seem on the long side or to have a red tint but it was slicked straight back and dark, though that, Kohl reasoned, might have been due to oil or lotion. He said he had been wearing not a suit but light-colored casual clothing, though the driver couldn't describe it in detail.

The man had got out at Lützow Plaza and vanished into the crowds. This was one of the busiest, most congested intersections in the city; there were few hopes of picking up the suspect's trail there. However, the cabdriver added that the man had asked directions to November 1923 Square and wondered if he could walk to it from Lützow Plaza.

"Did he ask anything more about the square? Anything specific? His business? Comrades he was hoping to meet? Anything?"

"No, Inspector. Nothing. I told him that it would be a long, long hike to the square. And he thanked me and got out. That was all. I was not looking at his face," he explained. "Only at the road."

Blindness, of course, Kohl had thought sourly.

They had returned to headquarters and picked up printed handbills of the Dresden Alley victim. They then had raced here, to the monument in honor of the failed putsch in 1923 (only the National Socialists could turn such an embarrassing defeat into an unqualified victory). While Lützow Plaza was too large to search effectively, this was a far smaller square and could be more easily canvassed.

Kohl now looked over the people here: beggars, vendors, hookers, shoppers, unemployed men and women in small cafés. He inhaled the air, pungent, ripe with the scent of trash, and asked, "Do you sense our quarry nearby, Janssen?"

"I . . ." The assistant seemed uncomfortable with this comment.

"It's a feeling," Kohl said, scanning the street as he stood in the shadow of a courageous, defiant bronze Hitler. "I myself don't believe in the occult. Do you?"

"Not really, sir. I'm not religious, if that's what you mean."

"Well, I haven't given up on religion completely. Heidi would not approve. But what I'm speaking of is the *illusion* of the spiritual based on our perceptions and experience. And I have such a feeling now. He's near."

"Yes, sir," the inspector candidate said. "Why do you think so?"

An appropriate query, Kohl thought. He believed young detectives should always question their mentors. He explained: because this neighborhood was part of Berlin North. Here you could find large numbers of War wounded and poor and unemployed and closet Communists and Socis and anti-Party Edelweiss Pirate gangs, petty thieves and supporters of labor who'd gone to ground after the unions were outlawed. It was populated by those Germans who sorely missed the early days: not Weimar, of course (*no* one liked the Republic), but the glory of Prussia, of Bismarck, of Wilhelm, of the Second Empire. Which meant few members of the Party and its sympathizers. Few denouncers, therefore, ready to run squealing to the Gestapo or the local Stormtrooper garrison.

"Whatever business he's up to, it's in places like this that he'll find support and comrades. Stand back somewhat, Janssen. It is always easier to spot a person on the *lookout* for a suspect, such as us, than to spot that suspect himself."

The young man moved into the shadows of a fishmonger's store, whose stinking bins were mostly empty. Gamy eels, carp and sickly canal trout were all he had for sale. The officers studied the streets for a few moments, looking for their quarry.

"Now let us think, Janssen. He got out of the taxi with his suitcase—and the incriminating satchel—at Lützow Plaza. He did not have the car drive him directly here from the Olympics possibly because he dropped his bags off where he is now staying and came here for some other purpose. Why? To meet someone? To deliver something, perhaps the satchel? Or to collect something or someone? He has been to the Olympic Village, Dresden Alley, the Summer Garden, Rosenthaler Street, Lützow Plaza and now here? What ties these settings together? I wonder."

"Shall we survey all the stores and shops?"

"I think we must. But I will tell you, Janssen, the food-deprivation concern is now serious. I am actually feeling light-headed. We will first query the cafés and, at the same time, get some sustenance for ourselves."

Inside his shoes Kohl's toes flexed against the pain. The lamb's wool had migrated and his feet were stinging once again. He nodded to the closest restaurant, the one he'd parked in front of, the Edelweiss Café, and they stepped inside.

It was a dingy place. Kohl noted the averted eyes that typically greeted the appearance of an official. When they were through looking over the patrons on the off-chance that their Manny's New York suspect might be here, Kohl displayed his ID to a waiter, who snapped instantly to attention. "Hail Hitler. How may I assist?"

In this smoky dive, Kohl doubted anyone had even heard of the position of maître d', so he asked for the manager.

"Mr. Grolle, yes, sir. I will get him at once. Please, sit at this table, sirs. And if you wish some coffee and something to eat, please let me know."

"I will have a coffee and apple strudel. Perhaps a double-size piece. And my colleague?" He lifted an eyebrow at Janssen.

"Just a Coca-Cola."

"Whipped cream with the strudel?" the manager asked.

"But of course," Willi Kohl said in a surprised voice, as if it were a sacrilege to serve it without.

As they were walking back from the gun dealer toward the Edelweiss Café, where Morgan would call his contact at the information ministry, Paul asked, "What will he get us? About Ernst's whereabouts?"

"He told me that Goebbels insists on knowing where all the senior officials will be appearing in public. He then decides if it is important to have a filming crew or a photographer present to record the event." He gave a sour laugh. "You go to see, say, *Mutiny on the Bounty*, and you don't even get a Mickey Mouse cartoon until twenty minutes of tedious reels of Hitler coddling babies and Göring parading in his ridiculous uniforms before a thousand Labor Service workers."

"And Ernst will be on that list?"

"That's what I'm hoping. I hear the colonel doesn't have much patience for propaganda, and he detests Goebbels as much as Göring, but he has learned to play the game. One does not succeed in the government in this day and age without playing the game."

As they approached the Edelweiss Café, Paul noticed a cheap black car sitting on the curb beside the statue of Hitler, in front of the restaurant.

Detroit still seemed to have one up on the German auto industry. While he'd seen some beautiful Mercedes and BMW models, most of the cars in Berlin were like this one, boxy and battered. When he returned to the United States, and had the ten G's, he'd get the car of his dreams, a shiny black Lincoln. Marion would look swell in a car like that.

Paul was suddenly very thirsty. He decided he'd get a table while Morgan made his call. The café seemed to specialize in pastry and coffee but on a hot day like this, those had no appeal to him. Nope, he decided; he'd continue his education in the fine art of German beer making.

Chapter Fourteen

Sitting at a rickety table at the Eidelweiss Café, Willi Kohl finished his strudel and coffee. Much better, he thought. His hands had actually been shaking from the hunger. It wasn't healthy to go without food for so long.

Neither the manager nor anyone else had seen a man fitting the suspect's description. But Kohl hoped someone in this unfortunate area had seen the victim from the Dresden Alley shooting. "Janssen, do you have the pictures of our poor, dead man?"

"In the DKW, sir."

"Well, fetch them."

"Yes, sir."

The young man finished his Coca-Cola and walked to the car.

Kohl followed him out the door, absently tapping the pistol in his pocket. He wiped his brow and looked up the street to his right toward the sound of yet another siren. He heard the DKW door slam and he turned back, glancing toward Janssen. As he did, the inspector noticed a fast movement just beyond his assistant, to Kohl's left.

It appeared that a man in a dark suit, carrying a fiberboard musical instrument case or suitcase, had turned and stepped quickly into the courtyard of a large, decrepit apartment building next door to the Edelweiss Café. There was something unnatural about the abruptness with which the man had veered off the sidewalk. It struck him as somewhat odd as well that a man in a suit would be going into such a shabby place.

"Janssen," Kohl called, "did you see that?"

"What?"

"That man going into the courtyard?"

The young officer shrugged. "Not clearly. I just saw some men on the sidewalk. Out of the corner of my eye."

"Men?"

"Two, I believe."

Kohl's instincts took over. "We must look into this!"

The apartment building was attached to the structure on the right and, looking down the alley, the inspector could see that there were no side doors. "There'll be a service entrance in the back, like at the Summer Garden. Cover it again. I'll go through the front. Assume that both men are armed and desperate. Keep your pistol in your hand. Now run! You can beat them if you hurry."

The inspector candidate sprinted down the alley. Kohl too armed himself. He slowly approached the courtyard.

Trapped.

Just like at Malone's apartment.

Paul and Reggie Morgan stood, panting from the brief sprint, in a gloomy courtyard, filled with trash and a dozen browning juniper bushes. Two teenage boys in dusty clothes tossed rocks at pigeons.

"Not the same police?" gasped Morgan. "From the Summer Garden? Impossible."

"The same." Paul wasn't sure they'd been spotted, but the younger officer, in the green suit, had glanced their way just as Paul had pulled Morgan into the courtyard. They had to assume they'd been seen.

"How did they find us?"

Paul ignored the question, looking around him. He ran to the wooden entrance door in the center of the U of the building; it was closed and locked. The first-floor windows were eight feet off the ground, a tough climb. Most were closed but Paul saw one was open and the apartment it let onto appeared deserted.

Morgan noticed Paul's glance and said, "We could hide there, yes. Pull the blinds. But how do we climb up?"

"Please," Paul called to one of the boys who'd been pitching rocks, "do you live here?"

"No, sir, we just come to play."

"Do you want to earn a whole mark?"

"Greet God, sir," one said. His eyes went wide and he trotted over to the men. "Yes, we do."

"Good. But you must act quickly."

Willi Kohl paused outside the courtyard entrance.

He waited a moment until he was sure Janssen would be in position in the back and then turned the corner. No sign of the suspect from Dresden Alley or the man with the suitcase. Only some teenage boys standing around a pile of wooden milk crates across the courtyard. They glanced up uneasily at the officers and began to walk out of the courtyard.

"You, boys!" Kohl called.

They stopped, looked at each other uneasily. "Yes?"

"Did you just see two men?"

Another uncomfortable shared glance. "No."

"Come here."

There was a brief pause. Then simultaneously they began sprinting, vanishing from the courtyard, raising puffs of dust beneath their feet. Kohl didn't even try to pursue them. Gripping his pistol, he looked around the courtyard. All of the apartments on the ground floor had curtained windows or anemic plants resting on the sills, suggesting they were occupied. One, though, was curtainless and dark.

Kohl approached it slowly and noticed that on the dusty ground below the window were indentations—from the milk cartons, he understood. The suspect and his companion had paid the boys to carry the crates to the window then replace them *after* the men had climbed into the apartment.

The inspector, gripping his pistol tightly, pressed the button for the building's janitor.

A moment later a harried man arrived. The wiry, gray janitor opened the door and glanced with a nervous blink at the pistol in Kohl's hand.

Kohl stepped inside, looking past the man into the dark corridor. There was motion at the far end of the hall. Kohl prayed that Janssen would remain vigilant. The inspector had at least been tested on the battlefield. He'd been shot at and had, he believed, shot one or two enemy soldiers. But Janssen? Though he was a talented marksman, the boy had fired only at paper targets. How would he do if the matter came to a gunfight?

He whispered to the janitor, "The apartment on this floor, two to the right." He pointed. "It is unoccupied?"

"Yes, sir."

Kohl stepped back so he could keep an eye on the courtyard in case the suspects tried to leap out the window and run. He told the janitor, "There's another officer at your back entrance. Go fetch him at once."

"Yes, sir."

But just as he was leaving, a stocky old woman in a purple dress and blue head scarf waddled toward them. "Mr. Greitel, Mr. Greitel! Quickly, you must call the police!"

Kohl turned to her.

The janitor said, "The police are here, Mrs. Haeger."

"Ach, how can that be?" She blinked.

The inspector asked her, "What do you require the police for?"

"Theft!"

Instinct told Kohl that this had something to do with the pursuit. "Tell me, ma'am. Quickly now."

"My apartment is in the front of the building. And from my window I noted two men hiding behind the stack of milk crates, which I must point out you have been promising for weeks you will cart away, Mr. Greitel."

"Please continue. This matter could be most urgent."

"These two were skulking. It was obvious. Then, just a moment ago, I saw them stand and take two bicycles from the rack next to the front entrance. I don't know about one of the bicycles but the other was clearly Miss Bauer's, and she has had no male companion for two years, so I know she would not have been lending him the bicycle."

"No!" Kohl muttered and hurried outside. Now he realized that the suspect had paid the boys simply to drop a couple of the crates beneath the window to leave the marks in the dust but then to return them to the pile, behind which the men had hidden. The boys then were probably told to act furtive or uneasy, making Kohl think this was how the suspects had gotten into the building.

He burst from the courtyard and looked up and down the street, seeing living proof of a statistic that he, as a diligent police officer, knew well: The most popular form of transportation in Berlin was the bicycle, hundreds of which clogged the streets here, hiding their suspects' escape as effectively as a cloud of dense smoke.

They'd ditched the bikes and were walking down a busy street a half mile from November 1923 Square.

Paul and Morgan looked for another café or tap room with a phone.

"How did you know they were in the Edelweiss Café?" Morgan asked, breathing hard from the fast cycling.

"The car, the one parked on the curb."

"The black one?"

"Right. I didn't think anything of it at first. But something clicked in my mind. I remembered a couple of years ago, when I was on my way to a job. It turned out that I wasn't the only one going to visit Bo Gillette. Some cops from Brooklyn got there first. But they were lazy and parked outside, halfway up over the curb, figuring it was an unmarked car, so who'd notice? Well, Bo noticed. He shows up, understands they're looking for him and vanishes. It took me a month to find him again. In the back of my mind I was thinking, police car. So when the younger guy stepped outside I realized right away it was the same man I'd seen on the patio of the Summer Garden."

"They've tracked us from Dresden Alley to the Summer Garden to here. . . . How on earth?"

Paul thought back. He hadn't told Käthe Richter he was coming here and he'd checked a dozen times to make sure nobody had been following him from the boardinghouse to the cab stand. He'd told nobody at the Olympics. The pawnbroker might have betrayed them here, but he wouldn't have known about the Summer Garden. No, these two industrious cops had trailed them on their own.

"Taxis," Paul finally said.

"What?"

"That's the only link. To the Summer Garden and here. From now on, if we can't shank it, we have the driver drop us two, three blocks from where we're going."

They continued away from November 1923 Square. Some blocks farther on they found a beer hall with a public phone. Morgan went inside to make the call to his contact while Paul ordered ales and, edgy and vigilant, kept watch outside. He wouldn't have been surprised to see the two cops hurrying up the street, still on their trail.

Who the hell *were* they?

When Morgan returned to the table he was troubled. "We have a problem." He took a sip of the beer and wiped his mustache. He leaned forward. "They're not releasing any information. Word came from Himmler or Heydrich—my man's not sure who—but no information about public appearances of Party or government officials is to be released until further notice. No press conferences. Nothing. The announcement went out just a few hours ago."

Paul drank down half the beer. "What do we do? Do you know *anything* about Ernst's schedule?"

"I don't even know where he lives, except somewhere in Charlottenburg. We could stake him out at the Chancellory maybe, follow him. But that'll be very hard. If you're within five hundred feet of a senior party official you can be expected to be stopped for your papers and detained if they don't like what they see."

Paul reflected for a moment. He said, "I have a thought. I might be able to get some information."

"About what?"

"Ernst," Paul said.

"You?" Morgan asked, surprised.

"But I'll need a couple of hundred marks."

"I have that, yes." He counted out bills and slipped them to Paul.

"And your man in the information ministry? Do you think he could find out about people who *aren't* officials?"

Morgan shrugged. "I can't say for certain. But I can tell you one thing without doubt—that if the National Socialists have any skill at all, it is gathering information on their citizens."

Janssen and Kohl left the courtyard building.

Mrs. Haeger could offer no descriptions of the suspects, though, ironically, this was due to literal, not political, blindness. Cataracts in her eyes had allowed the busybody to observe the men hiding, then making off with the bicycles but rendered her unable to give any more details.

Discouraged, they returned to November 1923 Square and resumed their search, making their way up and down the street, talking to shop vendors and waiters, flashing the etching of the victim and inquiring about their suspect.

They had no success—until they came to a bakery across from the park, hidden in the shadow of Hitler's statue. A round man in a dusty white apron admitted to Kohl that he'd seen a taxi pull up across the street an hour or so ago. A taxi here was an unusual occurrence, he said, since residents could not afford them and there was no earthly reason for anyone from outside the neighborhood to come here, at least not in a cab.

The man had noticed a big man with slicked-down hair climb out, look around and then walk to the statue. He'd sat down on a bench for a short time then left.

"He was wearing what?"

"Some light clothing. I didn't see very clearly."

"Any other features you noticed?"

"No, sir. I had a customer."

"Did he have a suitcase or satchel with him?"

"I don't believe so, sir."

So, Kohl reflected, his assumption was correct: most likely he was staying somewhere near Lützow Plaza and had come here on an errand of some sort.

"Which way did he go?"

"I didn't see, sir. Sorry."

Blindness, of course. But at least this was a confirmation that their suspect had indeed arrived here recently.

Just then a black Mercedes turned the corner and braked to a stop.

"Ach," Kohl muttered, watching Peter Krauss get out of the vehicle and look around. He knew how the man had tracked him down. Regulations required that he inform the department's desk officers every time he left the Alex during duty hours and where he would be. He'd debated about not sharing this information today. But ignoring rules was hard for Willi Kohl and before he left he'd jotted down, *November 1923 Square*, and the time he expected to return.

Krauss nodded a greeting. "Just making the rounds, Willi. Wondering how the case is coming."

"Which case?" Kohl asked, solely to be petulant.

"The body in Dresden Alley, of course."

"Ach, it seems our department resources are diminished." He added in a wry tone, "For some unknown reason. But we think the suspect might have come here earlier."

"I told you I would check with my contacts. I'm pleased to report that my informant has it on good information that the killer is indeed a foreigner."

Kohl took out his pad and pencil. "And what is the suspect's name?"

"He doesn't know."

"What is his nationality?"

"He wasn't able to say."

"Well, who is this informant?" Kohl asked, exasperated.

"Oh, I can't release that."

"I need to interview him, Peter. If he's a witness."

"He's not a witness. He has his own sources, which are—"

"—also confidential."

"Indeed. I'm merely telling you this because it was encouraging to learn that your suspicions have been confirmed."

"*My* suspicions."

"That he was not German."

"I never said that."

"Who are you?" Krauss asked, turning to the baker.

"The inspector here was asking me about a man I saw."

"Your suspect?" Krauss asked Kohl.

"Perhaps."

"Ach, you are good, Willi. We're kilometers from Dresden Alley and yet you've tracked the suspect to this hellhole." He glanced toward the witness. "Is he cooperating?"

The baker spoke in a shaking voice. "I didn't see anything, sir. Not really. Just a man getting out of a taxi."

"Where was this man?"

"I don't—"

"Where?" Krauss growled.

"Across the street. Really, sir, I didn't see anything. His back was to me. He—"

"Liar."

"I swear to . . . I swear to the Leader."

"A man who swears a false oath is still a liar." Krauss gestured toward one of his own young assistants, a round-faced officer. "We'll take him to Prince Albrecht Street. A day there and he'll give us a complete description."

"No, please, sir. I want to help. I promise you."

Willi Kohl shrugged. "But the fact is you have *not* helped."

"I told you—"

Kohl asked for the man's identity card.

With shaking hands, he handed the inspector his ID, which Kohl opened and examined.

Krauss glanced at his assistant again. "Cuff him. Take him back to head-quarters."

The young Gestapo officer pulled the man's hands behind him and clamped on the irons. Tears filled his eyes. "I tried to recall. I honestly—"

"Well, you *will* recall. I assure you that."

Kohl said to him, "We are dealing with matters of great importance here. I would rather you cooperated now. But if my colleague wants to take you to Prince Albrecht Street"—the inspector lifted an eyebrow to the ter-rified man—"things will go badly for you, Mr. Heydrich. Very badly."

The man blinked and wiped his tears. "But, sir—"

"Yes, yes, they will indeed . . ." Kohl's voice faded. He looked at the ID card again. "You are . . . where were you born?"

"Göttburg, outside of Munich, sir."

"Ah." Kohl's face remained placid. He nodded slowly. Krauss glanced at him.

"But, sir, I think—"

"And the town is small?"

"Yes, sir. I—"

"Please, silence," Kohl said, continuing to stare at the identity card.

Krauss finally asked, "What is it, Willi?"

Kohl gestured the Gestapo inspector aside. He whispered, "I think the Kripo is no longer interested in this man. You can do with him as you wish."

Krauss was silent for a moment, trying to make sense of Kohl's sudden change of heart. "Why?"

"And, please, as a favor, don't mention that Janssen and I detained him."

"Again, I must ask why, Willi?"

After a moment Kohl said, "SD Leader Heydrich came from Göttburg."

Reinhard Heydrich, head of the SS's intelligence division and Himmler's number two, was considered the most ruthless man in the Third Empire. Heydrich was a heartless machine (he'd once impregnated a girl then aban-doned her because he detested women with loose morals). It was said that Hitler disliked inflicting pain but tolerated its use if it suited his needs. Heinrich Himmler enjoyed inflicting pain but was inept at using it to fur-ther his goals. Heydrich both enjoyed inflicting pain and was a craftsman at its application.

Krauss glanced at the baker and asked uneasily, "Are they . . . are you saying they're related, you think?"

"I prefer not to take the chance. At the Gestapo you have a far better relation with SD than the Kripo does. You can question him without much risk of consequence. If they see my name connected to him in an investigation, my career could be over."

"But still . . . interrogating one of Heydrich's relatives?" Krauss looked down at the sidewalk. He asked Kohl, "Do you think that he knows anything valuable?"

Kohl studied the miserable baker. "I think there is perhaps more he knows but nothing particularly helpful to us. I have a feeling what you sense him being evasive about is nothing more than his practice of thinning flour with sawdust or using black-market butter." The inspector glanced around the neighborhood. "I'm sure that if Janssen and I keep at it here we can learn whatever information might be found regarding the Dresden Alley incident and at the same time"—he lowered his voice—"keep our jobs."

Pacing, Krauss was perhaps trying to recall if he'd mentioned his own name to this man, who might in turn relay it to his cousin Heydrich. He said abruptly, "Remove the cuffs." As the young officer did, Krauss said, "We'll need a report on the Dresden Alley matter soon, Willi."

"Of course."

"Hail Hitler."

"Hail."

The two Gestapo officers climbed into their Mercedes, circled the statue of the Leader and sped into traffic.

When the car had gone Kohl handed the baker back his ID card. "Here you are, Mr. Rosenbaum. You may go back to work now. We will not trouble you again."

"Thank you, oh, thank you," the baker said effusively. His hands were shaking and tears dripped into the creases around his mouth. "God bless you, sir."

"Shhhhh," Kohl said, irritated at the indiscreet gratitude. "Now get back into your store."

"Yes, sir. A loaf of bread for you? Some strudel?"

"No, no. Now, your store."

The man hurried back inside.

As they walked to their car Janssen asked, "His name was not Heydrich? It was Rosenbaum?"

"Regarding this matter, Janssen, it is better for you not to inquire. It will not help you become a better inspector."

"Yes, sir." The young man nodded in a knowing way.

"Now," Kohl continued, "we know that our suspect got out of a taxi there and sat in the square before he went on his mission here, whatever that might have been. Let's ask the benchwarmers if they saw anything."

They had no luck with this crowd, many of whom were, as Kohl had explained to Janssen, not the least sympathetic to the Party or police. No luck, that is, until they came to one man sitting in the shadow of the bronze Leader. Kohl looked him over and smelled soldier—either regular army or Free Corps, the informal militia that was formed after the War.

He nodded energetically when Kohl asked about the suspect. "Ach, yes, yes, I know who you mean."

"Who are you, sir?"

"I am Helmut Gershner, former corporal in Kaiser Wilhelm's army."

"And what can you tell us, Corporal?"

"I was speaking to this man not forty-five minutes ago. He fit your description."

Kohl felt his heart pound quickly. "Is he still around here, do you know?"

"Not that I've seen."

"Well, tell us about him."

"Yes, Inspector. We were speaking of the War. At first I thought we were comrades but then I sensed something was odd."

"What was that, sir?"

"He spoke of the battle of St. Mihiel. And yet he was not troubled."

"Troubled?"

The man shook his head. "We lost fifteen thousand captured at that battle and many, many dead. To me it was the black-letter day for my unit, Detachment C. Such a tragedy! The Americans and the French pushed us back to the Hindenburg Line. He knew much of the fighting, it seemed. I suspect he was there. But the battle was not a horror to him. I could see in his eyes he found those terrible days as nothing. And"—the man's eyes flared in indignation—"he would not share my flask in honor of the dead. I don't know why you are looking for him but this reaction alone made me suspicious. I suspect that he was a deserter. Or a coward. Perhaps he was even a backstabber."

Or perhaps, Kohl thought wryly, he was the enemy. The inspector asked, "Did he say anything of his business here? Or anywhere?"

"No, sir, he did not. We spoke for only a few moments."

"Was he alone?"

"I think not. He seemed to join another man, somewhat smaller than he. But I didn't see clearly. I'm sorry. I wasn't paying attention, sir."

"You're doing fine, soldier," Janssen said. To Kohl, the inspector candidate offered, "Perhaps that man we saw in the courtyard was his colleague. A dark suit, smaller."

Kohl nodded. "Possibly. One of the companions at the Summer Garden." He asked the veteran, "What was his age, the larger man?"

"About forty, plus a year or two. The same as myself."

"And you got a good look at him?"

"Oh, yes, sir. I was as close to him as I am to you right now. I can describe him perfectly."

Greet God, Kohl thought; the plague of blindness is over. He glanced up the street, looking for someone he'd observed on their search of the area a half hour earlier. He took the veteran by the arm and, holding up one hand to stop traffic, led the limping man across the street.

"Sir," he said to a vendor in a paint-stained smock, sitting beside a cheap pushcart displaying pictures. The street artist looked up from a floral still life he was painting. He set down his brush and rose in alarm when he saw Kohl's identification card.

"I am sorry, Inspector. I promise you I have tried many times to obtain a permit but—"

Kohl snapped, "Can you use a pencil or only paints?"

"I—"

"Pencil! Can you use one?"

"Yes, sir. I often began with a pencil to do the preliminary sketch and then I—"

"Yes, yes, fine. Now, I have a job for you." Kohl deposited the limping corporal in the shabby canvas chair and shoved a pad of paper toward the artist.

"You wish me to do a drawing of this man?" the vendor asked, game but confused.

"No, I wish you to do a drawing of the man *this* man is about to describe."

Chapter Fifteen

The taxi sped past a large hotel, from which fluttered black-white-and-red Nazi flags.

"Ach, that's the Metropol," the driver said. "You know who is there presently? The great actress and singer Lillian Harvey! I saw her myself. You must enjoy her musicals."

"She's good." Paul had no idea who the woman was.

"She is making a film just now in Babelsberg for UFA Studios. I would love to have her as a fare but, of course, she has a limousine."

Paul glanced absently at the posh hotel—just the sort of place where a movie starlet would stay. Then the Opel turned north, and abruptly the neighborhood changed, growing seamier by the block. Five minutes later Paul told the driver, "Please, here will do."

The man dropped him at the curb and, alert to the risks of taxis now, Paul waited until the vehicle had disappeared in traffic before walking two blocks to Dragoner Street then continuing to the Aryan Café.

Inside he didn't have to search hard for Otto Webber. The German was sitting at a table in the front bar, arguing with a man in a dirty light blue suit and a flat-topped straw boater hat. Webber glanced up and beamed a great smile toward Paul then quickly dismissed his companion.

"Come here, come here, Mr. John Dillinger! How are you, my friend?" Webber rose to embrace him.

They sat. Before Paul could even unbutton his jacket, Liesl, the attractive young waitress who'd served them earlier, made a beeline for him. "Ach, you're back," she announced, resting a hand on his shoulder, squeezing hard. "You could not resist me! I knew it! What will it be now?"

"Pschorr for me," Paul said. "For him a Berlin beer."

Her fingers brushed the back of his neck as she stepped away.

Webber's eyes followed Liesl. "It seems that you have yourself a special friend. And what *does* bring you back? The allure of Liesl? Or have you been beating up more dung-shirts and need my help?"

"I thought we might be able to do some business, after all."

"Ach, your words are like Mozart's music to me. I knew you were a sharp one."

Liesl brought the beers immediately. Paul noted that at least two customers who'd ordered earlier had not been served. She wrinkled her face, looking around the bar. "I must work now. Otherwise I would sit and join you and let you buy me schnapps." Resentfully she strode off.

Webber slammed his glass into Paul's. "Thank you for this." He nodded after the man in the baby-blue suit, who was now at the bar. "Such problems I have. You wouldn't believe them. Hitler announced a new car at the Berlin Auto Show last year. Better than the Audi, cheaper than the DKW. The Folks-Wagon, it is to be called. A car for everybody. You can pay by installments then pick it up when you've paid in full. Not a bad idea. The company can make use of the money and they still keep the car in case you don't complete the payments. Is that not brilliant?"

Paul nodded.

"Ach, I was lucky enough to find thousands of tires."

"*Find?*"

Webber shrugged. "And now I learn that the damn engineers have changed the wheel size of the piss-ant little car. My inventory is useless."

"How much did you lose?"

Webber regarded the foam in his beer. "I haven't actually lost money. But I will not *make* money. That is just as bad. Automobiles are one thing this country's done well. The Little Man's rebuilt all the roads. But we have a joke: You can travel anywhere in the country in great speed and comfort. But why would you want to? All you find at the other end of the road are more National Socialists." He roared with laughter.

Liesl was looking at Paul expectantly from across the room. What did she want? Another order for beer, a roll in the hay, a marriage proposal? Paul turned back to Webber. "I will admit you were right, Otto. I am something more than a sportswriter."

"If you are a sportswriter at all."

"I have a proposal."

"Fine, fine. But let us talk among four eyes. You understand the meaning? Just the two of us. There's a better place to speak and I need to deliver something."

They drained their beers and Paul left some marks on the table. Webber picked up a cloth shopping bag with the words *KaDeWe—the World's Finest Store* printed on the side. They escaped without saying good-bye to Liesl.

"Come this way." Outside they turned north, away from downtown, from the shops, from the fancy Metropol Hotel, and plunged into the increasingly tawdry neighborhood.

There were a number of nightclubs and cabarets here but they'd all been boarded up. "Ach, look at this. My old neighborhood. It's all gone now. Listen, Mr. John Dillinger, I will tell you that I was very famous in Berlin. Just like your mobs that I read about in the crime shockers, we had our *Ringvereine* here."

Paul was not familiar with the word, whose literal translation was "ring association," but, with Webber's explanation, decided it meant "gang rings."

Webber continued. "Ach, we had many of them. Very powerful. Mine was called after your Wild West. We were the Cowboys." He used the English word. "I was president of it for a time. Yes, *president*. You look surprised. But we held elections to choose our leaders."

"Democracy."

Webber grew serious. "You must remember, we were a republic then, our German government was. It was *President* Hindenburg. Our gang rings were very well run. They were grand. We owned buildings and restaurants and had elegant parties. Even costume balls, and we invited politicians and police officials. We were criminals, yes, but we were respectable. We were proud and we were skillful too. Someday I may boast to you of my better cons.

"I don't know much about your mob, Mr. John Dillinger—your Al Capone, your Dutch Schultz—but ours began as boxing clubs. Laborers would meet to box after work and they began protection rings. We had years of rebellion and civil unrest after the War, fighting with the Kosis. Madness. And then dreadful inflation . . . It was cheaper to burn banknotes for heat than to spend them on wood. One of your dollars would buy billions of marks. Times were terrible. We have an expression in our country: 'The devil plays in the empty pocket.' And all of our pockets were empty. It's why the Little Man came to power. And it's how I made myself a success. The world was barter and the black market. I bloomed in such an atmosphere."

"I can imagine," Paul said. Then he nodded at a boarded-up cabaret. "And the National Socialists have cleaned everything up."

"Ach, that's one way to put it. Depends on what you mean by 'cleaned up.' The Little Man isn't right in the head. He doesn't drink, doesn't smoke, doesn't like women. Or men. Watch how he holds his hat over his crotch at rallies. We say he's protecting the last of Germany's unemployed!" Webber laughed hard. Then the smile faded. "But it's no joke. Thanks to him, the inmates have taken over the prison."

They continued in silence for a time. Then Webber stopped and pointed proudly to a decrepit building.

"Here we are, my friend. Look at the name."

The faded sign read in English, *The Texas Club*.

"This used to be our headquarters. Of my gang ring, the Cowboys, I was telling you. It was far, far nicer then. Watch your step, Mr. John Dillinger. There are sometimes men sleeping off hangovers in the entryway. Ach, did I lament already how times have changed?"

Webber had delivered his mysterious shopping bag to the bartender and collected an envelope.

The room was filled with smoke and stank of garbage and garlic. The floor was littered with cigarette and cigar butts, smoked down to tiny nubs.

"Have only beer here," Webber warned. "They can't adulterate the kegs. They come sealed from the brewery. As for everything else? Well, they mix the schnapps with ethyl and food extract. The wine . . . Ach, do not even ask. And as for food . . ." He nodded at sets of knives, forks and spoons chained to the wall next to each table. A young man in filthy clothing was walking around the room rinsing the used ones in a greasy pail. "Far better to leave hungry," Webber said. "Or you might not leave at all."

They ordered and found seats. The bartender, staring darkly at Paul the whole time, brought beers. Both men wiped the lips of the glasses before drinking. Webber happened to glance down and then frowned. He lifted his solid leg over his opposite knee and examined his trousers. The bottom of his cuff had frayed through, threads dangling.

He examined the damage. "Ach. And these trousers were from England! Bond Street! Well, I'll get one of my girls to fix it."

"Girls? You have daughters?"

"I may. Sons too perhaps. I don't know. But I am referring to one of the women I live with."

"*Women?* All together?"

"Of course not," Webber said. "Sometimes I'm at one's apartment, sometimes at another's. A week here, a week there. One of them is a cook possessed by Escoffier, one sews as Michelangelo sculpted, one is a woman of considerable experience in bed. Ach, they're all pearls, each in her own way."

"Do they . . ."

"Know of each other?" Webber shrugged. "Perhaps, perhaps not. They don't ask, I don't say." He leaned forward. "Now, Mr. John Dillinger. What can I do for you?"

"I am going to say something to you, Otto. And you may choose to stand up and leave. I'll understand if you do. Or you can stay and hear me out. If so, and if you can help me, there will be some very good money in it for you."

"I'm intrigued. Keep talking."

"I have an associate in Berlin. He just had a contact of his do some research on you."

"On me? I'm flattered." And he truly seemed to be.

"You were born in Berlin in 1886, moved to Cologne when you were twelve and back here three years later after your school expelled you."

Now Webber frowned. "I left voluntarily. The story is often misreported."

"For theft of kitchen goods and a liaison with a chambermaid."

"*She* was the seductress and—"

"You have been arrested seven times and served a total of thirteen months in Moabit."

Webber beamed. "So many arrests, such short sentences. Which attests to the quality of my connections in high places."

Paul concluded: "And the British are none too happy with you because of that rancid oil you sold their embassy cook last year. The French, as well, because of the horsemeat you passed off as lamb. They have a notice posted not to deal with you anymore."

"Ach, the French," he sneered. "So you are telling me that you wish to make sure you can trust me and that I am the clever criminal I purport to be, not a stupid criminal like a National Socialist spy. You are merely being prudent. Why would I be insulted at this?"

"No, what you may be insulted about is that my associate has arranged to make some people in Berlin aware of you, some people in our government. Now, you're free to choose to have nothing more to do with me. A disappointment but understandable. But if you do decide to help us, and you betray me, these people will find you. And the consequences will be unpleasant. Do you understand what I'm saying?"

Bribery and threat, the cornerstones of trust in Berlin, as Reggie Morgan had said.

Webber wiped his face, lowered his gaze and muttered, "I save your life and this is how you treat me?"

Paul sighed. Not only did he like this improbable man but he saw no other way to get any wire on Ernst's whereabouts. But he'd had no choice in having Morgan's contacts look into Webber's background and to make arrangements to ensure he didn't betray them. These were precautions that were vital in this dangerous city. "So, I suppose we finish our beers in silence and go our separate ways."

After a moment, though, Webber's face broke into a smile. "But I will admit I am not as insulted as I ought to be, Mr. Schumann."

Paul blinked. He'd never told Webber his name.

"You see, I had my doubts about you too. At the Aryan Café, our first meeting, when you walked past me to refresh your makeup, as my girls would say, I palmed your passport and had a look. Ach, you didn't smell like a National Socialist but, as you suggest, one can never be too careful in this mad town of ours. So *I* made inquiries about *you*. You have no connection with Wilhelm Street that *my* contact was able to uncover. How was my skill, by the way? You felt nothing, did you, when I took your passport?"

"No," Paul said, smiling ruefully.

"So I think we have achieved enough mutual *respect*"—he laughed wryly—"to be able to consider a business proposition. Please continue, Mr. John Dillinger. Tell me what you have in mind."

Paul counted out a hundred of the marks Morgan had given him and passed them to Webber, whose eyebrow rose.

"What do you wish to buy?"

"I need some information."

"Ach, information. Yes, yes. That *could* cost one hundred marks. Or it could cost much more. Information about what or whom?"

He regarded the dark eyes of the man sitting across from him. "Reinhard Ernst."

Webber's lower lip jutted out and he cocked his head. "So at last the pieces fall into place. You are here for a very interesting new Olympic event. Big-game hunting. And you have made a good choice, my friend."

"Good?" Paul asked.

"Yes, yes. The colonel is making many changes here. And not for the country's benefit. He's getting us ready for mischief. The Little Man's a fool but he gathers smart people around him and Ernst is one of the smartest." Webber lit up one of his foul cigars. Paul, a Chesterfield, breaking only two matches from the cheap box to get a flame this time.

Webber's eyes were distant. "I served the Kaiser for three years. Until the surrender. Oh, I did some brave things, I'll tell you. My company once advanced over a hundred meters against the British and it only took us two months to do it. Earned us some medals, that one did. Those of us who survived. There are plaques in some villages that say only, *To the fallen.* The towns couldn't afford enough bronze to put all the names of the dead on them." He shook his head. "You Yankees had the Maxims. We had our Machine-Gun. Same as the Maxims. We stole the design from you, or you stole it from us. I don't recall which. But the Britons, ach, *they* had the Vickers. Water-cooled. Now, that was a snuff grinder, for you. That was quite a piece of metalwork. . . . No, no, we don't want another war, whatever the Little Man says, none of us do. That would be the end of everything. And that's what the colonel is up to." Webber slipped the hundred marks into his pocket and puffed on his vile ersatz cigar. "What do you need to know?"

"His schedule at Wilhelm Street. When he arrives for work, when he leaves, what kind of car he drives, where he parks, will he be there tomorrow, Monday or Tuesday, what routes he takes, any cafés he favors in the area."

"One can find out anything, given enough time. And egg."

"Egg?"

He tapped his pocket. "Money. I must be honest, Mr. John Dillinger. We are not talking about palming off three-day-old canal trout from the Landwehr as fresh from the Havel. This is a matter that will require me to retire for a time. There will be serious repercussions and I will have to go underground. There will be—"

"Otto, just give me a number."

"Very dangerous . . . Besides, what is money to you Americans? You have your FDR." In English he said, "You're rolling on dough."

"*In* dough," Paul corrected. "A number?"

"A thousand U.S. dollars."

"*What?*"

"Not marks. They say the Inflation's over but nobody who's lived through that time believes it. Why, in 1928 a liter of petrol cost five hundred thousand marks. And in—"

Paul shook his head. "That's a lot of money."

"But it's really not—if I get you your information. And I guarantee I will. You pay me only half up front."

Paul pointed to Webber's pocket, where the marks resided. "*That's* your down payment."

"But—"

"You get paid the rest when and if the information pans out. And if I get approval."

"I'll have expenses."

Paul slipped him the remaining hundred. "There."

"Hardly enough but I'll make do." Then Webber looked over Paul closely. "I'm curious."

"About what?"

"About *you,* Mr. John Dillinger. What's your tale?"

"There is no tale."

"Ach, there's *always* a tale. Go ahead, tell Otto your story. We're in business together now. That's closer than being in bed. And remember, he sees all, the truth and the lies. You seem an unlikely candidate for this job. Though perhaps that is why you were chosen to visit our fair city. Because you seem unlikely. How did you get into this noble profession of yours?"

Paul said nothing for a moment, then: "My grandfather came to America years ago. He'd fought in the Franco-Prussian War and wanted no more fighting. He started a printing company."

"What was his name?"

"Wolfgang. He said printing ink was in his veins and claimed that his ancestors had lived in Mainz and worked with Gutenberg."

"A grandfather's stories," Webber said, nodding. "Mine said he was Bismarck's cousin."

"His company was on the Lower East Side of New York in the German-American area of the city. In 1904 there was a tragedy—over a thousand people from there were killed in an excursion ship fire in the East River. *The General Slocum.*"

"Ach, what a sad thing."

"My grandfather was on the boat. He and my grandmother weren't killed but he was badly burned saving people and he couldn't work any longer. Then most of the German community moved to Yorkville, farther north in Manhattan. People were too sad to stay in Little Germany. His business was going to fail, with Grandpapa being so sick and fewer people around to order printing. So my father took over. He didn't want to be a printer; he wanted to play baseball. You know baseball?"

"Ach, of course."

"But there was no choice. He had a wife and my sister and my brother and me to feed—my grandparents now too. But he, we would say, rose to the occasion. He did his duty. He moved to Brooklyn, added English-language printing and expanded the company. Made it very successful. My brother couldn't go into the army during the War and they ran the shop together when I was in France. After I got back I joined them and we built the place up real nice." He laughed. "Now I don't know if you heard about this, but our country had this thing called Prohibition. You know—"

"Yes, yes, of course. I read the crime shockers, remember. Illegal to drink liquor! Madness!"

"My father's plant was right on the river in Brooklyn. It had a dock and a large warehouse for storing paper and the finished jobs. One of the gangs wanted to take it over and use it to store whisky they'd smuggle in from the harbor. My father said no. A couple of thugs came to see him one day. They beat up my brother and, when my father still resisted, they put his arms in our big letterpress."

"Oh, no, my friend."

Paul continued. "He was mangled badly. He died a few days later. And my brother and mother sold the plant to them the next day for a hundred dollars."

"So you were out of work and you fell in with a difficult crowd?" Webber nodded.

"No, that's not what happened," Paul said softly. "I went to the police. They weren't interested in helping find these particular killers. You understand?"

"Are you asking if I know about corrupt police?" Webber laughed hard.

"So I found my old army Colt, my pistol. I learned who the killers were. I followed them for a week straight. I learned everything about them. And I touched them off."

"You—?"

He realized that he'd translated the phrase literally; it would have no meaning in German. "We say 'touching off.' I put a bullet into the backs of their heads."

"Ach, yes," Webber whispered, unsmiling now. "'Snuffing,' we'd say."

"Yes. Well, I also knew whom they worked for, the bootlegger who'd ordered my father tortured. I touched him off too."

Webber fell silent. Paul realized he'd never told the story to anyone.

"You got your company back?"

"Oh, no, the place had been raided by the feds, the government, before that and confiscated. As for me, I disappeared underground in Hell's Kitchen in Manhattan. And I got ready to die."

"To die?"

"I'd killed a very important man. This mob leader. I knew that his associates or someone else would come to find me and kill me. I'd covered my tracks very well, the police wouldn't get me. But the gangs knew I was the one. I didn't want to lead anybody to my family—my brother'd started his own printing company by then—so instead of going back into business with him I took a job in a gym, sparring and cleaning up in exchange for a room."

"And you waited to die. But I can't help but notice that you're still extremely alive, Mr. John Dillinger. How did that transpire?"

"Some other men—"

"Gang leaders."

"—heard what I'd done. They hadn't been happy with the man I'd killed, the way he'd done business, like torturing my father and killing policemen. They thought criminals should be professionals. Gentlemen."

"Like me," Webber said, thumping his chest.

"They heard how I'd killed the gangster and his men. It had been clean, with no evidence left behind. And no one innocent was hurt. They asked me to do the same to another man, another very bad man. I didn't want to but I found out what he'd done. He'd killed a witness and the man's family, even his two children. So I agreed. And I touched him off too. They paid me a lot of money. Then I killed someone else. I saved up the money they paid me and bought a small gym. I was going to quit. But do you know what it means to get into a rut?"

"Indeed I do."

"Well, this rut has been my life for years. . . ." Paul fell silent. "So that's my story. All truth, no lies."

Finally Webber asked, "It bothers you? Doing this for a living?"

Paul was silent for a moment. "It should bother me more, I think. I felt worse touching off your boys during the war. In New York, I only touch off other killers. The bad ones. The ones who do what those men did to my father." He laughed. "I say that I'm only correcting God's mistakes."

"I like that, Mr. John Dillinger." Webber nodded. "God's mistakes. Oh, we've got a few of those around here, yes, we do." He finished his beer. "Now, it's Saturday. A difficult time to get information. Meet me tomorrow morning at the Tiergarten. There is a small lake at the end of Stern Alley. On the south side. What time would be good for you?"

"Early. Say eight."

"Ach, very well," Webber said, frowning. "That *is* early. But I will be on the moment."

"There's one more thing I need," Paul said.

"What? Whisky? Tobacco? I can even find some cocaine. There's not much left in town. Yet I—"

"It's not for me. It's for a woman. A present."

Webber grinned broadly. "Ach, Mr. John Dillinger, good for you! In Berlin only a short time and already your heart has spoken. Or perhaps the voice is from another part of your body. Well, how would your friend like a nice garter belt with stockings to match? From France, of course. A bustier in red and black? Or is she more modest? A cashmere sweater. Perhaps some Belgian chocolates. Or some lace. Perfume is always good. And for you, of course, my friend, a very special price."

Chapter Sixteen

Busy times.

There were dozens of matters that might have been occupying the mind of the huge, sweating man who, late this Saturday afternoon, sat in his appropriately spacious office within the recently completed 400,000-square-foot air ministry building at 81–85 Wilhelm Street, bigger even than the Chancellory and Hitler's apartments combined.

Hermann Göring could, for instance, resume work on the creation of the massive industrial empire that he was currently planning (and that would be named after him, of course). He could be drafting a memorandum to rural gendarmeries throughout the country, reminding them that the State Law for the Protection of Animals, which he himself had written, was to be strictly enforced and anyone caught hunting foxes with hounds would be severely punished.

Or there was the vital matter of his party for the Olympics, for which Göring was constructing his own village within the air ministry itself (he'd managed to get a look at the plans for Goebbels's event and upped his own gala to outdo the mealworm by tens of thousands of marks). And, of course, there was the ever-vital matter of what he would wear to the party. He could even be meeting with his adjutants regarding his present mission within the Third Empire: building the finest air force in the world.

But what forty-three-year-old Hermann Göring was now preoccupied with was a pensioner widow twice his age, who lived in a small cottage outside Hamburg.

Not that the man whose titles included minister without portfolio, commissioner for air, commander in chief of the air force, Prussian minister president, air minister and hunting master of the empire was himself doing any of the legwork regarding Mrs. Ruby Kleinfeldt, of course. A dozen of his minions and Gestapo officers scurried about on Wilhelm Street and in Hamburg, digging through records and interviewing people.

Göring himself was staring out the window of his opulent office, eating a massive plate of spaghetti. This was Hitler's favorite dish and Göring had watched the Leader picking at a bowl of it yesterday. Seeing the unconsumed portion triggered an itch within Göring that had festered into a fierce craving; so far he'd had three large helpings today.

What will we find about you? he silently asked the elderly woman, who knew nothing of the bustling inquiry about her. The investigation seemed absurdly digressive, considering the many vital projects currently on his calendar. Yet this one was vitally important because it could lead to the downfall of Reinhard Ernst.

Soldiering was at the core of Hermann Göring, who often recalled the happy days of the War, flying his all-white Fokker D-7 biplane over France and Belgium, engaging any Allied pilot foolish enough to be in the skies nearby (a confirmed twenty-two had paid for that mistake with their lives, though Göring remained convinced he'd killed many more). He might now be a behemoth who couldn't even fit into the cockpit of his old plane, a man whose life was painkillers, food, money, art, power. But if you asked him who he was at heart, Göring's answer would be: I am a soldier.

And a soldier who knew how best to turn his country into a nation of warriors once again—you showed your muscle. You didn't negotiate, you didn't pad around like a youth making for the bushes behind a barn to secretly puff away on his father's pipe—the behavior of Colonel Reinhard Ernst.

The man had a woman's touch about this business. Even the faggot Roehm, the head of the Stormtroopers killed by Göring and Hitler in the putsch two years ago, was a bulldog compared with Ernst. Secret arm's-length deals with Krupp, nervously shifting resources from one shipyard to another, forcing their present "army," such as it was, to train with wooden guns and artillery in small groups, so they wouldn't draw attention. A dozen other such prissy tactics.

Why the hesitancy? Because, Göring believed, the man's loyalty to National Socialist views was suspect. The Leader and Göring were not naive. They knew their support was not universal. You can win votes with fists and guns; you cannot win hearts. And many hearts within their country were not devoted to National Socialism, among them people at the top of the armed forces. Ernst could very well be intentionally dragging his Prussian heels to keep Hitler and Göring from having the one institution they needed desperately: a strong military. It was likely Ernst himself even hoped to accede to the throne if the two rulers were deposed.

Thanks to his soft voice, his reasonable manner, his smooth ways, his two fucking Iron Crosses and dozens of other decorations, Ernst was currently in Wolf's favor (because it made him feel close to the Leader, Göring liked to use the nickname women sometimes referred to Hitler by, though the minister, of course, uttered the intimacy only in his thoughts).

Why, look at how the colonel had attacked Göring yesterday on the issue of the Me 109 fighter at the Olympics! The air minister had lain awake half the night, enraged over that exchange, picturing again and again Wolf turning his blue eyes to Ernst and agreeing!

Another burst of rage swept through him. "God in heaven!" Göring swept the spaghetti dish to the floor. It shattered.

One of his orderlies, a veteran of the War, came running, stiff on his game leg.

"Sir?"

"Clean that up!"

"I'll get a pail—"

"I didn't say *mop* the floor. Just pick up the pieces. They'll mop this evening." Then the huge man glanced at his blousy shirt and saw tomato stains on it. His anger doubled. "I want a clean shirt," he snapped. "The china is too small for the portions. Tell the cook to find bigger. The Leader has that Meissen set, the green and white. I want plates like those."

"Yes, sir." The man was bending down to the shards.

"No, my shirt first."

"Yes, Air Minister." The man scurried off. He returned a moment later, bearing a dark green shirt on a hanger.

"Not *that* one. I told you when you brought it to me last month that it makes me look like Mussolini."

"That was the black one, sir. Which I've discarded. This is green."

"Well, I want white. Get me a white shirt! A silk one!"

The man left then came back once more, with the correct color.

A moment later one of Göring's senior aides stepped inside.

The minister took the shirt and set it aside; he was self-conscious of his weight and would never think of undressing in front of a subordinate. He felt another flash of rage, this time at Ernst's slim physique. As the orderly picked up the shards of china, the senior aide said, "Air Minister, I think we have good news."

"What?"

"Our agents in Hamburg have found some letters about Mrs. Kleinfeldt. They suggest that she is a Jew."

"'Suggest'?"

"*Prove*, Mr. Minister. They *prove* it."

"Pure?"

"No. A half-breed. But from the mother's side. So it's indisputable."

The Nuremberg Laws on Citizenship and Race, enacted last year, removed Jews' German citizenship and made them "subjects," as well as criminalized marriage or sex between Jews and Aryans. The law also defined exactly who was a Jew in the case of ancestral intermarriage. With two Jewish and two non-Jewish grandparents, Mrs. Kleinfeldt was a half-breed.

This was not as damning as it could be but the discovery delighted Göring because of the man who was Mrs. Kleinfeldt's grandson: Doctor-professor Ludwig Keitel, Reinhard Ernst's partner in the Waltham Study. Göring still didn't know what this mysterious study was all about. But the facts were sufficiently damning: Ernst was working with a man descended from Jews and they were using the writings of the Jew mind-doctor Freud. And, most searing of all, Ernst had kept the study secret from the two most important people in the government, himself and Wolf.

Göring was surprised that Ernst had underestimated him. The colonel had assumed that the air minister wasn't monitoring telephones in the cafés around Wilhelm Street. Didn't the plenipotentiary know that in this paranoia-soaked district those were the very phones that yielded the most gold? He'd gotten the transcript of the call Ernst had made to Doctor-professor Keitel this morning, urgently requesting a meeting.

What happened in that meeting wasn't important. What was critical was that Göring had learned the good professor's name and had now found out that he had Yid blood in his veins. The consequences of all this? That largely depended on what Göring wished those consequences to be. Keitel, a part-Jew intellectual, would be sent to the camp at Oranienburg. There was no doubt about that. But Ernst? Göring decided it would be better to keep him visible. He'd be ousted from the top ranks of government but retained in some lackey position. Yes, by next week the man would be lucky to be employed scurrying after Defense Minister von Blomberg, carting the bald man's briefcase.

Ebullient now, Göring took several more painkillers, shouted for another plate of spaghetti and rewarded himself for his successful intriguing by turning his attention back to his Olympic party. Wondering: Should he appear in the costume of a German hunter, an Arab sheik, or Robin Hood, complete with a quiver and a bow on his shoulder?

Sometimes it was next to impossible to make up one's mind.

Reggie Morgan was troubled. "I don't have the authority to approve a thousand dollars. Jesus Lord. A *thousand?*"

They were walking through the Tiergarten, past a Stormtrooper on a soapbox sweating fiercely as he hoarsely lectured a small group of people. Some clearly wished to be elsewhere, some looked back with disdain in their eyes. But some were mesmerized. Paul was reminded of Heinsler on the ship.

I love the Führer and I'd do anything for him and the Party. . . .

"The threat worked?" Morgan asked.

"Oh, yes. In fact, I think he respected me more for it."

"And he can actually get us useful information?"

"If anybody can, he's the one. I know his sort. It's astonishing how resourceful some people can be when you wave money toward them."

"Then let's see if we can come up with some."

They left the park and turned south at the Brandenburg Gate. Several blocks farther on they passed the ornate palace that would, when the repairs after the fire were finished, become the U.S. embassy.

"Look at it," Morgan said. "Magnificent, isn't it? Or it will be."

Even though the building wasn't officially the U.S. embassy yet, an American flag hung from the front. The sight stirred Paul, made him feel good, more at ease.

He thought of the Hitler Youth back at the Olympic Village.

And the black . . . the hooked cross. You would say swastika. . . . Ach, surely you know. . . . Surely you know . . .

Morgan turned down an alleyway and then another and, with a look behind them, unlocked the door. They entered the quiet, dark building and walked down several corridors until they came to a small door beside the kitchen. They stepped inside. The dim room was sparse: a desk, several chairs and a large radio, bigger than any Paul had ever seen. Morgan flipped on the unit and as the tubes warmed up it began to hum.

"They listen to all the overseas shortwave," Morgan said, "so we're going to transmit via relays to Amsterdam and then London and then be routed through a phone line to the States. It'll take the Nazis a while to get the frequency," the man said, pulling on earphones, "but they could get lucky so you have to assume they're listening. Everything you say, keep that in mind."

"Sure."

"We'll have to go fast. Ready?"

Paul nodded and took the set of headphones Morgan offered him, then plugged the thick jack into the socket he pointed to. A green light finally came to life on the front of the unit. Morgan stepped to a window, glanced out into the alleyway, let the curtain fall back. He pulled the microphone close to his mouth and pushed the button on the shaft. "I need a transatlantic connection to our friend in the south." He repeated this then released the transmit button and said to Paul, "Bull Gordon's 'our friend in the south.' Washington, you know. 'Our friend in the north' is the Senator."

"Roger that," said a young voice. It was Avery's. "Be a minute. Hold on. Placing the call."

"Howdy," Paul said.

A pause. "Hey there," Avery responded. "How's life treating you?"

"Oh, just swell. Good to hear your voice." Paul couldn't believe that he'd said good-bye to him just yesterday. It seemed like months. "How's your other half?"

"Staying out of trouble."

"That's hard to believe." Paul wondered if Manielli had been mouthing off to any Dutch soldiers the same way he wisecracked in America.

"You're on a speaker here," came Manielli's irritated voice. "Just to let you know."

Paul laughed.

Then staticky silence.

"What time is it in Washington?" Paul asked Morgan.

"Lunchtime."

"It's Saturday. Where's Gordon?"

"We don't have to worry about that. They'll find him."

Through the headset a woman's voice said, "One moment, please. Placing your call."

A moment later Paul heard a phone ring. Then another woman's voice answered, "Yes?"

Morgan said, "Your husband, please. Sorry to trouble you."

"Hold the line." As if she knew not to ask who was calling.

A moment later Gordon asked, "Hello?"

"It's us, sir," Morgan said.

"Go ahead."

"Setback in the arrangements. We've had to approach somebody local for information."

Gordon was silent for a moment. "Who is he? General terms."

Morgan gestured to Paul, who said, "He knows somebody who can get us close to our customer."

Morgan nodded at his choice of words and added, "My supplier has run out of product."

The commander asked, "This man, he works for the other company?"

"No. Works for himself."

"What other options do we have?"

Morgan said, "The only other choice is to sit and wait, hope for the best."

"You trust him?"

After a moment Paul said, "Yes. He's one of us."

"Us?"

"Me," Paul explained. "He's in my line of work. We've, uhm, arranged for a certain level of trust."

"There's money involved?"

Morgan said, "That's why we're calling. He wants a lot. Immediately."

"What's a lot?"

"A thousand. Your currency."

A pause. "That could be a problem."

"We don't have any choice," Paul said. "You've got to make it work."

"We could bring you back from your trip early."

"No, you don't want to do that," Paul said emphatically.

The sound from the radio could have been a wave of static or could have been Bull Gordon's sigh.

"Sit tight. I'll get back to you as soon as I can."

"So what would we get for my money?"

"I don't know the details," Bull Gordon said to Cyrus Adam Clayborn, who was in New York on the other end of the phone. "They couldn't go into it. Worried about eavesdropping, you know. But apparently the Nazis have cut off access to information Schumann needs to find Ernst. That's my take."

Clayborn grunted.

Gordon found himself surprisingly at ease, considering that the man he was speaking to was the fourth- or fifth-richest human being in the country. (He had ranked number two but the stock market crash had pulled him down a couple of notches.) They were very different men but they shared two vital characteristics: they had military in their blood and they were both patriots. That made up for a lot of distance in income and station.

"A thousand? Cash?"

"Yes, sir."

"I like that Schumann. That was pretty sharp, his reelection comment. FDR's scared as a rabbit." Clayborn chuckled. "Thought the Senator was going to crap right there."

"Looked like it."

"Okay. I'll arrange the funds."

"Thank you, sir."

Clayborn preempted Gordon's next question. "'Course, it's late Saturday in Hun-ville. And he needs the money now, right?"

"That's right."

"Hold on."

Three long minutes later the magnate came back on the line.

"Have 'em go to the clerk at the usual pickup spot in Berlin. Morgan'll know it. The Maritime Bank of the Americas. Number eighty-eight Udder den Linden Street, or however the hell you say it. I can never get it right."

"*Unter den Linden.* It means 'Under the Linden Trees.'"

"Fine, fine. The guard'll have the package."

"Thanks, sir."

"Bull?"

"Yes, sir?"

"We don't have enough heroes in this country. I want that boy to come home in one piece. Considering our resources . . ." Men like Clayborn would never say, "my money." The businessman continued. "Considering our resources, what can we do to improve the odds?"

Gordon considered the question. Only one thing came to mind.

"Pray," he said and pressed down the cradle on the phone then paused for a moment and lifted it once more.

Chapter Seventeen

Inspector Willi Kohl sat at his desk in the gloomy Alex, attempting to understand the inexplicable, a game played nowhere more often than in the halls of police departments everywhere.

He had always been a curious man by nature, intrigued, say, by how the blend of simple charcoal, sulfur and nitrate produced gunpowder, how undersea boats worked, why birds clustered together on particular parts of telegraph lines, what occurred within human hearts to whip otherwise rational citizens into a frenzy when some weasely National Socialist spoke at a rally.

His mind was presently preoccupied with the question of what sort of man could take another's life? And why?

And, of course, "Who?" as he now whispered aloud, thinking of the drawing done by the street artist at November 1923 Square. Janssen was now having it too printed up downstairs, as they'd done with the photo of the victim. It wasn't a bad sketch by any means, Kohl reflected. There were some erasures from the false starts and corrections but the face was distinctive: a handsome square jaw, thick neck, hair a bit wavy, a scar on the chin and a sticking plaster on his cheek.

"Who are you?" he whispered.

Willi Kohl knew the facts: the man's size and age and hair color and probable nationality, even his likely city of residence. But he'd learned in his years as an investigator that to find certain criminals, you needed far more than details like this. To truly understand them, something more was required, intuitive insights. This was one of Kohl's greatest talents. His mind made connections and leaps that occasionally startled even himself. But now, none of these was forthcoming. Something about this case was out of balance.

He sat back in his chair, examining his notes as he sucked on his hot pipe (one advantage of being with the ostracized Kripo was that Hitler's disdain for smoking did not reach here, to these unhallowed halls). He shot smoke toward the ceiling and sighed.

The results from his earlier requests had not been forthcoming. The laboratory technician had not been able to find any fingerprints on the Olympic guidebook that they'd found at the scene of the brawl with the Stormtroopers, and the FPE (yes, Kohl noted angrily, still only one examiner) hadn't found matches for the prints from Dresden Alley. And still nothing from the coroner. How the hell long does it take to cut a man open, to analyze his blood?

Of the dozens of missing persons reports that had flooded into the Kripo today, none matched the description of the man who was certainly a son and maybe a father, maybe a husband, maybe a lover. . . .

Some telegrams had arrived from precincts around Berlin, reporting the names of those who'd bought Spanish Star Modelo A pistols or Largo ammunition in the past year. But the list was woefully incomplete and Kohl was discouraged to learn that he'd been wrong; the murder weapon was not as rare as he'd thought. Perhaps because of the close connection between Germany and Franco's Nationalist forces in Spain, many of these powerful and efficient guns had been sold here. The list as of the moment totaled fifty-six people in Berlin and environs, and a number of gun shops remained to be polled. Officers had also reported that some shops kept no records or were closed for the weekend.

Besides, if the man had come to town only yesterday, as it now seemed, he most likely hadn't bought the gun himself. (Though the list might yet prove valuable: The killer could have stolen the gun, taken it from the victim himself or gotten it from a comrade who had been in Berlin for some time.)

Understanding the inexplicable . . .

Still hoping for the passenger manifest for the *Manhattan,* Kohl had sent telegrams to port officials in Hamburg and to the United States Lines, the owner and operator of the vessel, requesting a copy of the document. But Kohl wasn't optimistic; he wasn't even sure if the port master *had* a copy. As for the ship line itself, they would have to locate the document, create a copy and then post or Teletype it to Kripo headquarters; that could take days. In any event, there'd so far been no response to these requests.

He had even sent a telegram to Manny's Men's Wear in New York, asking about recent purchasers of Stetson Mity-Lites. This plea too was presently unanswered.

He glanced impatiently at the brass clock on his desk. It was getting late and he was starving. Kohl wished either for a break in the case or to return home for dinner with his family.

Konrad Janssen stepped into his doorway. "I have them, sir."

He held up a printed sheet of the street artist's rendering, fragrant with the scent of ink.

"Good . . . Now, sadly, Janssen, you have one more task tonight."

"Yes, sir, whatever I can do."

One further quality of serious Janssen was that he had no aversion to working hard.

"You will take the DKW and return to the Olympic Village. Show the artist's picture to everyone you can find, American or otherwise, and see if anybody recognizes him. Leave some copies along with our telephone number. If you have no luck there, take some copies to the Lützow Plaza precinct. If they happen to find the suspect tell them to detain him as a witness only and to call me at once. Even at home."

"Yes, sir."

"Thank you, Janssen. . . . Wait, this is your first murder investigation, is it not?"

"Yes, sir."

"Ah, you never forget the first one. You're doing well."

"I appreciate that, sir."

Kohl gave him the keys to the DKW. "A delicate hand on the choke. She likes air as much as petrol. Perhaps more."

"Yes, sir."

"I'll be at home. Telephone me with any developments."

After the young man had gone Kohl unlaced and removed his shoes. He opened his desk drawer, extracted a box of lamb's wool and wound several pieces around his toes to cushion the sensitive areas. He placed a few strategic wads in his shoes themselves and, wincing, slipped his feet back inside.

He glanced past the picture of the suspect to the grim photographs of the murders in Gatow and Charlottenburg. He'd heard nothing more about the report from the crime scene or interviews of any witnesses. He supposed that his fiction about the Kosi conspiracy he'd pitched to Chief of Inspectors Horcher had had no effect.

Gazing at the pictures: a dead boy, a woman trying to grasp the leg of a man lying just out of reach, a worker clutching his worn shovel . . . Heart-breaking. He stared for some moments. He knew it was dangerous to pursue the case. Certainly dangerous for his career, if not his life. And yet he had no choice.

Why? he wondered. Why this compulsion he invariably felt to close a murder case?

Willi Kohl supposed it was that, ironically, in death he found his sanity. Or, more accurately, in the process of bringing to justice those who caused death. This was his purpose on earth, he felt, and to ignore any killing—of a fat man in an alley or a family of Jews—was to ignore his nature and was therefore a sin.

The inspector now put the photographs away. Taking his hat, he stepped into the hallway of the old building and proceeded down the length of Prussian tile and stone and wood worn down over the years but nonetheless spotlessly clean and polished to a shine. He walked through shafts of low, rosy sun, which was the main source of illumination at headquarters this time of year; the grande dame of Berlin had become a spendthrift under the National Socialists ("Guns before butter," Göring proclaimed over and over and over), and the building's engineers did all they could to conserve resources.

Since he'd given his car to Janssen and would have to take a tram home, Kohl continued down two flights to a back door of headquarters, a shortcut to the stop.

At the bottom of the stairs signs pointed the way to the Kripo's holding cells, to the left, and to the old-case archives straight ahead. It was in this latter direction that he headed, recalling spending time there in his days as a detective-inspector assistant, reading the files not only to learn what he could from the great Prussian detectives of the past but simply because he enjoyed seeing the history of Berlin as told through its law enforcers.

His daughter's fiancé, Heinrich, was a civil servant but his passion was police work. Kohl decided he would bring the young man here sometime and they could browse through the files together. The inspector might even show him some of the cases Kohl himself had worked on years ago.

But, as he pushed through the doorway, he stopped fast; the archives were gone. Kohl was startled to find himself in a brilliantly lit corridor in which stood six armed men. They were not, however, in the green uniforms of the Schupo; they wore SS black. Almost as one, they turned toward him.

"Good evening, sir," one said, the closest to him. A lean man with an astonishingly long face. He eyed Kohl carefully. "You are . . . ?"

"Detective Inspector Kohl. And who are you?"

"If you're looking for the archives they are now on the second floor."

"No. I'm simply using the rear exit door." Kohl started forward. The SS trooper took a subtle step toward him. "I'm sorry to report that it is no longer in use."

"I didn't hear about that."

"No? Well, it has been the case for the past several days. You will have to go back upstairs."

Kohl heard a curious sound. What was it? A mechanical *clap, clap* . . .

A burst of sunlight filled the hallway as two SS men opened the far door and wheeled in dollies holding cartons. They turned into one of the rooms at the end of the corridor.

He said to the guard, "That door is the one I'm speaking of. It appears to be in use."

"Not in *general* use."

The sounds . . .

Clap, clap, clap and, beneath it, the rumbling of a motor or engine . . .

He glanced to his right, through a partially open doorway, where he glimpsed several large mechanical devices. A woman in a white coat was feeding stacks of paper into one of them. This must be part of the Kripo's printing department. But then he observed that, no, they weren't sheets of paper but cards with holes punched in them and they were being sorted by the device.

Ah, Kohl understood. An old mystery had been answered. Some time ago he'd heard that the government was leasing large calculating and sorting machines, called DeHoMags, after the firm that made them, the German subsidiary of the American company International Business Machines. These devices used punched cards to analyze and cross-reference information. Kohl had been delighted when he'd learned of the leases. The machines could be invaluable in criminal investigations; they might narrow down fingerprint categories or ballistics information a hundred times faster than a technician could by hand. They could also cross-reference modus operandi to link criminal and crime and could keep track of parolees or recidivist offenders.

The inspector's enthusiasm soon soured, though, when he learned that the devices were not available for use by the Kripo. He'd wondered who'd gotten them and where they were. But now, to his shock, it seemed that at least two or three were less than a hundred meters from his office and guarded by the SS.

What was their purpose?

He asked the guard.

"I couldn't tell you, sir," the man replied in a brittle voice. "I have not been informed."

From inside the room the woman in white looked out. Her hands paused and she spoke to someone. Kohl couldn't hear what was said, nor see the person she was speaking to. The door slowly swung shut as if by magic.

The guard with the vertical face stepped past Kohl and opened the door that led back up the stairs. "Again, Inspector, as I said, there is no exit here. You will find another door up one flight and—"

"I'm familiar with the building," Kohl said testily and returned to the stairs.

"I brought you something," he said.

Standing in Paul's living room in the Magdeburger Alley boardinghouse, Käthe Richter took the small package with a curious look: cautious awe, as if it had been years since anyone had given her a present. She rubbed her thumbs on the brown paper covering what Otto Webber had located for him.

"Oh." She uttered a faint exhalation as she looked at the leather-bound book on whose jacket was stamped *Collected Poems of Johann Wolfgang von Goethe*.

"My friend said it's not illegal but it's not legal either. That means it will soon be illegal."

"Limbo," she said, nodding. "It was the same with American jazz here for a time, which is now forbidden." Continuing to smile, Käthe turned the volume over and over in her hands.

He said, "I didn't know his names run in my family."

She glanced up with a quizzical look on her face.

"My grandfather was Wolfgang. My father was Johann."

Käthe smiled at the coincidence and flipped through the book.

"I was wondering," he said. "If you're not busy, perhaps some dinner."

Her face went still. "As I told you, I am able to serve only breakfast, not—"

He laughed. "No, no. I want to take you out to dinner. Perhaps see some sights in Berlin."

"You want to . . ."

"I would like to take you out."

"I . . . No, no, I couldn't."

"Oh, you have a friend, a husband. . . ." He'd glanced at her hand and seen no rings but he wasn't sure how one declared commitment in Germany. "Please, ask him to come too."

Käthe was at a loss for words. Finally she said, "No, no, there is no one. But—"

Paul said firmly, "No 'but's. I'm not in Berlin for very long. I could use somebody to show me around town." He gave her a smile. In English: "I'll tell you, miss, I ain't taking no for an answer."

"I don't understand 'ain't,'" she said. "But I have not been to a restaurant for a long time. Perhaps such an evening could be enjoyable."

Paul frowned. "You've got the English wrong."

"Oh, what should it be?" she asked.

"The proper word is 'will' be enjoyable, not 'could.'"

She gave a faint laugh and agreed to meet him in a half hour. She returned to her room, while Paul showered and changed.

Thirty minutes later, a knock on the door. When he opened it he blinked. She was an entirely different person.

Käthe was wearing a black dress that would have satisfied even fashion goddess Marion in Manhattan. Close fitting, made from a shimmery material, a daring slit up the side and tiny sleeves that barely covered her shoulders. The garment smelled faintly of mothballs. She seemed slightly ill at ease, embarrassed almost to be wearing such a stylish gown, as if all she'd worn recently were housedresses. But her eyes shone and he had the same thought as earlier: how a subdued beauty and passion radiated from within her, wholly negating the matte skin and the bony knuckles and pale complexion, the furrowed brow.

As for Paul, his hair was still dark with lotion but was now combed differently. (And when they went out, it would be hidden by a hat very different from his brown Stetson: a dark, broad-brimmed trilby he'd purchased that afternoon after leaving Morgan.) He was wearing a navy blue linen double-breasted suit and a silver tie over his white Arrow shirt. At the department store where he'd bought the hat he'd also picked up more makeup to cover the bruise and cut. He'd discarded the sticking plaster.

Käthe picked up the book of poems, which she'd left in his room to go change, and flipped through the pages. "This is one of my favorites. It's called 'Proximity of the Beloved One.'" She read it aloud.

I think of you when upon the sea the sun flings her beams.
    I think of you when the moonlight shines in silvery streams.
I see you when upon the distant hills the dust awakes;
At night when on a fragile bridge the traveler quakes.

I hear you when the billows rise on high,
    With murmur deep.
To tread the silent grove where wander I,
    When all's asleep.

She read in a low voice and Paul could picture her up in front of a class-room, her students spellbound by her obvious love of the words.

Käthe laughed and looked up with bright eyes. "This is very kind of you." She then took the book in both strong hands and ripped the leather binding off. This part she threw into the trash bin.

He stared at her, frowning.

She smiled sadly. "I will keep the poems but should dispose of the portion that shows most obviously the title and the poet's name. That way a visitor or guest will not accidentally see who wrote it and won't be tempted to turn me in. What a time we live in! And I will leave it in your room for now. Best not to carry some things with you on the streets, even a naked book. Now, let's go out!" she said with girlish excitement. She switched to English as she said, "I want to do the town. That is what you say, is it not?"

"Yep. Do the town. Where do you want to go? . . . But I've got two requirements."

"Please?"

"First, I'm hungry and I eat a lot. And, second, I'd like to see your famous Wilhelm Street."

Her face again went still for a moment. "Ach, the seat of our government."

He supposed that, being someone persecuted by the National Socialists, she would not enjoy that particular sight. Yet he needed to find the best location for touching off Ernst, and he knew that a man by himself was always far more suspicious than one with a woman on his arm. This had been Reggie Morgan's second mission today—not only had he looked into Otto Webber's past but he'd gotten the wire on Käthe Richter too. She had indeed been fired from a teaching job and had been marked down as an intellectual and a pacifist. There was no evidence that she'd ever informed for the National Socialists.

Now, watching her gaze at the poetry book, he felt pangs of guilt about employing her in this way, but he consoled himself with the thought that she was no fan of the Nazis, and by helping him in this unwitting way she'd be doing her part to stop the war Hitler was planning.

She said, "Yes, of course. I will show you. And for your first requirement I have just the restaurant in mind. You will like it." She added with a mysterious smile, "It's just the place for people like you and me."

You and me . . .

He wondered what she meant.

They walked out into the warm evening. He was amused to note that as they took the first step toward the sidewalk both their heads swiveled from side to side, looking to see if anyone was watching.

As they walked, they spoke about the neighborhood, the weather, the shortages, the Inflation. About her family: Her parents had passed away and she had one sister, who lived in nearby Spandau with her husband and four children. She asked him about his life too, but the cautious button man gave vague answers and continually steered the conversation back to her.

Wilhelm Street was too far to walk to, she explained. Paul knew this, recalling the map. He was still cautious about taxis but, as it turned out, none was available; this was the weekend before the Olympics began and people were pouring into town. Käthe suggested a double-decker bus. They climbed aboard the vehicle and walked up to the top deck, where they sat close together on the spotless leather seat. Paul looked around carefully but could see no one paying particular attention to them (though he half-expected to see the two policemen who'd been tracking him all day, the heavy cop in the off-white suit, the lean one in green).

The bus swayed as they drove through the Brandenburg Gate, narrowly missing the stone sides, and many of the passengers gave a gasp of humorous alarm, like on the roller coaster at Coney Island; he supposed the reaction was a Berlin tradition.

Käthe pulled the rope and they disembarked on Under the Lindens at Wilhelm Street, then walked south along the wide avenue that was the center of the Nazi government. It was nondescript, with monolithic gray office buildings on either side. Clean and antiseptic, the street exuded an unsettling power. Paul had seen pictures of the White House and Congress. They seemed picturesque and amiable. Here the facades and tiny windows of the rows upon rows of stone and concrete buildings were forbidding.

And, more to the point tonight, they were heavily guarded. He'd never seen such security.

"Where's the Chancellory?" he asked.

"There." Käthe pointed toward an old, ornate building with a scaffolding covering much of the front.

Paul was discouraged. His quick eyes took in the place. Armed guards in front. Dozens of SS and what appeared to be regular soldiers were patrolling the street, stopping people and asking for papers. On the tops of the buildings were other troops, armed with guns. There must have been a hundred uniformed men nearby. It would be virtually impossible to find a shooting position. And even if he were able to, there was no doubt that he'd be captured or killed trying to get away.

He slowed. "I think I've seen enough." He eyed several large, black-uniformed men demanding papers from two men on the sidewalk.

"Not as picturesque as you'd expected?" She laughed and started to say something—perhaps "I told you so," but then thought better of it. "If you have more time, don't worry; I can show you many parts of our city that are quite beautiful. Now, shall we go to dinner?" she asked.

"Yes, let's."

She directed him back to a tram stop on Under the Lindens. They got aboard and rode for a brief while then climbed off at her direction.

Käthe asked what he'd thought of Berlin so far in his short time here. Paul again gave some innocuous answers and turned the conversation back to her. He asked, "Are you going with anyone?"

"'Going'?"

He'd translated literally. "I mean romantically involved."

Straightforward, she answered, "Most recently I had a lover. We no longer are together. But he still owns much of my heart."

"What does he do?" he asked.

"A reporter. Like you."

"I'm not really a reporter. I write stories and hope to sell them. Human interest, we'd say."

"And you write about politics?"

"Politics? No. Sports."

"Sports." Her voice was dismissive.

"You don't like sports?"

"I am sorry to say I dislike sports."

"Why?"

"Because there are so many important questions facing us, not just here, but everywhere in the world. Sports are . . . well, they're frivolous."

Paul replied, "So is strolling down the streets of Berlin on a nice summer evening. But we're doing it."

"Ach," Käthe said testily. "The sole point of education in Germany now is to build strong bodies, not minds. Our boys, they play war games, they march everywhere. Did you hear we've started conscription?"

Paul recalled that Bull Gordon had described the new German military draft to him. But he said, "No."

"One out of three boys fails because they have flat feet from all the marching they do at school. It's a disgrace."

"Well, you can overdo anything," he pointed out. "I enjoy sports."

"Yes, you seem athletic. Do you body-build?"

"Some. Mostly I box."

"Box? You mean the sort where you hit other people?"

He laughed. "That's the only kind of boxing there is."

"Barbaric."

"It can be—if you let your guard down."

"You joke," she said. "But how can you encourage people to strike each other?"

"I couldn't really tell you. But I like it. It's fun."

"Fun," she scoffed.

"Yeah, fun," he said, growing angry too. "Life's hard. Sometimes you need to hold on to something fun, when the rest of the world is turning to shit around you. . . . Why don't you go to a boxing match sometime? Go see Max Schmeling. Drink some beer, yell till you're hoarse. You might enjoy it."

"*Kakfif*," she said bluntly.

"What?"

"*Kakfif*," Käthe repeated. "It's a shortening for 'Completely out of the question.'"

"Suit yourself."

She was silent for a moment. Then she said, "I'm a pacifist, as I was telling you today. All my friends in Berlin are pacifists. We don't combine the idea of fun with hurting people."

"I don't walk around like a Stormtrooper and beat up the innocent. The guys I spar with? They want to do it."

"You encourage causing pain."

"No, I *discourage* people from hitting me. That's what sparring is."

"Like children," she muttered. "You're like children."

"You don't understand."

"And why do you say that? Because I'm a woman?" she snapped.

"Maybe. Yeah, maybe that's it."

"I'm not stupid."

"I'm not talking about intelligence. I only mean that women aren't inclined to fight."

"We aren't inclined to be the *aggressor.* We will fight to protect our homes."

"Sometimes the wolf isn't *in* your home. Don't you go out and kill him first?"

"No."

"You ignore him and hope he goes away?"

"Yes. Exactly. And you teach him he doesn't need to be destructive."

"That's ridiculous," Paul said. "You can't talk a wolf into being a sheep."

"But I think you can if you wish to," she said. "And if you work hard at it. Too many men don't want that, however. They *want* to fight. They *want* to destroy because it gives them pleasure." Dense silence between them for a long moment. Then, her voice softening, she said, "Ach, Paul, please forgive me. Here you are, being my companion, doing the town with me. Which I haven't done for so many months. And I repay you by being like a shrew. Are American women shrews like me?"

"Some are, some aren't. Not that you *are* one."

"I'm a difficult person to be with. You have to understand, Paul—many women in Berlin are this way. We have to be. After the War there were no men left in the country. We had to become men and be as hard as they. I apologize."

"Don't. I enjoy arguing. It's just another way of sparring."

"Ach, sparring! And me a pacifist!" She gave a girlish laugh.

"What would your friends say?"

"What indeed?" she said and took his arm as they crossed the street.

Chapter Eighteen

Even though he was a "lukewarm"—politically neutral, not a member of the Party—Willi Kohl enjoyed certain privileges reserved for devout National Socialists.

One of these was that when a senior Kripo official had moved to Munich, Kohl had been offered the chance to take his large four-bedroom apartment in a pristine, linden-lined cul-de-sac off Berliner Street near Charlottenburg. Berlin had had a serious housing shortage since the War and most Kripo inspectors, even many at his level, were relegated to boxy, nondescript folk-apartments, thrown together in boxy, nondescript neighborhoods.

Kohl wasn't quite sure why he'd been so rewarded. Most likely because he was always ready to help fellow officers analyze crime scene information, make deductions from the evidence or interview a witness or suspect. Kohl knew that the most invaluable man in any job is the one who can make his colleagues—and superiors especially—appear invaluable as well.

These rooms were his sanctuary. They were as private as his workplace was public and were populated by those closest to his heart: his wife and children and, on occasion (sleeping always in the parlor, of course), Charlotte's fiancé, Heinrich.

The apartment was on the second floor and as he walked, wincing, up the stairs, he could make out the smells of onions and meat. Heidi kept to no schedule in preparing her food. Some of Kohl's colleagues would solemnly declare Saturdays, Mondays and Wednesdays, for instance, to be State Loyalty Meat-free Days. The Kohl household, at least seven strong, went without meat often, owing to scarcity as well as cost, but Heidi refused to be bound by a ritual. This Saturday night they might have aubergine with bacon in cream sauce or kidney pudding or sauerbraten or even an Italian-style dish of pasta with tomatoes. Always a sweet, of course. Willi Kohl liked his linzertorte and strudel.

Wheezing from the walk up the stairs, he opened the door just as eleven-year-old Hanna raced to him. Every inch the little blonde Nordic maid, despite her parents' brown hair, she wrapped her arms around the large man. "Papa! Can I carry your pipe for you?"

He fished out the meerschaum for her. She carried it to the rack in the den where dozens of others sat.

"I'm home," he called.

Heidi stepped into the doorway and kissed her husband on both cheeks. A few years younger than he, she'd become round over the course of their marriage, developing a smooth extra chin and huge bosom, adding pounds with each child. But this was as it should be; Kohl felt you should grow both in soul and in girth with your partner. Five children had earned her a certificate from the Party. (Women with more offspring had higher accolades; producing nine children won you a gold star. Indeed, a couple with fewer than four offspring were not allowed to call themselves a "family.") But Heidi had angrily stuffed the parchment into the bottom of her bureau. She had children because she enjoyed them, enjoyed everything about them—giving them life, raising them, directing their course—not because the Little Man wished to swell the population of his Third Empire.

His wife vanished then returned a moment later, bearing a snifter of schnapps. She let him have only one glass of the potent drink before dinner. He grumbled about the rationing occasionally but he secretly welcomed it. He knew far too many policemen who didn't stop with the second glass. Or second bottle.

He said hello to Hilde, his seventeen-year-old, lost as always in a book. She rose and hugged him and then returned to the divan. The willowy girl was the family scholar. But she'd been having a difficult time lately. Goebbels himself said that a woman's sole purpose was to be beautiful and populate the Third Empire. The universities were largely closed to girls now, and those admitted were limited to two courses of study: domestic science (which earned what was contemptuously called the "pudding degree") or education. Hilde, however, wished to study mathematics and science and ultimately become a university professor. But she would be allowed to teach only lower grades. Kohl believed both of his older daughters were equally smart but learning came more easily to Hilde than to vivacious and athletic Charlotte, four years older. He was often amazed at how he and Heidi had produced such similar and yet vastly different human beings.

The inspector walked out onto his small balcony, where he would sometimes sit and smoke his pipe late at night. It faced west and now he gazed at the fierce red-and-orange clouds, lit by the vanished sun. He took a small sip of the harsh schnapps. The second was kinder and he sat down comfortably in his chair, trying hard not to think about fat, dead men, about the tragic deaths in Gatow and Charlottenburg, about Pietr—forgive me, Peter—Krauss, about the mysterious churning of the DeHoMags in the basement of the Kripo. Trying not to think about their clever Manny's New York suspect.

Who are you?

A clamor from the front hall. The boys were returning. Feet thudded powerfully on the stairs. Younger Herman was first through the doorway, swinging it shut on Günter, who blocked the door and started for a tackle. They then noticed their father, and the wrestling match ceased.

"Papa!" Herman cried and hugged his father. Günter lifted his head in greeting. The sixteen-year-old had stopped hugging his parents exactly eighteen months ago. Kohl supposed sons had behaved according to that schedule since the days of Otto I, if not forever.

"You will wash before dinner," Heidi called.

"But we swam. We went to the Wilhelm Marr Street pool."

"Then," their father added, "you will wash the swimming water off of you."

"What are we having for supper, Mutti?" Herman asked.

"The sooner you bathe," she announced, "the sooner you'll find out."

They charged off down the corridor, teenage-calamity-in-motion.

A few moments later Heinrich arrived with Charlotte. Kohl liked the fellow (he would never have let a daughter marry someone he did not respect). But the handsome blond man's fascination with police matters prompted him to query Kohl enthusiastically and at length about recent cases. Normally the inspector enjoyed this but the last thing he wanted tonight was to talk about his day. Kohl brought up the Olympics—a sure conversation deflector. Everyone had heard different rumors about the teams, favorite athletes, the many nations represented.

Soon they were seated at the table in the dining room. Kohl opened two bottles of Saar-Ruwer wine and poured some for everyone, including small amounts for the children. The conversation, as always in the Kohl household, went in many different directions. This was one of the inspector's favorite times of the day. Being with those you loved . . . and being able to speak freely. As they talked and laughed and argued, Kohl looked from face to face. His eyes were quick, listening to voices, observing gestures and expressions. One might think he did this automatically because of his years as a policeman. But in fact, no. He made his observations and drew his conclusions because this was an aspect of parenthood. Tonight he noted one thing that troubled him but filed it away in his mind, the way he might a key clue from a crime scene.

Dinner was over relatively early, in about an hour; the heat had dampened everyone's appetite, except Kohl's and his sons'. Heinrich suggested card games. But Kohl shook his head. "Not for me. I will smoke," he announced. "And soak my feet, I think. Please, Günter, you will bring a kettle of hot water."

"Yes, Father."

Kohl fetched his foot-soaking pan and the salts. He dropped into his leather chair in the den, the very chair his father had sat in after a long day working in the fields, charged a pipe and lit it. A few minutes later his oldest son walked into the room, easily carrying the steaming kettle, which must have weighed ten kilos, in one hand. He filled the basin. Kohl rolled up his cuffs, removed his socks and, avoiding looking at the gnarled bunions and yellow calluses, eased his feet into the hot water and poured in some salts.

"Ach, yes."

The boy turned to go but Kohl said, "Günter, wait a moment."

"Yes, Father."

"Sit down."

The boy did, cautious, and set the kettle on the floor. In his eyes was a flash of adolescent guilt. Kohl wondered, with amusement, what transgressions were fluttering through his son's mind. A cigarette, a bit of schnapps, some fumbling exploration of young Lisa Wagner's undergarments?

"Günter, what is the matter? Something was bothering you at dinner. I could see it."

"Nothing, Father."

"Nothing?"

"No."

In a soft but firm voice Willi Kohl now said, "You will tell me."

The boy examined the floor. Finally he said, "School will start soon."

"Not for a month."

"Still . . . I was hoping, Father. Can I be transferred to a different one?"

"But why? The Hindenburg School is one of the best in the city. Head-master Muntz is very respected."

"Please."

"What's wrong with it?"

"I don't know. I just dislike it."

"Your grades are good. Your teachers say you are a fine student."

The boy said nothing.

"Is it something other than your lessons?"

"I don't know."

What could it be?

Günter shrugged. "Please, can't I just go to a different school until December?"

"Why then?"

The boy wouldn't answer and avoided his father's eyes.

"Tell me," Kohl said kindly.

"Because . . ."

"Go on."

"Because in December everyone must join the Hitler Youth. And now . . . well, you won't let me."

Ah, this again. A recurring problem. But was this new information true? Would Hitler Youth be mandatory? A frightening thought. After the National Socialists came to power they folded all of Germany's many youth groups into the Hitler Youth and the others were outlawed. Kohl believed in children's organizations—he'd been in swimming and hiking clubs in his teen years and loved them—but the Hitler Youth was nothing more than a pre-army military training organization, manned and operated, no less, by the youngsters themselves, and the more rabidly National Socialist the junior leaders, the better.

"And now you wish to join?"

"I don't know. Everyone makes fun of me because I'm not a member. At the football game today, Helmut Gruber was there. He's our Hitler Youth leader. He said I better join soon."

"But you can't be the only one who isn't a member."

"More join every day," Günter replied. "Those of us who aren't mem-bers are all treated badly. When we play Aryans and Jews in the school yard, I'm always a Jew."

"*What* do you play?" Kohl frowned. He had never heard of this.

"You know, Father, the game Aryans and Jews. They chase us. They aren't supposed to hurt us—Doctor-professor Klindst says they aren't. It's supposed to be tag only. But when he isn't looking they push us down."

"You're a strong boy and I've taught you how to defend yourself. Do you push them back?"

"Sometimes, yes. But there are many more who play the Aryans."

"Well, I'm afraid you can't go to another school," Kohl said.

Günter looked at the cloud of pipe smoke rising to the ceiling. His eyes brightened. "Maybe I could denounce someone. Maybe then they'd let me play on the Aryan side."

Kohl frowned. Denunciation: another National Socialist plague. He said firmly to his son, "You will denounce no one. They would go to jail. They could be tortured. Or killed."

Günter frowned at his father's reaction. "But I would only denounce a Jew, Father."

His hands trembling, heart pounding, Kohl was at a loss for words. Forcing himself to be calm, he finally asked, "You would denounce a Jew for no reason?"

His son seemed confused. "Of course not. I would denounce him because he *is* a Jew. I was thinking . . . Helen Morrell's father works at Karstadt department store. His boss is a Jew but he tells everyone he's not. He *should* be denounced."

Kohl took a deep breath and, weighing his words like a rationing butcher, said, "Son, we live in a very difficult time now. It is very confusing. It's confusing to me and it must be far more confusing to you. The one thing that you must always remember—but never must say out loud—is that a man decides for himself what is right and wrong. He knows this from what he sees about life, about how people live and act together, how he feels. He knows in his heart what is good and bad."

"But Jews *are* bad. They wouldn't teach us that in school if it weren't true."

Kohl's soul shivered in rage and pain to hear this. "You will not denounce anyone, Günter," he said sternly. "That is my wish."

"All right, Father," the boy said, walking away.

"Günter," Kohl said.

The boy paused at the door.

"How many in your school have not joined the Youth?"

"I can't say, Father. But more join every day. Soon there won't be anyone left to play the Jew but me."

The restaurant that Käthe had in mind was the Lutter and Wegner wine bar, which, she explained, was well over a hundred years old and an institution in Berlin. The rooms were dark, smoky and intimate. And the place was devoid of Brownshirts, SS and suited men wearing red armbands with the hooked, surely-you-know cross.

"I brought you here because, as I said, it used to be the haunt of people like you and me."

"You and me?"

"Yes. Bohemians. Pacifists, thinkers, and, like you, writers."

"Ah, writers. Yes."

"E.T.A. Hoffmann would find inspiration here. He drank copious champagne, whole bottles of it! And would then write all night. You've read him, of course."

Paul hadn't. He nodded yes.

"Can you think of a better writer of the German romantic era? I can't. *The Nutcracker and the Mouse King*—so much darker and more real than what Tchaikovsky did with it. That ballet is pure puff, don't you think?"

"Definitely," Paul agreed. He thought he'd seen it one Christmas as a boy. He wished he'd read the book so he could discuss it intelligently. How he enjoyed simply talking with her. As they sipped their cocktails, he reflected on the "sparring" he'd done with Käthe on the walk here. He'd meant what he'd said about arguing with her. It was exhilarating. He didn't think he'd had a disagreement with Marion in all the months they'd gone out. He couldn't even remember her getting angry. Sometimes a new stocking would run and she'd let go with a "darn" or "damnation." Then she'd press her fingers to her mouth, like the prelude to blowing someone a kiss—and apologize for cussing.

The waiter brought menus and they ordered: pig knuckles and spaetzle and cabbage and bread ("Ach, real butter!" she whispered in astonishment, staring at the tiny yellow rectangles). To drink, she ordered a sweet, golden wine. They ate leisurely, talking and laughing the whole time. After they'd finished, Paul lit a cigarette. He noticed she seemed to be debating. As if speaking to her students she said, "We have been too serious today. I will tell a joke." Her voice fell to a whisper. "Do you know Hermann Göring?"

"Some official in the government?"

"Yes, yes. He is Hitler's closest comrade. He's an odd man. Very obese. And he parades around in ridiculous costumes in the company of celebrities and beautiful women. Well, he finally got married last year."

"Is that the joke?"

"Not yet, no. He really did get married. *This* is the joke." Käthe gave an exaggerated pout. "Did you hear about Göring's wife? The poor thing's given up religion. You must ask me why."

"Please, tell me: Why has Göring's wife given up religion?"

"Because after their wedding night she lost her belief in the resurrection of the flesh."

They both laughed hard. He saw that she was blushing crimson. "Ach, my, Paul. I've told a naughty joke to a man I don't know. And one that could land us in jail."

"Not *us*," he said, straight-faced. "Only you. *I* didn't tell it."

"Oh, even *laughing* at a joke like that will get you arrested."

He paid the bill and they left, forgoing the tram and returning to the boardinghouse on foot, along the sidewalk that skirted the south boundary of the Tiergarten.

Paul was tipsy from the wine, which he rarely drank. The sensation was nice, better than a corn whisky zing. The warm breeze felt good. So did the pressure of Käthe's arm through his.

As they walked, they spoke of books and politics, arguing some, laughing some, an unlikely couple maneuvering through the streets of this immaculate city.

Paul heard voices, men coming their way. About a hundred feet ahead he saw three Stormtroopers. They were boisterous, joking. In their brown uniforms, with their youthful faces, they resembled happy schoolboys. Unlike the belligerent thugs he'd taken on earlier in the day, this trio seemed bent only on enjoying the fine night. They paid no attention to anyone on the street.

Paul felt Käthe slowing. He looked down at her. Her face was a mask and her arm began to tremble.

"What's the matter?"

"I don't wish to pass them."

"You don't have anything to worry about."

She looked to the left, panicked. The traffic on the street was busy and they were some blocks from a pedestrian crossing. To avoid the Brownshirts they had only one choice: the Tiergarten.

He said, "Really, you're safe. There's no need to worry."

"I can feel your arm, Paul. I can feel you ready to fight them."

"That's why you're safe."

"No." She looked at the gate that led into the park. "This way."

They turned into the park. The thick foliage cut out much of the sound of the traffic, and soon the *creek-creek* of insects and the baritone call of frogs from the ponds filled the night. The Stormtroopers continued along the sidewalk, ignoring everything but their ebullient conversation and their singing. They passed by without even glancing into the park. Still, Käthe kept her head down. Her stiff gait reminded Paul of the way he'd walked after breaking a rib in a sparring session.

"Are you all right?" he asked.

Silence.

She looked around, shivering.

"Are you afraid here?" he asked. "Do you want to leave?"

Still, she said nothing. They came to an intersection of sidewalks, one of which would take them to the left, south, out of the park and back to the boardinghouse. She stopped. After a moment she said, "Come. This way." Turning, Käthe led him farther into the park, north, along winding paths. They finally came to a small boathouse on a pond. Dozens of for-hire boats rested upside down, nestled against one another. Now, in the hot night, the area was deserted.

"I haven't been inside the Tiergarten for three years," she whispered.

Paul said nothing.

At last she continued. "That man who has my heart?"

"Yes. Your journalist friend."

"Michael Klein. He was a reporter for the *Munich Post*. Hitler got his start in Munich. Michael covered his rise and wrote much about him, about his tactics—the intimidation, the beatings, the murders. Michael kept a running count of the unsolved murders of people who were opposed to the Party. He even believed that Hitler had his own niece killed in thirty-two because he was obsessed with her and she loved someone else.

"The Party and the Stormtroopers threatened him and everybody at the *Post*. They called the paper the 'Poison Kitchen.' But before the National Socialists came to power they never hurt him. Then there was the Reichstag fire. . . . Oh, look, you can just see it. There." She pointed to the northeast. Paul caught a glimpse of a tall domed building. "Our parliament. Just weeks after Hitler was named chancellor, someone lit a fire inside. Hitler and Göring blamed the Communists and they rounded up thousands of them, Social Democrats too. They were arrested under the emergency decree. Michael was among them. He went to one of the temporary prisons set up around the city. They kept him there for weeks. I was frantic. No one told me what happened, no one told me where he was. It was terrible. He told me later that they beat him, fed him once a day at the most, made him sleep naked on a concrete floor. Finally a judge let him go since he hadn't committed any crime.

"After he was released I met him at his apartment, not far from here. It was a spring day in May, a beautiful day. Two in the afternoon. We were going to hire a boat. Right here, at this lake. I'd brought some stale bread to feed the birds. We were standing there and four Stormtroopers came up to us and pushed me to the ground. They'd followed us. They said they'd been watching him since he'd been released. They told him that the judge had acted illegally in releasing him and they were now going to carry out the sentence." She choked for a moment. "They beat him to death right in front of me. Right there. I could hear his bones break. You see that—"

"Oh, Käthe. No . . ."

"—you see that square of concrete? That was where he fell. That one. The fourth square from the grass. That was where Michael's head lay as he died."

He put his arm around her. She didn't resist. But neither did she find any comfort in the contact; she was frozen.

"May is now the worst month," she whispered. Then she looked around, at the textured canopy of summer trees. "This park is called the Tiergarten."

"I know."

In English she said, "'Tier' means 'animal' or 'beast.' And 'Garten,' of course, is 'garden.' So, this is the garden of beasts, where the royal families of imperial Germany would hunt game. But in our slang 'Tier' also means thug, like a criminal. And that's who killed my lover, criminals." Her voice grew cold. "Here, right here in the garden of beasts."

His grip tightened around her.

She glanced once more at the pond then at the square of concrete, the fourth from the grass. Käthe said, "Please take me home, Paul."

In the hallway outside his door they paused.

Paul slipped his hand into his pocket and found the key. He looked down at her. Käthe in turn was staring at the floor.

"Good night," he whispered.

"I've forgotten so much," she said, looking up. "Walking through the city, seeing lovers in cafés, telling ribald jokes, sitting where famous writers and thinkers have sat . . . the pleasure in things like those. I've forgotten what that's like. Forgotten so much . . ."

His hand went to the tiny scallop of cloth covering her shoulder, and then he touched her neck, felt her skin move against her bones. So thin, he thought. So thin.

With his other hand he brushed her hair out of her face. Then he kissed her.

She stiffened suddenly and he realized he'd made a mistake. She was vulnerable, she'd seen the site of her lover's death, she'd walked through the garden of beasts. He started to back away but suddenly she flung her arms around him, kissing him hard, teeth met his lip and he tasted blood. "Oh," she said, shocked. "I'm sorry." But he laughed gently and then she did too. "I said I've forgotten much," she whispered. "I'm afraid this is one more thing lost from my memory."

He pulled her to him and they remained in the dim hallway, their lips and hands frantic. Images flashing past: a halo around her golden hair from the lamp behind her, the cream lace of her slip over the lighter lace of her brassiere, her hand finding the scar left by a bullet fired from Albert Reilly's hidden Derringer, a .22 only but it tumbled when it hit bone and exited his biceps sideways, her keening moan, hot breath, the feel of silk, of cotton, his hand sliding down and finding her own fingers waiting to guide him through complicated layers of cloth and straps, her garter belt, which had been worn threadbare and stitched back together.

"My room," he whispered. In a few seconds the door was open and they were staggering inside, where the air seemed hotter even than in the hot corridor.

The bed was miles away but the rose-colored couch with gull-wing arms was suddenly beneath them. He fell backward onto the cushions and heard a crack of wood. Käthe was on top of him, holding him in a vise grip by the arms as if, were she to let go, he might sink beneath the brown water of the Landwehr Canal.

A fierce kiss, then her face sought his neck. He heard her whisper to him, to herself, to no one, "How long has this been?" She began to unbutton his shirt frantically. "Ach, years and years."

Well, he thought, not such a long time in his case. But as he lifted off her dress and slip in one smooth sweep, his hands sliding to the sweating small of her back, he realized that, while, yes, there'd been others recently, it *had* been years since he'd felt anything like this.

Then, gripping her face in his hands, bringing her closer, closer, losing himself entirely, he corrected himself once more.

Maybe it had been forever.

Chapter Nineteen

The evening rituals in the Kohl household had been completed. Dishes dried, linens put away, laundry done.

The inspector's feet were feeling better and he poured out the water from the tub and then dried and replaced it. He tied the salts closed and put them back under the sink.

He returned to the den, where his pipe awaited. A moment later Heidi joined him and sat down in her own chair with her knitting. Kohl explained to her about his conversation with Günter.

She shook her head. "So that's what it was. He was upset when he got home from the football field yesterday too. But he would say nothing to me. Not to a mother, not about such things."

Kohl said, "We need to talk to them. Someone has to teach them what *we* learned. Right and wrong."

Moral quicksand . . .

Heidi clicked the thick wooden needles together expertly; she was knitting a blanket for Charlotte's and Heinrich's first child, which she assumed would arrive approximately nine and a half months after their wedding next May. She asked in a harsh whisper, "And then what happens? In the school yard Günter mentions to his friends that his father says it's wrong to burn books or that we should allow American newspapers in the country? Ach, then *you're* taken away and never heard from again. Or they send me your ashes in a box with a swastika on it."

"We tell them to keep what we say to themselves. Like playing a game. It must be secret."

A smile from his wife. "They're *children*, my darling. They can't keep secrets."

True, Kohl thought. How true. What brilliant criminals the Leader and his crowd are. They kidnap the nation by seizing our children. Hitler said his would be a thousand-year empire. This is how he will achieve it.

He said, "I will speak to—"

A huge pounding filled the hall—the bronze bear knocker on Kohl's front door.

"God in heaven," Heidi said, standing up, dropping the knitting and glancing toward the children's rooms.

Willi Kohl suddenly realized that the SD or Gestapo had a listening device in his house and had heard the many questionable exchanges between himself and his wife. This was the Gestapo's technique—to gather evidence on the sly then arrest you in your home either early in the morning or during the dinner hour or just after, when you would least expect them. "Quickly, put the radio on, see if there's a broadcast," he said. As if listening to Goebbels's rantings would deter the political police.

She did. The dial glowed yellow but no sound yet came through the speakers. It took some moments for the tubes to heat up.

Another pounding.

Kohl thought of his pistol, but he kept it at the office; he never wanted the weapon near his children. Yet even if he had it, what good would it do against a company of Gestapo or SS? He walked into the living room and saw Charlotte and Heinrich, standing side by side, looking uneasily at each other. Hilde appeared in the doorway, her book drooping in her hand.

Goebbels's passionate baritone began surging out of the radio, talking about infections and health and disease.

As he walked to the door, Kohl wondered if Günter had already made some casual comment about his parents to a friend. Perhaps the boy *had* denounced someone—his father, albeit unknowingly. Kohl glanced back at Heidi, who was standing with her arm around her youngest daughter. He unbolted the lock and swung open the heavy oak slab.

Konrad Janssen stood in the doorway, looking fresh as a child at holy communion. He looked past the inspector and said to Heidi, "Forgive the intrusion, Mrs. Kohl. It's unforgivable at this late hour."

Mother of God, Kohl thought, hands and heart vibrating. He wondered if the inspector candidate could hear the pounding in his chest. "Yes, yes, Janssen, the hour is not a problem. But next time, a lighter touch on the door, if you please."

"Of course." The young face, usually so calm, bristled with enthusiasm.

"Sir, I showed the picture of the suspect all over the Olympics and half the rest of the city, it seemed."

"And?"

"I found a reporter for a British newspaper. He'd come over from New York on the S.S. *Manhattan*. He's been writing a story on athletic fields around the world and—"

"This Briton is our suspect, the man in the artist's picture?"

"No, but—"

"Then this portion of your story doesn't interest us, Janssen."

"Of course, sir. Forgive me. It's sufficient to say that this reporter recognized our man."

"Ah, well done, Janssen. Tell me, what did he have to say?"

"Not a great deal. All he knew was that he *is* an American."

This paltry confirmation was worth a burst heart? Kohl sighed.

But the inspector candidate, it seemed, was only pausing to catch his breath. He continued. "And his name is Paul Schumann."

Words spoken in the dark.

Words spoken as if in a dream.

They were close, finding in each other a comfortable opposite, knee to back of knee, swell of belly to back, chin to shoulder. The bed assisted; the feather mattress in Paul's bedroom formed a V under their joint weight and seated them firmly. They could not have moved apart had they wanted to.

Words spoken in the anonymity of new romance, the passion past, though only momentarily.

Smelling her perfume, which was in fact the source of the lilac he'd smelled when he'd first met her.

Paul kissed the back of Käthe's head.

Words spoken between lovers, speaking of everything, of nothing. Whims, jokes, facts, speculations, hopes . . . a torrent of words.

Käthe was telling him of her life as a landlady. She fell silent. Through the open window they could hear Beethoven once again, growing louder as someone in a nearby apartment turned up the volume. A moment later a firm voice echoed through the damp night.

"Ach," she said, shaking her head. "The Leader speaks. That's Hitler himself."

It was yet more talk about germs, about stagnant water, about infections.

Paul laughed. "Why's he so obsessed with health?"

"Health?"

"All day long, everybody's been talking about germs and cleanliness. You can't get away from it."

She was laughing. "Germs?"

"What's so funny?"

"Don't you understand what he's saying?"

"I . . . No."

"It's not germs he's talking about. It's *Jews*. He's changed all his speeches during the Olympics. He doesn't say 'Jew' but that's what he means. He doesn't want to offend the foreigners but he can't let us forget the National Socialist dogma. Paul, don't you know what is happening here? Why, in the basements of half the hotels and boardinghouses in Berlin are signs that were taken down for the Olympics and that will be put back up the day the foreigners leave. They say *No Jews*. Or *Jews Not Welcome Here*. There is a sharp turn on the road to my sister's home in Spandau. The sign warns, *Dangerous Curve. 30 Kilometers Per Hour. Jews Do 70*. It is a road sign! Not painted by vandals but by our government!"

"You're serious?"

"Serious, Paul. Yes! You saw the flags on the houses of Magdeburger Alley, the street here. You commented on ours when you arrived."

"The Olympic flag."

"Yes, yes. Not the National Socialist flag, like on most of the other homes on this street. Do you know why? Because this building is owned by a Jew. It's illegal for him to fly Germany's flag. He wants to be proud of his fatherland like everyone else. But he can't be. And how could he fly the National Socialist flag anyway? The swastika? The broken cross? It stands for anti-Semitism."

Ah, so that was the answer.

Surely you know. . . .

"Have you heard of Aryanization?"

"No."

"The government takes a Jewish home or business. It's theft, pure and simple. Göring is the master of it."

Paul recalled the empty houses he'd passed that morning on the way to meet Morgan at Dresden Alley, the signs saying that the contents were to be sold.

Käthe moved closer yet to him. After a long silence she said, "There is a man. . . . He performs at a restaurant. 'Fancy,' it would be called. That is to say the name of the establishment is Fancy. But it *is* fancy too. Very nice. I went to this restaurant once and this man was in a glass cage in the middle of the dining room. Do you know what he was? A hunger artist."

"What?"

"A hunger artist. Like in the Kafka story. He had climbed into his cage some weeks before and had survived on nothing except water. He was there for everyone to see. He never ate."

"How does—"

"He is allowed to go to the lavatory. But someone always accompanies him and verifies that he has had nothing to eat. Day after day . . ."

Words spoken in the dark, words between lovers.

What those words mean is often not important. But sometimes it is.

Paul whispered, "Go on."

"I met him after he had been in the glass cage for forty-eight days."

"No food? Was he a skeleton?"

"He was very thin, yes. He looked sick. But he came out of the cage for some weeks. I met him through a friend. I asked him why he chose to do this for a living. He told me he had worked in the government for some years, something in transportation. But when Hitler came to power he left his job."

"He was fired because he wasn't a National Socialist?"

"No, he quit because he couldn't accept their values and wouldn't work for their government. But he had a child and he needed to make money."

"A child?"

"And needed money. But everywhere he looked, he could find no position that wasn't tainted with the Party. He found that the only thing he could do with any integ— What is that word?"

"Integrity."

"Yes, yes, integrity. Was to be a hunger artist. It was pure. It could not be corrupted. And do you know how many people come to see him? Thousands! Thousands come to see him because he is *honest*. And there is so little honesty in our lives now." A faint shudder told him she was shivering with tears.

Words between lovers . . .

"Käthe?"

"What have they done?" She gasped for breath. "What have they done? . . . I don't understand what has happened. We are a people who love music and talk and who rejoice in sewing the perfect stitch in our men's shirts and scrubbing our alley cobblestones clean and basking in the sun on the beach at Wannsee and buying our children clothing and sweets, we're moved to tears by the 'Moonlight' Sonata, by the words of Goethe and Schiller—yet we are possessed now. Why?" Her voice faded. "Why?" A moment later she whispered, "Ach, that is a question for which, I'm afraid, the answer will come too late."

"Leave the country," Paul whispered.

She rolled about to face him. He felt her strong arms, strengthened from scrubbing tubs and sweeping floors, snake around him, he felt her heel rise and find the small of his back, pulling him closer, closer.

"Leave," he repeated.

The shivering stopped. Her breathing grew more regular. "I cannot leave."

"Why not?"

"It's my country," she whispered simply. "I can't abandon it."

"But it's *not* your country any longer. It's theirs. What did you say? *Tier.* Beasts, thugs. It's been taken over by beasts. . . . Leave. Get away before it gets worse."

"You think it will get worse? Tell me, Paul. Please. You're a writer. The way of the world isn't my way. It isn't teaching or Goethe or poetry. You're a clever man. What do you think?"

"I think it will get worse. You have to get out of here. As soon as you can."

She relaxed her desperate grip on him. "Even if I wanted to I cannot. After I was fired my name went on a list. They took my passport. I'll never get exit papers. They're afraid we'll work against them from England or Paris. So they keep us close."

"Come back with me. I can get you out."

Words between lovers . . .

"Come to America." Had she not heard? Or had she decided no already? "We have wonderful schools. You could teach. Your English is as good as anyone's."

She inhaled deeply. "What are you asking?"

"Leave with me."

A harsh laugh. "A woman cries, a man says anything to stop the tears. Ach, I don't even know you."

Paul said, "And I don't know you. I'm not proposing, I'm not saying we live together. I'm just saying you have to get the hell out of here. I can arrange that."

In the silence that followed, Paul was thinking that, no, he wasn't proposing. Nothing of the sort. But, truth be told, Paul Schumann couldn't help but wonder if his offer wasn't about more than helping her escape from this difficult place. Oh, he'd had his share of women—good girls and bad girls and good girls playing at being bad. Some of them he'd thought he'd loved, and some he'd *known* he had. But he knew he'd never felt for them what he felt for this woman after such a short period of time. Yes, he loved Marion in a way. He'd spend an occasional night with her in Manhattan. Or she with him in Brooklyn. They'd lie together, they'd share words— about movies, about where hemline lengths would go next year, about Luigi's restaurant, about her mother, about his sister. About the Dodgers. But they weren't lovers' words, Paul Schumann realized. Not like he'd spoken tonight with this complicated, passionate woman.

Finally she said dismissively, irritated, "Ach, I can't go. How can I go? I told you about my passport and exit papers."

"This is what I'm saying. You don't have to worry about that. I have connections."

"You do?"

"People in America owe me favors." This much was true. He thought of Avery and Manielli in Amsterdam, ready at a moment's notice to send the plane to collect him. Then he asked her, "Do you have ties here? How about your sister?"

"Ach, my sister . . . She's married to a Party loyalist. She doesn't even see me. I'm an embarrassment." After a moment Käthe said, "No, I have only ghosts here. And ghosts are no reason to remain. They're reasons to leave."

Outside, laughter and drunken shouts. A slurring male voice sang, *"When the Olympic Games are done, the Jews will feel our knife and gun. . . ."* Then the crash of breaking glass. Another song, several voices singing this time. *"Hold high the banner, close the ranks. The SA marches on with firm steps. . . . Give way, give way to the brown battalions, as the Stormtroopers clear the land. . . ."*

He recognized the song that the Hitler Youth had sung yesterday as they lowered the flag at the Olympic Village. The red, the white and the black hooked cross.

Ach, surely you know. . . .

"Oh, Paul, you can really get me out of the country, without papers?"

"Yes. But I'll be leaving soon. Tomorrow night, I hope. Or the night after."

"How?"

"Leave the details to me. Are you willing to leave immediately?"

After a moment of silence: "I can do that. Yes."

She took his hand, stroked his palm and interlaced her fingers with his. This was by far the most intimate moment between them tonight.

He gripped her tightly, stretched his arm out and struck something hard under the pillow. He touched it and, from the size and feel, realized that it was the volume of Goethe's poems that he'd given her earlier.

"You won't—"

"Shhhh," he whispered. And stroked her hair.

Paul Schumann knew that there are times for lovers' words to end.

IV
SIX TO FIVE AGAINST

SUNDAY, 26 JULY, TO MONDAY, 27 JULY, 1936

Chapter Twenty

He had been in his office at the Alex for an hour, since 5 A.M., painstakingly writing out the English-language telegram that he had composed in his mind as he lay sleepless in bed beside peaceful Heidi, fragrant with the powder she dusted on before retiring.

Willi Kohl now looked over his handiwork:

> I AM BEING SENIOR DETECTIVE INSPECTOR WILLI
> KOHL OF THE KRIMINALPOLIZEI (CRIMINAL POLICE) IN
> BERLIN STOP WE SEEK INFORMATION REGARD AMERI-
> CAN POSSIBLY FROM NEW YORK PRESENTLY IN BERLIN
> PAUL SCHUMANN IN CONNECTION OF HOMICIDE STOP
> ARRIVED WITH AMERICAN OLYMPIC TEAM STOP PLEASE
> TO REMIT ME INFORMATION ABOUT THIS MAN AT KRIM-
> INALPOLIZEI HEADQUARTERS ALEXANDERPLATZ
> BERLIN TO DIRECTION OF INSPECTOR WILLI KOHL
> STOP MOST URGENT STOP THANKING YOU REGARDS

He'd struggled hard with the wording. The department had translators but none worked on Sunday and he wanted to send the telegram immediately. It would be earlier in America; he wasn't sure about the time zones and he guessed the hour to be about midnight overseas but he hoped that the law enforcers there would keep the same long shifts as police in most countries.

Kohl read the telegram once again and decided that, though flawed, it was good enough. On a separate sheet of paper he wrote instructions to send it to the International Olympic Committee, the New York City Police Department and the Federal Bureau of Investigation. He walked down to the telegraph office. He was disappointed to find that no one was as yet on duty. Angrily, he returned to his desk.

After a few hours' sleep, Janssen was presently en route back to the Olympic Village to see if he could pick up any more leads there. What else could Kohl himself do? Nothing occurred to him, except hounding the medical examiner for the autopsy and FPE for the fingerprint analysis. But they, of course, were not in their offices yet either and might not come in at all on Sunday.

He felt the frustration acutely.

His eyes dropped down to the hard-worked-on telegram.

"Ach, this is absurd." He would wait no longer. How difficult could it be to man a Teletype machine? Kohl rose and hurried back to the department, figuring he would do the best he could to transmit the telegram to the United States himself. And if, because of his clumsy fingers, it ended up being sent by mistake to a hundred different places in America, well, so much the better.

She had returned to her own room not long before, around 6 A.M., and was now back in his, wearing a dark blue housedress, pins holding her hair flat to her head, a little blush on her cheeks. Paul stood in the doorway, wiping the remnants of the shaving froth from his face. He put the cover on his safety razor and dropped it into his stained canvas bag.

Käthe had brought coffee and toast, along with some pale margarine, cheese, dried sausage and soupy marmalade. She walked through the low, dusty light streaming into the front window of his living room and set the tray on the table near the kitchen.

"There," she announced, nodding at the tray. "No need for you to come to the breakfast room." She looked at him once quickly. Then away. "I have chores."

"So, you still game?" he asked in English.

"What is 'game'?"

He kissed her. "It means what I asked you last night. Are you still willing to come with me?"

She ordered the china on the tray, which had seemed to him already perfectly ordered. "I'm game. Are you?"

He shrugged. "I wouldn't have let you change your mind. It would be *Kakfif.* Out of the question."

She laughed. Then a frown. "One thing I wish to say."

"Yeah?"

"I give opinions quite often." She looked down. "And quite strongly. Michael called me a cyclone. I want to say, regarding the subject of sports: I could learn to like them too."

Paul shook his head. "I'd rather you didn't."

"No?"

"Then I'll feel I had to like poetry."

She pressed her head to his chest. He believed she was smiling.

"You will like America," he said. "But if you don't, when all this blows over you can come back. You aren't necessarily leaving the country forever."

"Ah, my wise writer-man. You think this will—the expression?—will blow over?"

"Yes, I do. I think they won't be in power much longer." He looked at the clock. The time was nearly seven-thirty. "Now I have to meet my associate."

"On Sunday morning? Ach, I finally understand your secret."

He looked at her with a cautious smile.

"You're writing about priests who play sports!" She laughed. "That's your big story!" Then her smile faded. "And why must you leave so quickly if you are writing about sports or the cubic meters of concrete used for the stadium?"

"I don't *have* to leave quickly. I have some important meetings back in the United States." Paul drank his coffee quickly and ate one piece of toast and sausage. "You finish what's left. I'm not hungry now."

"Well, hurry back to me. I will pack. But only one bag, I think. If I take too many, perhaps a ghost will try to hide in one." A laugh. "Ach, I am sounding like someone out of a story by our macabre friend E.T.A. Hoffmann."

He kissed her and left the boardinghouse, stepped out into the morning, already hot, already painting a damp coat on the skin. With a glance up and down the empty street, he made his way north, over the canal, and into the Tiergarten, the Garden of Beasts.

Paul found Reggie Morgan sitting on a bench in front of the very pond where Käthe Richter's lover had been beaten to death three years ago.

Even at this early hour, dozens of people were here. A number of walkers and bicyclists. Morgan's jacket was off and his shirt sleeves partly rolled up.

Paul sat down beside him. Morgan flicked an envelope inside his jacket pocket. "Got the greenbacks okay," he whispered in English.

They reverted to German. "They cashed a check on Saturday night?" Paul asked, laughing. "I'm living in a whole new world."

"You think Webber will show up?" Morgan asked skeptically.

"Oh, yes. If there's money involved he'll be here. But I'm not sure how helpful he'll be. I looked over Wilhelm Street last night. There are dozens of guards, hundreds maybe. It'd be far too risky to do the job there. We'll have to see what Otto says. Maybe he's found another location."

They sat in silence for a moment.

Paul watched him look around the park. Morgan seemed wistful. He said, "I will miss this country very much." For a moment the man's face lost its keenness and the dark eyes were sad. "There are good people here. I find them kinder than the Parisians, more open than the Londoners. And they spend far more time enjoying life than New Yorkers. If we had time I'd take you to the Lustgarten and Luna Park. And I love to walk here, in the Tiergarten. I enjoy watching birds." The thin man seemed embarrassed at this. "A foolish diversion."

Paul laughed to himself, thinking of the model airplanes sitting on his bookshelf in Brooklyn. Foolishness is in the eye of the beholder.

"So you'll leave?" Paul asked.

"I can't stay. I've been here far too long. Every day there's another chance of a mistake, some carelessness that will tip them off to me. And after what we're about to do they'll look very closely at every foreigner who's had business here recently. But after life returns to normal and the National Socialists are gone I can return."

"What will you do when you come back?"

Morgan brightened. "I would like to be a diplomat. That's why I am in this business. After what I saw in the trenches . . ." He nodded at a bullet scar on his arm. "After that, I decided I was going to do whatever I could to stop war. The diplomatic corps made sense. I wrote the Senator about it. He suggested Berlin. A country in flux, he called it. So here I am. I hope to be a liaison officer in a few years. Then ambassador or a consul. Like our Ambassador Dodd here. He's a genius, a true statesman. I won't be posted *here*, of course, not at first. Too important a country. I could start out in Holland. Or maybe Spain, well, after their civil war is over, of course. If there's any Spain left. Franco's as bad as Hitler. It'll be brutal. But, yes, I would like to come back here when sanity returns."

A moment later Paul spotted Otto Webber coming down the path, walking slowly, a bit unsteadily and squinting against the powerful sunlight.

"There he is now."

"Him? He looks like a *Bürgermeister*. And one who spent the evening in his cups. We're relying on *him?*"

Webber approached the bench and sat down, breathing hard. "Hot, hot day. I didn't know it could be this hot in the morning. I'm rarely up at this hour. But neither are the dung-shirts so we can meet without much concern. You are Mr. John Dillinger's associate?"

"Dillinger?" Morgan asked.

"I am Otto Webber." He shook Morgan's hand vigorously. "You are?"

"I'll keep my name to myself if you don't mind."

"Ach, me, yes, that's fine." Webber examined Morgan closely. "Say, I have some nice trousers, several pair. I can sell them to you cheap. Yes, yes, very cheap. The best quality. From England. I can have one of my girls alter them to fit you perfectly. Ingrid is available. And very talented. Quite pretty too. A real pearl."

Morgan glanced down at his gray flannel slacks. "No. I don't need any clothes."

"Champagne? Stockings?"

"Otto," Paul said. "I think the only transaction we're interested in involves what we were talking about yesterday."

"Ach, yes, Mr. John Dillinger. Except I have some news you may not like. All of my contacts report that a veil of silence has descended on Wilhelm Street. Something has made them cautious. Security has become higher than ever. And all this in the last day. There is no information anyone has about this person you were mentioning."

Paul's face twisted in disappointment.

Morgan muttered, "I spent half of last night coming up with the money."

"Good," Webber said brightly. "Dollars, correct?"

"My friend," the slim American added caustically, "you don't get paid if we don't get results."

"But the situation is not hopeless. I can still be of some assistance."

"Go on," Morgan said impatiently. He looked down again at his slacks, brushing at a smudge.

The German continued. "I can't tell you where the chicken is but what would you say if I can get you into the henhouse and you could find out for yourself?"

"The—"

He lowered his voice. "I can get you into the Chancellory. Ernst is the envy of all the ministers. Everyone tries to snuggle close to the Little Man and get offices in the building but the best that most of them can do is to find space nearby. That Ernst abides there is a source of anguish to many."

Paul scoffed. "I looked it over last night. There're guards everywhere. You couldn't get me in there."

"Ah, but I am of a different opinion, my friend."

"How the hell can you do it?" Paul had lapsed into English. He repeated the question in German.

"We have the Little Man to thank. He is obsessed with architecture. He has been renovating the Chancellory since he came to power. Laborers are there seven days a week. I will provide a workman's outfit, a forged identification card and the two passes that will get you into the building. One of my contacts is doing the plastering there and he has access to all the documentation."

Morgan considered this and nodded, now less cynical about the idea.

"My friend tells me that Hitler wishes rugs in all the offices on the important floors. That will include Ernst's. The carpet suppliers are measuring the offices. Some have been measured, some have not. We will hope Ernst's has not. In the event it has been, you can make some excuse about having to measure again. The pass I will give you is from a company that is known for, among other things, its fine carpeting. I will also provide a meter stick and a notebook."

"How do you know you can trust this man?" Paul asked.

"Because he's been using cheap plaster and pocketing the difference between its cost and what the state is paying him. That's a death offense when you're building Hitler's seat of power. So I have some leverage with him; he wouldn't lie to me. Besides, he thinks only that we're running some scam to undercut the price of carpets. Of course, I did promise him a bit of egg."

"Egg?" Morgan asked.

It was for Paul to interpret. "Money."

Whose bread I eat is whose song I sing. . . .

"Take it out of the thousand dollars."

"I wish to point out that I don't *have* the thousand dollars."

Morgan shook his head, reached into his pocket and counted out a hundred.

"That's fine. See, I'm not greedy."

Morgan rolled his eyes at Paul. "Not greedy? Why, he's like Göring."

"Ach, I take that as a compliment, sir. Our air minister is a very resource-ful businessman." Webber turned to Paul. "Now, there will be some officials in the building, even on Sunday. But my man tells me they will be senior people and will be mostly in the Leader's portion of the building, to the left, which you will not be allowed near. To the right are the lower-level-officials' offices—that's where Ernst's is. They, and their secretaries and aides, will most likely not be there. You should have some time to browse through his office and, with luck, find his calendar or a memo or notation about his appointments in the next few days."

"This is not bad," Morgan said.

Webber said, "It will take me an hour or so to put everything in place. I will pick up the coveralls and your papers and a truck. I'll meet you by that statue there, the woman with the large bosom, at ten A.M. And I'll bring some pants for *you*," he added to Morgan. "Twenty marks. Such a good price." He smiled then said to Paul, "Your friend here eyes me with a very particular look, Mr. John Dillinger. I don't believe he trusts me."

Reggie Morgan shrugged. "I will tell you, Otto Wilhelm Friedrich Georg Webber." A glance at Paul. "My colleague here told you about the precautions we've taken to make certain you don't betray us. No, my friend, trust is not the issue. I'm looking at you this way because I wish to know what the hell you think is wrong with these trousers of mine?"

He saw Mark's face in the young boy's before him.

This was to be expected, of course, seeing the father in the son. But it was still unsettling.

"Come here, Rudy," Reinhard Ernst said to his grandson.

"Yes, Opa."

The hour was early on Sunday and the housekeeper was removing breakfast dishes from the table, on which sunlight fell as yellow as pollen. Gertrud was in the kitchen, examining a plucked goose, which would be dinner later that day. Their daughter-in-law was at church, lighting candles to the memory of Mark Albrecht Ernst, the very same young man the colonel saw now echoed in his grandson.

He tied the laces of Rudy's shoes. He glanced once more at the boy's face and saw Mark again, though noted a different look on his face this time: curious, discerning.

It was uncanny really.

Oh, how he missed his son . . .

It was eighteen months since Mark had said good-bye to his parents, wife and Rudy, all of them standing behind the rail at Lehrter Station. Ernst had given the twenty-seven-year-old officer a salute—a real salute, not the fascist one—as his son had boarded the train to Hamburg to take command of his ship.

The young officer was fully aware of the dangers of the ramshackle vessel yet he'd wholly embraced them.

Because that is what soldiers and sailors do.

Ernst thought about Mark daily. But never before had the spirit of his son come so close to him as now, seeing these familiar expressions in his own grandson's face, so direct, so confident, so curious. Were they evidence that the boy had his father's nature? Rudy would be subject to the draft in a decade. Where would Germany be then? At war? Peace? Back in possession of the lands stolen away by the Treaty of Versailles? Would Hitler be gone, an engine so powerful that it quickly seizes and burns? Or would the Leader still be in command, burnishing his vision of the new Germany? Ernst's heart told him he should be vitally concerned about these questions. Yet he knew he couldn't worry about them. All he could focus on was his duty.

One *had* to do one's duty.

Even if that meant commanding an old training ship not meant to carry powder and shells, whose jerry-rigged magazine was too close to the galley or engine room or a sparking wire (no one would ever know), the consequences being that one moment the ship was practicing war maneuvers in the cold Baltic and the next she was a cloud of acrid smoke over the water, her shattered hull dropping through the blackness of water to the sea floor.

Duty . . .

Even if that meant spending half one's days battling in the trenches of Wilhelm Street, all the way to the Leader, if necessary, to do what was best for Germany.

Ernst gave a final tug on Rudy's shoelace to make sure it wouldn't come undone and trip the boy. Then he stood and looked down at this tiny version of his son. Acting on impulse, very unusual for Ernst, he asked, "Rudy, I have to see someone this morning. But later, would you like to come with me to the Olympic stadium? Would you like that?"

"Oh, yes, Opa." The boy's face blossomed into a huge smile. "I could run around the tracks."

"You run quickly."

"Gunni at my child-school and I ran a race from the oak tree to the porch and he's two years older than I but I won."

"Good, good. Then you will enjoy the afternoon. You'll come with me and you can run on the same track that our Olympians will race on. Then when we see the Games next week you can tell everyone that you ran on the same track. Won't that be fun?"

"Oh, yes, Opa."

"I have to go now. But I'll return at noontime and pick you up."

"I'll practice running."

"Yes, you do that."

Ernst walked to his den, collected several files on the Waltham Study, then found his wife in the pantry. He told her that he would pick up Rudy later that day. And for now? Yes, yes, it was Sunday morning but still he had to attend to some important matters. And, no, they couldn't wait.

Whatever else they said about him, Hermann Göring was tireless.

Today, for instance, he'd arrived at his desk in the air ministry at 8 A.M. A Sunday, no less. And he'd had a stop to make on the way.

Sweating furiously, he had marched into the Chancellory a half hour before that, making his way to Hitler's office. It was possible that Wolf was awake—*still* awake, that is. An insomniac, the man often stayed up past dawn. But, no, the Leader was in bed. The guard reported that he'd retired about five, with instructions not to be disturbed.

Göring had thought for a moment then jotted a note and left it with the guard.

> My Leader,
> I have learned of a matter of concern at the highest level.
> Betrayal might be involved. Significant future plans are at stake.
> I will relate this information in person as soon as it suits.
> Göring

Good choice of words. "Betrayal" was always a trigger. The Jews, the Communists, the Social Democrats, the Republicans—the backstabbers, in short—had sold out the country to the Allies at the end of the War and still threatened to play Pilate to Hitler's Jesus.

Oh, Wolf got hot when he heard that word.

"Future plans" was good, as well. Anything that threatened setbacks to Hitler's vision of the Third Empire would get the man's immediate attention.

Though the Chancellory was merely around the corner, it had been unpleasant to make the trip, a large man on a hot morning. But Göring'd had no choice. He couldn't telephone or send a runner; Reinhard Ernst wasn't a competent enough intriguer to have his own intelligence network to spy on colleagues but any number of others would be delighted to steal Göring's revelation about Ludwig Keitel's Jewish background and hand it to the Leader as if it were their own discovery. Goebbels, for instance, Göring's chief rival for Wolf's attention, would do so in a heartbeat.

Now, close to 9 A.M., the minister was turning his attention to a discouragingly large file about Aryanizing a large chemical company in the west and folding it into the Hermann Göring Works. His phone buzzed.

From the anteroom his aide answered. "Minister Göring's office."

The minister leaned forward and looked out. He could see the man standing to attention as he spoke. The aide hung up and walked to the doorway. "The Leader will see you in a half hour, sir."

Göring nodded and walked to the table across his office. He sat and served himself food from the heaped-high tray. The aide poured coffee. The air minister flipped through the financial information on the chemical company but he had trouble concentrating; the image that kept emerging from the charts of numbers was of Reinhard Ernst being led from the Chancellory by two Gestapo officers, a look of bewilderment and defeat on the colonel's otherwise irritatingly placid face.

A frivolous fantasy, to be sure, but it provided some pleasant diversion while he scarfed down a huge plate of sausage and eggs.

Chapter Twenty-One

In a spacious but dusty and unkempt Krausen Street apartment, which had been in existence from the days of Bismarck and Wilhelm, a half kilometer southeast of the government buildings, two young men sat at an ornate dining room table. For hours they'd been engaged in a debate. The discussion had been lengthy and fervent because the subject was nothing less than their survival.

As with so many matters nowadays the ultimate question they'd been wrestling with was that of trust.

Would the man deliver them to salvation, or would they be betrayed and pay for that gullibility with their lives?

Tink, tink, tink . . .

Kurt Fischer, the older of the two blond-haired brothers, said, "Stop making that noise."

Hans had been tapping the knife on the plate that had held an apple core and some rinds from cheese, the remnants of their pathetic breakfast. He continued the *tink* for a moment more and then set the utensil down.

Five years separated the brothers but there were other gulfs far wider between them.

Hans said, "He could denounce us for money. He could denounce us because he's drunk on National Socialism. He could denounce us because it's Sunday and he simply takes a fancy to denounce someone."

This was certainly true.

"And, as I keep saying, what's the hurry? Why today? I would like to see Ilsa again. You remember her, don't you? Oh, she is as beautiful as Marlene Dietrich."

"You are making a joke, aren't you?" Kurt replied, exasperated. "We're concerned for our lives and you're pining away for a big-titted girl you've known for less than a month."

"We can leave tomorrow. Or why not after the Olympics? People will leave the Games early, toss away their day tickets. We can get in for the afternoon events."

This was the crux of the matter, most likely: the Olympics. For a handsome youth like Hans, there would be many Ilsas in his life; she was not particularly pretty or bright (though she did seem particularly loose by National Socialist standards). But what troubled Hans the most about their escape from Germany was missing the Games.

Kurt sighed in frustration. His brother was nineteen, an age at which many men held responsible positions in the army or a trade. But his brother had always been impulsive and a dreamer, and a bit lazy, as well.

What to do? Kurt thought, taking up the debate with himself. He chewed on a piece of dry bread. They'd had no butter for a week. In fact, they had little of any food left. But Kurt hated to go outside. Ironically, he felt more vulnerable there—when in fact it was probably far more dangerous to be in the apartment, which was undoubtedly watched from time to time by the Gestapo or the SD.

Reflecting again: It all came down to trust. Should they or should they not?

"What was that?" Hans asked, lifting an eyebrow.

Kurt shook his head. He hadn't realized he'd spoken out loud. The question had been addressed to the only two people in the world who would have answered honestly and with sound judgment. Their parents. But Albrecht and Lotte Fischer were not present. Social Democrats, pacifists, the couple had attended a worldwide peace conference in London two months ago. But just before they returned, they'd learned from a friend that their names were on a Gestapo list. The secret police were planning to arrest them at Tempelhof when they arrived. Albrecht made two attempts to slip into the country and get his sons out, once through France and once through the Czech Sudetenland. He was refused entry both times, nearly arrested the second.

Ensconced in London, taken in by like-minded professors and working part-time as translators and teachers, the distraught parents had managed to get several messages to the boys, urging them to leave. But their passports had been lifted and their identity cards stamped. Not only were they the children of pacifists and ardent Socis, but the Gestapo had files on the boys themselves, it seemed. They held their parents' political beliefs, and the police had noted their attendance at the forbidden swing and jazz clubs, where American Negro music was played and girls smoked and the punch was spiked with Russian vodka. They had friends who were activists.

Hardly subversive. But it was merely a matter of time until they were arrested. Or they starved. Kurt had been dismissed from his job. Hans had completed his mandatory six-month Labor Service stint and was back home now. He'd been drummed out of university—the Gestapo had seen to that, as well—and, like his brother, he too was unemployed. Their future might very well see them becoming beggars on Alexander Plaza or Oranienburger Square.

And so the question of trust had arisen. Albrecht Fischer managed to contact a former colleague, Gerhard Unger, from the University of Berlin. A pacifist and Soci himself, Unger had quit his job teaching not long after the National Socialists had come to power and returned to his family confectionary company. He often traveled over borders and, being firmly anti-Hitler, was more than happy to help smuggle the boys out of Germany in one of his company's trucks. Every Sunday morning Unger made a run to Holland to deliver his candy and pick up ingredients. It was felt that with all the visitors coming into the country for the Olympics the border guards would be preoccupied and pay no attention to a commercial truck leaving the country on a regular run.

But could they trust him with their lives?

There was no apparent reason *not* to. Unger and Albrecht had been friends. They were like-minded. He hated the National Socialists.

Yet nowadays there were so many excuses for betrayal.

He could denounce us because it's Sunday. . . .

And there was another reason behind Kurt Fischer's hesitation to leave. The young man was a pacifist and Social Democrat mostly because of his parents and his friends; he'd never been very active politically. Life to him had been hiking and girls and traveling and skiing. But now that the National Socialists were in power, he was surprised to find within him a strong desire to fight them, to enlighten people about their intolerance and evil. Perhaps, he debated, he should stay and work to bring them down.

But they were so powerful, so insidious. And so deadly.

Kurt looked at the clock on the mantelpiece. It had run down. He and Hans were always forgetting to wind it. This had been their father's job and the image of the still timepiece made Kurt's heart ache. He pulled his pocket watch out and checked the time. "We have to go now or call him and tell him we're not doing it."

Tink, tink, tink . . . The knife resumed its cymbal tapping on the plate.

Then long silence.

"I say we stay," Hans said. But he looked at his brother expectantly; there'd always been rivalry between the two, yet the younger would abide by any decision the older made.

But will I decide correctly?

Survival . . .

Kurt Fischer finally said, "We're going. Get your pack."

Tink, tink . . .

Kurt shouldered his knapsack and glared defiantly at his brother. But Hans's mood changed like spring weather. He suddenly laughed and gestured at their clothing. They were dressed in shorts, short-sleeved shirts and hiking boots. "Look at us: Paint us brown and we'd be Hitler Youth!"

Kurt couldn't help but smile. "Let's go, comrade," he said sarcastically, the term the same one used by Stormtroopers and Youth to refer to their fellows.

Refusing a last look around the apartment, for fear he'd start to cry, Kurt Fischer opened the door and they stepped into the corridor.

Across the hallway was stocky, apple-cheeked Mrs. Lutz, a War widow, scrubbing her doormat. The woman usually kept to herself but would sometimes stop by certain residents' apartments—only those who met her strict standards of neighborliness, whatever those might be—to deliver her miraculous foodstuffs. She considered the Fischers her friends and over the years had left presents of lung pudding, prune dumplings, head cheese, pickled cucumbers, garlic sausage and noodles with tripe. Just seeing her now, Kurt began to salivate.

"Ach, the Fischer brothers!"

"Good morning, Mrs. Lutz. You're hard at work early."

"It will be hot again, I've heard. Ach, for some rain."

"Oh, we don't want anything to interfere with the Olympics," Hans said with a hint of irony. "We're so looking forward to seeing them."

She laughed. "Silly people running and jumping in their undergarments! Who needs them when my poor plants are dying of thirst? Look at my John-go-to-bed-at-noons outside the door. And the begonias! Now, tell me, where are your parents? Still on that trip of theirs?"

"In London, yes." Their parents' political difficulties were not common knowledge and the brothers were naturally reluctant to mention them to anyone.

"It's been several months. They better get home soon or they won't recognize you. Where are you off to now?"

"Hiking. In the Grünewald."

"Oh, it's lovely there. And much cooler than in the city." She returned to her diligent scrubbing.

As they walked down the stairs Kurt glanced at his brother and noticed that Hans had quickly grown sullen again.

"What's the matter?"

"You seem to think this city is the devil's playground. But it's not. There are millions of people like her." He nodded back up the stairs. "Good people, kind people. And we're leaving all of them behind. And to go to what? A place where we know no one, where we can hardly speak the language, where we have no jobs, a place we were at war with only twenty years ago? How well do you think we'll be received?"

Kurt had no rebuttal for this. His brother was one hundred percent correct. And there were probably a dozen more arguments to be made against their leaving.

Outside, they looked up and down the hot street. None of the few people out at this hour paid any attention to them. "Let's go," Kurt said and strode down the sidewalk, reflecting that, in a way, he'd been honest with Mrs. Lutz. They were going on a wander—only not to any rustic hostel in the fragrant woods west of Berlin but toward an uncertain new life in a wholly alien land.

He jumped when his phone buzzed.

Hoping it was the medical examiner on the Dresden Alley case, he grabbed the receiver. "Kohl here."

"Come see me, Willi."

Click.

A moment later, his heart beating solidly, he was walking up the hall to Friedrich Horcher's office.

What now? The chief of inspectors was at headquarters on a Sunday morning? Had Peter Krauss learned that Kohl had made up the story about Reinhard Heydrich and Göttburg (the man came from Halle) to save the witness, the baker Rosenbaum? Had someone overheard him make an improvident comment to Janssen? Had word come down from on high that the inspector inquiring about dead Jews in Gatow was to be reprimanded?

Kohl stepped into Horcher's office. "Sir?"

"Come in, Willi." He rose and closed the door, gestured Kohl to sit.

The inspector did so. He held the man's eye, as he'd told his sons to do whenever they looked at another human being with whom difficulty might arise.

There was silence as Horcher resumed his seat and rocked back and forth in the sumptuous leather chair, playing absently with the brilliant red armband on his left biceps. He was one of the few senior Kripo officials who actually wore one in the Alex.

"The Dresden Alley case . . . keeping you busy, is it?"

"An interesting one, this."

"I miss the days of investigating, Willi."

"Yes, sir."

Horcher meticulously ordered papers on his desk. "You will go to the Games?"

"I got my tickets a year ago."

"Did you? Your children are looking forward to it?"

"Indeed. My wife too."

"Ach, good, good." Horcher had not heard a single word of Kohl's. More silence for a moment. He stroked his waxed mustache, as he was accustomed to do when not playing with his crimson armband. Then: "Sometimes, Willi, it's necessary to do difficult things. Especially in our line of work, don't you think?" Horcher avoided his eyes when he said this. Through his concern, Kohl thought: This is why the man will not advance very far in the Party; he's actually troubled to deliver bad news.

"Yes, sir."

"People within our esteemed organization have been aware of you for some time."

Like Janssen, Horcher was incapable of being sardonic. "Esteemed" would be meant sincerely, though which organization he might be referring to was a mystery, given the incomprehensible hierarchy of the police. To his shock he learned the answer to this question when Horcher continued. "The SD has quite some file on you, wholly independent of the Gestapo's."

This chilled Kohl to his core. Everyone in government could count on a Gestapo file. It would be insulting *not* to have one. But the SD, the elite intelligence service for the SS? And its leader was none other than Reinhard Heydrich himself. So the story he'd spun to Krauss about Heydrich's hometown had returned. And all to save a Jew baker he didn't even know.

Breathing hard, palms staining his trousers with sweat, Willi Kohl numbly nodded, as the end of his career—and perhaps his life—began to unfold before him.

"Apparently there have been discussions about you at high levels."

"Yes, sir." He hoped his voice didn't quaver. He locked his eyes onto Horcher's, which tore themselves away after an electric few seconds and examined a Bakelite bust of Hitler on a table near the door.

"There is a matter that has come up. And unfortunately I can do nothing about it."

Of course there would be no help from Friedrich Horcher, who was not only merely Kripo, the lowest rung of the Sipo, but was a coward as well.

"Yes, sir, what might this matter be?"

"It is desired . . . it actually is *ordered* that you represent us at the ICPC in London this February."

Kohl nodded slowly, waiting for more. But, no, this seemed to be the entire volley of bad news.

The International Criminal Police Commission, founded in Vienna in the twenties, was a cooperative network of police forces throughout the world. They shared information about crime, criminals and law enforcement techniques via publications, telegram and radio. Germany was a member and Kohl had been delighted to learn that, though America was not, representatives from the FBI would be attending the conference, with an eye toward joining.

Horcher scanned his desktop, upon whose surface Hitler, Göring and Himmler also gazed down from their wooden frames on the wall.

Kohl took several breaths to steady himself. He said, "It would be an honor."

"Honor?" Horcher scowled. Leaning forward, he said softly, "Generous of you."

Kohl understood his superior's scorn. Attendance at the conference would be a waste of time. Because the hue and cry of National Socialism was a self-reliant Germany, an alliance of international law enforcement organizations sharing information was the last thing Hitler wanted. There was a reason that "Gestapo" was an acronym for "*secret* state police."

Kohl was being sent as a figurehead, merely to keep up appearances. No one higher would dare go—for a National Socialist official to leave the country for two weeks meant he might not find his job awaiting him when he returned. But Kohl, since he was merely a worker bee, with no intent to rise in the Party ranks, could disappear for a fortnight and return with no loss—aside, of course, from the little matter that a dozen cases would be delayed, and rapists and killers might go free.

Which was not their concern, of course.

Horcher was relieved at the detective's reaction. He asked with animation, "When was your last holiday, Willi?"

"Heidi and I go to Wannsee and the Black Forest frequently."

"I mean abroad."

"Ah, well . . . some years now. France. And one trip to Brighton in England."

"You should take your wife with you to London."

The suggestion alone was enough to expiate Horcher's guilt; after a judicious moment he said to Kohl, "I'm told the ferry and train fares are quite reasonable at that time of year." Another pause. "Though we will, of course, provide for *your* travel and accommodations."

"Most generous."

"Again, I'm sorry you must bear this cross, Willi. But you'll eat and drink well. British beer is much better than what one hears. And you can see the Tower of London!"

"Yes, I would enjoy that."

"What a treat, the Tower of London," the chief of inspectors repeated enthusiastically. "Well, good day to you, Willi."

"Good day, sir."

Through the halls, eerie and gloomy, despite shafts of bright sunlight falling on the oak and marble, Kohl returned to his office, calming slowly from the scare.

He sat heavily in his chair and glanced at the box of evidence and his notes regarding the Dresden Alley incident.

Then his eyes slid to a folder sitting next to it. He lifted the telephone receiver and placed a call to the operator in Gatow and asked to be connected to a private residence.

"Yes?" a young man's voice answered cautiously, unaccustomed perhaps to calls on Sunday morning.

"This is Gendarme Raul?" Kohl asked.

A pause. "Yes."

"I am Inspector Willi Kohl."

"Ah, yes, Inspector. Hail Hitler. You are telephoning me at home. On a Sunday."

Kohl chuckled. "Indeed I am. Forgive the interruption. I'm calling regarding the crime scene report from the shootings in Gatow and the other, the Polish workers."

"Forgive me, sir. I am inexperienced. The report, I'm sure, was shoddy compared to what you are used to. Certainly nothing of the quality you yourself could produce. I did the best I could."

"You mean the report is completed?"

Another hesitation, longer than the first. "Yes, sir. And it was submitted to Gendarmerie Commander Meyerhoff."

"I see. When was that?"

"Wednesday last, I believe. Yes. That is correct."

"Has he reviewed it?"

"I noticed a copy on his desk Friday evening, sir. I had also asked that one be sent to you. I'm surprised you haven't received it yet."

"Well, I will follow this matter up with your superior. . . . Tell me, Raul. Were you satisfied with your handling of the crime scene?"

"I believe I did a thorough job, sir."

"Did you reach any conclusions?" Kohl asked.

"I . . ."

"Speculation is perfectly acceptable at this stage of an investigation."

The young man said, "Robbery did not seem to be the motive?"

"You are asking me?"

"No, sir. I'm stating my conclusion. Well, speculation."

"Good. Their belongings were on them?"

"Their money was missing. But jewelry and other effects were not taken. Some of them appeared quite valuable. Though . . ."

"Go on."

"The items were on the victims when they were brought into our morgue. I'm sorry to say the effects have since disappeared."

"That does not interest, or surprise, me. Did you find any suggestion that they had enemies? Any of them?"

"No, sir, at least not regarding the families in Gatow. Quiet, hardworking, apparently decent folk. Jews, yes, but they did not practice their religion. They were, of course, not involved in the Party but they were not dissidents. As for the Polish workers, they had come here from Warsaw only three days before their deaths to plant trees for the Olympics. They were not Communists or agitators that anyone knew."

"Any other thoughts?"

"There were at least two or three killers involved. I noted the footprints, as you instructed me. Both incidents, the same."

"The type of weapon used?"

"No idea, sir. The casings for the shells were gone when I arrived."

"Gone?" An epidemic of conscientious murderers, it seemed. "Well, the lead slugs may tell us. Did you recover any in good shape?"

"I searched the ground carefully. But I couldn't find any."

"The coroner must have recovered some."

"I asked him, sir, and he said none were found."

"None?"

"I'm sorry, sir."

"My irritation is not directed at you, Gendarme Raul. You are a credit to your profession. And forgive me for disturbing you at home. You have children? I think I hear an infant in the background. Did I awaken him?"

"Her, sir. But when she is old enough I will tell her of the honor of being awakened from her dreams by such a famed investigator as yourself."

"Good day."

"Hail Hitler."

Kohl dropped the phone in the cradle. He was confused. The facts in the murders suggested an SS, Gestapo or Stormtrooper killing. But had that been the case, Kohl and the gendarme would have been ordered at once to stop the investigation—the way Kripo detectives had been told instantly to cease looking into a recent black-market food case when the investigation found leads to Admiral Raeder of the navy and Walter von Brauchitsch, a senior army officer.

They weren't being prevented from pursuing the case but they *were* encountering foot-dragging. What to make of the ambiguity?

It was almost as if the killings, whatever the motive, had been dangled before Kohl as a test of his loyalty. Had Commander Meyerhoff called the Kripo at the behest of the SD to see if the inspector would refuse to handle cases involving Jew and Pole killings? Could this be the case?

But, no, no, that was too paranoid. He was thinking of this only because he'd learned of the SD file on him.

Kohl could come up with no answers to these questions and so he rose and wandered through the silent halls once more to the Teletype room to learn if another miracle had occurred and his counterparts in America had seen fit to respond to his urgent inquiries.

The battered van, hot as an oven inside, pulled up on Wilhelm Square and parked in an alley.

"How do I address people?" Paul asked.

"'Sir,'" Webber said. "Always 'sir.'"

"There won't be any women?"

"Ach, good question, Mr. John Dillinger. Yes, there may be a few. But they will not be in official positions, of course. They'll be your peers. Secretaries, cleaners, file clerks, typists. They will be single—no married women may work—so you will say 'Miss.' And you may flirt a little if you like. That would be appropriate from a workman but they will also understand if you ignore them, wishing only to get your job done as efficiently as possible and get back home to your Sunday meal."

"Do I knock on doors or just enter?"

"Always knock," Morgan offered. Webber nodded.

"And I say 'Hail Hitler'?"

Webber scoffed. "As often as you like. One has never gone to prison for saying that."

"And that salute you do. The arm in the air?"

"Not necessary," Morgan said. "Not from a workman." He reminded, "And remember your *G*'s. Soften them. Speak as a Berliner. Lull suspicions before they arise."

In the back of the sweltering van Paul stripped off his clothes and pulled on the coveralls Webber had provided. "Good fit," the German said. "I can sell them to you if you wish to keep them."

"Otto," Paul said, sighing. He examined the battered identity card, which contained a picture of a man resembling himself. "Who's this?"

"There is a warehouse, not much used, where the Weimar stored files of soldiers who fought in the War. There are millions of them, of course. I use them from time to time for forging passes and other documents. I locate a picture that resembles the person buying the documents. The photographs are older and worn but so are *our* identity cards because we must keep them with us at all times." He looked at the picture then up at Paul. "This is a man who was killed at Argonne-Meuse. His file notes that he won several medals before he died. They were considering an Iron Cross. You look good for a dead man."

Webber then handed him the two work permits that would allow him access to the Chancellory. Paul had left his own passport and the fake Russian one at the boardinghouse, had bought a pack of German cigarettes and carried the cheap, unmarked matches from the Aryan Café; Webber had assured him he'd be searched carefully at the front of the building. "Here." Webber handed him a notebook and pencil and a battered meter stick. He also gave him a short steel rule, which he could use as a jimmy on the lock in Ernst's office door if need be.

Paul looked these items over. He asked Webber, "They're really going to fall for this?"

"Ach, Mr. John Dillinger, if you want certainty, aren't you in the wrong line of work?" He took out one of his cabbage cigars.

"You're not going to smoke that here?" Morgan asked.

"Where would you have me smoke it? On the door stoop of the Leader's abode, striking the match on an SS guard's ass?" He lit the stogie, nodded at Paul. "We will be waiting here for you."

Hermann Göring strode through the Chancellory building as if he owned it.

Which, he believed, he one day would.

The minister loved Adolf Hitler the way Peter loved Christ.

But Jesus eventually got nailed to a T of wood and Peter took over the operation.

That is what would happen in Germany, Göring knew. Hitler was an unearthly creation, unique in the history of the world. Mesmerizing, brilliant beyond words. And because of that he would not survive to see old age. The world cannot accept visionaries and messiahs. Wolf would be dead within five years and Göring would weep and beat his breast, pierced by pitched, genuine sorrow. He would officiate during the lengthy mourning. And then he would lead the country to its position as the greatest nation in the world. Hitler said that this would be a thousand-year empire. But Hermann Göring would steer *his* regime on the course to forever.

But, for now, smaller goals: tactical measures to make certain that it *was* he who stepped into the role of Leader.

After he'd finished his eggs and sausage, the minister had changed clothes again (he normally went through four or five outfits a day). He was now in a flamboyant green military uniform, encrusted with braids, ribbons and decorations, some earned, many bought. He had dressed for the part because he felt like he was on a mission. And his goal? To tack Reinhard Ernst's head to the wall (Göring was, after all, hunting master of the empire).

The file exposing Keitel's Jewish heritage tucked under his arm like a riding crop, he strode down the dim corridors. Turning a corner, he winced in pain from his wound—the bullet he'd taken in the groin during the November '23 Beer Hall Putsch. He'd swallowed his pills only an hour before—he was never without them—but already the numbness was wearing off. Ach, the pharmacist must have gotten the strength wrong. He would berate the man about this later. He nodded to the SS guards and stepped into the Leader's outer office, smiling to the secretary.

"He asked that you go in at once, Mr. Minister."

Göring strode across the carpet and then entered the Leader's office. Hitler was leaning against the edge of his desk, as he often did. Wolf was never comfortable sitting still. He would pace, he would perch, he'd rock back and forth, gazing out windows. He now sipped his chocolate, set the cup and saucer on the desktop, and nodded gravely to someone sitting in a high-backed armchair. Then he looked up. "Ah, Mr. Air Minister, come in, come in."

Hitler held up the note Göring had penned earlier. "I must hear more about this. It's interesting that you mention a conspiracy. . . . Our comrade here, it seems, has brought similar news of such a matter too."

Halfway through the large office, Göring blinked and stopped abruptly, seeing the other visitor to the Leader's office rise from the armchair. It was Reinhard Ernst. He nodded and offered a smile. "Good morning, Mr. Minister."

Göring ignored him and asked Hitler, "A conspiracy?"

"Indeed," Hitler said. "We have been discussing the colonel's project, the Waltham Study. It seems some enemies have falsified information about his associate, Doctor-professor Ludwig Keitel. Can you imagine? They've gone so far as to suggest that the professor has Jewish blood in him. Please, sit, Hermann, and tell me about this conspiracy *you've* uncovered."

Reinhard Ernst believed that for as long as he lived he would never forget the look on Hermann Göring's puffy face at that moment.

In the ruddy, grinning moon of flesh, the eyes registered utter shock. A bully cut down.

Ernst took no particular pleasure in the coup, however, because once the shock bled out, the visage turned to one of pure hatred.

The Leader didn't seem to notice the silent exchange between the men.

He tapped several documents on the desk. "I asked Colonel Ernst for information about his study on our military he is currently conducting, which he will deliver tomorrow. . . ." A sharp look at Ernst, who nodded and assured him, "Indeed, my Leader."

"And in preparing it he learned that someone has altered records of the relatives of Doctor-professor Keitel and others working with the government. Men at Krupp, Farben, Siemens."

"And," Ernst muttered, "I was shocked to find that the matter goes beyond that. They have even altered records of the relatives and ancestors of many prominent officials in the Party itself. Planting information in and around Hamburg, mostly. I saw fit to destroy much of what I came across." Ernst looked Göring up and down. "Some lies referred to people quite high up. Suggestions of liaisons with Jewish tinkers, bastard children and the like."

Göring frowned. "Terrible." His teeth were close together—furious not only at the defeat but at Ernst's hint that Jewish ancestry might have figured in the air minister's past, as well. "Who would do such a thing?" He began fidgeting with the folder he held.

"Who?" Hitler muttered. "Communists, Jews, Social Democrats. I myself have been troubled lately by the Catholics. We must never forget they oppose us. It's easy to be lulled, considering our common hatred for the Jews. But who knows? We have many enemies."

"Indeed we do." Göring again cast a look at Ernst, who asked if he could pour the minister some coffee or chocolate.

"No, thank you, Reinhard," was the chilly reply.

As a soldier Ernst had learned early that of all the weapons in the arsenal of the military the single most effective was accurate intelligence. He insisted on knowing exactly what his enemy was up to. He'd made a mistake in thinking that the phone kiosk some blocks away from the Chancellory was not monitored by Göring's spies. Through that carelessness, the air minister had learned the name of the coauthor of the Waltham Study. But fortunately Ernst—while appearing to be naive in the art of intrigue—nonetheless had good people placed where they were quite useful. The man who regularly provided information to Ernst about goings-on at the air ministry had last night reported, just after he'd cleaned up a broken spaghetti plate and fetched the minister a clean shirt, that Göring had unearthed information about Keitel's grandmother.

Disgusted to have to be playing such a game, yet aware of the deadly risk the situation posed, Ernst had immediately gone to see Keitel. The doctor-professor had supposed that the woman's Jewish connection was true but he'd had nothing to do with that side of the family for years. Ernst and Keitel had themselves spent hours last night creating forgeries of documents suggesting that businessmen and government officials who were pure-blooded Aryan had Jewish roots.

The only difficult part of Ernst's strategy was to make certain that he got to Hitler before Göring did. But one of the techniques of warfare that Ernst was committed to in strategic military planning was what he called the "lightning strike." By this he meant moving so quickly that your enemy had no time to prepare a defense, even if he was more powerful than you. The colonel blustered his way into the Leader's office early this morning and laid out *his* conspiracy, proffering the forgeries.

"We will get to the bottom of it," Hitler now said and stepped away from the desk to pour himself more hot cocoa and take several zwiebacks from a plate. "Now, Hermann, what about your note? What have *you* uncovered?"

With a smiling nod toward Ernst, the huge man refused to acknowledge defeat. Instead he shook his head, with a massive frown, and said, "I've heard of unrest at Oranienburg. Particular disrespect for the guards there. I'm worried about the possibility of rebellions. I would recommend reprisals. Harsh reprisals."

This was absurd. Being extensively rebuilt with slave labor and renamed Sachsenhausen, the concentration camp was perfectly secure; there was no chance for rebellion whatsoever. The prisoners were like penned, declawed animals. Göring's comments were told for one purpose only: out of vindic-tiveness, to lay a series of deaths of innocent people at Ernst's feet.

As Hitler considered this, Ernst said casually, "I know little about the camp, my Leader, and the air minister has a good point. We must make absolutely certain there is no dissent."

"But . . . I sense some hesitation, Colonel," Hitler said.

Ernst shrugged. "Only that I wonder if such reprisals would be better inflicted *after* the Olympics. The camp is not far from the Olympic Village, after all. Particularly with the foreign reporters in town, it could be quite awkward if stories leaked out. I would think it best to keep the camp as secret as possible until later."

This idea didn't please Hitler, Ernst could see at once. But before Göring could protest, the Leader said, "I agree it's probably best. We'll deal with the matter in a month or two."

When he and Göring would have forgotten about the matter, Ernst hoped.

"Now, Hermann, the colonel has more good news. The British have completely accepted our warship and undersea boat quotas under last year's treaty. Reinhard's plan has worked."

"How fortunate," Göring muttered.

"Air Minister, is that file for my attention?" The Leader's eyes, which missed little, glanced at the documents under the man's arm.

"No, sir. It's nothing."

The Leader poured himself yet more chocolate and walked to the scale model of the Olympic stadium. "Come, gentlemen, and look at the new additions. They're quite nice, don't you think? Elegant, I would say. I love the modern styling. Mussolini thinks he invented it. But he is a thief, of course, as we all know."

"Indeed, my Leader," Göring said.

Ernst too murmured his approval. Hitler's dancing eyes reminded him of Rudy's when the boy had shown his Opa an elaborate sand castle he'd built at the beach last year.

"I'm told the heat might be breaking today. Let us hope that will be the case, for our picture-taking session. Colonel, you will wear your uniform?"

"I think not, my Leader. I am, after all, merely a civil servant now. I wouldn't want to appear ostentatious in the company of my distinguished colleagues." Ernst kept his eyes on the mock-up of the stadium and, with some effort, avoided a glance at Göring's elaborate uniform.

The office of the plenipotentiary for domestic stability—the sign painted in stark Gothic German characters—was on the third floor of the Chancellory. The renovations on this level seemed largely completed, though the smell of paint and plaster and varnish was heavy in the air.

Paul had entered the building without difficulty, though he'd been carefully searched by two black-uniformed guards armed with bayonet-mounted rifles. Webber's paperwork passed muster, though he was stopped and searched again on the third floor.

He waited until a patrol had walked down the hallway and knocked respectfully on the rippled-glass window in the door to Ernst's office.

No answer.

He tried the knob and found it unlocked. He walked through the dark anteroom and toward the door that led to Ernst's private office. He stopped suddenly, alarmed that the man might be here, since the light under the door was so bright. But he knocked again and heard nothing. He opened the door and found that the brilliance was sunlight; the office faced east and the morning light streamed viciously into the room. Debating about the door, he decided to leave it open; closing it was probably against regulations and would be suspicious, if guards made rounds.

His first impression was how cluttered the office was: papers, booklets, account sheets, bound reports, maps, letters. They covered Ernst's desk and a large table in the corner. Many books sat on the shelves, most dealing with military history, apparently arranged chronologically, starting with Caesar's *Gallic Wars*. After what Käthe had told him about German censorship, he was surprised to find books by and about Americans and Englishmen: Pershing, Teddy Roosevelt, Lord Cornwallis, Ulysses S. Grant, Abraham Lincoln, Lord Nelson.

There was a fireplace, empty this morning, of course, and scrubbed clean. On the black-and-white marble mantel were plaques of war decorations, a bayonet, battle flags, pictures of a younger, uniformed Ernst with a stout man sporting a fierce mustache and wearing a spiked helmet.

Paul opened his notebook, in which he'd sketched a dozen room plans, then paced off the perimeter of the office, drew it and added dimensions. He didn't bother with the measuring stick; he needed credibility, not accuracy. Walking to the desk, Paul looked over it. He saw several framed pictures. These showed the colonel with his family. Others were of a handsome brunette woman, probably his wife, and a threesome: a young man in uniform with, apparently, his own young wife and infant. Then there were two of the same young woman and the child, taken several years apart and more recently.

Paul looked away from the pictures and quickly read over dozens of papers on the desk. He was about to reach for one of the piles of documents and dig through it, but he paused, aware of a sound—or perhaps an absence of sound. Just a softening of the loose noises floating about him. Instantly Paul dropped to his knees and set the measuring stick on the floor, then began walking it from one side of the room to the other. He looked up as a man slowly entered, glancing at him with curiosity.

The photographs on the mantel and the ones that Morgan's contact, Max, had shown him had been several years old but there was no doubt that the man standing in front of him was Reinhard Ernst.

Chapter Twenty-Two

"Hail Hitler," Paul said. "Forgive me if I am disturbing you, sir."

"Hail," the man replied lethargically. "You are?"

"I am Fleischman. I am measuring for carpets."

"Ah, carpets."

Another figure glanced into the room, a large, black-uniformed guard. He asked to see Paul's papers, read them carefully and then returned to the ante-office, pulling up a chair just outside the door.

Ernst asked Paul, "And how big a room do I have here?"

"Eight by nine and a half meters." Paul's heart was pounding; he'd nearly said "yards."

"I would have thought it bigger."

"Oh, it is bigger, sir. I was referring to the size of the rug. Generally with fine floors like this our customers want a border of wood visible."

Ernst glanced at the floor as if he'd never seen the oak. He took his jacket off and hung it on a suit form beside his desk. He sat back in his chair, closed his eyes and rubbed them. Then he sat forward, pulled on some wire-rimmed glasses and read some documents.

"You are working on Sunday, sir?" Paul asked.

"As you," Ernst replied with a laugh, not looking up.

"The Leader is eager to finish the renovations to the building."

"Yes, that is certainly true."

As he bent to measure a small alcove Paul glanced sideways at Ernst, noting the scarred hand, the creases around the mouth, the red eyes, the demeanor of someone with a thousand thoughts percolating in his mind, someone carrying a thousand burdens.

A faint squeal as Ernst swiveled in his chair to face the window, removing his glasses. He seemed to soak up the glare and heat of the sun hungrily, with pleasure, but with a hint of regret, as well, as if he were a man of the outdoors not happy that his duty kept him desk-bound.

"How long have you done this work, Fleischman?" he asked without turning.

Paul stood, clutching the notebook at his side. "All my life, sir. Since the War."

Ernst continued to bask in the sun, leaning back slightly, eyes closed. Paul walked quietly to the mantel. The bayonet was a long one. It was dark and had not been sharpened recently but it was still quite capable of death.

"And you enjoy it?" Ernst asked.

"It suits me."

He could snatch the grisly weapon up and step to Ernst's back in one second, kill him quickly. He'd killed with a blade before. Using a knife is not like fencing in a Douglas Fairbanks movie. The blade is merely a deadly extension of the fist. A good boxer is a good knife man.

Touching the ice . . .

But what about the guard outside the door? That man would have to die too. Yet Paul never killed his touch-off's bodyguards, never even put himself in a situation where he might have to. He might kill Ernst with the blade, then knock the guard out. But with all the other soldiers around, somebody might hear the ruckus and they'd arrest him. Besides, his orders were to make sure the death was public.

"It suits you," Ernst repeated. "A simple life, with no conflicts and no difficult choices."

The phone buzzed. Ernst lifted it. "Yes? . . . Yes, Ludwig, the meeting went to our advantage. . . . Yes, yes . . . Now, have you found some volunteers? Ach, good. . . . But perhaps another two or three . . . Yes, I'll meet you there. Good afternoon."

Hanging up the phone, Ernst glanced at Paul then toward the mantel. "Some of my mementos. I've known soldiers all my life, and we all seem to be pack rats of memorabilia like this. I have many more items at home. Isn't it odd how we keep souvenirs of such horrendous events? It sometimes seems mad to me." He looked at the clock on his desk. "Are you finished, Fleischman?"

"Yes, sir, I am."

"I have some work to do now in private."

"Thank you for allowing the intrusion, sir. Hail Hitler."

"Fleischman?"

Paul turned at the doorway.

"You are a lucky man to have your duty coincide with your circumstance and your nature. How rare that is."

"I suppose it is, sir. Good day to you."

"Yes, hail."

Outside, into the hallway.

With Ernst's face and his voice burned into Paul's mind, he walked down the stairs, eyes forward, moving slowly, passing invisibly among the men here, in black or gray uniforms or suits or the coveralls of laborers. And everywhere the stern, two-dimensional eyes staring down at him from the paintings on the walls: the trinity whose names were etched into brass plates, *A. Hitler, H. Göring* and *P. J. Goebbels.*

On the ground floor he turned toward the glaring front doorway that opened onto Wilhelm Street, footsteps echoing loudly. Webber had provided used boots, a good addition to the costume, except that a hobnail had worn through the leather and tapped loudly with every step, no matter how Paul twisted his foot.

He was fifty feet from the doorway, which was an explosion of sunlight surrounded by a halo.

Forty feet.

Tap, tap, tap.

Twenty feet.

He could see outside now, cars streaming past on the street.

Ten feet . . .

Tap . . . tap . . .

"You! You will stop."

Paul froze. He turned to see a middle-aged man in a gray uniform striding quickly to him.

"You came down those stairs. Where were you?"

"I was only—"

"Let me see your documents."

"I was measuring for carpets, sir," Paul said, digging Webber's papers out of his pocket.

The SS man looked them over quickly, compared the photo and read the work order. He took the meter stick from Paul's hand, as if it were a weapon.

He returned the work order then looked up. "Where is your special permit?"

"Special permit? I wasn't told I needed one."

"For access upstairs, you must have one."

"My superior never told me."

"That's not our concern. Everyone with access to floors above the ground needs a special permit. Your party membership card?"

"I . . . I don't have it with me."

"You are not a member of the Party?"

"Of course, sir. I am a loyal National Socialist, believe me."

"You're not a loyal National Socialist if you don't carry your card." The officer searched him, flipped through the notebook, glanced at the sketches of the rooms and the dimensions. He was shaking his head.

Paul said, "I am to return later in the week, sir. I can bring you a special permit and Party card then." He added, "And at that time I can measure your office as well."

"My office is on the ground floor, in the back—the area not scheduled for renovation," the SS officer said sourly.

"All the more reason to have a fine Persian carpet. Of which we happen to have several more than have been allotted. And nothing to do but let them rot in a warehouse."

The man considered this. Then he glanced at his wristwatch. "I don't have time to pursue this matter. I am Security Underleader Schechter. You will find my office down the stairs and to the right. The name is on the door. On with you now. But when you come back, have the special permit or it will be Prince Albrecht Street for you."

As the three men sped away from Wilhelm Square, a siren sounded nearby. Paul and Reggie Morgan looked uneasily out the windows of the van, which stank of burned cabbage and sweat.

Webber laughed. "It's an ambulance. Relax." A moment later the medical vehicle turned the corner. "I know the sounds of all the official vehicles. It's helpful knowledge in Berlin nowadays."

After a few moments Paul said quietly, "I met him."

"Met whom?" Morgan asked.

"Ernst."

Morgan's eyes widened. "He was there?"

"He came into the office just after I got there."

"Ach, what do we do?" Webber said. "We can't get back inside the Chancellory. How will we find out where he'll be?"

"Oh, I found that out," Paul said.

"You did?" Morgan asked.

"I had time to look over his desk before he arrived. He'll be at the stadium today."

"Which stadium?" Morgan asked. "There are dozens in the city."

"The *Olympic* stadium. I saw a memorandum. Hitler's having photographs of senior Party officials taken there this afternoon." He glanced at a nearby clock tower. "But we have only a few hours to get me into place. I think we'll need your help once again, Otto."

"Ach, I can get you anywhere you wish, Mr. John Dillinger. I work the miracles . . . and you pay for them. That is why we are such good partners, of course. And speaking of which, my American cash, if you please." And he let the transmission of the van scream in second gear as he held out his right hand, palm up, until Morgan dropped the envelope into it.

After a moment Paul was aware that Morgan had been looking him over. The man asked, "What was Ernst like? Did he seem like the most dangerous man in Europe?"

"He was polite, he was preoccupied, he was weary. And sad."

"Sad?" Webber asked.

Paul nodded, recalling the man's fast yet burdened eyes, the eyes of someone waiting for arduous trials to be over with.

The sun finally sets. . . .

Morgan glanced at the shops and buildings and flags on the wide avenue of Under the Lindens. He asked, "Is that a problem?"

"Problem?"

"Will meeting him make you hesitate to . . . to do what you've come here for? Will it make a difference?"

Paul Schumann wished to God that he could say it would. That seeing someone up close, that talking to him, would melt the ice, would make him hesitate to take that man's life. But he answered truthfully. "No. It will make no difference."

They sweated from the heat, and Kurt Fischer, at least, sweated from fear.

The brothers were now two blocks from the square where they would meet Unger, the man who was to spirit them away from this foundering country and reunite them with their parents.

The man they were trusting with their lives.

Hans stooped down, picked up a stone and skipped it across the waters of the Landwehr Canal.

"Don't!" Kurt whispered harshly. "Don't draw attention to us."

"You should relax, brother. Skipping stones doesn't draw attention. Everybody does it. God, it's hot. Can we stop for a ginger beer?"

"Ach, you think we are on holiday, don't you?" Kurt glanced around. There were not many people out. The hour was early, the heat already fierce.

"See anyone following us?" his brother asked with some irony.

"Do you want to stay in Berlin? All things considered?"

"All I know is that if we give up our house, we'll never see it again."

"If we don't give it up, we'll never see Mother and Father again. Probably we'll never see *anyone* again."

Hans scowled and picked up another stone. He got three skips this time. "Look! Did you see that?"

"Hurry up."

They turned into a market street, where vendors' booths were being set up. There were a number of trucks parked on the streets and sidewalks. The vehicles were filled with turnips, beets, apples, potatoes, canal trout, carp, cod oil. None of the most-in-demand items, of course, like meat, olive oil, butter and sugar. Even so, people were already queuing up to find the best—or rather the least unappetizing—purchases.

"Look, there he is," Kurt said, crossing the street and making for an old truck parked off the side of the square. A man with curly brown hair leaned against it, smoking as he looked through a newspaper. He glanced up, saw the boys and nodded subtly. He tossed the paper inside the cab of the truck.

It all comes down to trust. . . .

And sometimes you're not disappointed. Kurt had had doubts that he would even show up.

"Mr. Unger!" Kurt said as they joined him. They shook hands warmly. "This is my brother, Hans."

"Ach, he looks just like his father."

"You sell chocolates?" the boy asked, looking at the truck.

"I manufacture *and* sell candy. I was a professor but that is not a lucrative job any longer. Learning is sporadic but eating sweets is a constant, not to mention politically safe. We can talk later. Now we should get out of Berlin. You can ride in the cab with me until we get near the border. Then you will climb into a space in the back. I use ice to keep the chocolate from melting on days like this, and you will lie under boards covered with ice. Don't worry, you won't freeze to death. I've cut holes in the side of the truck to let in some warm air. We'll cross the border, as I do every week. I know the guards. I give them chocolate. They never search me."

Unger walked to the back of the truck and closed the gate.

Hans climbed into the cab, picked up the newspaper and started reading. Kurt turned, wiped his brow and looked out one last time over the city in which he'd spent his entire life. In the heat and the haze, it seemed Italian, reminding him of a trip he'd taken to Bologna with his parents when his father was lecturing for a fortnight at the old university there.

The young man was turning back to climb into the truck next to his brother when there was a collective gasp from the crowd.

Kurt froze, eyes wide.

Three black cars skidded to a stop around Unger's truck. Six men jumped out, in black SS uniforms.

No!

"Hans, run!" Kurt shouted.

But two of the SS troops raced to the passenger side of the vehicle. They ripped the door open and dragged his younger brother onto the street. He fought back until one struck him in the gut with a truncheon. Hans yelped and stopped struggling, rolling on the ground, clutching his belly. The soldiers pulled him to his feet.

"No, no, no!" Unger cried. Both he and Kurt were shoved against the side of the truck.

"Papers! Empty your pockets."

The three captives did as they were told.

"The Fischers," said the SS commander, looking over their identity cards and nodding in recognition.

Tears running down his cheeks, Unger said to Kurt, "I didn't betray you. I swear I didn't!"

"No, he didn't," said the SS officer, who unholstered his Luger, worked the toggle to cock it and shot the man in the head. Unger dropped to the pavement. Kurt gasped in horror. "*She* did," the SS man added, nodding toward a large, middle-aged woman leaning out of the SS car's window.

Her voice, filled with fury, raged at the boys: "Betrayers! Swine!"

It was Mrs. Lutz, the war widow who lived on their floor in the apartment building, the woman who had just wished them a good day!

Shocked, staring at Unger's limp body, from which blood flowed copiously, Kurt heard her breathless scream, "You ungrateful pigs. I've been watching you, I know what you've done, I know who's been to your apartment. I write down what I've seen. You've betrayed our Leader!"

The SS commander grimaced with irritation at the woman. He nodded toward a younger officer and he pushed her back into the car.

"You have been on our list, both of you, for some time."

"We've done nothing!" Staring at Unger's blood, unable to look away from the growing crimson pool, Kurt whispered, "Nothing. I swear. We were just trying to be with our parents."

"Illegally escaping the country, pacifism, anti-Party activities . . . all capital offenses." He pulled Hans closer, aimed the pistol at his head. The boy whimpered. "Please, no. Please! . . ."

Kurt stepped forward fast. A guard slugged him in the belly and he doubled over. He saw the commander touch the gun to the back of his brother's head.

"No!"

The commander squinted and leaned back to avoid the spray of blood and flesh.

"Please, sir!"

But then another officer whispered, "We have those orders, sir. During the Olympics, restraint." He nodded toward the market, where a crowd had gathered, watching. "Foreigners might be present, perhaps reporters."

Hesitating for a long moment, the commander muttered impatiently, "All right. Take them to Columbia House."

Although it was being phased out in favor of the more ruthlessly efficient, and less visible, Oranienburg camp, Columbia House was still the most notorious jail in Berlin.

The man nodded at Unger's corpse. "And dump that somewhere. Find out if he's married and if so send his wife his bloody shirt."

"Yes, my leader. With what message?"

"The shirt will be the message." The commander put his gun away and strode back to his car. He glanced briefly at the Fischer brothers but his eyes didn't really see them; it was as if they were already dead.

"Where are you, Paul Schumann?"

Like his question yesterday to the then anonymous suspect—*Who are you?*—Willi Kohl posed this query aloud and in frustration, with no immediate hope of an answer. The inspector had thought that knowing the man's name would speed the resolution of the case. But this was not so.

Kohl had received no reply to his telegrams to the Federal Bureau of Investigation or the International Olympic Committee. He'd gotten a brief response from the New York City Police Department but it said only that they would look into the matter when "practicable."

This was not a word that Kohl was familiar with but when he looked it up in the department's English-German dictionary an angry scowl filled his face. Over the past year he'd sensed a reluctance by American law enforcers to cooperate with the Kripo. Some of this was due to anti–National Socialist sentiment in the United States. Some too, he believed, might have roots in the Lindbergh baby kidnapping; Bruno Hauptmann had escaped from police custody in Germany and fled to America, where he'd murdered the child.

Kohl had sent a second, brief telegram in his halting English, thanking the NYPD and reminding them of the urgency of the matter. He'd alerted the border guards to detain Schumann if he tried to leave but word would get only to the major crossings.

Nor had Janssen's second trip to the Olympic Village proved fruitful. Paul Schumann had not been officially connected to the American team. He had come to Berlin as a writer with no known affiliation. He'd left the Olympic Village the day before and no one had seen him since, nor did anyone know where he might have gone. Schumann's name wasn't on the list of those who had bought Largo ammunition or Modelo A's recently but this was no surprise since he'd only arrived with the team on Friday

Rocking back in his chair, looking through the box of evidence, reading his penciled notes . . . Kohl looked up to see that Janssen had paused in the doorway, chatting with several other young plainclothed assistant inspectors and inspector candidates.

Kohl frowned at the noisy coffee klatch.

The younger officers paid their respects.

"Hail Hitler."

"Hail, Inspector Kohl."

"Yes, yes."

"We are on our way to the lecture. Are you coming?"

"No," Kohl muttered. "I'm working." Since the Party's ascension in '33, one-hour talks on National Socialism were held weekly in the main assembly hall of the Alex. Attendance by all Kripo officers was mandatory. Lukewarm Willi Kohl rarely went. The last one he'd attended was two years ago and had been entitled "Hitler, Pan-Germanism and the Roots of Funda-mental Social Change." He'd fallen asleep.

"SD Leader Heydrich himself may show up."

"We're not sure," another added enthusiastically. "But he might. Can you imagine? We could shake his hand!"

"As I said, I'm working." Kohl looked past their youthful, enthusiastic faces. "What do you have, Janssen?"

"Good day, Inspector," one young officer said exuberantly. They went off, loudly, down the hall.

Kohl fixed his frown on Janssen, who winced. "Sorry, sir. They attach themselves to me because I'm attached to . . ."

"Me?"

"Well, yes, sir."

Kohl nodded in the direction they'd gone. "They're members?"

"Of the Party? Several are, yes."

Before Hitler came to power it was illegal for a police officer to be a member of any political party. Kohl said, "Don't be tempted to join, Janssen. You think it will help your career but it won't. It will only get you stuck further in the spiderweb."

"Moral quicksand," Janssen quoted back his boss.

"Indeed."

"Anyway, how could I possibly join?" he asked gravely then offered one of his rare smiles. "Working with you leaves me no time for the rallies."

Kohl smiled back then asked, "Now what do you have?"

"The postmortem from Dresden Alley."

"It's about time." Twenty-four hours to perform an autopsy. Inexcusable.

The inspector candidate handed his boss the thin folder, which con-tained only two pages.

"What's this? Did the coroner do the autopsy in his sleep?"

"I—"

"Never mind," Kohl muttered and read through the document. It first stated the obvious, of course, as autopsies always did, in the dense language of physiology and morphology: that the cause of death was severe trauma to the brain due to the passage of a bullet. No sexual diseases, a bit of gout, a bit of arthritis, no war wounds. He and Kohl had in common bunions, and the calluses on the victim's feet suggested that he was indeed an ardent walker.

Janssen looked over Kohl's shoulder. "Look, sir, he had a broken finger that set badly."

"That does not interest us, Janssen. It's the little finger, which is prone to breaking under many circumstances, as opposed to an injury that is unique and might help us understand the man better. A recent break might be helpful—we could call upon physicians in northwest Berlin for leads to patients—but this fracture is old." He turned back to the report.

The alcohol in his blood suggested that he'd had some liquor not long before he'd died. The stomach contents revealed chicken, garlic, herbs, onion, carrots, potatoes, a reddish-colored sauce of some sort and coffee, all digested to the point that suggested the meal had been enjoyed about a half hour before death.

"Ah," Kohl brightened, jotting all these facts down in pencil in his battered little notebook.

"What, sir?"

"Here is something that *does* interest us, Janssen. While we can't be positive, it appears that the victim ate a very sublime dish for his last meal. It is probably coq au vin, a French delicacy that marries chicken with the unlikely partner of red wine. Usually a Burgundy such as Chambertin. We don't see it here often, Janssen. You know why? Because we Germans make piss-bad red wines, and the Austrians, who make brilliant reds, don't send us very much. Oh, yes, this is good." He thought for a moment then rose and walked to a map of Berlin on his wall. He found a pushpin and stuck it into Dresden Alley. "He died here at noon and he had lunch at a restaurant about thirty minutes before that. You recall he was a good walker, Janssen: his leg muscles, which put mine to shame, and the calluses on his feet. So, while he might have taken a taxi or tram to his fatal encounter, we will assume that he walked. Allowing him a few minutes after the meal for a cigarette . . . you recall his yellow-stained fingertips?"

"Not exactly, sir."

"Be more observant, then. Allowing him time for a cigarette and to pay the check and savor his coffee, we will assume that he walked on his sturdy legs for twenty minutes before he came to Dresden Alley. How far could a brisk walker go in that time?"

"I would guess a kilometer and a half."

Kohl frowned. "I too would guess that." He examined the legend of the Berlin map and drew a circle around the site of the killing.

Janssen shook his head. "Look at that. It's huge. We need to take the photograph of the victim to every restaurant in that circle?"

"No, only to those serving coq au vin, and of those only the ones that do so at lunchtime on Saturday. A fast look at the hours of service and the menu in front will tell us if we need to inquire further. But it will still be a huge task and one that must be undertaken immediately."

The young officer stared at the map. "Is it up to you and me, sir? Can we visit all of them ourselves? How can we?" He shook his head, discouraged.

"Of course we can't."

"Then?"

Willi Kohl sat back, his eyes floating around the room. They settled momentarily on his desktop. Then he said, "You wait here for any telegrams or other messages about the case, Janssen." Kohl took his Panama hat from the rack in the corner of his office. "And me, I have a thought."

"Where will you be, sir?"

"On the trail of a French chicken."

Chapter Twenty-Three

The anxious atmosphere that hung about the three men in the boarding-house was like cold smoke.

Paul Schumann knew the sensation well—from those moments as he waited to step into the boxing ring, trying to remember everything he knew about his opponent, picturing the guy's defenses, planning when best to dance under them, when to rise onto his toes and deliver a roundhouse or jab, figuring out how to exploit his weaknesses—and how best to compensate for your own.

He knew it from other times too: as a button man planning his touch-offs. Looking at maps drawn in his own careful handwriting, double-checking the Colt and his backup pistol, looking over the notes he'd assembled of his victim's schedules, preferences, dislikes, routines, acquaintances.

This was the Before.

The hard, hard Before. The stillness preceding the kill. The moment when he chewed the facts amid a feeling of impatience and edginess. Fear too, of course. You never got away from that. The good button men didn't, in any case.

And always the growing numbness, the crystalizing of his heart.

He was starting to touch the ice.

In the dim room, windows closed, shades down—phone unplugged, of course—Paul and Morgan looked over a map and two dozen publicity photos of the Olympic stadium, which Webber had dug up, along with a pair of sharply creased gray flannel trousers for Morgan (which the American had examined skeptically at first but then decided to keep).

Morgan tapped one of the photos. "Where do you—?"

"Please, one moment," Webber interrupted. He rose and walked across the room, whistling. He was in a jovial mood, now that he had a thousand dollars in his pocket and wouldn't have to worry about lard and yellow dye for a while.

Morgan and Paul exchanged frowns. The German dropped to his knees and began pulling records out from the cabinet beneath a battered gramophone. He grimaced. "Ach, no John Philip Sousa. I look all the time but they are hard to find." He glanced up at Morgan. "Say, Mr. John Dillinger here tells me that Sousa is American. But I think he is joking. Please, the bandleader is English, is he not?"

"No, he's American," the slim man said.

"I have heard otherwise."

Morgan lifted an eyebrow. "Perhaps you're right. Maybe a wager would be in order. A hundred marks?"

Webber considered then said, "I will look into the matter further."

"We don't really have time for music," Morgan added, watching Webber examining the stack of disks.

Paul said, "But I think we have time to cover up the sounds of our conversation?"

"Exactly," Webber said. "And we shall use . . ." He examined a label. "A collection of our stolid German hunting songs." He turned on the device and set the needle in the groove of the disk. A rousing, scratchy tune filled the room. "This is 'The Deer-stalker.'" A laugh. "Appropriate, considering our mission."

The mobsters Luciano and Lansky did exactly the same in America—usually playing the radio, to cover up conversation in the event Dewey's or Hoover's boys had a mike in the room where they were meeting.

"Now, you were saying?"

Morgan asked, "Where is the photography session?"

"Ernst's memorandum says the pressroom."

"That's here," Webber said.

Paul examined the drawing carefully and wasn't pleased. The stadium was huge and the press box must have been two hundred feet long. It was located near the top of the building's south side. He could take up position in the stands on the north side but that meant a very long shot across the entire width of the facility.

"Too far. A little breeze, the distortion of the window . . . No. I couldn't guarantee a fatal shot. And I might hit someone else."

"So?" Webber asked lethargically. "Maybe you could shoot Hitler. Or

Göring . . . why, he's as big a target as a dirigible. A blind man could hit him." He looked over the map again. "You could get Ernst when he got out of the car. What do you think of that, Mr. Morgan?" The fact that Webber had gotten Paul into and out of the Chancellory safely had given the gang leader sufficient credibility to be trusted with Morgan's name.

"But we don't know exactly when and where he'll be arriving," Morgan pointed out. There were a dozen walks and passages he could take. "They might not use the main entrance. We couldn't anticipate that and you should be in hiding before he gets there. The entire National Socialist pantheon will be assembled; security is going to be massive."

Paul continued to peruse the map. Morgan was right. And he noticed from the map that there was an underground driveway that seemed to circle the entire stadium, probably for the leaders to use for protected entrances and exits. Ernst might never be outside at all.

They stared silently for a time. An idea occurred to Paul and, touching the photos, he explained it: The back walkways of the stadium were open. Leaving the pressroom, one would walk either east or west along this corridor then down several flights of stairs to the ground level, where there was a parking area, a wide drive and sidewalks that led to the railway station. About a hundred feet from the stadium, overlooking the parking lot and drive, was a cluster of small buildings, labeled on the map *Storage Facilities*.

"If Ernst came out onto that walkway and down the stairs I could shoot from that shed. The one there."

"You could make the shot?"

Paul nodded. "Yes, easily."

"But, as we were saying, we don't know that Ernst will arrive or leave that way."

"Maybe we can force him outside. Flush him out like a bird."

"And how?" Morgan asked.

Paul said, "We ask him."

"Ask him?" Morgan frowned.

"We get a message to him in the pressroom that he's urgently needed. There's someone who needs to see him in private about something important. He walks out the corridor onto the porch, into my sights."

Webber lit one of his cabbage cigars. "But would any message be so urgent that he'd interrupt a meeting with the Leader, Göring and Goebbels?"

"From what I've learned about him he's obsessed with his job. We tell him that there's a problem having to do with the army or navy. I know that'll get his attention. What about this Krupp, the armorer that Max told us about. Could a message from Krupp be urgent?"

Morgan nodded. "Krupp. Yes, I'd think so. But how do we get the message to Ernst while he's in the photography session?"

"Ach, easy," Webber said. "I'll telephone him."

"How?"

The man drew on his ersatz cigar. "I will find out the number of one of the telephones in the pressroom and place a call. I will do this myself. I will ask for Ernst and tell him that there is a driver downstairs with a message. Only for him to see. From Gustav Krupp von Bohlen himself. I will call from a post office so when the Gestapo dials seven afterward to find the source of the call, there'll be no lead to me."

"How can you get the number?" Morgan asked.

"Contacts."

Paul asked cynically, "Do you really have to bribe someone to find the number, Otto? I would suspect that half the sports journalists in Berlin have them."

"Ach," Webber said, smiling in delight. He tried English. "You are hitting the head on the nail." Back to his native tongue: "Of course that's true. But the most important aspect of any venture is knowing *which* individual to approach and what his price is."

"All right," Morgan said, exasperated. "How much? And remember, we are not a bottomless well."

"Another two hundred. Marks will be fine. And for that I will add, for no extra charge, a way to get into and out of the stadium, Mr. John Dillinger. A full SS uniform. You can sling your rifle over your shoulder and walk straight into the stadium like Himmler himself and no one will stop you. Practice your 'Hail's and your Hitler salute, flapping your limp arm in the air like our goat-peeing Leader."

Morgan frowned. "But if they catch him masquerading as a soldier they'll shoot him for a spy."

Paul glanced at Webber and they both broke into laughter. It was the gang leader who said, "Please, Mr. Morgan. Our friend is about to kill the national military tzar. If he is caught he could be dressed like George Washington and whistling 'Stars and Stripes Forever' and they would still shoot him quite dead, do you not think?"

"I was only considering ways to make it less obvious," Morgan grumbled.

"No, it's a good plan, Reggie," Paul said. "After the shot they'll get all the officials back to Berlin as fast as possible. I'll ride with the guards protecting them. Once we're in town, I'll get lost in the crowd." Afterward he'd slip into the embassy building near the Brandenburg Gate and radio Andrew Avery and Vince Manielli in Amsterdam, who'd send the plane out to the aerodrome for him.

As their eyes returned to the maps of the stadium Paul decided it was time. He said, "I want to tell you. There's someone coming with me."

Morgan glanced at Webber, who laughed. "Ach, what are you thinking? That I could possibly live anywhere but this Prussian Garden of Eden? No, no, I will leave Germany only for heaven."

Paul said, "A woman."

Morgan's mouth tightened. "The one here." Nodding toward the hallway of the boardinghouse.

"That's right. Käthe." Paul added, "You looked into her. You know she's legitimate."

"What have you told her?" asked the troubled American.

"The Gestapo has her passport and it's only a matter of time until they arrest her."

"It's a matter of time until they arrest a *lot* of people here. What have you *told* her, Paul?" Morgan repeated.

"Just our cover story about sportswriting. That's all."

"But—"

"She's coming with me," he said.

"I should call Washington, or the Senator."

"Call who you like. She's coming."

Morgan looked at Webber.

"Ach, I have been married three times, possibly four," the German said. "And I now have a . . . complicated arrangement. Expect no advice from me on matters of the heart."

Morgan shook his head. "Jesus, we're running an airways service."

Paul fixed his fellow American with a gaze. "One other thing: At the stadium I'll only have the Russian passport for ID. If I don't make it she'll never hear what happened. Will you tell her something—about me having to leave? I don't want her thinking that I ditched her. And do what you can to get her out."

"Of course."

"Ach, you'll make it, Mr. John Dillinger. You're the American cowboy with big balls, right?" Webber wiped his sweating forehead. He rose and found three glasses in the cupboard. From a flask he poured some clear liquid into them and passed them around. "Austrian obstler. You have heard of it? It is the best of all liquors, good for the blood and good for the soul. Now, drink up, gentlemen, then let us go out and change the fate of my poor nation."

"I will need as many of them as you can find," Willi Kohl said.

The man nodded cautiously. "It isn't really a question of finding them. They are always quite findable. It's a question of how out-of-the-ordinary this matter is. There is really no precedent for it."

"It *is* out of the ordinary," Kohl agreed. "That much is true. But Police Chief Himmler has branded this an unusual case and an important one. Other officers are occupied throughout the city with equally pressing matters and he left it to me to be resourceful. So I have come to you."

"Himmler?" asked Johann Muntz. The middle-aged man stood in the doorway of a small house on Grün Street in Charlottenburg. Shaved and trimmed and wearing a suit, he looked as if he'd just returned from church this Sunday morning, a risky outing, to be sure, if you wished to retain your job as headmaster of one of the best schools in Berlin.

"Well, as you know, they're autonomous. Completely self-governed. I cannot dictate anything to them. They might say no. And there is nothing I can do about that."

"Ah, Dr. Muntz, I'm just asking for an opportunity to appeal to them in hopes they will volunteer to help the cause of justice."

"But today is Sunday. How can I contact them?"

"I suspect you need only call the leader at home and he will arrange for their assembly."

"Very well. I will do it, Inspector."

Three-quarters of an hour later, Willi Kohl found himself in Muntz's backyard, looking over the faces of nearly two dozen boys, many of whom were dressed in brown shirts, shorts and white socks, black ties dangling from a braided leather clasp at the throat. The youngsters were, for the most part, members of the Hindenburg School's Hitler Youth brigade. As the school's headmaster had just reminded Kohl, the organization was completely independent of any adult supervision. The members selected their own leaders and it was they who determined the activities of their group, whether that was hiking, football or denouncing backstabbers.

"Hail Hitler," Kohl said and was greeted with a number of outstretched right hands and a surprisingly loud echo of the salutation. "I am Senior Detective-inspector Kohl, with the Kripo."

Some of the faces broke into looks of admiration. And some of the youthful faces remained as emotionless as the face of the fat dead man in Dresden Alley.

"I need your assistance in the furtherance of National Socialism. A matter of the highest priority." He looked at a young blond boy, who had been introduced to him as Helmut Gruber, who, Koul recalled, was the leader of the Hindenburg brigade. He was smaller than most of the others but he had an adult confidence about him. A steely look filled his eyes as he gazed back at a man thirty years older than he. "Sir, we will do whatever is necessary to help our Leader and our country."

"Good, Helmut. Now listen, everyone. You may think this is an odd request. I have here two bundles of documents. One is a map of an area near the Tiergarten. The other is a picture of a man we are trying to identify. Written on the bottom of the man's picture is the name of a particular dish one would order at a restaurant. It's called coq au vin. A French term. You don't need to know how it's pronounced. All you need to do is go to every restaurant in the circled area on the map and see if the establishment was open yesterday and if that dish is on the luncheon menu. If it is you will ask if the manager of the restaurant knows the person in this picture or remembers him dining there recently. If so, contact me at Kripo headquarters at once. Will you do this?"

"Yes, Inspector Kohl, we will," Squad Leader Gruber announced, not bothering to poll his troops.

"Good. The Leader will be proud of you. I will now distribute these sheets." He paused and caught the eye of one particular student in the back, one of the few not dressed in a uniform. "One other matter. It is necessary that you all be discreet regarding something."

"Discreet?" the boy asked, frowning.

"Yes. It means you must refrain from mentioning a fact I am about to share with you. I have come to you for this assistance because of my son Günter, in the back there." Several dozen eyes swiveled toward the boy, whom Kohl had called at home not long before and instructed to come to his headmaster's house. Günter blushed fiercely and looked down. His father continued. "I suspect you do not know that my son will in the future be assisting me in important matters of state security. This, by the way, is why I cannot let him join your fine organization; I prefer that he remain behind the scenes, as it were. In this way he will be able to continue to help me work for the glory of the fatherland. Please keep this fact among yourselves. You will do that?"

Helmut's eyes grew still as he glanced back at Günter, thinking perhaps of recent Aryan and Jew games that possibly should not have been played. "Of course, Mr. Inspector Kohl," he said.

Kohl looked at his son's face and its repressed smile of joy and then said, "Now line up in a single queue and I will distribute the papers. My son and Squad Leader Gruber will decide how you divide the labor."

"Yes, sir. Hail Hitler."

"Hail Hitler." Kohl forced himself to offer a firm, outstretched-arm salute. He gave the handouts to the two boys. He added, "Oh, and gentlemen?"

"Yes, sir?" Helmut responded, standing to attention.

"Mind the traffic. Look carefully when crossing streets."

Chapter Twenty-Four

He knocked on the door and she let him into her room.

Käthe seemed embarrassed by her living space in the boardinghouse. Bare walls, no plants, rickety furniture; she or the landlord had moved all the better items into the rooms to be let. Nor did anything here seem personal. Maybe she'd been pawning off her possessions. Sunlight hit the faded carpet but it was a small, solitary trapezoid and pale; the light was reflected from a window across the alley.

Then she gave a girlish laugh and flung her arms around him. She kissed him hard. "You smell of something different. I like it." She sniffed his face.

"Shaving soap?"

"Perhaps that's it, yes."

He'd used some he'd found in the lavatory, a German brand, rather than his Burma Shave, because he was afraid a guard at the stadium might smell the unfamiliar scent of the American soap and grow suspicious.

"It's nice."

He noticed a single suitcase on the bed. The Goethe book was on the bare table, a cup of weak coffee next to it. There were white lumps floating on the surface and he asked her if there was such a thing as Hitler milk from Hitler cows.

She laughed and said that the National Socialists had plenty of asses among them, but to her knowledge they'd created no ersatz cows. "Even real milk curdles when it's old."

Then he said, "We're leaving tonight."

She nodded, frowning. "Tonight? When you say 'immediately,' you mean it."

"I will meet you here at five."

"Where are you going now?" Käthe asked him.

"Just doing one final interview."

"Well, good luck, Paul. I will look forward to reading your article, even if it *is* about, oh, perhaps the black market, and not sports." She gave him a knowing look. Käthe was a clever woman, of course; she suspected he had business here other than writing stories—probably, like half the town, putting together some semi-legal ventures. Which made him think she'd already accepted a darker side to him—and that she wouldn't be very upset if he eventually told her the truth about what he was doing here. After all, his enemy was her enemy.

He kissed her once more, tasting her, smelling lilac, feeling the pressure of her skin against him. But he found that, unlike last night, he wasn't the least stirred. This didn't trouble him, though; it was the way things had to be. The ice had taken him completely.

"How could she have betrayed us?"

Kurt Fischer answered his brother's question with a despairing shake of his head.

He too was heartsick at the thought of what their neighbor had done. Why, Mrs. Lutz! To whom they took a loaf of their mother's warm stollen, lopsided and overfilled with candied fruit, every Christmas Eve, whom their parents had comforted as she cried on the anniversary of Germany's surrender—that date a surrogate for the day her husband was killed during the War, since no one knew exactly when he died.

"How could she do it?" Hans whispered again.

But Kurt Fischer was unable to explain.

If she had denounced them because they had been planning to post dissident billboards or to attack some Hitler Youth, he might have understood. But all they wanted to do was leave a country whose leader had said, "Pacifism is the enemy of National Socialism." Like so many others, he supposed, Mrs. Lutz had become intoxicated by Hitler.

The prison cell at Columbia House was about three by three meters, made of rough-hewn stone, windowless, with metal bars for a door, opening onto the corridor. Water dripped and the young men heard the scuttle of rats nearby. There was a single bare, glaring bulb overhead in the cell, yet none in the corridor so they could see few details of the dark forms that occasionally passed. Sometimes the guards were alone, other times they escorted prisoners, who were barefoot and made no sound except their occasional gasps or pleas or sobs. Sometimes the silence of their fear was more chilling than the noises they uttered.

The heat was unbearable; it made their skin itch. Kurt couldn't understand why—they were underground and it should have been cool here. Then he noticed a pipe in the corner. Hot air streamed out fiercely. The jailors were pumping it in from a furnace to make sure the prisoners didn't get even a small respite from their discomfort.

"We shouldn't've left," Hans muttered. "I told you."

"Yes, we should have stayed in our apartment—*that* would have saved us." He was speaking with sharp irony. "Until when? Next week? Tomorrow? Don't you understand she's been watching us? She's seen the parties, she heard what we've said."

"How long will we be here?"

And how does one answer that question? Kurt thought; they were in a place where every moment was forever. He sat on the floor—there was nowhere else to perch—as he stared absently into the dark, empty cell across the corridor from theirs.

A door opened and boots sounded on the concrete.

Kurt began counting the steps—one, two, three . . .

At twenty-eight the guard would be even with their cell. Counting footsteps was something he'd already learned about being a prisoner; captives are desperate for *any* information, for *any* certainty.

Twenty, twenty-one, twenty-two . . .

The brothers regarded each other. Hans balled up his fists. "They'll hurt. They'll taste blood," he muttered.

"No," Kurt said. "Don't do anything foolish."

Twenty-five, twenty-six . . .

The steps slowed.

Blinking against the glare from the light overhead, Kurt saw two large men in brown uniforms appear. They looked at the brothers.

Then turned away.

One of them opened the cell opposite and harshly called, "Grossman, you will come out."

The darkness in the cell moved. Kurt was startled to realize that he'd been staring at another human being. The man staggered to his feet and stepped forward, using the bars as support. He was filthy. If he'd gone inside clean-shaven, the stubble on his face told Kurt that he had been in the cell for at least a week.

The prisoner blinked, looked around him at the two large men, then at Kurt across the hallway.

One of the guards glanced at a piece of paper, "Ali Grossman, you have been sentenced to five years in Oranienburg camp for crimes against the State. Step outside."

"But I—"

"Remain quiet. You are to be prepared for the trip to the camp."

"They deloused me already. What do you mean?"

"I said quiet!"

One guard whispered something to the other, who replied, "Didn't you bring yours?"

"No."

"Well, here, use mine."

He handed some light-colored leather gloves to the other guard, who pulled them on. With the grunt of a tennis player delivering a powerful serve, the guard swung his fist directly into the thin man's belly. Grossman cried out and began to retch.

The guard's knuckles silently struck the man's chin.

"No, no, no."

More blows, finding their targets on his groin, his face, his abdomen. Blood flowed from his nose and mouth, tears from his eyes. Choking, gasping. "Please, sir!"

In horror, the brothers watched as the human being was turned into a broken doll. The guard who'd been doing the hitting looked at his comrade and said, "I'm sorry about the gloves. My wife will clean and mend these."

"If it's convenient."

They picked the man up and dragged him up the hall. The door echoed loudly.

Kurt and Hans stared at the empty cell. Kurt was speechless. He believed he'd never been so frightened in his life. Hans finally asked, "He probably did something quite terrible, don't you think? To be treated like that."

"A saboteur, I'd guess," Kurt said in a shaky voice.

"I heard there was a fire in a government building. The transportation ministry. Did you hear that? I'll bet he was behind it."

"Yes. A fire. He was surely the arsonist."

They sat paralyzed with terror, as the blistering stream of air from the pipe behind them continued to heat the tiny cell.

It was no more than a minute later that they heard the door open and slam closed again. They glanced at each other.

The footsteps began, echoing as leather met concrete.

. . . six, seven, eight . . .

"I will kill the one who was on the right," Hans whispered. "The bigger. I can do it. We can get the keys and—"

Kurt leaned close, shocking the boy by gripping his face in both of his hands. "No!" he whispered so fiercely that his brother gasped. "You will do nothing. You will not fight them, you will not speak back. You will do exactly what they say and if they hit you, you will take the pain silently." All his earlier thoughts of fighting the National Socialists, of trying to make some difference, had vanished.

"But—"

Kurt's powerful fingers pulled Hans close. "You will do as I say!"

. . . thirteen, fourteen . . .

The footsteps were like a hammer on the Olympic bell, each one sending a jolt of fear vibrating within Kurt Fischer's soul.

. . . seventeen, eighteen . . .

At twenty-six they would slow.

At twenty-eight they would stop.

And the blood would begin to flow.

"You're hurting me!" But even Hans's strong muscles couldn't shake off his brother's grip.

"If they knock out your teeth you will say nothing. If they break your fingers you can cry and wail and scream. But you will say nothing to them. We are going to survive this. Do you understand me? To survive we cannot fight back."

Twenty-two, twenty-three, twenty-four . . .

A shadow fell on the floor in front of the bars.

"Understand?"

"Yes," Hans whispered.

Kurt put his arm around his brother's shoulder and they faced the door.

The men stopped at the cell.

But they weren't the guards. One was a lean gray-haired man in a suit. The other was heavier, balding, wearing a brown tweed jacket and a waistcoat. They looked the brothers over.

"You are the Fischers?" the gray-haired man asked.

Hans looked at Kurt, who nodded.

He pulled a piece of paper from his pocket and read. "Kurt." He looked up. "You would be Kurt. And you, Hans."

"Yes."

What was this?

The man looked up the hallway. "Open the cell."

More footsteps. The guard appeared, glanced in and unlocked the door. He stepped back, his hand on the truncheon that hung from his belt.

The two men stepped inside.

The gray-haired man said, "I am Colonel Reinhard Ernst."

The name was familiar to Kurt. He occupied some role in Hitler's government, though he wasn't sure what exactly. The second man was introduced as Doctor-professor Keitel, from some military college outside of Berlin.

The colonel asked, "Your arrest document says 'crimes against the State.' But they all do. What exactly *were* your crimes?"

Kurt explained about their parents and about trying to leave the country illegally.

Ernst cocked his head and regarded the boys closely. "Pacifism," he muttered and turned to Keitel, who asked, "You've committed anti-Party activities?"

"No, sir."

"You are Edelweiss Pirates?"

These were informal anti–National Socialist clubs of young people, some said gangs, rising up in reaction to the mindless regimentation of the Hitler Youth. They'd meet clandestinely for discussions about politics and art—and to sample some of the pleasures of life that the Party, publicly at least, condemned: drinking, smoking and unmarried sex. The brothers knew some young people who were members but they themselves were not. Kurt told the men this.

"The offense may seem minor, but"—Ernst displayed a piece of paper— "you have been sentenced to three years at Oranienburg camp."

Hans gasped. Kurt felt stunned, thinking of the terrible beating they'd just seen, poor Mr. Grossman pounded into submission. Kurt knew too that people sometimes went to Oranienburg or Dachau to serve a short sentence but were never seen again. He sputtered, "There was no trial! We were arrested an hour ago! And today is Sunday. How can we have been sentenced?"

The colonel shrugged. "As you can see, there *was* a trial." Ernst handed him the document, which contained dozens of prisoners' names, Kurt's and Hans's among them. Next to each was the length of sentence. The heading on the document said simply "The People's Court." This was the infamous tribunal that consisted of two real judges and five men from the Party, the SS or the Gestapo. There was no appeal from its judgment.

He stared at it, numb.

The professor spoke. "You are in general good health, both of you?"

The brothers glanced at each other and nodded.

"Jewish to any degree?"

"No."

"And you have done Labor Service?"

Kurt said, "My brother has. I was too old."

"As to the matter at hand," Professor Keitel said, "we are here to offer you a choice." He seemed impatient.

"Choice?"

Ernst's voice lowered and he continued. "It is the thinking of some people in our government that particular individuals should not participate in our military. Perhaps they are of a certain race or nationality, perhaps they are intellectuals, perhaps they tend to question decisions of our government. I, however, believe that a nation is only as great as its army, and that for an army to be great it must be representative of all its citizens. Professor Keitel and I are doing a study that we think will support some shifts in how the government views the German armed forces." He glanced back into the hall and said to the SA guard, "You can leave us."

"But, sir—"

"You can leave us," Ernst repeated in a calm voice and yet it seemed to Kurt as strong as Krupp steel.

The man glanced again at Kurt and Hans and then receded down the hall.

Ernst continued. "And this study may very well ultimately determine how the government values its citizens in general. We have been looking for men in your circumstances to help us."

The professor said, "We need healthy young men who would otherwise be excluded from military service for political or other reasons."

"And what would we do?"

Ernst gave a brief laugh. "Why, you'd become soldiers, of course. You would serve in the German army, navy or air force for one year, regular duty."

He glanced at the professor, who continued. "Your service will be as any other soldier's. The only difference is that we will monitor your performance. Your commanding officers will keep notes on your record. The information will be compiled and we will analyze it."

Ernst said, "If you serve the year, your criminal record will be erased." A nod at the court's sentencing list. "You will be free to emigrate if you wish. But the currency regulations will remain in place. You can only take a limited number of marks and you will not be allowed back into the country."

Kurt was thinking about something he'd heard a moment ago. *Perhaps they are of a certain race or nationality. . . .* Did Ernst foresee that Jews or other non-Aryans would someday be in the German army?

And, if so, what did that mean for the country in general? What changes did these men have in mind?

"You are pacifists," Ernst said. "Our other volunteers who've agreed to help us have had less of a difficult choice than you. Can a pacifist morally join a military organization? That's a hard decision to make. But we would like you to participate. You are Nordic in appearance, are in excellent health and have the bearing of soldiers. With people like you involved, I believe certain elements in the government would be more inclined to accept our theories."

"Regarding these beliefs of yours," Keitel added, "I will say this: Being a professor at a war college and a military historian, I find them naive. But we will take your sentiments into account, and your duties in the service would be commensurate with your views. We would hardly make a flier out of a man terrified of heights or put a claustrophobic in an undersea boat. There are many jobs in the military that a pacifist could hold. Medical service comes to mind."

Ernst said, "And, as I said, after some time you may find that your feelings about peace and war become more realistic. There is no better crucible for becoming a man than the army, I feel."

Impossible, Kurt thought. He said nothing.

"But if your beliefs dictate that you cannot serve," Ernst said, "you have another option." A gesture toward the sentencing document.

Kurt glanced at his brother. "May we discuss this between ourselves?"

Ernst said, "Certainly. But you only have a few hours. There is a group

being inducted late this afternoon, with basic training to start tomorrow."
He looked at his watch. "I have a meeting now. I'll be back here by two or
three to learn your decision."

Kurt handed the sentencing document to Ernst.

But the colonel shook his head. "Keep that. It might help you make up
your mind."

Chapter Twenty-Five

Twenty minutes from downtown Berlin, just past Charlottenburg, the white van turned north at Adolf Hitler Plaza, Reggie Morgan behind the wheel. He and Paul Schumann, beside him, gazed at the stadium to the left. Two massive rectangular columns stood at the front, the five Olympic rings floating between them.

As they turned left onto Olympic Street, Paul again noted the massive size of the complex. According to the directional signs, in addition to the stadium itself were a swimming facility, a hockey rink, a theater, a sports field and many outbuildings and parking areas. The stadium was white, toweringly high and long; it didn't remind Paul of a building as much as an impregnable battleship.

The grounds were crowded: mostly workmen and provisioners but also many gray- and black-uniformed soldiers and guards, security for the National Socialist leaders attending the photography session. If Bull Gordon and the Senator wanted Ernst to die in public, then this was the place for it.

It appeared that one could drive right up to the front plaza of the stadium. But for an SS lieutenant (the commission was courtesy of Otto Webber, no extra cost) to climb out of a private van would be suspicious, of course. So they decided to skirt the stadium. Morgan would drop Paul off in some trees near a parking lot, which he would "patrol," examining trucks and workmen as he slowly made his way to the shed overlooking the press office on the south side of the stadium.

The van now pulled off the road onto a grassy patch and rocked to a stop, invisible from the stadium. Paul climbed out and assembled the Mauser. He took the telescopic sight off the rifle—it was not the sort of accessory a guard would have—and slipped it into his pocket. He slung the gun over his shoulder and put his black helmet on his head.

"How do I look?" Paul asked.

"Authentic enough to scare me. Good luck to you."

I'll need it, Paul thought grimly, peering through the trees at the scores of workmen on the grounds, ready and able to point out an intruder, and at the hundreds of guards who'd be happy to gun him down.

Six to five against . . .

Brother. He glanced at Morgan and felt an impulse to lift his hand in an American salute, one veteran to another, but of course Paul Schumann was fully aware of his role. "Hail." And lifted his arm. Morgan repressed a smile and reciprocated.

As Paul turned to leave, Morgan said softly, "Oh, wait, Paul. When I spoke to Bull Gordon and the Senator this morning, they wished you luck. And the commander said to tell you you can print his daughter's wedding invitations as your first job. You know what he means?"

Paul gave a nod and, gripping the sling of the Mauser, started toward the stadium. He stepped through the line of trees and into a huge parking lot, which must have had room for twenty thousand cars. He strode with authority and determination, glancing sharply toward the vehicles parked here, every inch the diligent guard.

Ten minutes later Paul had made his way through the lot and was at the soaring entrance to the stadium. There were soldiers on duty here, carefully checking papers and searching anyone who wanted to enter, but on the surrounding grounds, Paul was merely another soldier and no one paid him any attention. With an occasional "Hail Hitler" and nods, he skirted the building, heading toward the shed. He passed a huge iron bell, on the side of which was an inscription: "I Summon the Youth of the World."

As he approached the shed he noticed that it had no windows. There was no back door; the escape after the shooting would be difficult. He'd have to exit by the front, in full view of the entire stadium. But he suspected the acoustics would make it very difficult to tell where the shot had come from. And there were many sounds of construction—pile drivers, saws, riveting machines and the like—to obscure the report of the rifle. Paul would walk slowly from the shed after firing, pause and look around, even call for help if he could do so without raising suspicion.

The time was one-thirty. Otto Webber, who was in the Potsdam Plaza post office, would place his call around two-fifteen. Plenty of time.

He strolled on slowly, examining the grounds, looking in parked vehicles.

"Hail Hitler," he said to some laborers, who were stripped to the waist and painting a fence. "It is a hot day for work like that."

"Ach, it's nothing," one replied. "And if it were, so what? We work for the good of the fatherland."

Paul said, "The Leader is proud of you." And continued on to his hunting blind.

He glanced at the shed curiously as if wondering if it posed any security threat. Pulling on the black leather gloves that were part of the uniform, he opened the door and stepped inside. The place was filled with cardboard cartons tied with twine. Paul recognized the smell immediately from his days as a printer: the bitter scent of paper, the sweet scent of ink. The shed was being used to store programs or souvenir booklets of the Games. He arranged some cartons to make a shooting position in the front of the shed. He then laid his open jacket to the right of where he'd be lying, to catch the ejected shells when he worked the bolt of the gun. These details—retrieving the casings and minding fingerprints—probably didn't matter. He had no record here and would be out of the country by nightfall. But nonetheless he went to the trouble simply because this was his craft.

You make sure nothing is out of kilter.

You check your *p*'s and *q*'s.

Standing well inside the small building, he scanned the stadium with the rifle's telescopic sight. He noted the open corridor behind the pressroom, which Ernst would take to reach the stairway and walk down to meet the messenger or driver that Webber would tell him about. He'd have a perfect shot as soon as the colonel stepped out of the doorway. There were large windows too, which he might shoot through if the man paused in front of one.

The time was one-fifty.

Paul sat back, legs crossed, and cradled the rifle in his lap. Sweat was dripping down his forehead in tickling rivulets. He wiped his face with the sleeve of his shirt then began to mount the telescopic sight onto the rifle.

"What do you think, Rudy?"

But Reinhard Ernst did not expect his grandson to answer. The boy was staring with smiling awe over the expanse of the Olympic stadium. They were in the long press facility on the south side of the building, above the Leader's reviewing stand. Ernst held him up so that he could look through the window. Rudy was virtually dancing with excitement.

"Ah, who is this?" a voice asked.

Ernst turned to see Adolf Hitler and two of his SS guards enter the room.

"My Leader."

Hitler walked forward and smiled at the boy.

Ernst said, "This is Rudy, my son's boy."

A faint look of sympathy on the Leader's face told Ernst that he was thinking of Mark's death in the war maneuvers accident. Ernst was momentarily surprised that the man remembered but realized that he should not have been; Hitler's mind was as expansive as the Olympic field, frighteningly quick, and it retained everything he wished to retain.

"Say hello to our Leader, Rudy. Salute as I taught you."

The boy gave a smart National Socialist salute and Hitler laughed in delight and tousled Rudy's hair. The Leader stepped closer to the window and pointed out some of the features of the stadium, talking in an enthusiastic voice. Hitler asked the boy about his studies and what subjects he liked, which sports he enjoyed.

More voices in the hallway. The two rivals Goebbels and Göring arrived together. What a drive *that* must have been, thought Ernst, smiling to himself.

After his defeat at the Chancellory that morning Göring remained desultory. Ernst could see it clearly, despite the smile. What a difference between the two most powerful men in Germany. . . . Hitler's tantrums, admittedly extreme, were rarely about personal matters; if his favorite chocolate was not available or he knocked his shin on a table he would shrug the matter off without anger. And as to reversals on issues of state, yes, he had a temper that could terrify his closest of friends, but once the problem was solved he was on to other matters. Göring, on the other hand, was like a greedy child. Anything that went against his wishes would infuriate him and fester until he found suitable revenge.

Hitler was explaining to the boy what sporting events would be played in which areas of the stadium. Ernst was amused to see that beneath his broad smile Göring was growing all the more angry that the Leader was paying such attention to his rival's grandson.

Over the next ten minutes other officials began arriving: Von Blomberg, the state defense minister, and Hjalmar Schacht, head of the state bank, with whom Ernst had developed a complicated system of financing rearmament projects using untraceable funds known as "Mefo bills." Schacht's middle name was Horace Greeley, after the American, and Ernst would joke with the brilliant economist about having cowboy roots. Here too were Himmler, block-faced Rudolf Hess and serpent-eyed Reinhard Heydrich, who greeted Ernst in a distracted way, which was how he greeted everyone.

The photographer meticulously set up his Leica and other equipment so that he could get both the subject in the foreground and the stadium in the back, yet the lights would not flare in the windows. Ernst had developed an interest in photography. He himself owned several Leicas and he'd planned to buy Rudy a Kodak, which was imported from America and easier to use than the German precision cameras. The colonel had recorded some of the trips he and his family had taken. Paris and Budapest in particular had been well documented, as had a hiking sojourn in the Black Forest and a boat trip down the Danube.

"Good, good," the photographer now called. "We can begin."

Hitler first insisted on taking a picture with Rudy and lifted the boy onto his knee, laughing and chatting with him like a good uncle. After this the planned pictures began.

Though he was pleased that Rudy was enjoying himself, Ernst was growing impatient. He found publicity absurd. Moreover, it was a bad tactical error—as was the whole idea of holding the Olympics in Germany, for that matter. There were far too many aspects of the rearmament that should have been kept secret. How could a foreign visitor *not* see that this was a military nation and becoming more so every day?

The flashes went off, as the celebrities of the Third Empire looked cheerful or thoughtful or ominous for the lens. When Ernst was not being photographed he talked with Rudy or stood by himself and, in his mind, composed his letter to the Leader about the Waltham Study, considering what to say and what not to.

Sometimes you couldn't share all. . . .

An SS guard appeared in the doorway. He spotted Ernst and called, "Mr. Minister."

A number of heads turned.

"Mr. Minister Ernst."

The colonel was as amused as Göring was irritated; Ernst was not officially a minister of state.

"Yes?"

"Sir, there is a phone call for you from the secretary of Gustav Krupp von Bohlen. There is a matter he needs to inform you of immediately. Something most important. Regarding your latest meeting."

What had they discussed then that was so urgent? Armor for the warships had been one topic. It hadn't seemed so critical. But now that England had accepted the new German shipbuilding figures, perhaps Krupp would have a problem meeting the production quotas. But then he reflected that, no, the baron had not been informed of the victory regarding the treaty. Krupp was as brilliant a capitalist as he was a technician. But he was also a coward, who'd shunned the Party until Hitler came to power then had become a rabid convert. Ernst suspected the crisis was minor at worst. But Krupp and his son were so important to the rearmament plans that they could not be ignored.

"You may take the call on one of those phones there. I will have it put through."

"Excuse me for one moment, my Leader."

Hitler nodded and returned to discussing the angle of the camera with the photographer.

A moment later one of the many phones against the wall buzzed. A glowing light indicated which it was and Ernst picked it up.

"Yes? This is Colonel Ernst."

"Colonel. I am Stroud, an aide to Baron von Bohlen. I apologize for the disturbance. He's sent some documents for you to examine. A driver has them at the stadium where you are now."

"What are these about?"

A pause. "I was instructed by the baron not to mention the subject over this telephone."

"Yes, yes, fine. Where is the driver?"

"In the driveway on the south side of the stadium. He will meet you there. It's better to be discreet. Alone, I am saying, sir. Those are my instructions."

"Yes, of course."

"Hail Hitler."

"Hail."

Ernst hung the phone in the cradle. Göring had been watching him like an obese falcon. "A problem, Minister?"

The colonel decided both to ignore the feigned sympathy and the irony in the title. Rather than lie, he admitted, "Some problem that Krupp's having. He's sent me a message about it."

As a maker primarily of armor, artillery and munitions, Krupp dealt more with Ernst and the naval and army commanders than with Göring, whose province was the air.

"Ach." The huge man turned back to the mirror the photographer had provided. He began moving a finger around his face, smoothing his makeup.

Ernst started for the door.

"Opa, may I come with you?"

"Of course, Rudy. This way."

The boy scurried after his grandfather and they stepped into the interior corridor that connected all the pressrooms. Ernst put his arm around the boy's shoulder. He oriented himself and noticed a doorway that would lead to one of the south stairways. They started toward it. He'd downplayed the concern at first but in fact he was growing troubled. Krupp steel was recognized as the best in the world; the spire of New York City's magnificent Chrysler building was made of his company's famed Enduro KA-2. But this meant too that foreign military planners were looking very carefully at Krupp's products and output. He wondered if the British or French had learned how much of his steel was going not to rails or washing machines or automobiles but to armor.

Grandfather and grandson made their way through a crowd of workers and foremen energetically finishing the construction here on the pressbooth floor, cutting doors to size, mounting hardware, sanding and painting walls. As they dodged around a carpentry station, Ernst glanced down at the arm of his suit and grimaced.

"What's wrong, Opa?" Rudy shouted over the scream of a saw.

"Oh, look at this. Look at what I've gotten on me." There was a sprinkling of plaster on it.

He brushed the dust away as best he could but some remained. He wondered if he should wet his fingers to clean it. But this might cause the plaster to set permanently in the cloth. Gertrud would not be pleased if that happened. He'd leave it for now. He put his hand on the door handle to step onto the outer walkway that led to the stairs.

"Colonel!" a voice called in his ear.

Ernst turned.

The SS guard had run up behind him. He shouted over the whine of the saw, "Sir, the Leader's dogs are here. He wonders if your grandson would like to pose with them."

"Dogs?" Rudy asked excitedly.

Hitler liked German shepherds and had several of them. They were genial animals, house pets.

"Would you like that?" Ernst asked.

"Oh, yes, please, Opa."

"Don't play roughly with them."

"No, I won't."

Ernst escorted the boy back down the hall and watched him run to the dogs, which were sniffing around the room, exploring. Hitler laughed, seeing the youngster hug the larger one and kiss him on top of the head. The animal licked Rudy with his huge tongue. With some difficulty, Göring bent down and petted the animals too, a childlike smile on his round face. Though he was heartless in many ways, the minister loved animals devoutly.

The colonel then returned to the corridor and walked toward the outer door once again. He blew again at the plaster dust on his sleeve then paused in front of one of the large, south-facing windows and looked outside. The sun fell on him fiercely. He'd left his hat back in the press booth. Should he get it?

No, he thought. It would—

His breath was knocked from his lungs as he felt a jarring blow to his body and found himself tumbling to the drop cloth covering the marble, gasping in agony . . . confused, frightened. . . . But the one thought most prominent in his mind as he struck the floor was: Now I'll get paint on my suit too! What will Gertrud say about *this*?

Chapter Twenty-Six

The Munich House was a small restaurant ten blocks northwest of the Tiergarten and five from Dresden Alley.

Willi Kohl had eaten here several times and recalled enjoying the Hungarian goulash, to which they added caraway seeds and raisins, of all things. He'd drunk a wonderful red Austrian Blaufrankisch wine with the meal.

He and Janssen parked the DKW in front of the place and Kohl tossed the Kripo card onto the dashboard to fend off eager Schupos armed with their traffic offense booklets.

Tapping spent tobacco from his meerschaum pipe, Kohl hurried toward the restaurant, Konrad Janssen close behind. Inside, the decor was Bavarian: brown wood and yellowing stucco plaster, with borders of wooden gardenias everywhere, clumsily carved and painted. The room was aromatic of sour spices and grilled meat. Kohl was instantly hungry; he had eaten only one breakfast that morning and it had consisted of nothing more than pastry and coffee. The smoke was dense, for the lunch hour was nearly over and people had exchanged empty plates for coffee and cigarettes.

Kohl saw his son Günter standing with the young Hitler Youth leader, Helmut Gruber, and two other teenagers, dressed in the group's uniform. The Youth had kept their army officer–style hats on, even though they were inside, either out of disrespect or ignorance.

"I received your message, boys."

Extending his arm in a salute, the Hitler Youth leader said, "Detective-inspector Kohl, Hail Hitler. We have identified the man you are seeking." He held up the picture of the body found in Dresden Alley.

"Have you now?"

"Yes, sir."

Kohl glanced at Günter and saw contradictory feelings in his son's face. He was proud to have elevated his status with the Youth but wasn't happy that Helmut had preempted the restaurant search. The inspector wondered if this incident would be a double benefit—the identification of the body for him and a lesson about the realities of life among the National Socialists for his son.

The maître d' or owner, a stocky, balding man in a dusty black suit and shabby gold-striped waistcoat, saluted Kohl. When he spoke he was clearly uneasy. Hitler Youth were among the most energetic of denouncers. "Inspector, your son and his friends here were inquiring about this individual."

"Yes, yes. And you, sir, are . . . ?"

"Gerhard Klemp. I am the manager and have been for sixteen years."

"Did this man eat lunch here yesterday?"

"Please, yes, he did. And almost three days a week. He first came in several months ago. He said he liked it because we prepare more than just German food."

Kohl wanted the boys to know as little about the murder as possible so he said to his son and the Hitler Youths, "Ah, thank you, son. Thank you, Helmut." He nodded to the others. "We will take over from here. You're a credit to your nation."

"I would do anything for our Leader, Detective-inspector," Helmut said in a tone fitting to his declaration. "Good day, sir." Again he lifted his arm. Kohl watched his son's arm extend similarly and, in response, the inspector himself gave a sharp National Socialist salute. "Hail." Kohl ignored Janssen's faint look of amusement at his gesture.

The youngsters left, chattering and laughing; they seemed normal for a change, boyish and happy, free from their usual visage—mindless automatons out of Fritz Lang's science fiction film *Metropolis*. He caught his son's eye and the boy smiled and waved as the cluster disappeared out the door. Kohl prayed his decision on his son's behalf was not a mistake; Günter could so easily be seduced by the group.

He turned back to Klemp and tapped the picture. "What time did he lunch here yesterday?"

"He came in early, about eleven, just as we were opening. He left thirty, forty minutes later."

Kohl could see that Klemp was troubled by the death but reluctant to express sympathy in case the man turned out to be an enemy of the state. He was also very curious but, as with most citizens these days, was afraid to ask questions about the investigation or to volunteer anything more than he was asked. At least he didn't suffer from blindness.

"Was he alone?"

"Yes."

Janssen asked, "But did you happen to observe him outside to see if he arrived with anyone or perhaps met someone when he left?" He nodded toward the restaurant's large, uncurtained windows.

"I didn't see anyone, no."

"Were there persons he dined with regularly?"

"No. He was usually by himself."

"And which way did he go after he finished eating yesterday?" Kohl asked, jotting it all down in his notebook after touching the pencil tip to his tongue.

"I believe to the south. That would be the left."

The direction of Dresden Alley.

"What do you know about him?" Kohl asked.

"Ach, a few things. For one, I have his address, if that helps."

"Indeed it does," said Kohl excitedly.

"After he began coming here regularly I suggested he open an account with us." He turned to a file box containing neatly penned cards and wrote down an address on a slip of paper. Janssen looked at it. "Two blocks from here, sir."

"Do you know anything else about him?"

"Not much, I'm afraid. He was secretive. We spoke rarely. It wasn't the language. No, it was his preoccupation. He was usually reading the newspaper or a book or business documents and didn't wish to converse."

"What do you mean by 'it wasn't the language'?"

"Oh, he was an American."

Kohl lifted an eyebrow at Janssen. "He was?"

"Yes, sir," the man replied, glancing once more at the picture of the dead man.

"And his name?"

"Mr. Reginald Morgan, sir."

"And you are who?"

Robert Taggert held up a cautionary finger in response to Reinhard Ernst's question, then looked carefully out the window Ernst had been standing at when Taggert had tackled the colonel a moment before to get him out of the line of sight of the shed, where Paul Schumann was waiting.

Taggert caught a glimpse of the black doorway in the shed and could vaguely make out the muzzle of the Mauser easing back and forth.

"No one go outside!" Taggert called to the workers. "Keep away from the windows and the doors!" He turned back to Ernst, who sat on a box containing cans of paint. Several of the laborers had helped him up from the floor and stood nearby.

Taggert had been late arriving at the stadium. Driving the white van, he'd had to circle far to the north and west to make certain Schumann didn't see him. After flashing his identity cards to the guards, he had run up the stairs to the press floor to find Ernst pausing in front of the window. The construction noise was loud and the colonel hadn't heard his shout over the screams of the power saws. So the American had sprinted down the hall past a dozen or so astonished workers and knocked Ernst away from the window.

The colonel was cradling his head, which had struck the tarpaulin-covered floor. There was no blood on his scalp, and he didn't seem badly hurt, though Taggert's tackle had stunned him and knocked the wind from his lungs.

Responding to Ernst's question, Taggert said, "I'm with the American diplomatic staff in Washington, D.C." He proffered his papers: a government identification card and an authentic American passport issued in his real name, not the forgery in the name of Reginald Morgan—the Office of Naval Intelligence agent he'd shot to death in front of Paul Schumann in Dresden Alley yesterday and had been impersonating ever since.

Taggert said, "I've come here to warn you about a plot against your life. An assassin is outside now."

"But Krupp . . . Is Baron von Bohlen involved?"

"Krupp?" Taggert feigned surprise and listened as Ernst explained about the phone call.

"No, that must have been one of the conspirators, who called to lure you out." He gestured out the door. "The killer is in one of the supply sheds south of the stadium. We've heard he's a Russian but dressed in an SS uniform."

"A Russian? Yes, yes, there was a security alert about such a man."

In fact, there would have been no danger had Ernst stayed at the window or stepped out onto the porch. The rifle that Schumann now held was the same one he'd tested at November 1923 Square yesterday but last night Taggert had plugged the barrel of the gun with lead so that if Schumann had fired, the bullet never would have left the muzzle. Yet had that happened, the American gangster would have known he'd been set up and might have escaped, even if he'd been injured by the exploding rifle.

"Our Leader could be in danger!"

"No," Taggert said. "It's only you he's after."

"Me? . . ." Then Ernst's head swiveled. "My grandson!" He rose abruptly. "My grandson is here. He could be at risk too."

"We have to tell everyone to stay away from the windows," Taggert said, "and to evacuate the area." The two men hurried down the hallway. "Is Hitler in the pressroom?" Taggert asked.

"He was a few minutes ago."

Oh, this was far better than Taggert could have hoped for. When Schumann had reported, back in the boardinghouse, that Hitler and the other leaders would be assembled here, he'd been ecstatic, though he'd obscured this reaction, of course. He now said, "I need to tell him what we've learned. We have to act fast before the assassin escapes."

They walked into the pressroom. The American blinked, stunned to find himself among the most powerful men in Germany, their heads turning to look at him in curiosity. The only ones in the room who ignored Taggert were two cheerful German shepherd dogs and a cute little boy of about six or seven.

Adolf Hitler noticed Ernst, still holding the back of his head, the paint and plaster on his suit. Alarmed, he asked, "Reinhard, you are hurt?"

"Opa!" The boy ran forward.

Ernst first put his arms around the child and ushered him quickly to the center of the room away from the doors and windows. "It's all right, Rudy. I just took a spill. . . . Everyone, keep back from the windows!" He gestured to an SS guard. "Take my grandson into the hallway. Stay with him."

"Yes, sir." The man did as ordered.

"What's happened?" Hitler called.

Ernst replied, "This man is an American diplomat. He tells me there's a Russian out there with a rifle. In one of the supply sheds south of the stadium."

Himmler nodded to a guard. "Get some men in here now! And assemble a detachment downstairs."

"Yes, my Police Chief."

Ernst explained about Taggert, and the German leader approached the American, who was nearly breathless with excitement to be in Hitler's presence. The man was short, about the same height as Taggert, but broader of body and with thicker features. A stern frown filled his wan face and he examined the American's papers carefully. The eyes of the dictator of Germany were surrounded by drooping lids above and bags below but they themselves were every bit the pale but piercing blue that he'd heard of. This man could mesmerize anyone, Taggert thought, feeling this force himself.

"Please, my Leader, may I see?" Himmler asked. Hitler handed him the documents. The man looked them over and asked, "You speak German?"

"Yes, I do."

"With all respect, sir, are you armed?"

"I am," Taggert said.

"With the Leader and the others here, I will take possession of your weapon until we learn what this matter is about."

"Of course." Taggert lifted his jacket and allowed one of the SS men to take the pistol from him. He'd expected this. Himmler was, after all, head of the SS, whose primary purpose was guarding Hitler and the government leaders.

Himmler told another SS trooper to take a look at the sheds and see if he could observe the purported assassin. "Hurry."

"Yes, my Police Chief."

As he left the pressroom, a dozen armed SS guards filed into the room and spread out, protecting the assembly. Taggert turned to Hitler and nodded respectfully. "State Chancellor-President, several days ago we learned of a potential plot by the Russians."

Nodding, Himmler said, "The intelligence we received Friday from Hamburg—about the Russian doing some 'damage.'"

Hitler waved him silent and nodded for Taggert to continue.

"We thought nothing particular of this information. We hear it all the time from the damn Russians. But then we learned some specifics a few hours ago: that his target was Colonel Ernst and that he might be here at the stadium this afternoon. I assumed he was examining the stadium with an eye toward shooting the colonel during the Games themselves. I came here to see for myself and noticed a man slip into a shed south of the stadium. And then I learned to my shock that the colonel and the rest of you were here."

"How did he get on the grounds?" Hitler raged.

"An SS uniform and false identity papers, we believe," Taggert explained.

"I was about to step outside," Ernst said. "This man saved my life."

"What about Krupp? The phone call?" Göring asked.

"Krupp has nothing to do with this, I'm sure," Taggert said. "The call was undoubtedly from a confederate to lure the colonel outside."

Himmler nodded to Heydrich, who strode to the phone, dialed a number and spoke for several moments. He looked up. "No, it was not Krupp who called. Unless he now makes his calls from the Potsdam Plaza post office."

Hitler muttered ominously to Himmler, "Why did *we* not know about this?"

Taggert knew that conspiracy paranoia danced constantly in Hitler's head. He came to Himmler's defense, saying, "They were very clever, the Russians. We only learned about it from our sources in Moscow, by happenstance. . . . But, please, sir, we must move quickly. If he realizes we're onto him he'll escape and try again."

"Why Ernst?" Göring asked.

Meaning, Taggert supposed, why not *me?*

Taggert directed his response to Hitler, "State Leader, we understand that Colonel Ernst is involved in rearmament. We are not troubled with that—in America we consider Germany our greatest European ally and we want you to be militarily strong."

"Your countrymen feel this way?" Hitler asked. It was well known in diplomatic circles that he was very troubled by the anti-Nazi sentiment in America.

Now able to discard the placid demeanor of Reggie Morgan, Taggert spoke with an edge to his voice. "You don't always get the full story. Jews talk loudly—in your country and in mine—and the leftist element are forever whining, the press, the Communists, the Socialists. But they're a small fraction of the population. No, our government and the majority of Americans are firmly committed to being your ally and seeing you get out from under the yoke of the Versailles. It's the Russians who are concerned about your rearming. However, please, sir, we have only minutes. The assassin."

The SS guard returned just then. "It's as he said, sir. There are some sheds beside the parking plaza. The door to one is open and, yes, there's a rifle barrel protruding, scanning for a target at the stadium here."

Several of the men in the room gasped and muttered indignation.

Joseph Goebbels picked at his ear nervously. Göring had unholstered his Luger and was waving it around comically like a child with a wooden pistol.

Hitler's voice shook and his hands quivered in rage. "Communist Jew animals! They come to my country and do this to me! Backstabbers . . . And with our Olympics about to start! They . . ." He was unable to continue his diatribe, he was so furious.

To Himmler, Taggert said, "I speak Russian. Surround the shed and let me try to convince him to surrender. I'm sure the Gestapo or the SS can persuade him to tell us who and where the other conspirators are."

Himmler nodded then turned to Hitler. "My Leader, it is important that you and the others leave at once. By the underground route. Perhaps there is only the one assassin but perhaps too there are others that this American doesn't know about."

Like everyone who'd read the intelligence reports on Himmler, Taggert considered the former fertilizer salesman half insane and an incurable syco-phant. But the American's role here was clear and he said submissively, "Police Chief Himmler is correct. I'm not sure how complete our informa-tion is. Go to safety. I will help your troops capture the man."

Ernst shook Taggert's hand. "My thanks to you."

Taggert nodded. He watched Ernst collect his grandson from the corri-dor and then join the others, who took an internal stairway down to the underground driveway, surrounded by a squad of guards.

Only when Hitler and the others were gone did Himmler return Tag-gert's pistol. The police chief then called to the SS officer who had arranged the detachment downstairs, "Where are your men?"

The guard explained that two dozen were deployed to the east, out of view of the shed.

Himmler said, "SD Leader Heydrich and I will remain here and call a general alert for the area. Bring us that Russian."

"Hail Hitler." The guard turned on his heels and hurried down the stair-case, Taggert behind him. They jogged to the east side of the stadium, joined the troops there and, in a wide arc to the south, approached the shed.

The men ran quickly, surrounded by the emotionless SS troops, amid the sound of gun bolts and toggles, snapping bullets into place. But despite the apparent tension and drama, Robert Taggert was at ease for the first time in days. Like the man he'd killed in Dresden Alley—Reggie Morgan—Taggert was one of those people who exist in the shadows of government and diplomacy and business, doing the bidding for their principals in ways sometimes legal and often not. One of the few truthful things he'd told Schumann was his passion for a diplomatic posting either in Germany or elsewhere (Spain would indeed be nice). But such plums were not easy to come by and had to be earned, often in mad and risky situations. Such as the plan involving the poor sap Paul Schumann.

His instructions from the United States had been simple: Reggie Morgan would have to be sacrificed. Taggert would kill him and take over his identity. He would help Paul Schumann plan Reinhard Ernst's death and then, at the last moment, Taggert would dramatically "rescue" the German colonel, proof of how firmly the U.S. supported the National Socialists. Word of the rescue and Taggert's comments about that support would trickle up to Hitler. But as it turned out, the results were far, far better: Taggert had actually performed his routine for Hitler and Göring themselves.

What happened to Schumann was irrelevant now, whether he died, which would be cleaner and more convenient, or was caught and tortured. In the latter case, Schumann would eventually talk . . . and tell an unlikely tale of being hired by the American Office of Naval Intelligence to kill Ernst, which the Germans would instantly dismiss since it was Taggert and the Americans who turned him in. And if he turned out to be a German-American gangster and not a Russian? Ah, well, he must've been *recruited* by the Russians.

A simple plan.

But there had been setbacks from the beginning. He'd planned to kill Morgan several days ago and impersonate him at the first meeting with Schumann yesterday. But Morgan had been a very cautious man and talented at leading a covert life. Taggert had had no chance to murder him before Dresden Alley. And how tense *that* had been. . . .

Reggie Morgan had had only the old pass phrase—not the lines about the tram to Alexanderplatz—so when he'd met Schumann in the alley, they'd each believed the other was an enemy. Taggert had managed to kill Morgan just in time and convince Schumann that he was in fact the American agent—thanks to the right pass phrase, the forged passport, and the accurate description of the Senator. Taggert had also made sure he was the first to go through the dead man's pockets. He'd pretended to find proof that Morgan was a Stormtrooper, though the document he'd showed Schumann was, in fact, simply a card attesting that the bearer had donated a sum to a War veterans' relief fund. Half the people in Berlin had such cards since the Brownshirts were very adept at soliciting "contributions."

Schumann himself had also proved to be a source of concern. Oh, the man was smart, far smarter than the thug whom Taggert had expected. He had a suspicious nature and didn't tip off what he was really thinking. Taggert had had to watch what he said and did, constantly remind himself to be Reginald Morgan, the dogged, nondescript civil servant. When Schumann, for instance, had insisted they check Morgan's body for tattoos, Taggert was horrified. The most likely tattoo they'd find would have said "U.S. Navy." Or maybe the name of the ship he'd served on in the War. But fate had smiled; the man had never been under the needle.

Now, Taggert and the black-uniformed troops arrived at the shed. He could just see the barrel of the Mauser protruding, as Paul Schumann searched for his target. The men deployed quietly, the senior SS officer directing his soldiers with hand signals. Taggert was as impressed as ever with the brilliance of German tactical skills.

Closer now, closer.

Schumann was preoccupied, continuing to scan the balcony behind the press box. He would be wondering what had happened. Why the delay in getting Ernst outside? Had the phone call from Webber gone through properly?

As the SS men circled the shed, cutting off any chance of Schumann's escape, Taggert reminded himself that after he was finished here, he would have to return to Berlin and find Otto Webber and kill him. Käthe Richter too.

When the young soldiers were in position around the shed, Taggert whispered, "I will go speak to him in Russian and get him to surrender." The SS commander nodded. The American took his pistol from his pocket. He was in no danger, of course, because of the Mauser's plugged barrel. Still, he moved slowly, pretending to be cautious and uneasy.

"Keep back," he whispered. "I'll go in first."

The SS nodded, eyebrows raised, impressed at the American's courage.

Taggert lifted his pistol and stepped toward the doorway. The rifle muzzle still eased back and forth. Schumann's frustration at not finding a target was palpable.

In a swift motion, Taggert flung one of the doors open and lifted his pistol, applying pressure on the trigger.

He stepped inside.

Robert Taggert gasped. A chill ran through him.

The Mauser continued its scan of the stadium, moving back and forth slowly. The deadly rifle, though, was gripped not by a would-be assassin's hands but by lengths of twine torn from packing cartons and tethered to a roof beam.

Paul Schumann was gone.

Chapter Twenty-Seven

Running.

Not his favorite form of exercise by any means, though Paul often ran laps or jogged in place, to get the legs in shape and to work the tobacco and beer and corn whisky out of his system. And now he was running like Jesse Owens.

Running for his life.

Unlike poor Max, gunned down in the street as he sprinted away from the SS guards, Paul attracted little notice; he was wearing gymnasium clothes and shoes he'd stolen from the locker room of the Olympic stadium's swimming complex and he looked like any one of the thousands of athletes in and around Charlottenburg, in training for the Games. He was about three miles east of the stadium now, heading back to Berlin, pumping hard, putting distance between himself and the betrayal, which he had yet to figure out.

He was surprised that Reggie Morgan—if it *was* Morgan—had made a careless mistake after going to such elaborate efforts to set him up. There were certainly button men who didn't look over their tools every time they were going on a job. But that was nuts. When you were up against ruthless men, always armed, you made sure that your own weapons were in perfect shape, that nothing was out of kilter.

In the baking-hot shed Paul had mounted the telescopic sight and made sure the calibrations were set to the same numbers as at the pawnshop shooting range. Then, as a final check he'd slipped the bolt out of the Mauser and sighted up the bore. It was blocked. He thought at first this was some dirt or creosote from the fiberboard carrying case. But Paul had found a length of wire and dug inside. He looked closely at what he scraped off. Somebody had poured molten lead down the muzzle. If he'd fired, the barrel might have exploded or the bolt shot backward through Paul's cheek.

The gun had been in Morgan's possession overnight and was the same weapon; Paul had noted a unique configuration in the grain when he was sighting it in yesterday. So Morgan, or whoever he might be, had clearly sabotaged the gun.

Moving fast, he'd ripped twine from the cartons in the shed and hung the rifle from the ceiling to make it appear he was still there then slipped outside, joining a group of other troopers walking north. He'd split off from them at the swimming complex, found a change of clothing and shoes, thrown away the SS uniform and torn up and flushed the Russian passport down a toilet.

Now, a half hour from the stadium, running, running . . .

Sweating fiercely through the thick cloth, Paul turned off the highway and trotted into a small village center. He found a fountain made from an old horse trough and bent to the spigot, drinking a quart of the hot, rusty water. Then he bathed his face.

How far from the city was he? Probably four miles or so, he guessed. He saw two officers in green uniforms and tall green-and-black hats stopping a large man, demanding his papers.

He turned casually away from them and walked down side streets, deciding it was too risky to continue into Berlin on foot. He noticed a parking lot—rows of cars around a train station. Paul found an open-air DKW and, making sure he was out of sight, used a rock and a broken branch to knock the key lock into the dashboard. He fished underneath for the wires. Using his teeth, he cut through the cloth insulation and twined the copper strands together. He pushed the starter button. The engine ground for a moment but didn't catch. Grimacing, he realized he'd forgotten to set the choke. He adjusted it to rich and tried again. The engine fired to life and sputtered and he adjusted the knob until it was running smoothly. It took a moment to figure out the gears but soon he was easing east through the narrow streets of the town, wondering who'd sold him out.

And why? Had it been money? Politics? Some other reason?

But at the moment he could find no hint of the answers to those questions. Escaping occupied all his thoughts.

He shoved the accelerator to the floor and turned onto a broad, immaculate highway, passing a sign that assured him that the city center of Berlin was six kilometers away.

Modest quarters, off Bremer Street in the northwest portion of town. Typical of many dwellings in this neighborhood, Reginald Morgan's was in a gloomy stone four-flat that dated from the Second Empire, though this particular structure summoned up no Prussian glory whatsoever.

Willi Kohl and his inspector candidate climbed from the DKW. They heard more sirens and glanced up to see a truck of SS troops speeding along the roads—yet another installment of the secret security alert, even more extensive than earlier, it seemed, with random roadblocks now being set up throughout the city. Kohl and Janssen themselves were stopped. The SS guard glanced with disdain at the Kripo ID and waved them through. He didn't respond to the inspector's query about what was happening and merely snapped, "Move along."

Kohl now rang the bell beside the thick front door. The inspector tapped his foot with impatience as they waited. Two lengthy rings later a stocky landlady in a dark dress and apron opened the door, eyes wide at the sight of two stern men in suits.

"Hail Hitler. I'm sorry, sirs, that I didn't get here sooner but my legs aren't—"

"Inspector Kohl, with the Kripo." He showed his identity card so the woman would relax somewhat; at least they were not Gestapo.

"Do you know this man?" Janssen displayed the photo taken in Dresden Alley.

"Ach, that's Mr. Morgan, who lives here! He doesn't look . . . Is he dead?"

"Yes, he is."

"God in heav—" The politically questionable phrase died in her mouth.

"We'd like to see his rooms."

"Yes, sir. Of course, sir. Follow me." They walked into a courtyard so overwhelmingly bleak, Kohl thought, that it would sadden even Mozart's irrepressible Papageno. The woman rocked back and forth as she walked. She said breathlessly, "I always thought him a little strange, to tell the truth, sirs." This was served up with careful glances at Kohl, to make it clear that she was no confederate of Morgan's, in case he'd been killed by the

National Socialists themselves, and yet that his behavior wasn't *so* suspicious that she should have denounced him herself.

"We haven't seen him for a whole day. He went out just before lunch yesterday and he never returned."

They went through another locked door at the end of the courtyard and up two flights of stairs, which reeked of onion and pickle.

"How long had he lived here?" Kohl asked.

"Three months. He paid for six in advance. And tipped me . . ." Her voice faded. "But not much."

"The rooms were furnished?"

"Yes, sir."

"Any visitors you recall?"

"None that I knew of. None that I let into the building."

"Show her the drawing, Janssen."

He displayed the picture of Paul Schumann. "Have you seen this man?"

"No, sir. Is he dead too?" She added abruptly, "I mean, sir, no, I've never seen him."

Kohl looked into her eyes. They were evasive, but with fear, not deception, and he believed her. Under questioning, she told him that Morgan was a businessman, he took no phone calls here and picked up his mail at the post office. She didn't know if he had an office elsewhere. He never said anything specific about his job.

"Leave us now."

"Hail Hitler," she replied and scurried off like a mouse.

Kohl looked around the room. "So you see how I made an incorrect deduction, Janssen?"

"How is that, sir?"

"I assumed Mr. Morgan was German because he wore clothes made of Hitler cloth. But not all foreigners are wealthy enough to live on Under the Lindens and to buy top-of-the-line at KaDeWe, though that is our impression."

Janssen thought for a moment. "That's true, sir. But there could be another reason he wore ersatz clothes."

"That he wished to masquerade as a German?"

"Yes, sir."

"Good, Janssen. Though perhaps he wanted not so much to masquerade as one of us but more to not draw attention to himself. But either makes him suspicious. Now let's see if we can make our mystery less mysterious. Start with the closets."

The inspector candidate opened a door and began his examination of the contents.

Kohl himself chose the less demanding search and eased into a creaking chair to look through the documents on Morgan's desk. The American had been, it seemed, a middleman of sorts, providing services for a number of U.S. companies in Germany. For a commission he would match an American buyer with a German seller and vice versa. When American businessmen came to town Morgan would be hired to entertain them and arrange meetings with German representatives from Borsig, Bata Shoes, Siemens, I.G. Farben, Opel, dozens of others.

There were several pictures of Morgan and documents confirming his identity. But it was curious, Kohl thought, that there were no truly personal effects. No family photographs, no mementos.

. . . perhaps he was somebody's brother. And maybe somebody's husband or lover. And, if he was lucky, he was a father of sons and daughters. I would hope too that there are past lovers who think of him occasionally. . . .

Kohl considered the implications of this absence of personal information. Did it mean he was a loner? Or was there another reason for keeping his personal life secret?

Janssen dug through the closet. "And is there anything in particular I ought to be looking for, sir?"

Embezzled money, a married mistress's handkerchief, a letter of extortion, a note from a pregnant teenager . . . any of the indicia of motive that might explain why poor Mr. Morgan had died brutally on the immaculate cobblestones of Dresden Alley.

"Look for anything that enlightens us, in any way, regarding the case. I can describe it no better than that. It is the hardest part of being a detective. Use your instinct, use your imagination."

"Yes, sir."

Kohl continued his own examination of the desk.

A moment later Janssen called, "Look at this, sir. Mr. Morgan has some pictures of naked women. They were in a box here."

"Are they commercially made? Or did he take them himself?"

"No, they are postcards, sir. He bought them somewhere."

"Yes, yes, then they do not interest us, Janssen. You must discern between the times that a man's vices are relevant and when they are not.

And, I promise you, voluptuous postcards are not presently important. Please, continue your search."

Some men grow calm in direct proportion to their desperation. Such men are rare, and they are particularly dangerous, because, while their ruthlessness is not diminished, they are never careless.

Robert Taggert was one such man. He was livid that some goddamn button man from Brooklyn had out-thought him, had jeopardized his future, but he was not going to let emotion cloud his judgment.

He knew how Schumann had figured things out. There was a piece of wire on the floor of the shed and bits of lead next to it. Of course, he'd checked the bore of the gun and found it plugged. Taggert thought angrily, Why the hell didn't I empty the powder out of his shells and recrimp the bullets back into the brass casing? There'd have been no danger to Ernst that way and Schumann never would have figured out the betrayal until it was too late and the SS troops were around the shed.

But, he reflected, the matter wasn't hopeless.

After a second brief meeting in the Olympic pressroom with Himmler and Heydrich, during which he told them he knew little more of the plot than what he'd already explained, he left the stadium, telling the Germans that he would contact Washington at once and see if they had more details. Taggert left them both, muttering about Jewish and Russian conspiracies. He was surprised he'd been allowed out of the stadium without being detained—his arrest would not have been logical but was certainly a risk in a country top-heavy with suspicion and paranoia.

Taggert now considered his quarry. Paul Schumann was not stupid, of course. He'd been set up to be a Russian and he'd know that was whom the Germans would be looking for. He'd have ditched his fake identity by now and be an American again. But Taggert preferred not to tell the Germans that; it would be better to produce the dead "Russian," along with his confederates, a gang-ring criminal and a woman dissident—Käthe Richter undoubtedly had some Kosi-sympathizing friends, adding to the credibility of the Russian assassin scenario.

Desperate, yes.

But, as he steered the white van south over the Stormtrooper-brown canal then east, he remained calm as stone. He parked on a busy street and climbed out. There was no doubt that Schumann would return to the boardinghouse for Käthe Richter. He'd adamantly insisted on taking the woman with him back to America. Which meant that, even now, he wasn't going to leave her behind. Taggert also knew that he'd come in person, not call her; Schumann knew the dangers of tapped phones in Germany.

Continuing quickly through the streets, feeling the comforting bump of the pistol against his hip, he turned the corner and proceeded into Magdeburger Alley. He paused and examined the short street carefully. It seemed deserted, dusty in the afternoon heat. He casually walked past Käthe Richter's boardinghouse and then, sensing no threat, returned quickly and descended to the basement entrance. He shouldered open the door then slipped into the dank cellar.

Taggert climbed the wooden stairs, keeping to the sides of the steps to minimize the creaks. He came to the top, eased the doorway open and, pulling the pistol from his pocket, stepped out into the ground-floor hallway. Empty. No sounds, no movement other than the frantic buzzing of a huge fly trapped between two panes of glass.

He walked the length of the corridor, listening at each door, hearing nothing. Finally he returned to the door on which hung a crudely painted sign that read, *Landlady*.

He knocked. "Miss Richter?" He wondered what she looked like. It had been the real Reginald Morgan who'd arranged for these rooms for Schumann, and apparently they'd never met; she and Morgan had spoken on the phone and exchanged a letter of agreement and cash through the pneumatic delivery system that crisscrossed Berlin.

Another rap on the door. "I've come about a room. The front door was open."

No response.

He tried the door. It was not locked. He slipped inside and noted a suitcase resting open on the bed, clothes and books around it. This reassured him; it meant Schumann hadn't returned yet. Where was she, though? Perhaps she wanted to collect money she was owed or, more likely, borrow what she could from friends and family. Emigrating from Germany through proper channels meant leaving with nothing more than clothes and pocket money; thinking she'd be leaving illegally with Schumann, she'd get as much cash as she could. The radio was on, the lights. She'd be back soon.

Taggert noticed next to the door a rack containing keys for all the rooms. He found the set to Schumann's and stepped into the corridor again. He walked quietly up the hall. In a swift motion he unlocked the door, pushed inside and lifted his pistol.

The living room was empty. He locked the door then stepped silently into the bedroom. Schumann was not here, though his suitcase was. Taggert stood in the middle of the room, debating. Schumann was sentimental perhaps in his concern for the woman but he was a thorough professional. Before he entered he would look through the windows in the front and back to see if anybody was here.

Taggert decided to lie in wait. He settled on the only realistic option: the closet. He'd leave the door open an inch or two so he could hear Schumann enter. When the button man was in the midst of packing his bag, Taggert would slip out of the closet and kill him. If he was lucky Käthe Richter would be with him and he could murder her as well. If not, he'd wait in her room. She might arrive first, of course, in which case he could kill her then or wait until Schumann returned. He'd have to consider which was best. He'd then scour the rooms to make certain that there was no trace of Schumann's real identity and call the SS and Gestapo to let them know that the Russian had been stopped.

Taggert stepped inside the large closet, swung the door nearly shut and undid his top several shirt buttons to alleviate the terrible heat. He breathed deeply, sucking air into his aching lungs. Sweat dotted his forehead and prickled the skin in the pits of his arms. But that mattered not one iota. Robert Taggert was wholly sustained, no, *intoxicated,* by an element far better than damp oxygen: the euphoria of power. The boy from low, gray Hartford, the boy beaten simply because he was a sharper thinker but a slower runner than the others in his low, gray neighborhood had just met Adolf Hitler himself, the most savvy politician on the face of the earth. He had seen the man's searing blue eyes regard him with admiration and respect, a respect that would soon be echoed in America when he returned home and reported about the success of his mission.

Ambassador to England, to Spain. Yes, even here eventually, the country he loved. He could go anywhere he wished.

Wiping his face again, he wondered how long he would have to wait for Schumann to return.

The answer to that question came just a moment later. Taggert heard the front door of the boardinghouse open and heavy footsteps in the hall. They continued past this room. There was a knocking.

"Käthe?" came the distant voice.

It was Paul Schumann speaking.

Would he go inside her apartment to wait?

No . . . The footsteps returned in this direction.

Taggert heard the jangle of the key, the squeak of old hinges and then a click as the door closed. Paul Schumann had walked into the room where he would die.

Chapter Twenty-Eight

Heart pounding like any hunter close to his prey, Robert Taggert listened carefully.

"Käthe?" Schumann's voice called.

Morgan heard the creak of boards, the sound of water running in the sink. The gulp of a man drinking thirstily.

Taggert lifted his pistol. It would be better to shoot him in the chest, front on, as if he'd been attacking. The SS would want him alive, of course, to interrogate him and wouldn't be happy if Taggert shot the man in the back. Still, he could take no chances. Schumann was too large and too dangerous to confront face-to-face. He'd tell Himmler that he'd had no choice; the assassin had tried to escape or grab a knife. Taggert had been forced to shoot him.

He heard the man walk to the bedroom. And a moment later, the sounds of rummaging through drawers as he filled his suitcase.

Now, he thought.

Taggert pushed one of the two closet doors open further. This gave him a view of the bedroom. He raised the pistol.

But Schumann wasn't visible. Taggert could see only the suitcase on the bed. And scattered around it were some books, and other objects. Then he frowned, looking at a pair of shoes sitting in the bedroom doorway. They hadn't been there before.

Oh, no . . .

Taggert realized that Schumann had walked to the bedroom but had then slipped off his shoes and eased back into the living room in stocking feet. He'd been pitching books through the doorway onto the bed to make Taggert think he was still there! That meant—

The huge fist crashed through the closet door as if it were spun sugar. The knuckles struck Taggert in the neck and jaw and he saw searing red in his vision as he staggered into the living room. He dropped the pistol and grabbed his throat, pressing the agonized flesh.

Schumann gripped Taggert by the lapels and flung him across the room. He crashed into a table and fell to the floor, where he lay crumpled like the German bisque doll that had landed beside him, unbroken, staring at the ceiling with her eerie, violet eyes.

"You're a ringer, right? You're not Reggie Morgan."

Paul didn't bother to explain that he'd done what every smart button man has to do—memorize the appearance of a room when he left it and then match that memory with what the place looks like when he returned. He'd seen the closet door, which he'd left closed, was open a few inches. Knowing that Taggert would have to track him down and kill him, he knew that's where the man was hiding.

"I—"

"Who?" Paul growled.

When the man said nothing, Paul took him by the collar with one hand and, with the other, emptied his jacket pocket: a wallet, a number of American passports, a U.S. diplomatic identity card in the name of Robert Taggert and the Stormtrooper card he'd flashed at Paul in the alley when they'd met.

"Don't move," Paul muttered, then examined the find. The wallet was Reginald Morgan's; it contained an ID card, some business cards with his name and an address on Bremer Street in Berlin and one in Washington, D.C. There were several photographs too—all depicting the man who'd been killed in Dresden Alley. One photo had been taken at a social function. He stood between an elderly man and woman, his arms around them both, all smiling at the Kodak.

One of the passports, well used and filled with entry and exit stamps, was in Morgan's name. It too contained a picture of the man from the alley.

Another passport—the one he'd showed Paul yesterday—also contained the name Reginald Morgan but the picture was of the man in front of him. Now, he held it under a lamp and examined the document closely. It seemed phony. A second passport, which seemed genuine, contained dozens of stamps and visas and was in the name of Robert Taggert, like the diplomatic ID card. The two remaining passports, a U.S. one in the name of Robert Gardner and a German one in the name of Artur Schmidt, had pictures of the man here.

So this guy on the floor in front of him had killed his contact in Berlin and taken over his identity, Paul understood.

"Okay, what's the game?"

"Just settle down, buddy. Don't do anything stupid." The man had dropped the stiff Reggie Morgan persona. The one who emerged was slick, like one of Lucky Luciano's sharkskin-suited Manhattan underbosses.

Paul held up the passport he thought was genuine. "This's you. Taggert, right?"

The man pressed his jaw and neck where Paul had hit him and rubbed the reddened area. "You got me, Paulio."

"How'd it work?" He frowned. "You intercepted the pass codes about the tram, right? That's why Morgan did a double-take in the alley. He thought *I* was the rat because I flubbed the phrase about the tram, same as I thought about him. Then you swapped documents when you were searching the body." Paul read the Stormtrooper card. "'Veterans' Relief.' Crap," he snapped, furious he hadn't looked at it more closely when Taggert had first flashed it at him. "Who the hell are you, mister?"

"A businessman. I just do odd jobs for people."

"And you got picked because you looked a little like the real Reggie Morgan?"

This offended him. "I got picked because I'm good."

"What about Max?"

"He was legit. Morgan paid him a hundred marks to get him the wire on Ernst. Then I paid him *two* hundred to pretend I was Morgan."

Paul nodded. "That's why the sap was so nervous. It wasn't the SS he was afraid of; it was me."

But the history of the deception seemed to bore Taggert. He continued impatiently. "We've got some horse trading to do, my friend. Now—"

"What was the point of this?"

"Paulio, we don't exactly have time for chats, don't you think? Half the Gestapo's looking for you."

"No, Taggert. If I'm understanding this right, thanks to you, they're looking for some Russian. They don't even know what I look like. And you wouldn't lead 'em back here—at least not until after you'd killed me. So we've got all the time in the world. Now, spill."

"This is about bigger things than you and me, buddy." Taggert moved his jaw in a slow circle. "You fucking loosened my teeth."

"Tell me."

"It's not—"

Paul stepped closer, closing his hand into a fist.

"Okay, okay, calm down, big guy. You want to know the truth? Here's the lowdown: There're a lot of people back home that don't want to get into another fight over here."

"That's what I'm *doing,* for God's sake. Stopping the rearmament."

"Actually, we don't give a fig about Hun rearmament. What we care about is keeping Hitler happy. Get it? Show him the U.S. is on his side."

Paul finally understood. "So I was the Easter lamb. You set me up as a Russian killer, and then you rat me out—so it looks to Hitler like the U.S. is his good pal, is that it?"

Taggert nodded. "Pretty much on the money, Paulio."

"Are you goddamn blind?" Paul said. "Don't you see what he's doing here? How can anybody be on their side?"

"Christ, Schumann, what's the hitch? Maybe Hitler takes over part of Poland, Austria, the Sudetenland." He laughed. "Hell, he can even have France. No skin off our nose."

"He's murdering people. Doesn't anybody see that?"

"Just a few Jews—"

"*What?* Are you hearing what you're saying?"

Taggert held up his hands. "Look, I don't mean it like that. Things here are only temporary. The Nazis're like kids with a new toy: their country. They'll get tired of this Aryan crap before the year is out. Hitler's all talk. He'll calm down and realize eventually that he *needs* Jews."

"No," Paul said emphatically. "You're wrong there. Hitler's nuts. He's Bugsy Siegel times a thousand."

"Well, okay, Paulio, it's not for you or me to decide stuff like that. Let's concede you caught us. We tried to pull a fast one and, good for you, you tumbled to it. But you need me, buddy-boy. You're not getting out of this country without my help. So here's what we're going to do: Let's you and me find some Russian-looking sap, kill him and call the Gestapo. Nobody's seen you. I'll even let you play the hero. You can meet Hitler and Göring. Get a goddamn medal. You and the broad can go back home. And I'll sweeten the pot: I'll throw some business to your friend Webber. Black market dollars.

He'd love it. How's that sound? I can make it happen. And everybody wins. Or . . . you can die here."

Paul asked, "I've got one question. Was it Bull Gordon? Was he behind it?"

"Him? Naw. He wasn't part of it. It was . . . other interests."

"What the hell does that mean, 'interests'? I want an answer."

"Sorry, Paulio. I didn't get to where I am now by having a loose tongue. Nature of the business, you know."

"You're as bad as the Nazis."

"Yeah?" Taggert muttered. "And who're you to talk, button man?" He stood up, dusting his jacket off. "So whatta you say? Let's find ourselves some Slav hobo, cut his throat and give the Huns their Bolshevik. Let's do it."

Everybody wins. . . .

Without shifting his weight, without narrowing his eyes, without giving any hint of what he was about to do, Paul drove his fist directly into the man's chest. Taggert's eyes snapped wide as his breath stopped. He never even glanced toward Paul's left fist as it shot forward and crushed his throat. By the time Taggert dropped to the floor, his extremities were shivering in death throes and a rattle echoed from his wide-open mouth. Whether it was a ruptured heart or a broken neck that killed him, he was dead within thirty seconds.

Paul stared down at the body for a long moment, hands shaking—not from the powerful blows but from the fury within him at the betrayal. And at the man's words.

He can even have France . . . Just a few Jews . . .

Paul hurried into the bedroom, stripped off the sweat clothes he'd stolen at the stadium, sponged off with water from the basin in the bedroom and dressed. He heard a knocking on the door. Ah, Käthe had returned. He realized suddenly that Taggert's body still lay visible in the living room. He hurried out to move the corpse into the bedroom.

Just as he was bending down to drag it into the closet, though, the front door to the apartment opened. Paul looked up. It hadn't been Käthe knocking. He found himself staring at two men. One was round, mustachioed, wearing a wrinkled cream-colored suit with a waistcoat. A Panama hat was in his hand. A slim, younger man in a dark suit stood beside him, gripping a black automatic pistol.

No! It was the very same cops who'd been dogging him since yesterday. He sighed and slowly stood.

"Ach, at last, is Mr. Paul Schumann," said the older man in heavily accented English, blinking in surprise. "I am Detective-inspector Kohl. You are under arrest, sir, for the murder of Reginald Morgan in Dresden Alley yesterday." He glanced down at Taggert's body and added, "And now, it seems, for the murder of someone else as well."

Chapter Twenty-Nine

"Keep your hands still. Yes, yes, please, Mr. Schumann. Keep them raised."

The American was quite large, Kohl observed. Easily four inches taller than the inspector himself and broad. The street artist's rendering had been accurate but the man's face was marred with more scars than in the sketch, and the eyes . . . well, they were a soft blue, cautious yet serene.

"Janssen, see if that man is indeed dead," Kohl said, returning to German. He covered Schumann with his own pistol.

The young detective leaned down and examined the figure, though there was little doubt in Kohl's mind he was looking at a corpse.

The young officer nodded and stood up.

Willi Kohl was as shocked as he was pleased to find Schumann here. He'd never expected this. Just twenty minutes before, in Reginald Morgan's room on Bremer Street, the inspector had found a letter of confirmation taking rooms in this boardinghouse on behalf of Paul Schumann. But Kohl was sure that after he'd killed Morgan, Schumann would have been smarter than to remain in the residence his victim had arranged for him. He and Janssen had sped here in hopes of finding some witnesses or evidence that might lead to Schumann, but hardly the American himself.

"So, are you one of those Gestapo police?" Schumann asked in German. Indeed, as the witnesses had reported, he had just a trace of accent. The G was that of a born Berliner.

"No, we are with the Criminal Police." He displayed his identification card. "Janssen, search him."

The young officer expertly patted every place that a pocket—obvious or secret—might be. The inspector candidate discovered his U.S. passport, money, comb, matches and a pack of cigarettes.

Janssen handed everything over to Kohl, who told his assistant to hand-cuff Schumann. He then flipped open the passport and examined it care-fully. It appeared authentic. Paul John Schumann.

"I didn't kill Reggie Morgan. He did." A nod toward the body. "His name is Taggert. Robert Taggert. He tried to kill me too. That's why we were fighting."

Kohl wasn't sure that "fighting" was the right word to describe a con-frontation between this tall American, with red calloused knuckles and huge arms, and the victim, who had the physique of Joseph Goebbels.

"Fight?"

"He pulled a gun on me." Schumann nodded toward a pistol lying on the floor. "I had to defend myself."

"Our Spanish Star Modelo A, sir," Janssen said excitedly. "The murder weapon!"

The same *type* of gun as the murder weapon, Kohl thought. A bullet comparison would tell if it was the same gun or not. But he would not cor-rect a colleague, even a junior one, in front of a suspect. Janssen draped a handkerchief around the weapon, picked it up and noted the serial number.

Kohl licked his pencil, jotted the number into his notebook and asked Janssen for the list of people who had bought such guns, supplied by police precincts around town. The young man produced it from his briefcase. "Now get the fingerprint kit from the car and print the gun and our friends here. Both the live one and the dead one."

"Yes, sir." He stepped outside.

The inspector flipped through the names on the list, seeing no Schu-mann.

"Try Taggert," the American said, "or one of those names." He nodded toward a stack of passports sitting on the table. "He had those on him."

"Please, you may sit." The inspector helped the cuffed Schumann onto the couch. He'd never had a suspect assist him in an investigation before but Kohl picked up the stack of passports that Schumann suggested might be revealing.

And indeed they were. One passport was Reginald Morgan's, the man killed in Dresden Alley. It was clearly authentic. The others contained pic-tures of the man lying at their feet but were issued in different names. One could not be a criminal investigator in National Socialist Germany these days without being familiar with forged documents. Of the others, only the passport in the name of Robert Taggert seemed genuine to Kohl and was the only one filled with apparently legitimate stamps and visas. He compared all the names with those on the list of gun purchasers. He stopped at one entry.

Janssen appeared in the doorway with the fingerprint kit and the Leica. Kohl held up the list. "It seems the deceased *did* buy the Modelo A last month, Janssen. Under the name of Artur Schmidt."

Which still didn't preclude Schumann from being Morgan's killer; Taggert might simply have given or sold him the gun. "Proceed with the fingerprinting," Kohl instructed. The young officer opened the briefcase and began his task.

"I didn't kill Reggie Morgan, I'm telling you. He did."

"Please, say nothing now, Mr. Schumann."

Reginald Morgan's wallet was also here. Kohl looked through it. He paused and looked at the picture of the man at a social event, standing with two older people.

We know something else about him . . . that he was somebody's son. . . . And perhaps he was somebody's brother. And maybe somebody's husband or lover. . . .

The inspector candidate proceeded to dust powder on the gun and then took Taggert's prints. The young man said to Schumann, "Sir, if you could sit forward please." Kohl approved of his protégé's polite tone.

Schumann cooperated and the young man printed him then wiped the ink off his fingers with the astringent cleaner that was included in the kit. Janssen placed the gun and the two printed cards on a table for his boss's inspection. "Sir?"

Kohl pulled out his monocle. He examined the weapon and the men's prints closely. He was no expert but his opinion was that the only prints on the pistol were Taggert's.

Janssen's eyes narrowed and he nodded to the floor.

Kohl followed the glance. A battered leather bag there. Ah, the telltale satchel! Kohl walked over and opened the clasp. He leafed through the contents—deciphering the English as best he could. There were many notes about Berlin, sports, the Olympics, a press pass in the name of Paul Schumann, dozens of innocuous clippings from American newspapers.

So, the inspector thought, he's been lying. The bag placed him at the murder scene.

But as Kohl examined it carefully he noted that, while it was old, yes, the leather was supple, not flaking.

Then he glanced at the body in front of them. Kohl set the case down and crouched over the dead man's shoes. They were brown, worn, and shedding bits of leather. The color and shine were just like the ones they'd found on the cobblestones of Dresden Alley and on the floor of the Summer Garden restaurant. Schumann's shoes were not shedding such flakes. The inspector's face twisted in irritation at himself. Another erroneous assumption. Schumann *had* been telling the truth. Perhaps.

"Search *him* now, Janssen," Kohl said, rising. A nod toward the body.

The inspector candidate dropped to his knees and began examining the corpse carefully.

Kohl lifted an eyebrow at Janssen, who continued the search. He found money, a penknife, a packet of cigarettes. A pocket watch on a heavy gold chain. Then the young man frowned. "Look, sir." He handed the inspector some silk clothing labels, undoubtedly cut from the garments Reginald Morgan had worn in Dresden Alley. They bore the names of German clothing manufacturers or stores.

"I'll tell you what happened," Schumann said.

"Yes, yes, you may talk in a minute. Janssen, contact headquarters. Have someone there get in touch with the American embassy. Ask about this Robert Taggert. Tell them he's in possession of a diplomatic identity card. Say nothing about his death at this time."

"Yes, sir." Janssen located the phone, which Kohl noted was disconnected from the wall, a common sight nowadays. The Olympic flag on the building, unaccompanied by the National Socialist banner, told him the place was owned or managed by a Jew or someone else in disfavor; the phones might be tapped. "Call from the wireless in the DKW, Janssen."

The inspector candidate nodded and left the room again.

"Now, sir, you may enlighten me. And please spare me no details."

Schumann said in German, "I came over here with the Olympic team. I'm a sportswriter. A freelance journalist. Do you—?"

"Yes, yes, I am familiar with the term."

"I was supposed to meet Reggie Morgan and he'd introduce me to some people for the stories. I wanted what we call 'color.' Information about the livelier parts of the city, gamblers, hustlers, boxing clubs."

"And this Reggie Morgan did what? As a profession, I mean."

"He was just an American businessman I'd heard about. He'd lived here for a few years and knew the place pretty well."

Kohl pointed out, "You came over with the Olympic team and yet they seemed unwilling to tell me anything about you. That's curious, don't you think?"

Schumann laughed bitterly. "You live in this country and you ask *me* why anyone would be reluctant to answer a policeman's questions?"

It is a matter of state security. . . .

Willi Kohl allowed no expression to cross his face but he was momentarily embarrassed at the truth of this comment. He regarded Schumann closely. The American appeared at ease. Kohl could detect no signs of fabrication, which was one of the inspector's particular talents.

"Continue."

"I was to meet with Morgan yesterday."

"That would have been when? And where?"

"Around noon. Outside a beer hall on Spener Street."

Right next to Dresden Alley, Kohl reflected. And around the time of the shooting. Surely, if he had something to hide, he would not place himself near the scene of the killing. Or would he? The National Socialist criminals were by and large stupid and obvious. Kohl sensed he was in the presence of a very smart man, though whether he was a criminal or not, the inspector could not tell. "But, as you contend, the real Reginald Morgan did not show up. It was this Taggert."

"That's right. Though I didn't know it at the time. He claimed he was Morgan."

"And what happened at this meeting?"

"It was very brief. He was agitated. He pulled me into this alley, said something had come up and I was supposed to meet him later. At a restaurant—"

"The name?"

"The Summer Garden."

"Where the wheat beer was not to your liking."

Schumann blinked, then replied, "Is it to *anyone's* liking?"

Kohl refrained from smiling. "And you met Taggert again, as planned, at the Summer Garden?"

"That's right. A friend of his joined us there. I don't recall his name."

Ah, the laborer.

"He whispered something to Taggert, who looked worried and said we ought to beat it." A frown at the literal German translation of what would be an English idiom. "I mean, leave quickly. This friend thought there were some Gestapo or something around, and Taggert agreed. We slipped out the side door. I should've guessed then that something wasn't right. But it was kind of an adventure, you know. That's just what I was looking for, for my stories."

"Local color," Kohl said slowly, reflecting that it is so much easier to make a big lie believable when the liar feeds you small truths. "And did you meet this Taggert at any other times?" A nod toward the body. "Other than today, of course?" Kohl wondered if the man would admit going to November 1923 Square.

"Yes," Schumann said. "Some square later that day. A bad neighborhood. Near Oranienburger Station. By a big statue of Hitler. We were going to meet some other contact. But that guy never showed up."

"And you 'beat it' from there as well."

"That's right. Taggert got spooked again. It was clear something was off. That's when I decided I better cut things off with the guy."

"What happened," Kohl asked quickly, "to your Stetson hat?"

A concerned look. "Well, I'll be honest, Detective Kohl. I was walking down the street and saw some young . . ." A hesitation as he sought a word. "Beasts . . . toughs?"

"Yes, yes, thugs."

"In brown uniforms."

"Stormtroopers."

"Thugs," Schumann said with some disgust. "They were beating up a bookseller and his wife. I thought these men were going to kill them. I stopped them. The next thing I knew there were a dozen of them after me. I threw some clothes away, down the sewer, so they wouldn't recognize me."

This is a wiry man, Kohl thought. And clever.

"Are you going to arrest me for beating up some of your Nazi thugs?"

"That doesn't interest me, Mr. Schumann. But what does very much interest me is the purpose of this whole masquerade orchestrated by Mr. Taggert."

"He was trying to fix some of the Olympic events."

"Fix?"

The American thought for a moment. "To have a player lose intentionally. That's what he'd been doing here over the past several months, putting together gambling pools in Berlin. Taggert's colleagues were going to place bets against some of the American favorites. I have a press pass and can get close to the athletes. I was supposed to bribe them to lose on purpose. That's why he was so nervous for the past couple days, I guess. He owed some of your gang rings, he called them, a lot of money."

"Morgan was killed because this Taggert wished to impersonate him?"

"That's right."

"Quite an elaborate plot," Kohl observed.

"Quite a lot of money was involved. Hundreds of thousands of dollars."

Another glance at the limp body on the floor. "I noted that you said you decided to end your relationship with Mr. Taggert as of yesterday. And yet here he is. How did this tragic 'fight,' as you call it, transpire?"

"He wouldn't take no for an answer. He was desperate for the money— he'd borrowed a lot to place the bets. He came here today to threaten me. He said they were going to make it look like I killed Morgan."

"To extort you into helping them."

"That's right. But I said I didn't care. I was going to turn him in anyway. He pulled that gun on me. We struggled and he fell. It seems he broke his neck."

Kohl's mind instinctively applied the information Schumann had provided against the facts and the inspector's awareness of human nature. Some details fit; some were jarring. Willi Kohl always reminded himself to keep an open mind at crime scenes, refrain from reaching conclusions too quickly. Now, this process happened automatically; his thoughts were deadlocked. It was as if a punch card had jammed in one of the DeHoMag sorting machines.

"You fought to save yourself and he died in a fall."

A woman's voice said, "Yes, that is exactly what happened."

Kohl turned to the figure in the doorway. She was about forty, slim and attractive, though her face was tired, troubled.

"Please, your name?"

"Käthe Richter." She automatically handed her card to him. "I manage this building in the owner's absence."

Her papers confirmed her identity and he returned the ID. "And you were a witness to this event?"

"I was here. In the hallway. I heard some disturbance from inside and opened the door partway. I saw the whole thing."

"And yet you were gone when we arrived."

"I was afraid. I saw your car pull up. I didn't want to get involved."

So she was on a Gestapo or SD list. "And yet here you are."

"I debated for some moments. I took the chance that there are still some policemen in this city who are interested in the truth." She said this defiantly.

Janssen stepped inside. He eyed the woman but Kohl said nothing about her. "Yes?" the inspector asked.

"Sir, the American embassy said they have no knowledge of a Robert Taggert."

Kohl nodded as he continued to ponder the information. He stepped closer to Taggert's body and said, "Quite a fortuitous fall. Fortuitous from your perspective, of course. And you, Miss Richter, I'll ask you again—you saw the struggle firsthand? You must be honest with me."

"Yes, yes. That man had a gun. He was going to kill Mr. Schumann."

"Do you know the victim?"

"No, I don't. I've never seen him."

Kohl glanced again at the body then tucked his thumb into his vest watch pocket. "It's a curious business, being a detective, Mr. Schumann. We try to read the clues and follow where they lead. And in this case the clues put me on your trail—indeed they led me here, directly to you—and now it seems those very same clues suggest that it was actually this *other* man I have been seeking all along."

"Life's funny sometimes."

The phrase made no sense in German. Kohl assumed it was a translation of an American idiom but he deduced the meaning.

Which he certainly could not dispute.

He took his pipe from his pocket and, without lighting it, slipped it into his mouth and chewed on the stem for a moment. "Well, Mr. Schumann, I have decided not to detain you, not at this moment. I will let you leave, though I will retain your passport while I look into these matters in more depth. Do not leave Berlin. As you have probably seen, our various authorities are quite adept at locating people in our country. Now, I'm afraid, you will have to quit the boardinghouse. It's a crime scene. Do you have another place to stay where I can contact you?"

Schumann thought for a moment. "I'll get a room at the Hotel Metropol."

Kohl wrote this down in his notebook and pocketed the man's passport. "Very well, sir. Now, is there anything else you wish to tell me?"

"Not a thing, Inspector. I'll cooperate however I can."

"You may leave now. Take only your necessities. Uncuff him, Janssen."

The inspector candidate did so. Schumann walked to his suitcase. As Kohl watched carefully, he packed a shaving kit with a razor, shaving soap, toothbrush and dental cream. The inspector handed him back his cigarettes, matches, money and comb.

Schumann glanced at the woman. "Can you walk me to the tram stop?"

"Yes, of course."

Kohl asked, "Miss Richter, you live here in the building?"

"The back apartment on this floor, yes."

"Very well. I'll be in touch with you, as well."

Together, they walked out the door.

After they had gone Janssen frowned and said, "Sir, how can you let him go? Did you believe his story?"

"Some of it. Enough to allow me to release him temporarily." Kohl explained to the inspector candidate his concerns: He believed that the killing here had been in self-defense. And it did indeed appear that Taggert was the killer of Reginald Morgan. But there remained unanswered questions. If they had been in any other country, Kohl would have detained Schumann until he verified everything. But he knew that if he now ordered the man held while he investigated further, the Gestapo would peremptorily declare the American to be the guilty "foreigner" Himmler wanted and he'd be in Moabit Prison or Oranienburg camp by nightfall.

"Not only would a man die for a crime he probably did not commit but the case will be declared closed and we'll never find the complete truth—which is, of course, the whole point of our job."

"But shouldn't I at least follow him?"

Kohl sighed. "Janssen, how many criminals have we ever apprehended by following them? What do they say in the American crime shockers? 'Shadowing'?"

"Well, none, I would guess, but—"

"So we will leave that to fictional detectives. We know where we can find him."

"But the Metropol is a huge hotel with many exits. He could escape from us easily there."

"That does not interest us, Janssen. We'll continue to look into Mr. Schumann's role in this drama shortly. Our priority now, though, is to examine the room here carefully. . . . Ach, congratulations, Inspector Candidate."

"Why is that, sir?"

"You have solved the Dresden Alley murder." He nodded toward the body. "And, what's more, the perpetrator is dead; we need not be inconvenienced by a trial."

Chapter Thirty

Accompanied by an SS bodyguard, Colonel Reinhard Ernst had taken Rudy back home to Charlottenburg. He was grateful for the boy's young age; the child hadn't completely understood the peril at the stadium. The grim faces of the men, the urgency in the pressroom and the fast drive away from the complex had been troubling to him, but he could not fathom the significance of the events. All he knew was that his Opa had fallen and hurt himself slightly, even though his grandfather had made light of the "adventure," as he called it.

The highlights of the afternoon for the boy, in fact, had not been the magnificent stadium, nor meeting some of the most powerful men in the world, nor the alarm over the assassin. It had been the dogs; Rudy now wanted one himself, preferably two. He talked endlessly about the animals.

"Construction everywhere," Ernst muttered to Gertrud. "I've ruined my suit."

True, she wasn't pleased but she was more troubled that he'd taken a fall. She examined his head closely. "You have a bump. You must be more careful, Reinie. I'll bring you ice for it."

He hated to be less than honest with her. But he simply would not tell her that he'd been the target of an assassin. If she'd learned that, she would implore him to stay home, no, insist. And he would have to refuse, as he rarely did with his wife. Hitler may have buried himself beneath corpses during the November '23 rebellion to remain out of harm's way, but Ernst would never avoid an enemy when his duty required otherwise.

Under different circumstances, yes, he might have remained home for a day or two until the assassin was found, which surely he would be, now that the great mechanism of the Gestapo, SD and SS was in motion. But

Ernst had a vital matter to attend to today: conducting the tests at the college with Doctor-professor Keitel and preparing the memo about the Waltham Study for the Leader.

He now asked to have the housekeeper bring him some coffee, bread and sausage in the den.

"But Reinie," Gertrud said, exasperated, "it's Sunday. The goose . . ."

Afternoon meals on the day of rest were a long tradition in the Ernst household, not to be broken if at all possible.

"I'm sorry, my dear. I have no choice. Next week I will spend the entire weekend with you and the family."

He walked into the den and sat at his desk, then began jotting notes.

Ten minutes later Gertrud herself appeared, carrying a large tray.

"I won't have you eating a coarse meal," she said, lifting the cloth off the tray.

He smiled and looked over the huge plate of roast goose with orange marmalade, cabbage, boiled potatoes and green beans with cardamon. He rose and kissed her on the cheek. She left him and, as he ate, without much appetite, he began to peck out a draft of the memo on his typewriter.

HIGHEST CONFIDENTIALITY

Adolf Hitler,
> Leader, State Chancellor and President of the German
> Nation and Commander of the Armed Forces

Field Marshal Werner von Blomberg,
> State Minister of Defense

My Leader and my Minister:

You have asked for details of the Waltham Study being conducted by myself and Doctor-Professor Ludwig Keitel of Waltham Military College. I am pleased to describe the nature of the study and the results so far.

> This study arises out of my instructions from you to make ready the German armed forces and to help them achieve most expeditiously the goals of our great nation, as you have set forth.

He paused and organized his thoughts. What to share and what not to share?

A half hour later he finished the page-and-a-half document, made a few penciled corrections. This draft would do for now. He would have Keitel read the document as well and make corrections, then Ernst would retype the final version tonight and personally deliver it to the Leader tomorrow. He wrote a note to Keitel asking for his comments and clipped it to the draft.

Carrying the tray downstairs, he said good-bye to Gertrud then left. Hitler had insisted that guards be stationed outside his house, at least until the assassin was caught. Ernst had no objection to this but he now asked that they remain out of sight so as not to alarm his family. He also acquiesced to the Leader's demand that he not drive himself in his open Mercedes, as he preferred, but be driven in a closed auto by an armed SS bodyguard.

They drove first to Columbia House, at Tempelhof. The driver climbed out and looked around to make sure the entry area was safe. He walked to the other two guards, stationed in front of the door, spoke with them and they looked around too, though Ernst couldn't imagine anyone being so foolish as to attempt an assassination in front of an SS detention center. After a moment they waved and Ernst climbed out of the car. He stepped through the front door and was led down the stairs, through several locked doors, and then into the cell area.

Walking down the long hallway again, hot and dank, stinking of urine and shit. What a disgusting way to treat people, he thought. The British, American and French soldiers he'd captured during the War had been treated with respect. Ernst had saluted the officers, chatted with the enlisted men, made sure they were warm and dry and fed. He now felt a burst of contempt for the brown-uniformed jailer who accompanied him down the corridor, softly whistling the "Horst Wessel Song" and occasionally banging on bars with his truncheon, simply to frighten the prisoners.

When they came to a cell three-quarters of the way down the corridor Ernst stopped, looked inside, his skin itching in the heat.

The two Fischer brothers were drenched with sweat. They were frightened, of course—*everyone* was frightened in this terrible place—but he saw something else in their eyes: youthful defiance.

Ernst was disappointed. The look told him they were going to reject his offer: They'd chosen a spell in Oranienburg? He'd thought for certain that Kurt and Hans would agree to participate in the Waltham Study. They would have been perfect.

"Good afternoon."

The older one nodded. Ernst felt a strange chill. The boy resembled his own son. Why hadn't he noticed it before? Perhaps it was the self-confidence and the serenity that hadn't been there this morning. Perhaps it was just the lingering aftermath of the look in young Rudy's eyes earlier. In any case, the similarity unnerved him.

"I need your answer now regarding your participation in our study."

The brothers looked at each other. Kurt began to speak but it was the younger one who said, "We will do it."

So, he'd been wrong. Ernst smiled and nodded, genuinely pleased.

The older brother then added, "Provided you let us send a letter to England."

"A letter?"

"We wish to communicate with our parents."

"That is not allowed, I'm afraid."

"But you're a colonel, right? Aren't you someone who can decide what's allowed and what isn't?" Hans asked.

Ernst cocked his head and examined the boy. But his attention returned to the older brother. The resemblance to Mark was indeed uncanny. He hesitated then said, "One letter. But you must send it in the next two days, while you're under my supervision. Your training sergeants won't permit it, not a letter to London. They are definitely *not* someone who can decide what's allowed and what isn't."

Another glance passed between the boys. Kurt nodded. The colonel did too. And then he saluted them—just as he'd said good-bye to his son. Not with a fascist extended arm but in a traditional gesture, lifting his flat palm to his forehead, which the SA guard pretended not to notice.

"Welcome to the new Germany," Ernst said in a voice that was close to a whisper and belied the crisp salute.

They turned the corner and headed for Lützow Plaza, putting as much distance between them and the boardinghouse as possible before they found a taxi, Paul looking back often to make sure they weren't being followed.

"We aren't staying at the Metropol," he said, gazing up and down the street. "I'll find someplace safe. My friend Otto can do that. I'm sorry. But you'll have to just leave everything back there. You can't go back again."

On the busy street corner they stopped. Absently his arm slipped around Käthe's waist as he looked into traffic. But he felt her stiffen. Then she pulled away.

He glanced down at her, frowning.

"I *am* going back, Paul." She spoke in a voice that was devoid of emotion.

"Käthe, what's wrong?"

"I was telling the truth to the Kripo inspector."

"You . . ."

"I *was* outside the door, looking in. *You* were the one who lied. You murdered that man in the room. There was no fight. He didn't have a gun. He was standing there helpless, and you hit him and killed him. It was horrible. I haven't seen anything so horrible since . . . since . . ."

The fourth square from the grass . . .

Paul was silent.

An open truck drove past. A half dozen Stormtroopers were in the back. They shouted out something to a group of people on the street, laughing. Some of the pedestrians waved back. The truck disappeared fast around a corner.

Paul led Käthe to a bench in a small park but she wouldn't sit. "No," she whispered. Arms folded across her chest, she stared at him coldly.

"It's not as simple as you think," he whispered.

"Simple?"

"There's more to me, to why I'm here, yes. I didn't tell you because I didn't want you to be involved."

Now, at last, raw anger exploded. "Oh, *there's* an excuse for lying! You didn't want to get me involved. You asked me to come to America, Paul. How much more involved could I be?"

"I mean involved with my old life. This trip will be the end of that."

"Old life? Are you a soldier?"

"In a way." Then he hesitated. "No. That's not true. I was a criminal in America. I came here to stop them."

"Them?"

"Your enemies." He nodded at one of the hundreds of red-white-and-black flags that stirred nearby in the breeze. "I was supposed to kill someone in the government here to stop him from starting another war. But afterwards, that part of my life will be over with. I'd have a clean record. I'd—"

"And when were you going to tell me this little secret of yours, Paul? When we got to London? To New York?"

"Believe me. It's over with."

"You used me."

"I never—"

"Last night—that wonderful night—you had me show you Wilhelm Street. You were using me as cover, weren't you? You wished to find a place where you could murder this man."

He looked up at one of the stark, flapping banners and said nothing.

"And what if in America I did something that angered you? Would you hit *me*? Would you kill *me*?"

"Käthe! Of course not."

"Ach, you say that. But you've lied before." Käthe pulled a handkerchief from her purse. The smell of lilac touched him momentarily and his heart cried, as if it were the smell of incense at a loved one's wake. She wiped her eyes and stuffed the cloth away. "Tell me one thing, Paul. How are you different from them? Tell me. How? . . . No, no, you *are* different. You're crueller. Do you know why?" Choking on tears. "You gave me hope and then you took it away. With them, with the beasts in the garden, there is *never* any hope. At least they're not deceitful like you. No, Paul. Fly back to your perfect country. I'll stay here. I'll stay until the knock on the door. And then I'll be gone. Like my Michael."

"Käthe, I haven't been honest with you, no. But you have to leave with me. . . . Please."

"Do you know what our philosopher Nietzsche wrote? He said, 'He who fights monsters must take care that he does not become a monster himself.' Oh, how true that is, Paul. How true."

"Please, come with me." He took her by the shoulders, gripping her hard.

But Käthe Richter was strong too. She pulled his hands off and stepped back. Her eyes fixed on his and she whispered ruthlessly, "I'd rather share my country with ten thousand killers than my bed with *one*."

And turning on her heels, she hesitated for a moment then walked away quickly, drawing the glances of passersby, who wondered what might have caused such a fierce lovers' spat.

Chapter Thirty-One

"Willi, Willi, Willi. . . ."

Chief of Inspectors Friedrich Horcher drew the name out very slowly.

Kohl had returned to the Alex and was nearly to his office when his boss caught up with him. "Yes, sir?"

"I've been looking for you."

"Yes? Have you?"

"It's about that Gatow case. The shootings. You will recall?"

How could he forget? Those pictures would be burned into his mind forever. The women . . . the children . . . But now he felt the chill of fear again. Had the case in fact been a test, as he'd worried earlier? Had Heydrich's boys waited to see if he'd drop the matter and now learned that he'd done worse: He'd secretly called the young gendarme at home about it?

Horcher tugged at his blood-red armband. "I have good news for you. The case has been solved. Charlottenburg too, the Polish workers. They were both the work of the same killer."

Kohl's initial relief that he was not going to be arrested turned quickly to bewilderment. "Who closed the case? Someone at Kripo?"

"No, no, it was the head of the gendarmerie himself. Meyerhoff. Imagine."

Ach . . . The matter was beginning to crystalize—to Willi Kohl's disgust. He wasn't the least surprised at the rest of the tale that his boss laid out. "The killer was a Czech Jew. Deranged. Much like Vlad the Impaler. Was *he* Czech? Maybe Romanian or Hungarian, I don't recall. Ha, history was always my poorest subject. In any case, the suspect was caught and confessed. He was handed over to the SS." Horcher laughed. "They took time out from their *important,* and mysterious, security alert to actually do some police work."

"Was there one accomplice or more?" Kohl asked.

"Accomplice? No, no, the Czech was alone."

"Alone? But the gendarme in Gatow concluded there had to be at least two or three perpetrators, probably more. The pictures support that theory, and logic, as well, given the number of victims."

"Ach, as we know, Willi, being trained policemen, the eye can be fooled. And a young gendarme in the suburbs? They are not used to crime scene investigation. Anyway, the Jew confessed. He acted alone. The case is solved. And the fellow is on his way to the camp."

"I would like to interview him."

A hesitation. Then, smiling still, Horcher adjusted his armband once again. "I'll see what I can do about that. Though it's likely that he might already be in Dachau."

"Dachau? Why would they send him to Munich? Why not Oranienburg?"

"Overcrowding perhaps. In any event, the case is done, so there's really no reason to talk to him."

The man was, of course, dead by now.

"Besides, you need all your time to concentrate on the Dresden Alley matter. How is that coming?"

"We've had some breakthroughs," Kohl told his boss, trying to keep anger and frustration out of his voice. "A day or two and I think we'll have all our answers."

"Excellent." Horcher frowned. "Even more hubbub over on Prince Albrecht Street than before. Did you hear? More alerts, more security measures. Even mobilizing among the SS. Still haven't heard what's going on. Have *you* caught a glimmer, by any chance?"

"No, sir." Poor Horcher. Afraid everybody was better informed than he. "You'll have the report on the killing soon," Kohl told him.

"Good. It *is* leaning toward that foreigner, isn't it? I believe you said it was."

Kohl thought: No, *you* said it was. "The case is moving apace."

"Excellent. My, look at us, Willi: Here we are working Sundays. Can you imagine it? Remember when we actually had Saturday afternoon *and* Sunday off?" The man wandered back up the quiet hallway.

Kohl walked to the doorway of his office and saw the blank spaces where his notes and the photographs of the Gatow killings had rested. Horcher would have "filed them away"—meaning they'd had the same fate as the poor Czech Jew. Probably burned like the manifest of the *Manhattan* and floating over the city as particles of ash in the alkaline Berlin wind. He leaned wearily against the doorjamb, staring at the empty spaces on his desk, and he thought: This is the one thing about murder: It can never be undone. You return the stolen money, bruises heal, the burned-down house is rebuilt, you find the kidnap victim troubled but alive. But those children who had died, their parents, the Polish workers . . . their deaths were forever.

And yet here was Willi Kohl being told that this was not so. That the laws of the universe were somehow different in this land: The deaths of the families and the workers had been erased. Because, if they had been real, then honest people would not rest until the loss had been understood and mourned and—Kohl's role—vindicated.

The inspector hung his hat on the rack and sat heavily in his creaking chair. He looked over his incoming mail and telegrams. Nothing regarding Schumann. With his magnifying monocle, Kohl himself compared the fingerprints Janssen had taken of Taggert with the photos of those found on the cobblestones of Dresden Alley. They were the same. This relieved him somewhat; it meant that Taggert was indeed the murderer of Reginald Morgan, and the inspector had not let a killer go free.

It was just as well that he could make the comparison himself. A message from the Identification Department told him that all the examiners and analysts had been ordered to drop any Kripo investigation and make themselves available to the Gestapo and SS in light of "a new development in the security alert."

He walked to Janssen's desk and learned that the coroner's men still hadn't collected Taggert's body from the boardinghouse. Kohl shook his head and sighed. "We'll do what we can here. Have the ballistics technicians run tests on the Spanish pistol to make sure it *is* the murder weapon."

"Yes, sir."

"Oh, and, Janssen? If the firearms examiners too have been commandeered in the search for this Russian, then run the tests yourselves. You can do that, can you not?"

"I can, sir, yes."

After the young man had left, Kohl sat back and began to jot a list of questions about Morgan and the mysterious Taggert, which he would have translated and sent to the American authorities.

A shadow appeared in the doorway. "Sir, a telegram," said the floor runner, a young man in a gray jacket. He offered the document to Kohl.

"Yes, yes, thank you." Thinking it would be from the United States Lines about the manifest or Manny's Men's Wear, tersely explaining they could be of no help, he ripped the envelope open.

But he was wrong. It was from the New York City Police Department. The language was English but he could understand the meaning well enough.

TO DETECTIVE INSPECTOR W KOHL KRIMINALPOLIZEI
ALEXANDERPLATZ BERLIN IN RESPONSE TO YOUR
REQUEST OF EVEN DATE BE ADVISED THAT THE FILE
ON P SCHUMANN HAS BEEN EXPUNGED AND OUR
INVESTIGATION RE SAID INDIVIDUAL SUSPENDED
INDEFINITELY STOP NO MORE INFORMATION IS
AVAILABLE STOP REGARDS CAPT G O'MALLEY NYPD

Kohl frowned. He found the department's English-German dictionary and learned that "expunged" meant "obliterated." He read the telegram several times more, feeling his skin grow hot with each reading.

So the criminal police *had* been investigating Schumann. For what? And why had the file been destroyed and the investigation stopped?

What were the implications of this? Well, the most immediate was that while the man might not have been guilty of killing Reginald Morgan, he was possibly in town for some criminal venture.

And the other was that Kohl himself had let a potentially dangerous man loose in the city.

He needed to find Schumann, or at least more information about him, and fast. Without waiting for Janssen to return, Willi Kohl collected his hat and walked along the dim hallway, then down the stairs. So distracted was he that he took the stairway to the forbidden ground floor. He pushed the door open anyway and was immediately confronted by an SS soldier. Amid the flapping of the DeHoMag card sorters, the man said, "Sir, this is a restricted—"

"You will let me pass," Kohl growled with a fierceness that startled the young guard.

Another guard, armed with an Erma machine gun, glanced their way.

"I am leaving my building by the door at the end of that hallway. I don't have time to go the other way."

The young SS man looked uneasily around him. No one else in the hallway said a word. Finally he nodded.

Kohl stalked down the hall, ignoring the pain in his feet, and pushed outside into the brilliant, hot afternoon light. He oriented himself, lifted his foot to a bench and adjusted the lamb's wool to pad his right foot. Then the inspector started north in the direction of the Hotel Metropol.

"Ach, Mr. John Dillinger!" Otto Webber frowned, gesturing him to a chair in a dark corner of the Aryan Café. He gripped Paul's arm hard and whispered, "I was worried about you. No word! Was my phone call to the stadium successful? I haven't heard anything on the radio. Not that our rodent Goebbels would go on state radio to spread the word of an assassination."

Then the gang leader's smile faded. "What's the matter, my friend? Your face is not pleased."

But before he could say anything the waitress Liesl noticed Paul and moved in fast. "Hello, my love," she said. Then pouted. "Shame on you. Last time you left without kissing me good-bye. What can I get you?"

"A Pschorr."

"Yes, yes, I'm pleased to. I've missed you."

Ignored by the waitress, Webber said petulantly, "Excuse me, ach, excuse me. A lager for me."

Liesl bent and kissed Paul's cheek. He smelled powerful perfume. It hung around him even after she left. He thought of lilac, thought of Käthe. He pushed the thoughts aside abruptly then explained what had happened at the stadium and afterward.

"No! Our friend Morgan?" Webber was horrified.

"A man *pretending* to be Morgan. The Kripo has my name and passport but they don't think I killed him. And they haven't connected me with Ernst and the stadium."

Liesl brought them the beers. She squeezed Paul's shoulder as she stepped away and brushed against him flirtatiously, leaving another cloud of strong perfume around the table. Paul leaned away from it. She smiled lasciviously as she sashayed away.

"She just can't figure out I'm not interested, can she?" he muttered, all the angrier because he couldn't get Käthe out of his mind.

"Who?" Webber asked, drinking several large gulps.

"Her. Liesl." He nodded.

Webber frowned. "No, no, no, Mr. John Dillinger. Not her. *Him.*"

"*What?*"

Webber frowned. "You thought Liesl is a woman?"

Paul blinked. "She's a . . ."

"But of course." He drank more beer, wiped his mustache with the back of his hand. "I thought you knew. It's obvious."

"Jesus Lord." Paul rubbed his cheek hard where he'd been kissed. He glanced back. "Obvious to you maybe."

"For a man with your profession, you're a babe in the woods."

"I said I liked women, when you asked me about the rooms here."

"Ach, the *show* in here is women. But half the waitresses are men. Don't blame me if both sexes find you attractive. Besides, it's your fault—you tipped her like a prince from Addis Ababa."

Paul lit a cigarette to cover the scent of the perfume, which he now found revolting.

"So, Mr. John Dillinger, I see there are problems for you. Are the people behind this betrayal the ones who were to get you out of Berlin?"

"I don't know yet." He glanced around the nearly empty club but still leaned forward to whisper, "I need your help again, Otto."

"Ach, here I am, always ready to assist. Me, the saver-from-dung-shirts, the butter-maker, the champagne-dealer, the Krupp-impersonator."

"But I have no money left."

Webber gave a sneer. "Money . . . it's the root of all evil, after all. What do you need, my friend?"

"A car. Another uniform. And another gun. A rifle."

Webber was quiet. "Your hunt continues."

"That's right."

"Ach, what I could've done with a dozen men like you in my gang ring. . . . But Ernst's security will be higher than ever. He may leave town for a while."

"True. But perhaps not immediately. When I was in his office I saw that he had *two* appointments today. The first was at the stadium. The other is at a place called Waltham College. Where is that?"

"Waltham?" Webber asked. "It's—"

"Hello, darling, do you wish another beer? Or maybe you wish *me?*"

Paul jumped as hot breath blew against his ear and arms snaked around him. Liesl had come up from behind.

"The first time," the waitress whispered, "will be free. Perhaps even the second time."

"Stop it," he barked. The waitress's face went cold.

Now knowing the truth about him, Paul could see that while the creature's face was pretty it had clearly masculine angles.

"You needn't be rude, my darling."

"I'm sorry," Paul said, leaning away. "I'm not interested in men."

Liesl said coolly, "I'm not a man."

"You know what I mean."

"Well, then, you shouldn't have flirted," Liesl snapped. "You owe me four marks for the beers. No, five. I added wrong."

Paul paid and the waitress turned away coldly, muttering and noisily cleaning adjacent tables.

"My girls," Webber said dismissively, "they get the same way sometimes. It can be such a bother."

They resumed their conversation and Paul repeated, "Waltham College? What do you know about it?"

"A military school not far from here. It's on the way to Oranienburg, by the way—the home of our beautiful concentration camp. Why don't you just knock on the door while you're there and give yourself up. Save the SS the trouble of tracking you down."

"A car and a uniform," Paul repeated. "I want to be an official but not a soldier. That's what we did at the stadium and they might be anticipating it. Maybe—"

"Ach, I know! You can be an RAD leader."

"A what?"

"National Labor Service. A Soldier of the Spade. Every young man in the country must do a stint as a laborer, probably thought up by Ernst himself as another clever way to train soldiers. They carry their shovels like guns and practice marching as much as digging. You're too old to be in the service but you could be an officer. They have trucks to shuttle workers to job sites and parade grounds and they're common in the countryside. No one would notice you. I know where to find you one, a nice truck. And a uniform. They're a tasteful blue-gray. Just the color for you."

Paul whispered, "And the rifle?"

"That will be harder. But I have some thoughts." He finished his beer. "When do you wish to do this?"

"I should be at Waltham College by five-thirty. No later."

Webber nodded. "Then we must move quickly to turn you into a National Socialist official." He laughed. "Though you need no training. God knows the real ones have none."

Chapter Thirty-Two

He heard only static at first. Then the scratchy sounds coalesced into: "Gordon?"

"We don't use names," the commander reminded, pressing the Bakelite phone to his ear furiously so that he could hear the words from Berlin more clearly. It was Paul Schumann, calling via radio patched through London. The time was just before 10 A.M. on Sunday morning but Gordon was at his desk at the Office of Naval Intelligence in Washington, D.C., where he'd been all night, anxiously waiting to hear whether the man had succeeded in killing Ernst. "Are you all right? What's going on? We've been checking all the press, monitoring the radio broadcasts and nothing's—"

"Be quiet," Schumann snapped. "I don't have time for 'friends in the north' and 'friends in the south.' Just listen."

Gordon sat forward in his chair. "Go ahead."

"Morgan's dead."

"Oh, no." Gordon closed his eyes momentarily, feeling the loss. He hadn't known the man personally but his information had always been solid, and any man who risks his life for his country was okay in Gordon's book.

Then Schumann delivered a bombshell. "He was murdered by somebody named Robert Taggert, an American. You know him?"

"What? An American?"

"Do you *know* him?"

"No, never heard of him."

"He tried to kill me too. Before I could do what you sent me for. The guy you've been talking to for the past couple of days was Taggert, not Morgan."

"What was that name again?"

Schumann spelled it and told Gordon that he might have some connec-

333

tion with the U.S. diplomatic service but he wasn't sure. The commander wrote the name on a slip of paper and shouted, "Yeoman Willets!"

The woman appeared in the doorway a moment later. Gordon jammed the note into her palm. "Get me everything you can find about this guy," he said. She vanished instantly. Then into the phone: "Are you all right?"

"Were you part of it?" Despite the bad connection Gordon could feel the man's anger.

"What?"

"It was all a setup. From the beginning. Were you part of it?"

Gordon felt the swampy July morning air of Washington, D.C., float in and out of the open window. "I don't know what you're talking about."

After a pause Schumann told the whole story—about the murder of Morgan, Taggert's masquerading as him and the betrayal of Schumann to the Nazis.

Gordon was genuinely shocked. "My God, no. I swear. I'd never do that to one of my men. And I consider you one of them. I honestly do."

Another pause. "Taggert said you weren't involved. But I wanted to hear it from you."

"I swear. . . ."

"Well, you've got a traitor somewhere on your end, Commander. You need to find out who."

Gordon sat back, shattered at this news. He stared, numb, at the wall in front of him, on which were a number of citations, his Yale diploma and two pictures: President Roosevelt and Theodorus B.M. Mason, the solid-jawed naval lieutenant who'd been the first head of the Office of Naval Intelligence.

A traitor . . .

"What does this Taggert say?"

"All he said was that it was 'interests.' Nothing more specific. They wanted to keep the boss here happy. The overall boss, I mean."

"Can you talk to him again, find out more?"

A hesitation. "No."

Gordon understood the implication; Taggert was dead.

Schumann continued. "I got the pass phrases about the tram when I was on the ship. Taggert got the same phrases we did but Morgan didn't know them. How could that happen?"

"I sent the code to my men on the ship. It also went separately to where you are now. Morgan was supposed to pick it up there."

"So Taggert got the right message and had a different one sent to Morgan. That German-American Bund spy on board didn't transmit anything. It wasn't him. So who could've done that? Who knew the right phrase?"

Two names came immediately to Gordon's mind. A soldier before everything else, Gordon knew that a military commander had to consider all possibilities. But young Andrew Avery was like a son to him. He knew Vincent Manielli less well yet he'd seen nothing in the young officer's record that would make him doubt his loyalty.

As if he were a mind reader, Schumann asked, "How long have you worked with those two boys of yours?"

"It would be next to impossible."

"'Impossible' has a whole goddamn different meaning lately. Who the hell else knew about the code? Daddy Warbucks?"

Gordon considered. But the moneybags, Cyrus Clayborn, only knew in general what they had planned. "He didn't even know there *was* a pass code."

"Then who came up with the phrase?"

"We did, together, the Senator and me."

More static. Schumann said nothing.

But Gordon added, "No, it can't be him."

"Was he with you when you sent the codes?"

"No. He was in Washington."

Gordon was thinking: The moment he hung up with me, the Senator could have sent a message to Taggert in Berlin with the right code and arranged for the wrong one to go to Morgan. "Impossible."

"I keep hearing that word, Gordon. That doesn't cut it with me."

"Look, this whole thing was the Senator's idea in the first place. He had some talks with people in the administration and he came to me."

"All that means is he's been planning to set me up from the beginning." Schumann added ominously, "Along with those same 'people.'"

Facts cascaded through Gordon's mind. Could this be? Where could the betrayal lead?

Finally Schumann said, "Listen, you handle that situation the way you want. Are you still going to get me that plane?"

"Yes, sir. You have my absolute word on that. I'll contact my men in Amsterdam myself. We'll have it there in about three and a half hours."

"No, I'll need it later than that. About ten tonight."

"We can't land in the dark. The strip we're using's abandoned. It doesn't have lights. But there should be enough daylight left to set down around eight-thirty. How's that?"

"No. Then make it dawn tomorrow."

"Why?"

There was a pause. "I'm going to get him this time."

"Going to . . . ?"

"Do what I came here for," Schumann growled.

"No, no . . . You can't. It's too dangerous now. Come on home. Get that job you were talking about. You earned it. You—"

"Commander . . . you listening?"

"Go on."

"See, I'm here and you're there, and there's nothing you can do to stop me, so all of this jawing now's just a waste of time. Make sure that plane's at the field at dawn tomorrow."

Yeoman Ruth Willets appeared in the doorway. "Hold on," Gordon said into the phone.

"Nothing on Taggert yet, sir. Records'll call as soon as they find something."

"Where's the Senator?"

"In New York."

"Get me on any plane you can going up there now. Army, private. Whatever it takes."

"Yessir."

Gordon turned back to the phone. "Paul, we'll get you your lift out of there. But please listen to reason. Everything's changed now—you have any idea what the risks are?"

The noise on the line rose and swallowed most of Schumann's words but it seemed to Bull Gordon that he heard what might've been laughter and then the button man's voice again. Part of the phrase was something like "six to five against."

Then he was listening to a silence that was far louder than the static had ever been.

In a warehouse in eastern Berlin (which Otto Webber called "his" despite the fact they had to break a window to get inside) they found racks of

National Labor Service uniforms. Webber pulled a fancy one off a hanger. "Ach, yes, as I said, the blue-gray becomes you."

Maybe it did, but the color was also conspicuous, especially since his shooting blind at Waltham College would be an open field or forest, as Webber had described the landscape there. The uniform was also close-fitting, bulky and hot. It would get him close to the school but he took another set of more practical clothing as well, dungarees, a dark shirt and a pair of boots, to wear for the touch-off itself.

One of Webber's business associates had access to a motor pool of government trucks and, with the assurance that Webber would return the vehicle within one day (and not try to sell it back to the government when he did so), the key was handed over, in exchange for some Cuban cigars that had been made in Romania.

Now they needed only the rifle.

Paul had considered the pawnbroker near November 1923 Square, the one who'd supplied the Mauser. But he couldn't be sure whether the man had been part of Taggert's deceit or, even if not, whether the Kripo or Gestapo had traced the gun back to the shop and arrested him.

But Webber told him there were often rifles stored in a small warehouse on the Spree River, where he sometimes made deliveries of military supplies.

They drove north and, just after crossing the river at Wullenweber Street, turned west and headed through an area of low manufacturing and commercial buildings. Webber tapped Paul's arm and he pointed to a dark building to their left.

"That's it, my friend."

The place appeared deserted, which they'd expected, today being Sunday. ("Even godless dung-shirts insist on a day of rest," Webber explained.) But unfortunately the warehouse was set back behind a tall barbed-wire fence and had a spacious, now empty parking area in the front, which made it very visible from the well-traveled street.

"How do we—?"

"Relax, Mr. John Dillinger," Webber said. "I know what I'm doing. There's a waterside entrance for boats and barges. It's impossible to see from the street and you can't tell it's a National Socialist warehouse from that side—no eagles or hooked crosses on the dock—so no one will think twice about our visit."

They parked a half block past the warehouse and Webber led him through an alley, south, toward the water. The men stepped out onto a stone wall above the brown river, where the air was pungent with the scent of rotten fish. They walked down old stairs, carved into stone, and onto a concrete wharf. Several rowboats were tied up and Webber climbed into one. Paul joined him.

They cast off and in a few minutes had rowed their way to a similar dock beneath the back of the military warehouse.

Webber tied the boat up and climbed carefully onto the stone, slick with bird droppings. Paul followed. Looking around, he could see boats on the river, mostly pleasure craft, but Webber was right; no one was paying them any attention. They climbed a few steps to the back door and Paul took a fast look through the window. No lights were on inside and only dim sunlight filtered through several opaque skylights, but the large room appeared deserted. Webber extracted a key ring from his pocket and tried several skeleton keys until he found one that worked. Paul heard a soft click. Webber glanced at him and nodded. Paul pushed the door open.

They walked into the hot, musty room, filled with the eye-burning fumes of creosote. Paul looked around and noticed hundreds of crates. Against the wall were racks of rifles. The army or SS was using this place as an assembly station—taking the guns from the crates, ripping off the oil-paper wrapping and cleaning off the creosote, which had been smeared on to prevent rusting. They were Mausers, similar to the one that Taggert had arranged for him, though with longer barrels, which was good. This meant they were more accurate and, at Waltham, he might be quite far from Ernst. No telescopic sights. But Paul Schumann hadn't had one on his Springfield at St. Mihiel and Argonne Woods and his marksmanship there had been deadly accurate.

He walked to the rack, picked up one, looked it over and tried the bolt. It worked smoothly, giving the satisfying click of finely machined metal. He aimed and dry-fired it a few times, getting a feel for the trigger. They located crates labeled 7.92 *mm*, the caliber of ammunition for the Mauser. Inside were gray cardboard boxes, printed with swastikas and eagles. He opened one, took out five bullets, loaded the gun then chambered and ejected a round to make absolutely certain the bullets were right.

"Good, let's get out of here," he said, putting two boxes of the shells into his pocket. "Can we—"

His words were interrupted as the front door opened, casting a beam of fierce sunlight on them. They turned, squinting. Before Paul could lift the rifle, the young man in the doorway, wearing a black SS uniform, was pointing a pistol toward them. "You! Put that down at once. Hands up!"

Paul crouched, set the Mauser on the floor and slowly rose.

Chapter Thirty-Three

Otto Webber said gruffly, "What are you doing? We are from the Krupp Munitions Works. We were sent to make certain that the correct ammunition—"

"Quiet."

The young guard looked around nervously to see if anyone else was here.

"There was a problem with a delivery. We got a call from—"

"It's Sunday. Why are you working on Sunday?"

Webber laughed. "My young friend, when we deliver the wrong shipment to the SS, we will correct our error no matter what the day or the hour. My supervisor—"

"Quiet!" The young soldier spotted a telephone on a dusty workstation and moved toward it, keeping the pistol pointed toward them. When he was nearly to the table Webber lowered his hands and started walking in his direction.

"Ach, this is absurd." He was exasperated. "I have identification."

"You will stop right there!" He thrust the gun forward.

"I will show you the paperwork from my supervisor." Webber kept walking.

The SS guard pulled the trigger. A short metallic bang shook the walls.

Unsure if Webber was hit or not, Paul scooped the Mauser up from the floor and rolled behind a high stack of rifle crates, chambering a round.

The young trooper lunged for the phone and pulled the receiver off the cradle, then ducked back. "Please, listen," he cried into the handset. Paul rose fast. He had no view of the soldier but he fired a bullet into the phone unit, which exploded into a dozen Bakelite shards. The trooper cried out.

Paul slipped back behind cover. But not before he caught a glimpse of Otto Webber lying on the floor, writhing slowly as he gripped his belly, which was stained with blood.

No . . .

"You Jew!" the young trooper raged. "You will throw down your gun at once. There will soon be a hundred men here."

Paul made his way to the front of the building, where he could cover both the front and back doors. He glanced quickly out the window and saw a lone motorcycle parked in front. He knew the young man was merely making a routine check of the warehouse and there would be no others coming. But someone might have heard the shot. And the SS man could simply stay where he was, keeping Paul pinned down, until his superior realized he hadn't reported back and sent more troops to the warehouse.

He looked out from his end of the stack of crates. He had no idea where the soldier was. He—

Another gunshot echoed. Glass splintered the front window, nowhere near Paul.

The SS guard had fired through the glass to draw attention; he'd shot directly into the street, not caring if he hit anyone.

"You Jew pig!" the man raged. "Stand up and raise your hands or you'll die screaming in Columbia House!" The voice came from a different place this time, closer to the front of the warehouse. He'd crawled forward to put more crates between himself and his enemy.

Another shot through the window. Outside a car horn blared.

Paul moved into the next row, swinging the gun before him, finger on the trigger. The Mauser was ungainly—good for distance, bad for this. He looked fast. The aisle was empty. He jumped as another shot shattered a window. Someone *must* have heard by now. Or seen a bullet strike a wall or house across the street. Maybe a car or passerby had been hit.

He started for the next aisle. Fast, swinging the gun before him.

A glimpse of the man's black uniform, disappearing. The SS man had heard Paul, or anticipated him, and slipped behind another stack of crates.

Paul decided he couldn't wait any longer. He'd have to stop the guard. There was nothing to do but charge over the center row of crates, just like he'd gone over the top of the trenches in an assault during the War, and hope he could get off a fatal shot before the man sprayed bullets at him from the semiautomatic pistol.

Okay, Paul said to himself. He took a deep breath.

Another . . .

Go!

He leapt to his feet and climbed onto the crate in front of him, lifting the gun. His foot just touched the second crate when he heard a sound behind him and to his right. The soldier had flanked him! But as he turned, the grimy windows shook again from a gunshot. Paul froze.

The SS soldier stepped directly in front of him, twenty feet away. Paul frantically raised the Mauser but just before he fired, the soldier coughed. Blood sprayed from his mouth, and the Luger dropped to the floor. He shook his head. He fell heavily and lay still, blood turning his uniform ruddy.

To his right, Paul could see Otto Webber on the floor. He clutched his bloody gut with one hand. In his other was a Mauser. He'd managed to crawl to a rack of guns, load one and fire. The rifle slid to the floor.

"Are you crazy?" Paul whispered angrily. "Why did you go toward him like that? Didn't you think he'd shoot?"

"No," the white-faced, sweating man said, laughing. "I *didn't* think he'd do that." The man sighed in pain. "Go see if anybody has responded to his subtle call for help."

Paul ran to the front and noted the area was still deserted. Across the street was a tall, windowless building, a factory or warehouse, closed today. It was likely that the bullets had struck the wall unnoticed.

"It's clear," he said, returning to Webber, who had sat up and was looking down at the mass of blood on his belly. "Ach."

"We have to find a doctor." Paul slung the rifle over his shoulder. He helped Webber to his feet and they made their way out the back doorway and into the boat. Pale and sweating, the German lay back with his head against the bow as Paul rowed frantically to the dock near the truck.

"Where can I take you? For a doctor?"

"Doctor?" Webber laughed. "It's too late for that, Mr. John Dillinger. Leave me. Go on. I can tell. It's too late."

"No, I'm taking you for help," Paul repeated firmly. "Tell me where to find somebody who won't go running to the SS or Gestapo." He pulled the boat to the dock, tied it up and climbed out. He set the Mauser in a patch of grass nearby and turned back to help Webber out of the boat.

"No!" Paul whispered.

Webber had untied the rope and with his remaining strength pushed off from the dock. The dinghy was now ten feet away, drifting into the current.

"Otto! No!"

"As I say, too late," Webber called, gasping. Then he gave a sour laugh. "Look at me, a Viking's funeral! Ach, when you return home play some John Philip Sousa and think of me. . . . Though I still say he's English. You Americans take credit for far too much. Now, go on, Mr. John Dillinger. Do what you have come here for."

The last glimpse Paul Schumann had of his friend were the man's eyes closing as he slumped to the bottom of the boat, which gathered speed, drawn into the murky water of the Spree.

A dozen of them, all young men, who had chosen life and freedom over honor. Was it cowardice or intelligence that had motivated them to do this?

Kurt Fischer wondered if he was the only one among them plagued by this question.

They were being driven through the countryside northwest of Berlin in the same sort of bus that used to take them on outings as young students. The round driver piloted his vehicle smoothly over the winding road and tried, unsuccessfully, to get them to sing hunting and hiking songs.

Kurt sat next to his brother, as they shared stories with the others. Little by little he learned something about them. Mostly Aryan, all from middle-class families, all with degrees, attending universities or planning to do so after their Labor Service. Half were, like Kurt and Hans, marginally anti-Party for political and intellectual reasons: Socialists, pacifists, protestors. The other half were "swing kids," richer, rebellious too but not as political; their main complaint with the National Socialists was cultural: the censoring of movies, dance and music.

There were no Jews, Slavs or Roma gypsies among this crowd, of course. Nor any Kosis, either. Despite Colonel Ernst's enlightenment, Kurt knew that it would be many years before such ethnic and political groups would find a home in the military or German officialdom. Kurt's personal belief was that it would never happen as long as the triumvirate of Hitler, Göring and Goebbels was in power.

So here they were, he was thinking, these young men, brought together by the predicament of having to choose between a concentration camp and possible death or an organization they found morally wrong.

Am I a coward, Kurt wondered again, choosing as I did? He remembered Goebbels's call for the nationwide boycott of Jewish stores in April of

'33. The National Socialists thought it would receive an overwhelming show of support. In fact, the event went badly for the Party, with many Germans—his parents among them—openly defying the boycott. Thousands, in fact, sought out stores they hadn't previously been to, just to show support for their Jewish fellow citizens.

That was courage. Did he not have this bravery within him?

"Kurt?"

He looked up. His brother had been speaking to him. "You're not listening."

"What did you say?"

"When will we eat supper? I'm hungry."

"I don't have any clue. How would I know?"

"Is army food any good? I heard you eat well. I suppose it depends, though. If you're in the field, it'll be different than at a base. I wonder what it's like."

"What, the food?"

"No. Being in the trenches. Being—"

"We won't be in the trenches. There won't be another war. And if there is, you heard Colonel Ernst, we won't have to fight. We'll be given different duties."

His brother didn't look convinced. And more troubling, he didn't look that upset that he might be seeing combat. Why, he even seemed intrigued by the thought. This was a very new, and disturbing, side to his brother.

I wonder what it's like. . . .

Conversation in the bus continued—about sports, about the scenery, about the Olympics, about American movies. And girls, of course.

Finally they arrived, turning off the highway and easing down a long maple-lined drive that led to the campus of Waltham Military College.

What their pacifist parents would think to see them in such a place!

The bus squealed to a halt in front of one of the school's red-brick buildings. Kurt was struck by the incongruity: an institution devoted to the philosophy and practice of warfare, yet set in an idyllic vale with a rich carpet of grass, fluttering ivy crawling up the ancient buildings, forests and hills behind, which formed a gentle frame for the scene.

The boys gathered their rucksacks and climbed off the bus. A young soldier not much older than they identified himself as their recruitment officer and shook their hands, welcoming them. He explained that Doctor-professor Keitel would be with them shortly. He held up a football that he and another soldier had been kicking around and he tapped it toward Hans, who expertly sent it on its way to another of the recruits.

And, as always happens when young men and a ball end up together on a grassy field, it was only a matter of minutes before two teams had formed and a game begun.

Chapter Thirty-Four

At 5:30 P.M. the Labor Service truck eased over a smooth, immaculate highway that wove through tall stands of pine and hemlock. The air was flecked with motes of dust, and lazy insects died on the flat windshield.

Paul Schumann struggled to think only of Reinhard Ernst, of his target. Groping for the ice.

Don't think about Otto Wilhelm Friedrich Georg Webber.

This was, however, impossible. Paul was consumed with memories of the man he'd known only a day. Presently he was thinking that Otto would have fit in perfectly on the West Side of New York. Drinking with Runyon and Jacobs and the boxing crew. Maybe he'd even enjoy sparring a little. But what Webber really would have loved were the opportunities in America: the freedom to run countless scams and grifts.

Someday I may boast to you of my better cons. . . .

But then his thoughts faded as he turned around a slow curve and diverted down a side road. A kilometer along the highway he saw a carefully painted sign, *Waltham Military College*. Three or four young men in hiking outfits lounged on the grass, surrounded by packs, baskets and the remnants of their Sunday afternoon dinner. A sign beside them pointed down the wide drive to the main hall. A second road led to the stadium and gymnasium and Academic Buildings 1 through 4. Farther along was the driveway to Buildings 5 through 8. It was in Building 5 that Ernst would have his meeting in a half hour, Paul had read on his schedule. He continued past the turnoff, though, drove another hundred yards along the road and pulled onto a deserted unpaved byway, overgrown with grass. He nosed the truck into the woods so that it couldn't be seen from the main road.

A deep breath. Paul rubbed his eyes and wiped the sweat from his face.

Would Ernst actually show up? he wondered. Or would he be like Dutch Schultz that time in Jersey City, when the mobster had skipped out on a meeting where he'd instinctively—some said psychically—known he was going to be ambushed?

But what else could Paul do? He had to believe the colonel would go ahead with the meeting. And his assessment was that the man would in fact show up here. Everything he'd learned about him suggested someone who didn't shirk his obligations. The American climbed out of the truck. He stripped off the bulky blue-gray uniform and hat, folded them neatly and rested them on the front seat, beneath which he'd also hidden another suit, in case he needed to change identity yet again to escape. Paul dressed quickly in the working clothes he'd stolen from the warehouse. Then, collecting the rifle and the ammunition, he plunged into the thickest part of the woods, moving as silently as he could.

He slowly made his way through the quiet, fragrant forest, cautious at first, expecting more guards or troops, especially after the attempt that afternoon on Ernst's life, but he was surprised to find none at all. As he moved closer to the buildings, easing through brush and trees, he saw some people and vehicles near the front of one of the structures, which a sign reported was No. 5, the one he sought. Parked up the drive about one hundred feet from it was a black Mercedes sedan. A man wearing an SS uniform stood beside the car, looking around vigilantly, a machine gun over his shoulder. Was this Ernst's car? He couldn't see through the glare of the windows.

Paul also noted a small panel van and a bus, near which a dozen young men in civilian clothing and a soldier in a gray uniform were playing soccer. A second soldier leaned against the bus, watching the game and cheering the teams on.

Why would someone as senior as Ernst meet with this small group of students? Maybe they were a handpicked group of future officers; the boys looked like model National Socialists—fair, blond and in very good shape. Whoever they were, Paul assumed that Ernst would meet with them in the classroom, which would require him to walk the fifty feet or so from the Mercedes to Building 5. Paul would have plenty of time to touch him off. From where he now crouched, though, he had no good shooting angle. The trees and brush waved in the hot wind and not only impaired the sight of his prey but could deflect the bullet.

The door to the Mercedes opened and a balding man in a brown jacket climbed out. Paul looked past him into the backseat. Yes! Ernst *was* inside. Then the door slammed and he lost sight of the colonel, who remained in the car. The man in brown carried a large folder to a second car, an Opel, near Paul, where the wooded hill bottomed out. He set the folder in the backseat and returned to the far side of the field.

Paul's attention was drawn to the Opel; it was unoccupied. The car would give him a good shooting position, provide some cover from the soldiers and offer Paul a head start back into the woods to the truck for his escape afterward.

Yes, he decided, the car would be his hunting blind. Cradling the Mauser in the crook of his arm, Paul moved slowly forward, hearing the soft buzz of insects, the snap and crunch of the dusty July vegetation beneath his body and the shouts and laughter of young men enjoying their soccer game.

The faithful set of Auto Union wheels clattered along the highway at a paltry sixty kilometers per hour, rattling madly despite the mirror-smooth surface of the road. A backfire erupted and the engine gulped for air. Willi Kohl adjusted the choke and stomped on the accelerator once again. The car shuddered but finally picked up a bit of speed.

After he'd left Kripo headquarters through the forbidden back door—defiantly and, yes, foolishly—the inspector had walked toward the Hotel Metropol. As he'd approached he gradually became aware of music; the notes penned by Mozart so many years ago were dancing from the strings of a chamber quartet in the magnificent lobby.

He'd looked through the windows at the glittering chandeliers, the murals of scenes from Wagner's *Ring*, the waiters in perfect black trousers and perfect white jackets balancing silver trays on their palms. And he'd continued *past* the hotel, not even pausing. The inspector had known all along, of course, that Paul Schumann was lying about coming here. His investigation had revealed that the American was a man who was comfortable not with champagne and limousines and Mozart, but with Pschorr ale and sausages. He was a man with worn shoes and a love of boxing rings. A man with some connection with the fringe neighborhood around November 1923 Square. If a man had no hesitation to take on four Stormtroopers with his fists, he would not be checking into an effete place like the Metropol, nor could he afford it either.

Yet this place had been the first location Schumann had thought of in response to Kohl's question about his new address—which suggested that the American might have seen it recently. And since Miss Richter's boardinghouse was far across town, it was logical that he had seen the hotel on his way to Berlin North, the tough neighborhood that began just a block past the hotel. This was an area that *was* akin to Paul Schumann's temperament and tastes.

It was a large district; under most circumstances a half dozen investigators would be needed to canvass the locals and gather information on a suspect. But some evidence Kohl had found might, he believed, help him narrow his search considerably: At the boardinghouse he'd discovered in Schumann's pockets a limp box of cheap matches, tucked into the packet of German cigarettes. Kohl was familiar with these. He often found them in the possession of other suspects, who'd picked them up in establishments in bad areas of the city, like Berlin North.

Perhaps the American had no connection here, but it was a good place to start his search. Armed with Paul Schumann's passport, Kohl had made the rounds in the southern end of the neighborhood, noting first what kind of matches they gave away and, if they were the same, then showing the American's picture to waiters and bartenders.

"No, Inspector . . . I am so sorry. Greet God, Inspector . . . I have seen no one like that. Hail Hitler. I'll keep on the lookout for him. . . . Hail Hitler hail Hitler hail Hitler . . ."

He tried a restaurant on Dragoner Street. Nothing. Then walked a few doors farther on, to a club on the same street. He'd flashed his ID card to the man at the entrance and walked into the bar. Yes, the matches were the same as Schumann had had. He'd walked through the various rooms, flashing the American's passport, asking if anyone had seen him. The civilians in the audience were typically blind, and the SS typically uncooperative. (One barked, "You're blocking my view, Kripo. Move your ass!")

But then he'd shown the picture to a waitress. Her eyes had flashed in anger.

"You know him?" Kohl had asked.

"Ach, do I know him? Yes, yes."

"You are?"

"Liesl. He claimed his name was Hermann but I see that was a lie." She nodded at the passport. "I'm not surprised. He was here not an hour ago. With his toad of a companion, Otto Webber."

"Who is this Webber?"

"A toad, as I say."

"What were they doing here?"

"What else? Drinking, talking. Ach, and flirting . . . A man flirts with a girl and then rejects her coldly. . . . How cruel that is." Liesl's Adam's apple had quivered and Kohl deduced the whole sad story. "Will you arrest him?"

"Please, what do you know about him? Where he is staying, what his business is?"

Liesl had not known much. But one bit of information was golden. Schumann and Webber apparently planned to meet with someone later that afternoon. And a clandestine gathering it was to be, the spurned waitress had offered darkly. "A toad's business. At someplace called Waltham College."

Kohl had hurried from the Aryan Café, collected the DKW and sped to Waltham. He now saw the military college in front of him and eased the car gently onto the gravel shoulder near two low brick columns topped with statues of imperial eagles. Several students lounging on the grass beside backpacks and a picnic basket glanced at the dusty, black car.

Kohl gestured the students over to the car and the blond young men, sensing authority, trotted quickly forward.

"Hail Hitler."

"Hail," Kohl replied. "School is still in session? In the summer?"

"There are courses being taught, sir. Today, though, we have no classes, so we've been hiking."

Like his own sons, these students were caught in the great fever of Third Empire education, only more so, of course, since the whole point of this college was to produce soldiers.

What brilliant criminals the Leader and his crowd are. They kidnap the nation by seizing our children. . . .

He opened Schumann's passport and displayed the picture. "Have you seen this man?"

"No, Inspector," one said and glanced at his friends, who shook their heads no.

"How long have you been here?"

"Perhaps an hour."

"Has anyone arrived in that time?"

"Yes, sir. Not long ago, a school bus arrived and with it an Opel and a Mercedes. A black one. Five-liter. New."

"No, it was the seven-point-seven," a friend corrected.

"You're blind! It was much smaller."

A third said, "And that Labor Service truck. Only it didn't drive in here."

"No, it went past and then turned off the road." The boy pointed. "Near the entrance of some other academic buildings."

"Labor Service?"

"Yes, sir."

"Was the truck full of workers?"

"We couldn't see in the back."

"Did you get a look at the driver?"

"No, sir."

"Nor I."

Labor Service . . . Kohl pondered this. RAD workers were used primarily for farming and public works. It would be very unusual for them to be assigned to a college, especially on Sunday. "Has the Service been doing some work here?"

The boy shrugged. "I don't believe so, sir."

"I've heard of nothing either, sir."

"Don't say anything of my questions," Kohl said. "To anyone."

"A matter of Party security?" one boy asked with an intrigued smile.

Kohl touched his finger to his lips.

And left them gossiping excitedly about what the mysterious policeman might mean.

Chapter Thirty-Five

Closing in on the gray Opel.

Crawling, pause.

Then crawling again. Just like at St. Mihiel and the dense, ancient forests of Argonne.

Paul Schumann smelled hot grass and the old manure used to fertilize the field. Smelled the oil and creosote of the weapon. Smelled his own sweat.

Another few feet. Then pause.

He had to move slowly; he was very exposed here. Anyone on the field around Building 5 might have glanced his way and noticed the grass swaying unnaturally or caught the glint of low light reflecting off the rifle barrel.

Pause.

He looked over the field again. The man in brown was taking a stack of documents from the panel truck. The glare on the windows continued to obscure any view of Ernst in the Mercedes. The SS guard continued his vigil of the area.

Looking back toward the classroom building, Paul watched the balding man call the young men together. They reluctantly ended the soccer game and walked into the classroom.

With their attention focused away from him, Paul continued more quickly now to the Opel, opened the back door and climbed into the baking vehicle, feeling his skin prickle from the heat. Looking out through the back left window, he noted that this was the perfect vantage point to shoot from. He had an excellent view of the area around Ernst's car—a clear killing field of forty to fifty feet to bring the man down. And it would take the bodyguard and soldiers some time to figure out where the shot had come from.

Paul Schumann was touching the ice firmly. He clicked the Mauser's safety catch off and squinted toward Ernst's car.

"Greetings, future soldiers. Welcome to Waltham Military College."

Kurt Fischer and the others replied to Doctor-professor Keitel with various greetings. Most said, "Hail Hitler."

It was interesting that Keitel himself did not use that salutation, Kurt noted.

The recruitment soldier who'd been playing football with them stood beside the doctor-professor, in the front of the classroom, holding a stack of large envelopes. The man winked at Kurt, who'd just missed blocking a goal the soldier had scored.

The volunteers sat at oak desks. On the walls around them were maps and flags that Kurt didn't recognize. His brother was looking around too and he leaned over and whispered, "Battle flags of Second Empire armies."

Kurt shushed him, frowning in irritation, both at the interruption and because his younger brother knew something he did not. And how, he now wondered, troubled, did his brother, the son of pacifists, even know what a battle flag was?

The dowdy professor continued. "I'm going to tell you what is planned for the next few days. You will listen carefully."

"Yes, sir" and its variations filled the room.

"First, you will fill out a personal information form and application for induction into the armed forces. Then you will answer a questionnaire about your personality and your aptitudes. The answers will be compiled and analyzed and will help us determine your talents and mental preferences for certain duties. Some of you, for instance, will be better suited for combat, some for radio work, some for office detail. So it is vital that you answer honestly."

Kurt glanced toward his brother, who did not, however, acknowledge him. Their agreement had been that they would answer any such questions in a way as to be guaranteed of being assigned office tasks or even manual labor—anything to keep from having to kill another human being. But Kurt was troubled that Hans might be thinking differently now. Was he being seduced by the idea of becoming a combat soldier?

"After you are through with the forms, Colonel Ernst will address you. Then you will be shown to your dormitory and be given supper. Tomorrow you will begin your training and spend the next month marching and improving your physical condition before your classroom instruction begins."

Keitel nodded at the soldier, who began passing out the packets. The recruitment officer paused at Kurt's desk. They agreed to try for another game before supper, if the light held. The soldier then followed Keitel outside to get pencils for the inductees.

As he absently smoothed his hand over his documents, Kurt found himself oddly content, despite the harrowing circumstances of this hard, hard day. Yes, certainly some of this was gratitude—to Colonel Ernst and Doctor-professor Keitel—for providing this miraculous salvation. But more than that he was beginning to feel that he'd been given the chance to do something important after all, an act that transcended his own plight. Had Kurt gone to Oranienburg his imprisonment or death would have been courageous perhaps, but meaningless. Now, though, he decided that the incongruous act of volunteering for the army might prove to be exactly the gesture of defiance he'd been searching for, a small but concrete way of helping save his country from the brown plague.

With a smile toward his brother, Kurt ran his hand over the test envelope, realizing that for the first time in months his heart was truly content.

Chapter Thirty-Six

Willi Kohl parked the DKW not far from the Labor Service truck, which was about fifty meters off the road, parked in such a way that the driver clearly intended that the vehicle not be seen.

As he walked quietly to the truck, his Panama hat low to keep the glaring sun out of his eyes, he removed his pistol and listened for footsteps, voices. But he heard nothing out of the ordinary: only birds, crickets, cicadas. He approached the truck slowly. He looked into the back and found the burlap bags, shovels and hoes he'd expected—the "weapons" of the Labor Service. But in the cab he located some items that interested him considerably more. On the seat was an RAD officer's uniform—carefully folded as if it would be used again soon and the wearer was concerned that wrinkles might make him appear suspicious. More important, though, was what he found wrapped in paper beneath the seat: a blue double-breasted suit and a white shirt, both in large sizes. The shirt was an Arrow, made in the United States. And the suit? Kohl felt his heart thud as he looked at the label inside the jacket. *Manny's Men's Wear, New York City.*

Paul Schumann's favorite store.

Kohl replaced the clothes and looked around for any sign of the American, the toad Webber or anyone else.

No one.

The footsteps in the dust outside the door of the truck suggested that Schumann had gone into the woods toward the campus. An old service drive, leading in that direction, was overgrown with grass but more or less smooth. But it was also exposed; the hedgerows and brush on either side would be a perfect place for Schumann to lie in wait. The only other route was through the hilly woods, strewn with rocks and branches. Ach . . . His poor feet cried out at the very sight of it. But he had no choice. Willi Kohl started forward through the painful obstacle course.

Please, Paul Schumann prayed. Please, step out of the car, Colonel Ernst, and into clear view. In a country that has outlawed God, where there were fewer prayers to hear, perhaps He'd grant this one.

But apparently this was not the moment for divine help. Ernst remained inside the Mercedes. Glare from the windshield and windows kept Paul from seeing exactly where he was in the backseat. If he fired through the glass and missed he'd never have another chance.

He scanned the field again, reflecting: No breeze. Good light—from the side, not in his eyes—illuminating the killing field. A perfect opportunity to shoot.

Paul wiped the sweat off his forehead and sat back in frustration. He felt something pressing uncomfortably into his thigh and he glanced down. It was the folder of papers that the balding man had placed in the car ten minutes before. He pushed it to the floor but, as he did, he glanced at the document on top. He lifted it and, alternating between glancing at Ernst's Mercedes and the letter, he read:

> Ludwig:
> You will find annexed hereto my draft letter to the Leader about our study. Note that I've included a reference to the testing being done today at Waltham. We can add the results tonight.
>   At this early stage of the study I believe it is best that we refer to those killed by our Subject soldiers as state criminals. Therefore you will see in the letter that the two Jewish families we killed at Gatow will be described as Jew subversives, the Polish laborers killed at Charlottenburg as foreign infiltrators, the Roma as sexual deviants, and the young Aryans at Waltham today will be political dissidents. At a later point we can, I feel, be more forthright about the innocence of those exterminated by our Subjects but at the moment I do not believe the climate is right for this.
>   Nor do I refer to the questionnaires you administer to the soldiers as "psychological testing." This too, I feel, would be unfavorably received.

Please review this and contact me about alterations. I intend to submit the letter as requested, on Monday, 27 July.

—Reinhard

Paul frowned. What was this all about? He flipped to the next sheet and continued reading.

HIGHEST CONFIDENTIALITY

Adolf Hitler,
   Leader, State Chancellor and President of the German
   Nation and Commander of the Armed Forces
Field Marshal Werner von Blomberg,
   State Minister of Defense

My Leader and my Minister:

You have asked for details of the Waltham Study being conducted by myself and Doctor-Professor Ludwig Keitel of Waltham Military College. I am pleased to describe the nature of the study and the results so far.

This study arises out of my instructions from you to make ready the German armed forces and to help them achieve most expeditiously the goals of our great nation, as you have set forth.

In my years of commanding our courageous troops during the War, I learned much about men's behavior during combat. While any good soldier will follow orders, it became clear to me that men respond in different ways to the matter of killing, and this difference, I believe, is based on their nature.

In brief, our study involves asking questions of soldiers before and after they execute condemned enemies of the state and then analyzing their responses. These executions involve a number of different situations: various methods of execution, categories of prisoners, relationship of the soldier to the prisoners, the family background and personal history of the soldier, etc. The examples to date are as follows:

On 18 July of this year, in the town of Gatow, a soldier (Subject A) questioned at length two groups convicted of Jewish subversive activities. He was then ordered to carry out the execution order by automatic weapon fire.

On 19 July, a soldier in Charlottenburg (Subject B) similarly executed a number of Polish infiltrators. Although Subject B was the proximate cause of their deaths, he had had no communication with them prior to their extermination, unlike the Gatow executions.

On 21 July a soldier (Subject C) executed a group of Roma Gypsies engaged in sexually deviant behavior in a special facility we have had constructed at Waltham College. Carbon monoxide gas from vehicle exhaust was the means of death. Like Subject B, this soldier never conversed with the victims, but, unlike him, he did not witness their actual deaths.

Paul Schumann gasped in shock. He looked again at the first letter. Why, these people killed were innocent, by Ernst's own admission. Jewish families, Polish workers . . . He read the passages again to make sure he'd seen correctly. He thought he must have mistranslated the words. But, no, there wasn't any doubt. He looked across the dusty field at the black Mercedes, which still sheltered Ernst. He glanced down at the letter to Hitler and continued.

On 26 July a soldier (Subject D) executed a dozen political dissidents at the Waltham facility. The variation in this case was that these particular convicts were of Aryan extraction, and Subject D spent an hour or more conversing and playing sports with them immediately before he executed them, getting to know some of them by name. He was further instructed to observe them die.

Oh, Christ . . . that's here, today!

Paul leaned forward, squinting over the field. The gray-uniformed German soldier who'd been playing soccer with the boys gave a stiff-arm salute to the balding man in brown then he hooked a thick hose from the tailpipe of the bus into a fixture on the outside wall of the classroom.

We are presently compiling the responses provided by all of these Subject soldiers. Several dozen other executions are planned, each one a variation intended to provide us with as much helpful data as possible. The results of the first four tests are attached hereto.

Please be assured we reject out of hand the tainted Jew-thinking of traitors like Dr. Freud but feel that solid National Socialist philosophy and science will allow us to match the personality types of soldiers with the means of death, the nature of the victims and the relationship between them to more efficiently achieve the goals you have set forth for our great nation.

We will be submitting the complete report to you within two months.

With all humble respect,

Col. Reinhard Ernst,
Plenipotentiary
for Domestic Stability

Paul looked up, across the field, to see the soldier glance into the classroom at the young men, close the door, then walk calmly to the bus and turn on the engine.

Chapter Thirty-Seven

When the door to the classroom closed, the students looked around them. It was Kurt Fischer who got out of his seat and walked to the window. He rapped on it.

"You've forgotten the pencils," he called.

"There are some in the back," someone called.

Kurt found three stubby pencils sitting on a chalkboard ledge. "But not enough for us all."

"How can we take a test without pencils?"

"Open a window!" somebody called. "My God, it's hot in here."

A tall blond boy, jailed because he'd written a poem ridiculing the Hitler Youth, walked to the windows. He struggled to undo the latch.

Kurt returned to his seat and tore open his envelope. He pulled out the sheets of paper to see what sort of personal information they wanted and if there would be any questions about their parents' pacifism. But he laughed in surprise.

"Look at this," he said. "The printing didn't come out on mine."

"No, mine too."

"It's all of them! They're blank!"

"This is absurd."

The blond boy at the window called, "They don't open." He looked around the stifling room at the others. "None of them. The windows. They don't open."

"I can do it," said a huge young man. But the locks defeated him too. "They're sealed shut. Why would that be? . . ." Then he squinted at the window. "It's not normal glass, either. It's thick."

It was then that Kurt smelled the sweet, strong aroma of petrol exhaust flooding into the room from a vent above the door.

"What's that? Something's wrong!"

"They're killing us!" a boy shrieked. "Look outside!"

"A hose. Look!"

"Break it! Break the glass!"

The large boy who'd tried to open the windows looked around. "A chair, table, anything!"

But the tables and benches were bolted to the floor. And although the room had seemed to be a regular classroom, there were no pointers, no globes, not even ink bottles in the wells they might try to shatter the glass with. Several students tried to shoulder down the door but it was thick oak and barred from the outside. The faint blue cloud of exhaust smoke streamed steadily into the room.

Kurt and two other boys tried to kick the windows out. But the glass was indeed thick—far too strong to break without heavy tools. There was a second door but that too was securely closed and locked.

"Stuff something in the vents."

Two boys stripped off their shirts and Kurt and another student boosted them up. But their murderers, Keitel and Ernst, had anticipated everything. The vents were thick screening, a half meter by a meter in size. There was no way to block the smooth surface.

The boys began to choke. Everyone scrabbled away from the vent, into the corners of the room, some crying, some praying.

Kurt Fischer looked outside. The "recruitment" officer, who'd scored a goal against him just minutes earlier, stood with his arms crossed, gazing at them calmly, the same way someone might watch bears frolic in their pen at the Zoological Garden on Budapest Street.

Paul Schumann saw before him the black Mercedes, still protecting his prey.

He saw the SS guard looking around vigilantly.

He saw the balding man walk up to the soldier who'd fitted the hose to the classroom building, speaking to him, then jotting on a sheet of paper.

He saw an empty field where a dozen young men had just played a soccer game in their last minutes on earth.

And above all of these discrete images he saw what linked them: the appalling specter of indifferent evil. Reinhard Ernst was not simply Hitler's architect of war, he was a murderer of the innocent. And his motive: the handy collection of information.

The whole goddamn world here was out of kilter.

Paul swung the Mauser to the right, toward the bald man and the soldier. The second gray-uniformed trooper leaned against the van, smoking a cigarette. The two soldiers were some distance apart but Paul could probably touch them both off. The balding man—maybe the professor mentioned in the letter to Hitler—was probably not armed and would most likely flee at the first shot. Paul could then sprint to the classroom, open the door and give covering fire so the boys could get away to safety.

Ernst and his guard would escape or hunker down behind the car until help arrived. But how could Paul let these young men die?

The sights of the Mauser centered on the soldier's chest. Paul began applying pressure to the trigger.

Then he sighed angrily and swung the muzzle of the rifle back to the Mercedes.

No, he had come here for one purpose. To kill Reinhard Ernst. The young people in the classroom were not his concern. They'd have to be sacrificed. Once he shot Ernst the other soldiers would take cover and return fire, forcing Paul to escape back into the woods, while the boys suffocated.

Trying not to imagine the horror in the room, what those young men would be going through, Paul Schumann touched the ice once more. He steadied his breathing.

And, just at that moment, his prayer was finally answered. The back door to Ernst's car opened.

Chapter Thirty-Eight

I used to swim for hours at a time, and hike for days, Willi Kohl thought angrily, as he leaned against a tree and caught his breath. It was unjust to be given both a hearty appetite and a flair for a sedentary job.

Ach, and there was the matter of his age too, of course.

Not to mention the feet.

Prussian police training was the best in the world but tracking a suspect through the woods like Göring on a bear hunt had not been part of the curriculum. Kohl could find no signs of Paul Schumann's route, nor anyone else's. His own progress had been slow. He would pause from time to time as he approached a particularly dense thicket and make sure no one was sighting at him with a weapon. Then he'd resume his cautious pursuit.

Finally, through the brush ahead of him, he noticed a mowed field around a classroom building. Parked nearby were a black Mercedes, a bus and a van. An Opel too, on the opposite side of the field. Several men stood about, two soldiers among them, with an SS trooper beside the Mercedes.

Was this some sort of furtive black market business deal Schumann was involved in with this Webber? If so, where were they?

Questions, nothing but questions.

Then Kohl noted something unusual. He eased closer, pushing aside brush. He squinted the sweat from his eyes and looked carefully. A hose ran from the tailpipe of the bus into the school. Why would that be? Perhaps they were killing vermin.

Then he soon forgot this curious detail. His attention turned to the Mercedes, whose back door was open. A man was climbing out. Kohl realized with a shock that it was a government minister: Reinhard Ernst, the man in charge of what was dubbed "domestic stability," though everyone knew that he was the military genius behind rearming the country.

What was *he* doing here? Could it—

"Oh, no," Willi Kohl whispered aloud. "Good God . . ."

He suddenly understood exactly what the security alerts were all about, what the relationship between Morgan and Taggert and Schumann were, and what the American's mission in this country was.

Gripping his pistol, the inspector began jogging through the woods toward the clearing, cursing the Gestapo and the SS and Peter Krauss for not telling him what they knew. Cursing too the twenty years and twenty-five kilos that life had added to his body since he'd become a policeman. As for his feet, so urgent was his desire to prevent Ernst's death that he forgot about the pain completely.

All lies!

Everything they'd said was a lie. To get us to come willingly to their death chamber! Kurt had taken what he thought was the cowardly choice, agreeing to join the service, and he was now about to die for that decision— while if he and Hans had gone to the concentration camp they might very well have survived.

Listless and dizzy, Kurt Fischer sat in the corner of Academic Building 5, beside his brother. No less frightened than anyone else, no less desperate, he was not, however, trying to rip the iron desks from the floor or batter the door with his shoulder like the others. He knew Ernst and Keitel had thought this out ahead of time and had constructed an impregnable, airtight building to be their coffin. The National Socialists were as efficient as they were demonic.

Rather, he was wielding a different tool. With the stub of pencil from the back of the room, he was jotting unsteady words onto a page of blank paper ripped from the back of a book. Ironically, considering that it was pacifism that had brought them to this terrible place, the volume's title was *Cavalry Tactics During the War Between France and Prussia, 1870–1871.*

Whimpers of fear, shouts of anger around him, sobs.

Kurt hardly heard them. "Don't be afraid," he told his brother.

"No," the terrified younger man said, his voice cracking. "I'm not."

Rather than the letter of reassurance that he'd planned on writing to their parents that night, which Ernst had promised they could send, he now wrote a very different note.

Albrecht and Lotte Fischer
Prince George Street, No. 14
Swiss Cottage,
London, England

If by some miracle this reaches you, please know that you are in our thoughts now, at these last minutes of our lives. The circumstances of our deaths are as pointless as those of the ten thousand who have died before us here. We pray that you continue your work, with us in your thoughts, so that perhaps this madness can end. Tell everyone who will listen that the evil here is worse than the worst they can imagine and it will not end until somebody has the courage to stop it.

Know that we love you.

—Your sons

Around him the screams abated as the young men dropped to their knees or bellies and began kissing the scuffed oak floor and baseboards to suck whatever air they might from beneath the floors. Some simply prayed peacefully.

Kurt Fischer looked over his writing once more. He actually gave a soft laugh. For he'd realized suddenly that *this* was the essential purpose he'd been hoping for: delivering the message to his parents and ultimately, he prayed, the world. This is how he would fight the Party. His weapon was his death.

And, now at the end, he felt a curious optimism that this note would be found and delivered and perhaps, through his parents or others, it would be the final root that cracked the wall of the jail imprisoning his country.

The pencil fell from his hand.

Using his last morsels of thought and strength, Kurt folded the paper and put it into his wallet, which had the most chance of being removed from his body by a local mortician or doctor, who, God willing, might find the words he'd written and have the courage to send them on.

Then he took his brother's hand and closed his eyes.

Still, Paul Schumann had no target.

Reinhard Ernst was pacing erratically beside the Mercedes as he spoke into the microphone attached by a wire to the dashboard in the front seat. The man's tall bodyguard also blocked Paul's view.

He kept the gun steady, finger on the trigger, waiting for the man to stop.

Touching the ice . . .

Controlling his breathing, ignoring the flies buzzing into his face, ignoring the heat. Silently screaming to Reinhard Ernst: Stop moving, for Christ's sake! Let me do this thing and get away, back to my country, back to my printing plant, my brother . . . the family that I've had, the family that I may yet have.

An image of Käthe Richter came quickly into his head and he saw her eyes, felt her tears, heard the echo of her voice.

I'd rather share my country with ten thousand killers than my bed with one. . . .

His finger caressed the trigger of the Mauser, and her face and words vanished in a spray of ice.

And just at that moment Ernst stopped pacing, clipped the microphone back onto the dashboard of the Mercedes and stepped away from the car. He stood with arms folded, chatting amiably to his bodyguard, who nodded slowly, as they gazed at the classroom.

Paul rested the sights on the colonel's chest.

Chapter Thirty-Nine

Approaching the clearing, Willi Kohl heard a loud gunshot.

It echoed off the buildings and the landscape and was swallowed in the tall grass and juniper around him. The inspector ducked instinctively. He saw, across the clearing, the tall form of Reinhard Ernst drop to the ground beside the Mercedes.

No . . . The man is dead! It's my fault! Through my oversight, my stupidity, a man has been killed, a man vital to the fatherland.

The minister's SS bodyguard, crouching, looked for the assailant.

What have I done? the inspector thought.

But then another shot rang out.

Easing to the protective trunk of a thick oak at the edge of the clearing, Kohl saw one of the regular army soldiers slump to the ground. Kohl looked just beyond him and saw another soldier lying on the grass, blood on his chest. Nearby a balding man in a brown jacket scrabbled to safety under the bus.

The inspector then looked back to the Mercedes. What was this? He'd been wrong. The minister was unhurt! Ernst had dived to the ground for cover when he'd heard the first shot but was now rising cautiously, a pistol in his hand. His guard had unslung a machine pistol and he too was looking for a target.

Schumann *hadn't* killed Ernst.

Then a third shot rang through the clearing. It hit Ernst's Mercedes, shattering a window. A fourth, too, hitting the car's tire and inner tube. Then Kohl saw motion on the grassy field. It was Schumann, yes! He was running from the Opel toward the school, firing occasionally toward the Mercedes with a long rifle, forcing Ernst and his guard to remain low. He reached the front door of the classroom as Ernst's SS man rose and fired several times. The bus, however, protected the American from the shots.

But he was not protected from Willi Kohl.

The inspector wiped his hand on his slacks and aimed his revolver at Schumann. It was a long-range shot but not impossible and at least he could pin the man down until other troops arrived.

But just as Kohl began to squeeze the trigger, Schumann ripped the front door of the building open. He stepped inside and emerged a moment later, dragging out a young man. Several others followed, staggering, holding their chests, coughing, some vomiting. Another one, then three more.

God in Heaven! Kohl was stunned. It was *they* who'd been gassed, not rats or mice.

Schumann motioned the men toward the woods and, before Kohl could recover from the shock of what he'd seen and aim once more, the American was firing toward the Mercedes again, giving the young men cover with the rifle as they made for the safety of the dense forest.

The Mauser kicked hard against his shoulder as Paul fired again. He aimed low, hoping to hit Ernst's or his guard's legs. But their car was in a shallow gully and he couldn't find a target beneath it. He glanced inside the classroom quickly; the last of the young men were leaving. They staggered out and ran for the woods.

"Run!" Paul cried. "Run!"

He fired twice more to keep Ernst and the guard down.

Flinging sweat from his forehead with his fingers, Paul tried to get closer to the Mercedes but both Ernst and his guard were armed and good shots, and the SS man had a submachine gun. They fired repeatedly and Paul could make no headway toward them. As Paul worked the bolt to chamber a round, the guard peppered the bus and the ground nearby. Ernst leapt into the front seat of the Mercedes and grabbed the microphone then took cover again on the far side of the car.

How long would it be until help arrived? Paul had driven through Waltham only two miles up the road; he was sure the good-sized town would be home to a garrison of police. And the school itself might have its own security force.

If he wanted to survive he'd have to flee now.

He fired twice more, using up the last of the Mauser ammunition. He tossed the rifle to the ground then bent down and pulled a pistol from the belt of one of the dead soldiers. It was a Luger, like Reginald Morgan's. He worked the toggle to put a bullet in the chamber.

He looked down and saw, crouching, halfway under the bus, the balding mustachioed man who'd led the students into the building.

"What's your name?" Paul asked in German.

"Please, sir." His voice shook. "Do not—"

"Your *name*?"

"Doctor-professor Keitel, sir." The man was crying. "Please . . ."

Paul recalled that this was the name on the letter about the Waltham Study. He lifted the pistol and shot him once in the center of the forehead.

Then he took a final look toward Ernst's car and could see no target. Paul ran across the field, firing several shots into the Mercedes to keep Ernst and the guard down, and soon he plunged into the woods as bullets from the SS man's weapon chopped through the lush green foliage around him, none even close to its mark.

Chapter Forty

Willi Kohl had turned away from the clearing and now, drenched in sweat and sick from the heat and exertion, was heading back in the direction of the Labor Service truck, Schumann's means of escape, he assumed. He would flatten the tires to prevent him from leaving.

A hundred meters, two hundred, gasping, wondering: Who were the young people? Were they criminals? Were they innocent?

He paused to try to catch his breath. If he didn't, he was sure Schumann would easily hear the wheezing rasp as he approached.

He scanned the forest. He saw nothing.

Where was the truck? He was disoriented. This direction? No, it was the other way.

But perhaps Schumann wasn't making for the truck. Maybe he *did* have another way out. The man was brilliant, after all. He might have hidden—

Without a sound, without any warning, a piece of hot metal touched the back of his head.

No! His first thought was: Heidi, my love . . . how will you manage alone with the children in this mad world of ours? Oh, no, no!

"Don't move." In barely accented German.

"I won't. . . . Is you, Schumann?" he asked in English.

"Give me the pistol."

Kohl let the weapon go. Schumann took it from him.

A huge hand gripped his shoulder and turned the inspector around.

What eyes, Kohl thought, chilled. He reverted to his native language. "You are going to kill me, yes?"

Schumann said nothing but patted the inspector's pockets for other weapons. He stood back and then examined the field and forest around them. Apparently satisfied that they were alone, the American reached into his shirt pocket and withdrew several pieces of paper, damp with sweat. He handed them to Kohl, who asked, "What is this?"

"Read it," Schumann said.

Kohl said, "Please, my spectacles." Glancing down at his breast pocket. Schumann lifted the glasses out. He handed them to the inspector.

Placing them on his nose, he unfolded and read the documents quickly, shocked by the words. He looked up, speechless, staring into Schumann's blue eyes. He looked down and read the top page again.

> Ludwig:
>
> You will find annexed hereto my draft letter to the Leader about our study. Note that I've included a reference to the testing being done today at Waltham. We can add the results tonight.
>
> At this early stage of the study I believe it is best that we refer to those killed by our Subject soldiers as state criminals. Therefore you will see in the letter that the two Jewish families we killed at Gatow will be described as Jew subversives, the Polish laborers killed at Charlottenburg as foreign infiltrators, the Roma as sexual deviants, and the young Aryans at Waltham today will be political dissidents. . . .

Oh, our dear God in Heaven, he thought. The Gatow case, the Charlottenburg case! Another too: Gypsies murdered. And those young men today! With more planned . . . They were killed simply as fodder for this barbarous study, one sanctioned at the highest levels of government.

"I . . ."

Schumann took the sheets back. "On your knees. Close your eyes."

Kohl looked once more at the American. Ach, yes, these *are* the eyes of a killer, he realized. How had he missed the look earlier at the boarding-house? Perhaps because there are so many killers among us now that we have grown immune. Willi Kohl had acted humanely, letting Schumann go while he continued to investigate, rather than send the man to sure death in an SS or Gestapo cell. He'd saved the life of a wolf that had now turned on him. Oh, he could tell Schumann that he knew nothing about this horror. Yet why should the man believe him? Besides, Kohl thought with shame, despite his ignorance about this particular monstrosity, the inspector was undeniably linked to the people who had perpetrated it.

"Now!" Schumann whispered fiercely.

Kohl knelt in the leaves, thinking of his wife. Recalling that when they were young, first married, they would picnic in the Grünewald Forest. Ah, the size of the basket she packed, the salt of the meat, the resinous aroma of the wine, the sour pickles. The feel of her hand in his.

The inspector closed his eyes and said a prayer, thinking that at least the National Socialists hadn't found a way to make your spiritual communications a crime. He was soon lost in a fervent narrative, which God had to share with Heidi and their children.

And then he realized that some moments had passed.

Eyes still closed, he listened carefully. He heard only the wind through the trees, the buzzing of insects, an airplane's tenor motor high above him.

Another endless minute or two. Finally he opened his eyes. He debated. Then Willi Kohl slowly looked behind him, expecting to hear the crack of a pistol shot at any moment.

No sign of Schumann. The large man had slipped silently from the clearing. Not far away he heard an internal combustion engine start. Then the mesh of gears.

He rose and, as fast as his solid frame and difficult feet could manage, trotted toward the sound. He came to the grass service road and followed it toward the highway. There was no sign of the Labor Service truck. Kohl veered in the direction of his DKW. But he stopped quickly. The hood was up and wires dangled. Schumann had disabled it. He turned and hurried back down the road toward the academic building.

He arrived at the same time that two SS staff cars skidded to a stop nearby. Uniformed troops leapt out and immediately surrounded the Mercedes in which Ernst sat. They drew their pistols and gazed out into the woods, looking for threats.

Kohl hurried across the clearing toward them. The SS officers frowned at Kohl's approach and turned their weapons on him.

"I'm Kripo!" he called breathlessly and waved his identification card.

The SS commander gestured him over. "Hail Hitler."

"Hail," Kohl gasped.

"A Kripo inspector from Berlin? What are you doing here? You heard the wireless report of the assault on Colonel Ernst?"

"No, I followed the suspect here, Captain. I didn't know his designs on the colonel, though. I wanted him in connection with a different matter."

"The colonel and his guard didn't get a look at the assailant," the SS man said to the inspector. "Do you know what he looks like?"

Kohl hesitated.

A single word burned into the inspector's mind. It seated itself like a lamprey and would not leave.

That word was *duty*.

Finally Kohl said, "Yes, yes, I do know, sir."

The SS commander said, "Good. I've ordered roadblocks throughout the area. I'll send them his description. He's Russian, is he not? That's what we heard."

"No, he's American," Kohl said. "And I can do better than merely describe him. I know what vehicle he's driving and I have his photograph."

"You have?" the commander asked, frowning. "How?"

"He surrendered this to me earlier today." Willi Kohl knew he had no choice. Still his heart cried in agony as he dug into his pocket and handed the passport to the commander.

Chapter Forty-One

I'm a fool, thought Paul Schumann.

He was in despair and there was no bottom to it.

Piloting the Labor Service truck west along rough back roads that led to Berlin, looking in the mirror for signs that he was being followed.

A fool . . .

Ernst had been in my sights! I could have killed him! And yet . . .

Yet those others, the young men, would have died horrible deaths in that goddamn classroom. He'd told himself to forget them. To touch the ice. To do what he'd come to this troubled country for.

But he hadn't been able to.

Paul now slammed his palm against the steering wheel, shaking with anger. Now, how many others would die because of his decision? Every time he read that the National Socialists had expanded their army, that they had developed new weapons, that their soldiers had engaged in training exercises, that more people had disappeared from their homes, that they had died bloody on the fourth square of concrete from the grass in the Garden of Beasts, he would feel responsible.

And killing the monstrous Keitel didn't take the horror out of his choice. Reinhard Ernst, a far worse man than anyone had ever imagined, was still alive.

He felt tears fill his eyes. Fool . . .

Bull Gordon had picked him because he was so goddamn good. Oh, sure, he touched the ice. But a better man, a stronger man would not simply have gripped the cold; he would have taken it into his soul and made the correct decision, whatever the cost to those young men. His face burning with shame, Paul Schumann drove on, heading back toward

Berlin, where he would hide out until the rescue plane arrived in the morning.

Then he rounded a bend and braked hard. An army truck blocked the way. Standing beside it were six SS troopers, two with machine guns. Paul hadn't thought they would set up roadblocks this quickly or on small roads like this. He took both the pistols—his and the inspector's—and put them nearby on the seat.

Paul gave a limp salute. "Hail Hitler."

"Hail Hitler, Officer," was the crisp reply from the SS commander, though he glanced with a hint of derision at the Labor Service uniform, which Paul had put back on.

"Please, what is the problem?" Paul asked.

The commander approached the truck. "We are looking for someone in connection with an incident at Waltham Military College."

"Is that why I've seen all the official cars on the road?" Paul asked, heart slamming in his chest.

The SS officer grunted, then he studied Paul's face. He was about to ask a question when a motorcycle pulled up and the driver killed the engine, leapt off and hurried to the commander. "Sir," he said, "a Kripo detective has learned the assassin's identity. Here's his description."

Paul's hand slowly curled around the Luger. He could kill these two. But there were still the others nearby.

Handing a sheet of paper to the commander, the motorcyclist continued. "He's an American. But he speaks German fluently."

The commander consulted the note. He glanced at Paul then back down at the paper. He announced, "The suspect is about five feet six inches high and quite thin. Black hair and a mustache. According to his passport, his name is Robert E. Gardner."

Paul stared at the commander, nodding, silent. Gardner? he wondered.

"Ach," the SS officer asked, "why are you looking at me? Have you seen such a man or not?"

"No, sir. I'm sorry. I haven't."

Gardner? . . . Who was he? . . . Wait, yes, Paul remembered: It was the name on one of Robert Taggert's fake passports.

Kohl had given *that* documentation to the SS, not Paul's own.

The commander looked down at the sheet of paper again. "The detective reported that the man was driving a green Audi sedan. Have you seen this vehicle in the area?"

"No, sir."

In the mirror Paul noticed two of the other officers looking in the back of the truck. They called, "Everything's fine here."

The commander continued. "If you see him or the Audi, you will contact the authorities immediately." He shouted to the driver of the truck barricading the road. "Let him pass."

"Hail Hitler," Paul said with an enthusiasm he believed he hadn't heard anyone else use since he'd arrived in Germany.

"Yes, yes, hail Hitler. Now move along!"

An SS staff Mercedes skidded to a stop outside Building 5 of Waltham Military College, where Willi Kohl was watching dozens of troops prowl through the forest in search of the young men who'd escaped from the classroom.

The door of the car opened and no less than Heinrich Himmler himself climbed out, wiped his schoolteacher glasses with a handkerchief and strode up to the SS commander, Kohl and Reinhard Ernst, who was out of the car now and surrounded by a dozen guards.

Kohl raised his arm and Himmler responded with a brief salute and then studied the man closely with his tight eyes. "You are Kripo?"

"Yes, Police Chief Himmler. Detective-inspector Kohl."

"Ah, yes. So you are Willi Herman Kohl."

The detective was taken aback that the overlord of German police would know his name. He recalled his SD file and felt all the more uneasy at the recognition. The mousy man turned away and asked Ernst, "You are unharmed?"

"Yes. But he killed several officers and my colleague, Doctor-professor Keitel."

"Where is the assassin?"

The SS commander said sourly, "He escaped."

"And who is he?"

"Inspector Kohl has learned his identity." With a temerity that Ernst's rank allowed—but Kohl would not dare use—the colonel said abruptly, "Look at the passport picture, Heinrich. He was the same man who was at the Olympic stadium. He was standing *one* meter from the Leader, from all the ministers. He was that close to us all."

"Gardner?" Himmler asked uneasily, gazing at the booklet the SS commandant held up. "He was using a fake name at the stadium. Or this one is fake." The small man looked up and frowned. "But why did he save your life at the stadium?"

"Obviously he *didn't* save my life," Ernst snapped. "I wasn't in danger then. He must have rigged the gun in the shed himself to make it appear that he was our ally. To get under our defenses, of course. Who knows whom else he was going to target after he'd killed me. Perhaps the Leader himself.

"The report you told us about said that he was Russian," he added sharply. "But this is an American passport."

Himmler fell silent for a moment, eyes sweeping the dry leaves at their feet. "The Americans would have no incentive to harm you, of course. I would guess that the Russians hired him." He looked at Kohl. "How do you happen to know of this assassin?"

"Purely a coincidence, State Police Chief. I followed him as a suspect in another case. Only after I arrived here to conduct surveillance did I realize that Colonel Ernst was present at the college and that the suspect had designs to kill him."

"But surely you knew of the earlier attempt on Colonel Ernst's life?" Himmler asked quickly.

"The incident that the colonel was just referring to, at the Olympic stadium? No, sir. I was not apprised of that."

"You weren't?"

"No, sir. Kripo was not informed. And I just met with Chief of Inspectors Horcher no more than two hours ago. He knew nothing of it either." Kohl shook his head. "I wish we had been informed, sir. I could have coordinated my case with the SS and Gestapo so that this incident might not have happened and those soldiers not died."

"You're saying that you did not know that our security forces were looking for a possible infiltrator as of yesterday?" Himmler asked with the leaden delivery of a bad cabaret actor.

"That's correct, my Police Chief." Kohl looked into the man's tiny eyes, framed by round black-rimmed glasses, and knew that it had been Himmler himself who'd given the order to keep the Kripo in the dark about the security alert. He was, after all, the Third Empire's Michelangelo in the art of hoarding credit, plundering glory and deflecting blame, better even than Göring. Kohl wondered if he himself was somehow at risk here. A potentially disastrous security breach had occurred; would it benefit Himmler to sacrifice someone for the oversight? Kohl's stock seemed high, but sometimes a scapegoat was necessary, especially when your intrigue has nearly gotten Hitler's rearmament expert killed. Kohl made a quick decision and added, "And curiously I heard nothing from our Gestapo liaison officer either. We just met yesterday afternoon. I wish he'd mentioned the specific details of the security matter."

"And who *is* your Gestapo liaison?"

"That would be Peter Krauss, sir."

"Ah." The state chief of police nodded, filing the information away, and lost interest in Willi Kohl.

"There were some political prisoners here too," Reinhard Ernst said evasively. "A dozen or so young men. They have escaped into the woods. I've sent troops to find them." His eyes strayed again to the deadly classroom. Kohl too looked at the building, which seemed so benign, a modest facility of higher learning, dating from Second Empire Prussia, and yet which he now understood represented the purest of evils. He noticed that Ernst had had the soldiers remove the hose from the exhaust and drive the bus away. The clipboard and some documents that had been scattered on the ground, probably part of the abhorrent Waltham Study, were likewise gone.

Kohl said to Himmler, "With your permission, sir, I would like to prepare a report as soon as possible and assist in finding the killer."

"Yes, do so immediately, Inspector."

"Hail."

"Hail," Himmler said.

Kohl turned and started toward some SS troopers beside a van to arrange for a ride back to Berlin. As he walked painfully toward them, he decided that he could finesse the incident in such a way as to reduce the risk to himself. True, the picture in the passport matched the face of a man killed in a boardinghouse in southwest Berlin *before* the attempt on Ernst's life. But only Janssen, Paul Schumann and Käthe Richter knew that. The latter two would not be volunteering any information to the Gestapo and, as for the inspector candidate, Kohl would dispatch Janssen to Potsdam immediately for several days on one of the homicides that awaited their attention there and take control of all the files on Taggert and the Dresden Alley murder. Tonight Kohl would produce the body of the assassin, who died while trying to escape. The coroner would not, of course, have performed the autopsy yet—if the corpse had even been picked up—and Kohl could make sure, through favors or bribery, that the time of death would be noted as occurring *after* the assassination attempt here at the school.

He doubted there would be any further inquiry; the whole matter was now a dangerous embarrassment—to Himmler for being slack in state security and to Ernst because of the incendiary Waltham Study. He could—

"Oh, Kohl, Inspector Kohl?" Heinrich Himmler called.

He turned. "Yes, sir?"

"How soon will your protégé be ready, do you think?"

The inspector thought for a moment and could make no sense of this. "Ah, yes, Police Chief Himmler. My protégé?"

"Konrad Janssen. How soon will he be transferring to the Gestapo?"

What did he mean? Kohl's mind was blank for a moment.

Himmler continued. "Why, you knew that we accepted him into the Gestapo before his graduation from the police college, didn't you? But we wanted him to apprentice to one of the best investigators in the Alex before he began working on Prince Albrecht Street."

Kohl felt the blow in his chest, hearing this news. But he recovered quickly. "Forgive me, State Police Chief," the inspector said, shaking his head and smiling. "Of course I was aware. The incident here has wholly occupied my mind. . . . Regarding Janssen, he'll be ready soon. He's proving extremely talented."

"We've had our eye on him for some time, Heydrich and I both. You can be proud of that boy. He's going to the top quickly, I have a feeling. Hail Hitler."

"Hail Hitler."

Devastated, Kohl walked away. Janssen? He'd planned all along to work for the secret political police? The inspector's hands trembled with pain at this betrayal. So, the boy had lied about everything—his desire to be a criminal detective, about joining the Party (to rise through the Gestapo and the Sipo he would have to be a member). And, with a chill running through him, he thought of the many indiscretions he'd shared with the inspector candidate.

Janssen, you could have me arrested, you know, and sent to Oranien-burg for a year for saying what I just did. . . .

Still, he reflected, the inspector candidate needed Kohl to get ahead and could not afford to denounce him. Perhaps the danger was not as great as it cold have been.

Kohl looked up from the ground at the coterie of SS troops standing around the van. One of them, a huge man in a black helmet, asked, "Yes? Can we help you?"

He explained about his DKW.

"The killer disabled it? Why did he bother? He could have *outrun* you on foot!" The soldiers laughed. "Yes, yes, we'll give you a ride, Inspector. We'll leave in a few minutes."

Kohl nodded and, still numb with shock from learning about Janssen, climbed into the van and sat by himself. He stared into the orange disk of the sun, slipping behind a hillside bristling with the silhouettes of flowers and grass. He slouched, head against the back of the seat. The SS troops got into the vehicle and they started off, out of the college, heading southeast, back to Berlin.

The soldiers talked about the attempted assassination and the Olympic Games and plans for a big National Socialist rally outside of Spandau this coming weekend.

It was at this moment that the inspector came to a decision. His choice seemed absurdly impulsive, as fast as the sudden vanishing of the sun below the horizon, brilliant color in the sky one moment then nothing but a blue-gray dimness an instant later. But perhaps, he reflected, his was no conscious choice at all but was inevitable and had been determined long, long before, by immutable laws, in the same way that day had to become dusk.

Willi Kohl and his family would leave Germany.

Konrad Janssen's betrayal and the Waltham Study—both stark emblems of what the government was and where it was going—were reason enough. Yet what truly decided the matter was the American, Paul Schumann.

Standing with the SS officers outside Building 5, aware that he had both Schumann's real passport and Taggert's fake ones in his pocket, Kohl had agonized over doing his duty. And in the end he had done so. But the sorrow was that his obligation had dictated he act *against* his country.

As for how he would leave, he knew that too. He would remain ignorant of Janssen's choice (but would, of course, cease his improvident asides to the young man), he would mouth whatever lines Chief of Inspectors Horcher wished him to, he would stay well clear of the basement of Kripo headquarters with its busy DeHoMag card-sorting machines, he would handle murders like the one in Gatow exactly the way they wished him to—which was, of course, to handle them not at all. He would be the model National Socialist policeman.

And then in February he would take his entire family with him to the International Criminal Police Commission conference in London. And from there they would sail for New York, to which two cousins had emigrated some years ago and had made lives for themselves.

Being a senior official traveling on Kripo business he could easily arrange for exit documents and permission to take a good amount of money out of the country. There would be some tricky maneuvering, of course, in making the arrangements, but who in Germany nowadays did not have some skill at intrigue?

Heidi would welcome the change, of course, finding a haven for her children. Günter would be saved from his Nazi Youth classmates. Hilde could attend school once again and perhaps become the professor she wished to be.

His older daughter had a complication, of course: her fiancé, Heinrich Sachs. But Kohl decided he would convince the man to come with them. Sachs was vehemently anti–National Socialist, had no close relatives and was so completely in love with Charlotte that he would follow her anywhere. The young Sachs was a talented civil servant, spoke English well and, despite some bouts of arthritis, he was a tireless worker; Kohl suspected that he would have a far easier time finding a job in America than would Kohl himself.

As for the inspector—starting over in middle age! What an overwhelming challenge! He thought ironically of the Leader's nonsensical opus, *My Struggle*. Well, what a struggle he himself would have—a tired man with a family, beginning again at an age when he should be delegating cases to young inspectors and taking half-days off to escort his children to the wavemaking pool at Luna Park. Yet, it was not the thought of the effort and uncertainty awaiting him that made him choke quietly and that drew tears from his eyes, which he averted from the young SS troopers.

No, the tears were for what he was now looking at as they swept around a turn en route to Berlin: the plains of Prussia. And, though they were dusty and wan on this dry summer evening, they still exuded a grandeur and palpable significance, for they were the plains of *his* Germany, a great nation at heart, whose truths and ideals had somehow tragically been stolen by thieves.

Kohl reached into his pocket and pulled out his meerschaum pipe. He filled the bowl then searched his jacket but could find no match. He heard a rasp as the SS trooper sitting next to him struck one and held it out for him. "Thank you," Kohl said and sucked on the stem to ignite the tobacco. He sat back, filling the air around him with the scent of pungent cherries, and stared out the front windshield as the lights of Berlin came into view.

Chapter Forty-Two

The car wove like a dancer along the road to his home in Charlottenburg. Reinhard Ernst sat in the back, bracing himself against the turns, his head resting on the luxurious leather. He had a new driver and guard; Claus, the SS lieutenant with him at Waltham College, had been injured by glass flying from a window of the Mercedes and had been taken to a surgeon. Another SS car, filled with black-helmeted guards, was behind them.

He removed his glasses and rubbed his eyes. Ach, Keitel dead, along with the soldier taking part in the study. "Subject D" was how Ernst thought of him; he'd never even known the man's name. . . . What a disaster this day had been.

Yet the one thing that stood out most prominently in Ernst's thoughts was the choice that the killer had made outside Building 5. If he'd wanted to kill me, the colonel reflected, which was clearly his mission, he could have, easily. Yet he had decided not to; he'd rescued the young men instead. Reflecting on this act, the horror of what Ernst had been doing became clear. Yes, he realized, the Waltham Study *was* abominable. He had looked those young men in the face and told them: Serve in the army for a year and your sins will be absolved—all the while knowing that this was a lie; he'd spun the fiction solely to keep the victims relaxed and unsuspecting, so that the soldier could get to know them before he killed them.

Yes, he'd lied to the Fischer brothers, just as he'd lied to the Polish workers when he'd said they would receive double pay to transplant some trees near Charlottenburg for the Olympics. And he'd lied to the Jewish families in Gatow, telling them to assemble by the riverside, because there were some renegade Stormtroopers nearby and Ernst and his men would protect them.

Ernst didn't dislike Jews. He'd fought beside some in the War and found them as smart and courageous as everyone else. Indeed, based on the Jews he'd known then and since, he couldn't find any difference between them and Aryans. As for Poles, well, his reading of history told him they too were not so very different from their Prussian neighbors and indeed had a nobility that few National Socialists possessed.

Repugnant, what he was doing with the study. Horrifying. He felt a twist of razor-sharp shame within him, like the searing pain in his arm when the hot shrapnel had ripped into his shoulder in the War.

The road now straightened and they approached the neighborhood where he lived. Ernst leaned forward and gave the driver directions to his home.

Abominable, yes . . .

And yet . . . as he looked around him at the familiar buildings and cafés and parks of this portion of Charlottenburg, the horror began to dull, just as happened on the battlefield after the last Mauser or Enfield was fired, the cannon salvos ceased, the cries of the wounded abated. He recalled tonight watching the "recruitment officer," Subject D, who had willingly, cavalierly, hooked up the deadly hose to the school, even though he'd been playing soccer with the victims shortly before. Another soldier might have balked altogether. Had he not died, his answers to the doctor-professor's questionnaire would have been extremely helpful in establishing the criteria they would use to match soldiers and duties.

The weakness he'd felt a moment ago, the contrition prompted by the assassin's choice to forsake his own duty, vanished suddenly. He was once again convinced he was doing the right thing. Let Hitler have his fling with madness. Some innocents would die, yes, until the storm blew over, but eventually the Leader would be gone, while the army Ernst was creating would outlast him and be the backbone of a new German glory—and ultimately a new European peace.

Sacrifices had to be made.

Tomorrow Ernst would begin searching for another psychologist or doctor-professor who might help him continue the work. And this time he would find one who was more attuned to the spirit of National Socialism than Keitel—and one without Jewish grandparents, for God's sake. Ernst must be more clever. This was a time in history when one *had* to be clever.

The car pulled up in front of his house. Ernst thanked the driver and stepped out. The SS troops in the car behind his leapt out as well and joined the others already guarding his residence. The commander told him that the men would remain until the assassin was caught or it could be verified that he'd been killed or fled the country. Ernst politely thanked him as well and walked inside. He greeted Gertrud with a kiss. She glanced at the grass and mud stains on his pants.

"Ach, you are hopeless, Reinie!"

Without explaining, he smiled wanly. She returned to the kitchen, where she was cooking something fragrant with vinegar and garlic. Ernst climbed the stairs to wash and change his clothes. He saw his grandson in his room, drawing on a tablet of paper.

"Opa!" the boy cried and ran to him.

"Hello, Mark. Are we going to work on our boat tonight?"

He didn't respond and Ernst realized the little boy was frowning.

"What is the matter?"

"Opa, you called me Mark. That was Papa's name."

Had he? "I'm sorry, Rudy. I was not thinking clearly. I'm very tired today. I believe I need a nap."

"Yes, I take naps too," the boy said eagerly, happy to please his grandfather with his knowledge. "In the afternoon sometimes I get tired. Mutti gives me hot milk, cocoa sometimes, and then I have a nap."

"Exactly. That's how your foolish grandfather feels. It's been a long day and he needs a nap. Now you get the wood and knives ready. After supper we will work on our boat."

"Yes, Opa, I'll do it now."

Close to 3 P.M. Bull Gordon walked up the steps to The Room in Manhattan. The city was busy and vibrant in other neighborhoods, even on Sunday, but here the cross street was still.

The blinds were closed and the town house appeared deserted but as Gordon, wearing civvies today, approached, the front door opened before he even took the key from his pocket. "Afternoon, sir," the uniformed naval officer said in a soft voice.

Gordon nodded.

"The Senator's in the parlor, sir."

"Alone?"

"That's right."

Gordon walked inside, hung his topcoat on a rack in the hallway. He felt the weapon in his pocket. He wouldn't need it, probably, but he was glad it was there. He drew a deep breath and walked into the small room.

The Senator was sitting in an armchair beside a Tiffany floor lamp. He was listening to the Philco radio. When he saw Gordon he shut it off and asked, "Tiring flight?"

"They're always tiring. Seems that way."

Gordon walked to the bar and poured himself a scotch. Maybe not a good idea, what with the gun. But to hell with it. He added another finger to the glass. He offered a querying glance to the Senator.

"Sure. Only double that." He nodded at Gordon's glass.

The commander poured smoky liquid into another glass and handed it to the older man. He sat down heavily. His head still throbbed from the flight in the R2D-1, the naval version of the DC-2. It was just as fast but lacked the comfortable wicker chairs and soundproofing of the Douglas Commercial line.

The Senator was wearing a suit, waistcoat and stiff-collared shirt with a silk tie. Gordon wondered if it had been what he'd worn to church that morning. He'd once told the commander that whatever a politician personally believed, even if he was an atheist, he had to go to church. Image. It counts.

The Senator said gruffly, "So. You may as well tell me what you know. Get it over with."

The commander took a deep sip of whisky and did just what the old man asked.

Berlin sat under a veil of night.

The city was a huge expanse, flat except for the few cloud-catchers of the skyline and the Tempelhof airport beacon to the south. This view vanished as the driver piloted his vehicle over the crest of the hill and plunged into the ordered northwestern neighborhoods of the city, among cars apparently returning from their weekends at nearby Prussian lakes and mountains.

All of which made driving particularly difficult. And Paul Schumann wanted to make certain he was not stopped by the traffic police. No identification, a stolen truck . . . No, it was vital to be inconspicuous.

He turned down a street that led to a bridge across the Spree and worked his way south. Finally he found what he sought, an open lot in which dozens of delivery vehicles and vans were parked. He'd noticed this as he'd walked from Lützow Plaza to Käthe Richter's boardinghouse along the canal when he'd first arrived in the city.

Could that only have been yesterday?

He thought again about her. And about Otto Webber too.

As hard as it was to picture them, though, those images were better than dwelling on his pitiful decision at Waltham.

On the best day, on the worst day, the sun finally sets. . . .

But it would be a long, long time before the sun set on his failure today. Maybe it never would.

He parked between two large vans, killed the engine. He sat back, wondering if it was crazy to return here. But he concluded that it was probably a wise move. He wouldn't have to stay long. Smooth-faced Avery and bucking-for-a-fight Manielli would make sure the pilot took off promptly for the rendezvous at the aerodrome. Besides, he sensed instinctively he was safer here than anywhere outside the city. Beasts as arrogant as the National Socialists would never suspect that their prey was hiding squarely in the middle of their garden.

The door opened and the orderly let another man into The Room, where Bull Gordon and the Senator sat.

In his trademark white suit, looking every inch a plantation owner from a hundred years ago, Cyrus Clayborn walked inside and nodded to the two men with a casual smile on his ruddy face. Then he squinted and nodded once more. He glanced at the liquor cabinet but didn't make a move toward it; he was an abstainer, Bull Gordon knew.

"They have any coffee here?" Clayborn asked.

"No."

"Ah." Clayborn set his walking stick against the wall near the door and said, "You only ask me here when you need money, and I suspect you're not after alms today." He sat heavily. "It's the other thing, huh?"

"It's the other thing," Gordon echoed. "Where's your man?"

"My bodyguard?" Clayborn cocked his head.

"Right."

"Outside in the car."

Relieved that he wouldn't need his pistol after all—Clayborn's minder was notoriously dangerous—Gordon called one of the three navy men in an office near the front door and told him to make sure the fellow stayed inside the limo, not to let him into the town house. "Use any force you need to."

"Yes, sir. With pleasure, sir."

Gordon hung up and saw the financier chuckling. "Don't tell me you were thinkin' it'd come to six-guns, Commander." When the officer said nothing Clayborn asked, "So. How'd you tip to it?"

"Fellow named Albert Heinsler," Gordon replied.

"Who?"

"You oughta know," grumbled the Senator. "He was on the *Manhattan* because of you."

Gordon continued. "The Nazis're smart, sure, but we thought—why would they have a spy on the ship? That seemed bum to me. We knew Heinsler was with the Jersey division of the German-American Bund, so we had Hoover put some pressure on them."

"Doesn't that faggot have anything better to do with his time?" Clayborn grumbled.

"We found out you're a big contributor to the bund."

"Man's gotta put his money to work somehow," he said glibly, making Gordon detest him all the more. The magnate nodded. "Heinsler was his name, huh? Never knew it. He was just on board to keep an eye on Schumann and get a message to Berlin about a Russian being in town. Needed to keep the Huns on alert. Make our little play more credible, you know. All part of the act."

"How did you know Taggert?"

"Served with me in the War. Promised him some diplomatic postings if he helped me out here."

The Senator shook his head. "We couldn't figure out how you got the pass codes." He laughed and nodded toward Gordon. "At first the commander here thought I was the one sold Schumann out. That's okay, though. Didn't ruffle my feathers. But then Bull remembered your companies—you control every telephone and telegraph line on the East Coast. You had somebody listen in when I called the commander and we decided on the codes."

"That's baloney. I—"

Gordon said, "One of my men checked your company's files, Cyrus. You had transcripts of the conversations between the Senator and me. You found out everything."

Clayborn shrugged, more amused than troubled. Which really rubbed

Gordon the wrong way. The commander snapped, "We've got it all, Clayborn." He explained how the original idea to kill Reinhard Ernst had come from the magnate, who suggested it to the Senator. Patriotic duty, he'd said. He'd help fund the assassination. Hell, he'd fund the *whole* thing. The Senator had gone to certain people high in the administration and they'd approved the operation on the sly. But Clayborn had secretly called Robert Taggert and ordered him to kill Morgan, meet Schumann and help him plot to kill Ernst, then save the German colonel at the last minute. When Gordon had gone to him to ask for the extra thousand bucks, Clayborn had kept up the pretense that it was Morgan, not Taggert, whom Gordon was talking to.

"Why's it so important to you to keep Hitler happy?" Gordon asked.

Clayborn scoffed. "You're a fool if you're ignoring the Jew threat. They're plotting all over the world. Not to mention the Communists. And, for God's sake, the coloreds? We can't let our guard down for a minute."

Disgusted, Gordon snapped, "So that's what this's all about? Jews and Negroes?"

Before the old man could answer, though, the Senator said, "Oh, I'll betcha there's something else, Bull. . . . Money, right, Cyrus?"

"Bingo!" the white-haired man whispered. "The Germans owe us billions—all the loans we floated to keep them going over the past fifteen years. We have to keep Hitler and Schacht and the rest of the money boys over there happy so our notes keep getting paid."

"They're rearming to start another war," Gordon growled.

Clayborn said matter-of-factly, "All the better to be on their side then, don't you think? Bigger market for our arms." He pointed a finger at the Senator. "Provided you fools in Congress get rid of the Neutrality Act . . ." Then he frowned. "So what do the Huns think about the Ernst situation?"

"Oh, well, it's a goddamn mess," the Senator raged. "Taggert tells them about an assassination but the killer escapes and tries again. Then Taggert disappears. Publicly they're talking about the Russians hiring an American assassin. But in private they're wondering if we weren't behind the whole thing."

Clayborn grimaced in disgust. "And Taggert?" Then he nodded. "Dead. Sure. And Schumann did it. Well, that's the way it goes. . . . So, gentlemen, I suppose this is the end of our fine working relationship."

"Reggie Morgan's dead because of you. . . . You're guilty of some pretty bad crimes here, Cyrus."

The man brushed a white eyebrow. "How 'bout you funding this little outing with private money? Oh, that'd make a nice topic for a congressional hearing, don'tcha think? We have ourselves a standoff here, looks like. So I'm thinking it's best we *both* go our separate ways and keep mum. Good night now. Oh, and keep buying stock in my company if you civil servants can afford any. It's only going to go up." Clayborn stood slowly. He picked up his cane and headed for the door.

Gordon decided that, whatever the consequences, whatever happened to his own career, he'd make sure Clayborn get didn't away with this, not after the man had murdered Reginald Morgan and nearly killed Schumann. But larger justice would have to wait. There was only one matter that needed attention at the moment. "I want Schumann's money," the commander said.

"What money?"

"The ten thousand you promised him."

"Oh. He didn't produce. The Huns suspect us and my man's dead. Schumann's outa luck. No dough."

"You're not going to chisel him."

"Sorry," the businessman said, not looking the least contrite.

"Well, in that case, Cyrus," the Senator called, "good luck."

"We'll keep our fingers crossed for you," Gordon added.

The businessman stopped, looked back.

"I'm just thinking what might happen if Schumann finds out you not only tried to kill him but you stiffed him too."

"Knowing his line of work and all," Gordon chimed in again.

"You wouldn't dare."

"He'll be back here in a week, ten days."

The industrialist sighed. "All right, all right." He reached into his pocket and pulled out a booklet of bank drafts. He tore one out and started to write.

Gordon shook his head. "Nope. You're going to go dig up some good, old-fashioned scratch right now. Now. Not next week."

"Sunday night? Ten thousand?"

"Now," the Senator echoed. "If Paul Schumann wants greenbacks, greenbacks're what we're going to give him."

Chapter Forty-Three

They were sick of waiting.

During their weekend in Amsterdam, Lieutenants Andrew Avery and Vincent Manielli had seen tulips in every color imaginable and looked at plenty of fine paintings and flirted with page-boyed blondes who had round, rosy faces (Manielli, at least; Avery being contentedly married). They'd enjoyed the company of a dashing Royal Air Force flier named Len Aarons, who was in the country on his own intrigues (about which he was as evasive as the Americans). They'd drunk quarts of Amstel beer and cloying Genever gin.

But life on a foreign army base wears thin fast. And, in truth, they were also tired of hanging from tenterhooks, worrying about Paul Schumann.

Now, though, the waiting was over. At 10 A.M. Monday morning the twin-engine plane, streamlined as a gull, flared for a moment and then touched down on the grass field at Machteldt Aerodrome outside of Amsterdam. It settled onto its tail wheel and slowed, then taxied toward the hangar, weaving in a zigzag since the pilot couldn't see over the raised nose when the plane was on the ground.

Avery waved as the sleek, silver plane eased toward them.

"I think I'll go a few rounds with him," Manielli shouted over the sound of the engines and prop wash.

"Who?" Avery asked.

"Schumann. Do some sparring. I watched him; he's not as good as he thinks he is."

The lieutenant looked his colleague over and laughed.

"What?"

"He'd eat you like a box of Cracker Jack and spit out the prize."

"I'm younger, I'm faster."

"You're stupider."

The plane eased up to a parking strip and the pilot cut the engines. The props coughed to a stop and the ground crew ran out to chock the wheels under the big Pratt & Whitneys.

The lieutenants walked up to the door. They'd tried to think of something to get Schumann, a present, but couldn't figure out what. Manielli had said, "We'll tell him we gave him his first airplane ride. That'll be his present."

But Avery had said, "No. You can't tell somebody that something you've already done for them is a present."

Manielli figured the lieutenant would know this; married men knew all about the protocols of giving presents. So they bought him a carton of Packs o' Pleasure—Chesterfields—which had taken them some effort, and expense, to find in Holland. Manielli now held it under his arm.

One of the ground crew walked to the door of the plane and pulled it down. It became stairs. The lieutenants stepped forward, grinning, but stopped fast as a man in his early twenties, wearing filthy clothing, stepped into the doorway, hunched over because of the low clearance.

He blinked, held his hand up to shelter his eyes from the sun, then climbed down the stairs. *"Guten Morgen. . . . Bitte, Ich bin Georg Mattenberg."* He threw his arms around Avery and hugged him heartily. Then he walked past him, rubbing his eyes as if he'd just awakened.

"Who the hell's he?" Manielli whispered.

Avery shrugged and then stared at the door as other men emerged. There were five altogether. All in their twenties or late teens, in good shape, but exhausted and bleary-eyed, unshaven, their clothes tattered and stained with sweat.

"It's the wrong plane," Manielli whispered. "Jesus, where—"

"It's the right plane," his fellow officer said but he was no less confused.

"Lieutenant Avery?" an accented voice called from the doorway. A man a few years older than the others climbed out. Another, younger, joined him.

"That's me. Who are you?"

"I speak English better as the others. I will answer. I am Kurt Fischer and this is my brother, Hans." He laughed at the lieutenants' expression and said, "You are not expecting us, yes, yes. But Paul Schumann saved us."

He told a story about how Schumann had rescued a dozen young men from being gassed to death by the Nazis. The American had managed to round up some of them as they fled into a forest and offered them the chance to escape from the country. Some wanted to stay and take their chances but seven had agreed to leave, including the Fischer brothers. Schumann had loaded them into the back of a Labor Service truck, where they'd grabbed shovels and burlap bags and masqueraded as workers. He'd driven them through a roadblock to safety in Berlin, where they hid out for the night.

"At dawn he droved us out to a old aerodrome outside of the city, where we got on this airplane. And here we are."

Avery was about to pepper the man with more questions, but at that moment a woman appeared in the doorway of the airplane. She was around forty, quite thin, as tired as the others. Her brown eyes quickly snapped up everything around her. She climbed down the stairs. In one hand was a small suitcase, in the other a book whose cover had been torn off.

"Ma'am," Avery said, casting another perplexed gaze at his colleague.

"You are Lieutenant Avery? Or perhaps you are Lieutenant Manielli." Her English was perfect, with only a slight accent.

"I . . . well, yes, I'm Avery."

The woman said, "My name is Käthe Richter. This is for you."

She handed him a letter. He opened it and nudged Manielli. They both read:

> Gordon, Avery and Manelli (or however the hell you spell it):
>
> Get these people into England or America or wherever they want to go. Find homes for them, get them set up. I don't care how you do it but make sure it happens.
>
> And if you're thinking about sending them back to Germany, just remember that Damon Runyon or one of my buddies at the Sun or the Post would be pretty interested in what you sent me to Berlin for. Now that'd be one hell of a news story. Esp. in an election year.
>
> It's been swell, boys,
>
> Paul
>
> P.S.: There's a Negro living in the back room of my gym, Sorry Williams. Have the place signed over to him, however that works. And give him some dough too. Be generous.

"There is this as well," she said and gave Avery several tattered pages typed in German. "It's about something called the Waltham Study. Paul said the commander should see it."

Avery took the document and put it in his pocket. "I'll make sure he gets it."

Manielli walked to the airplane. Avery joined him and they looked into the empty cabin. "He didn't trust us. He thought we were going to hand him over to Dewey after all and had the pilot land somewhere else before they got here."

"France, you think?" Manielli suggested. "Maybe he got to know it during the War. . . . No, I know. I'll bet it was Switzerland."

Stung that Schumann had thought they'd renege on their deal, Avery called toward the cockpit, "Hey, where did you drop him off?"

"What?"

"Where did you land? To drop Schumann off?"

The pilot frowned as he glanced at the copilot. Then he looked back at Avery. His voice echoed through the tinny fuselage: "You mean he didn't tell you?"

EPILOGUE

A cold night in the Black Forest.

Two men trudged through the shallow snow. They were chilled certainly, but they were men who seemed to have a destination in mind and an important task to perform once they arrived.

Purpose, like desire, invariably numbs the body to discomfort.

As does the powerful Austrian liquor, obstler, which they'd been drinking liberally from a shared flask.

"How is your belly?" Paul Schumann asked his companion in German, noticing a particularly pronounced wince on the man's mustachioed face.

The man gave a grunt. "It hurts, of course. It will *always* hurt, Mr. John Dillinger."

After his return to Berlin, Paul had made a few subtle inquiries at the Aryan Café to learn where Otto Webber had lived; he'd wanted to do what he could to help any of the man's "girls." He'd gone to see one—Berthe—and learned to his shock and joy that Webber was still alive.

The bullet that had punctured the man's gut in the warehouse by the Spree had caused serious but not lethal damage during its brief transit through his substantial flesh. He had floated halfway down the river in his Viking funeral boat before some fishermen pulled him out and decided he wasn't as dead as he looked. They got him into a bed and stanched the bleeding. Soon he was in the care of an old gang-ring doctor, who, for a

395

price, of course, stitched him up, no questions asked. The later infection was worse than the wound. ("Lugers," Webber had griped. "They fire the filthiest of bullets. The toggle allows in germs.") But Berthe made up for her inability to cook or keep house by being an infinitely dedicated nurse and she spent some months, with Paul's help, getting the German gangster back to health.

Paul moved into another boardinghouse in a forgotten portion of the city, far from Magdeburger Alley and Alexander Plaza, and lay low for a time. He did some sparring in gyms, picked up some marks here and there in printing plants, and occasionally dated local women: mostly former Socis or artists or writers who'd gone to ground in places like Berlin North and November 1923 Square. During the first weeks of August he would go regularly to a post office or viewing hall to watch the Olympics live on the Telefunken or Fernseh television sets installed there for those who couldn't get tickets to the Games. Playing the good National Socialist (with his bleached Aryan hair, no less), he would have forced himself to scowl each of the four times Jesse Owens won a gold medal, but it turned out that most of the Germans sitting around him enthusiastically cheered the Negro's victories. The Germans won the most gold medals, which didn't surprise anybody, but the U.S. won plenty and came in second. The only shadow over the event, Paul had been troubled to see, was that America's Jewish runners, Stoller and Glickman, had indeed been pulled from the relay.

After the Games concluded and August moved toward September, Paul's holiday came to an end. Determined to make up for his lapse in judgment at the Waltham Military College, he resumed his quest to kill Germany's plenipotentiary for domestic stability.

But Webber's weathervane system of civil servants reported some interesting information: Reinhard Ernst had disappeared. All they could learn was that his office at the Chancellory had been vacated. It seemed that he'd moved out of Berlin with his family and was spending a great deal of time on the road. He was given a new title (like ribbons and medals, Paul had learned, titles were tossed out by National Socialists like corn to chickens). Ernst was now the "state overleader for special industrial liaison."

No other details about him could be learned. Did this mean that he'd been put out to pasture? Or were these merely security measures to protect the rearmament tzar?

Paul Schumann had no idea.

But one thing was clear. Germany's military buildup was proceeding at a breakneck pace. That fall the new fighter plane, the Me 109, manned by German pilots, made its combat debut in Spain, helping Franco and his Nationalist troops. The plane was stunningly successful, decimating Republican positions. The German army was conscripting more and more young men, and navy yards were working at full capacity to produce warships and submarines.

By October even the out-of-the-way neighborhoods of Berlin were growing more and more dangerous, and as soon as Otto Webber was well enough to travel he and Paul took to the road.

"How far to Neustadt?" the American now asked.

"Not far. Ten kilometers or so."

"Ten?" Paul grumbled. "God in heaven."

In fact, though, he was glad that their next destination wasn't nearby. Best to put some distance between them and St. Margen, their most recent stop, where Schupo officers were perhaps just now finding the body of a local National Socialist party boss. He'd been a brutal man who would order his thugs to round up and beat merchants then Aryanize their businesses. He had many enemies who wished to do him harm but the Kripo or Gestapo investigation would reveal that the circumstances of his death were hardly questionable; it was obvious that he had stopped his car by the road-side to relieve himself in the river and lost his footing on the icy shore. He'd fallen twenty feet and crushed his head on the rocks then drowned in the fast-flowing river. A half-empty bottle of schnapps was found beside him. A sorrowful accident. No need to look further.

Paul now considered their next destination. Neustadt, they had learned, would be the site of a speech by one of Hermann Göring's front men, the headliner at a miniature Nuremberg rally that was currently under way. Paul had heard the man speak, inciting citizens to destroy the houses of Jews in the vicinity. He called himself "doctor" but he was nothing but a big-oted criminal, a petty man, a dangerous man—and one who would prove to be just as accident-prone as the party leader in St. Margen if Paul and Web-ber were successful.

Perhaps another fall. Or maybe he would knock an electric lamp into the bathtub with him. There was always the possibility too that, being as unbalanced as many National Socialist leaders seemed to be, the man might be inclined to shoot or hang himself in a fit of madness. After Neustadt they would hightail it to Munich, where, God bless him, Webber had yet another of his "girls," with whom they could stay.

Headlights flared behind them and the two men took to the woods quickly and remained there until the truck passed. When the taillights vanished around a bend in the road the men continued on their way.

"Ach, Mr. John Dillinger, you know what this road was used for?"

"Tell me, Otto."

"This was the center of the cuckoo clock trade. You have heard of them?"

"Sure. My grandmother had one. My grandfather kept taking the weights off the chains so it wouldn't run. Hated that damn clock. Every hour, *coo-koo, coo-koo . . .*"

"And this is the very road that the traders used, to carry them to market. There are not so many clock makers now but at one time you would see carts going up and down this highway at all hours of the night and day. . . . Ach, and look there. You see that river? It feeds the Danube, and the rivers on the other side of the road feed the Rhine. This is the heart of my country. Isn't it a beautiful place in the moonlight?"

Nearby an owl called, the wind sighed and the ice coating the tree branches tapped like peanut shells on a barroom floor.

The man is right, Paul thought; it *is* a beautiful place. And he felt within him a contentment as crisp as the day-old snow beneath his boots. The most improbable turn of events had made him a resident of this alien land, but he'd come to decide that it was far less alien to him than the country where his brother's printing plant awaited, a world to which he knew he'd never return.

No, he'd left that life behind years ago, left behind *any* circumstance involving modest commerce, a neatly shingled house, a bright, loving wife, playful children. But this was perfectly fine with him. Paul Schumann wanted nothing more than what he had at this moment: to be walking under the coy eye of a half-moon, with a like-minded companion at his side, on a journey to fulfill the purpose God had given him—even if that role was the difficult and presumptuous task of correcting His mistakes.

AUTHOR'S NOTE

While the story of Paul Schumann's mission to Berlin is purely fiction—and the real-life individuals did not, of course, play the roles I gave them—the history, geography, technology and cultural and political institutions in the United States and Germany during the summer of 1936 are otherwise accurate. The Allies' naivete about and ambivalence toward Hitler and the National Socialists were as I have described them. German rearmament occurred very much as I portrayed it, though it was not a single individual, like my fictional Reinhard Ernst, but a number of men who had the task of making the country ready for the war that Hitler had long envisioned. There was indeed a place known as "The Room" in Manhattan, and the Office of Naval Intelligence was the country's CIA of its day.

Portions of Hitler's *Mein Kampf* were the inspiration for the radio broadcasts throughout the story, and while there was no Waltham Study per se, such research was undertaken, although somewhat later than I have it in the book, by SS troops responsible for mass exterminations (known as *Einstatzgruppen*), under the direction of Artur Nebe, who had at one time headed the Kripo. The Nazi government was using DeHoMag card-sorting machines for tracking its citizens in 1936, though they were not, to my knowledge, ever located at Kripo headquarters. The International Criminal Police Commission, which proved to be Willi Kohl's salvation, did in fact meet in London in early 1937; the organization ultimately became Interpol. Sachsenhausen concentration camp officially replaced the old camp at Oranienburg in the late summer of 1936. For the next nine years more than 200,000 political and racial prisoners were held there; tens of thousands were executed or died from beatings, abuse, starvation and illness. The occupying Russians in turn used the facility as a prison to house some sixty thousand Nazis and other political prisoners, of whom an estimated twelve thousand died before the camp was closed in 1950.

As for Otto Webber's favorite gin mill: The Aryan Café permanently closed its door shortly after the Olympic Games ended.

A brief note here regarding the fate of several characters appearing in the story: In the spring of 1945, as Germany lay in ruins, Hermann Göring came to the mistaken belief that Adolf Hitler was abdicating control of the country and asked to succeed him. To Göring's shame and horror, Hitler was incensed and labeled him a backstabber, casting him out of the Nazi party and ordering his arrest. At the Nuremberg war crimes trial Göring was sentenced to die. He killed himself two hours before his scheduled execution in 1946.

Despite being the supreme sycophant, Heinrich Himmler made independent peace overtures to the Allies (the head of the SS and architect of the Nazis' mass-murder programs actually suggested that Jews and the Nazis should forget the past and "bury the hatchet"). Like Göring he was labeled a traitor by Hitler. As the country fell, he tried to escape justice by fleeing in disguise—but for some reason the persona he chose to assume was that of a Gestapo military policeman, which meant automatic arrest. His real identity was immediately discovered. He killed himself before he could stand trial at Nuremberg.

Toward the end of the war, Adolf Hitler grew increasingly unstable, physically debilitated (it is believed he had Parkinson's disease) and despondent, planning military offensives with divisions that no longer existed, calling upon all citizens to fight to the death and ordering Albert Speer to institute a scorched-earth plan (which the architect refused to do). Hitler spent his last days in a bunker complex beneath the Chancellory garden. On April 29, 1945, he married his mistress, Eva Braun, and soon after they both committed suicide.

Paul Joseph Goebbels remained loyal to Hitler until the end and was appointed his successor. Following the Führer's suicide, Goebbels attempted to negotiate peace with the Russians. The efforts were futile and the former propaganda minister and his wife, Magda, also took their own lives (after she had murdered their six children).

Earlier in his career Hitler said of his military expansion that led to the Second World War, "It will be my duty to carry on this war regardless of losses. . . . We shall have to abandon much that is dear to us and today seems irreplaceable. Cities will become heaps of ruins; noble monuments of architecture will disappear forever. This time our sacred soil will not be spared. But I am not afraid of this."

The empire that Hitler claimed would survive for a thousand years lasted for twelve.

ACKNOWLEDGMENTS

With heartfelt thanks to the usual suspects, and a few new ones: Louise Burke, Britt Carlson, Jane Davis, Julie Deaver, Sue Fletcher, Cathy Gleason, Jamie Hodder-Williams, Emma Longhurst, Carolyn Mays, Diana Mackay, Mark Olshaker, Tara Parsons, Carolyn Reidy, David Rosenthal, Ornella Robiatti, Marysue Rucci, Deborah Schneider, Vivienne Schuster and Brigitte Smith.

Madelyn, too, of course.

For those interested in reading more about Nazi Germany, you'll find the following sources as interesting as I found them invaluable in my research: Louis Snyder, *Encyclopedia of the Third Reich;* Ron Rosenbaum, *Explaining Hitler;* John Toland, *Adolf Hitler;* Piers Brendon, *The Dark Valley;* Michael Burleigh, *The Third Reich: A New History;* Edwin Black, *IBM and the Holocaust;* William L. Shirer, *The Rise and Fall of the Third Reich* and *20th Century Journey, Volume II, The Nightmare Years;* Giles MacDonogh, *Berlin;* Christopher Isherwood, *The Berlin Stories;* Peter Gay, *Weimar Culture: The Outsider as Insider* and *My German Question;* Frederick Lewis Allen, *Since Yesterday;* Edward Crankshaw, *Gestapo: Instrument of Tyranny;* David Clay Large, *Berlin;* Richard Bessel, *Life in the Third Reich;* Nora Waln, *The Approaching Storm;* George C. Browder, *Hitler's Enforcers;* Roger Manvell, *Gestapo;* Richard Grunberger, *The 12-Year Reich;* Ian Kershaw, *Hitler 1889–1936: Hubris;* Joseph E. Persico, *Roosevelt's Secret War;* Adam LeBor and Roger Boyes, *Seduced by Hitler;* Mel Gordon, *Voluptuous Panic: The Erotic World of Weimar Berlin;* Richard Mandell, *The Nazi Olympics;* Susan D. Bachrach, *The Nazi Olympics;* Mark R. McGee, *Berlin: A Visual and Historical Documentation from 1925 to the Present;* Richard Overy, *Historical Atlas of the Third Reich;* Neal Ascherson, *Berlin: A Century of Change;* Rupert Butler, *An Illustrated History of the Gestapo;* Alan Bullock, *Hitler; A Study in Tyranny;* Pierre Aycoberry, *The Social History of the Third Reich, 1833–1945;* Otto Friedrich, *Before the Deluge.*

ABOUT THE AUTHOR

Former journalist, folksinger and attorney Jeffery Deaver's novels have appeared on a number of best-seller lists around the world, including those of *The New York Times,* the *Times of London* and *The Los Angeles Times.* The author of nineteen novels, he's been nominated for five Edgar Awards from the Mystery Writers of America, an Anthony Award and a Gumshoe Award, is a three-time recipient of the Ellery Queen Reader's Award for Best Short Story of the Year, and is a winner of the British Thumping Good Read Award. His book *A Maiden's Grave* was made into an HBO movie staring James Garner and Marlee Matlin, and his novel *The Bone Collector* was a feature release from Universal Pictures, starring Denzel Washington and Angelina Jolie. His most recent books are *The Vanished Man, The Stone Monkey* and *Twisted: Collected Stories.* And, yes, the rumors are true, he did appear as a corrupt reporter on his favorite soap opera, *As the World Turns.* Readers can visit his website at www.jefferydeaver.com.